MISSION CRITICAL

BAEN BOOKS by CHARLES E. GANNON

THE TERRAN REPUBLIC SERIES
Fire with Fire
Trial by Fire
Raising Caine
Caine's Mutiny
Marque of Caine
Mission Critical (with Griffin Barber,
Chris Kennedy & Mike Massa)
Endangered Species (forthcoming)
Protected Species (forthcoming)

THE VORTEX OF WORLDS SERIES
This Broken World
Into the Vortex (forthcoming)
Toward the Maw (forthcoming)

THE RING OF FIRE SERIES (WITH ERIC FLINT)
1635: The Papal Stakes
1636: Commander Cantrell in the West Indies
1636: The Vatican Sanction
1637: No Peace Beyond the Line
1636: Calabar's War (with Robert Waters)

JOHN RINGO'S BLACK TIDE RISING SERIES
At the End of the World
At the End of the Journey

THE STARFIRE SERIES (WITH STEVE WHITE)
Extremis
Imperative
Oblivion

To purchase Baen titles in e-book form,
please go to www.baen.com.

MISSION CRITICAL

CHARLES E. GANNON
GRIFFIN BARBER
CHRIS KENNEDY
MIKE MASSA

Mission Critical

This is a work of fiction. All the characters and events portrayed in this book are fictional, and any resemblance to real people or incidents is purely coincidental.

A Baen Books Original

Baen Publishing Enterprises
P.O. Box 1403
Riverdale, NY 10471
www.baen.com

ISBN: 978-1-9821-9260-0

Cover artist: Thomas Peters

First printing, January 2023

Distributed by Simon & Schuster
1230 Avenue of the Americas
New York, NY 10020

Library of Congress Cataloging-in-Publication Data

Names: Gannon, Charles E., author. | Barber, Griffin, author. | Kennedy,
    Chris, 1965– author. | Massa, Mike, 1967– author.
Title: Mission critical / Charles E Gannon, Griffin Barber, Chris Kennedy,
    Mike Massa.
Identifiers: LCCN 2022046597 (print) | LCCN 2022046598 (ebook) | ISBN
    9781982192600 (hardcover) | ISBN 9781625798985 (ebook)
Subjects: LCGFT: Science fiction. | Novels.
Classification: LCC PS3607.A556 M57 2023 (print) | LCC PS3607.A556
    (ebook) | DDC 813/.6—dc23/eng/20221025
LC record available at https://lccn.loc.gov/2022046597
LC ebook record available at https://lccn.loc.gov/2022046598

Printed in the United States of America
10 9 8 7 6 5 4 3 2 1

This book is dedicated to:

Toni Weisskopf, who enthusiastically encouraged the Murphy's Lawless series in its original incarnation at Chris Kennedy Publishing's dedicated Terran Republic imprint, Beyond Terra Press. Her ready embrace of new and innovative market models made possible Baen's release of this book (and the others in the series), thereby establishing a unique bridge between traditional and independent publishers. Thank you, Toni, for your support—and always, for your friendship. ❧

PART ONE

Chapter One

Colonel Rodger Murphy tapped the secure opening tab twice, the first touch releasing the lock so that the second could activate the mechanism.

Within the gray bulkheads, infrequently used motors growled to life. The compartment's faux-rock blast covers slid back, revealing the two stars that comprised the 55 Tauri binary system. The approaching F7 primary known as Jrar now appeared almost two-thirds the size of the orange K3 secondary Shex, although that may have been partially due to the intensity of the larger and hotter star's light. After a moment, the two-inch glass polarized enough to make the double-glare bearable.

Major Mara "Bruce" Lee folded her arms. "How long can we stay here?"

Murphy shrugged. "Ten minutes. The REMs aren't so bad at this distance and there's a gel-layer embedded in the glass that picks up a lot of the large-particle radiation."

Captain T. J. Cutter peered into the riot of untwinkling stars. "Where's R'Bak? I know we're on the same side of the sun—damn, Shex—right now, but to me, everything is just stars."

Murphy smiled. "You and me both." He gestured toward the left-hand margin of the cosmic mural that crept constantly, slowly downward. "I wouldn't have any idea if I didn't have Makarov showing me charts so I can keep track of our shuttle traffic and line-of-sight commo windows."

They gazed at the stars in an easy silence, but there was a thread of expectation underlying it; Murphy hadn't told them why he had asked them to meet him. *No time like the present.* "I want to share something with all of you. I wish Bowden and Tapper were with us—and even that pain Chalmers. But in a few hours, I'm going to be gone, too. So I guess it's now or never."

Bo raised an eyebrow. "What gives, Colonel? First the other guys go back dirtside, and now you're following them? I thought the handful who didn't get up here for the wedding were supposed to be extracted by the end of next week."

Murphy shook his head. "Several had to go back to tie up loose ends, and Kevin had to finish training some pilots, as well as gathering data for the simulators we need to use as long as we're hiding out here."

"That's a lot of new, and changed, plans," Bo said. He studied the faces around him. "And no one thought to tell me?"

Mara smiled. "You were busy...on your honeymoon."

Bo, badass tanker that he was, blushed just a shade shy of crimson. "Oh. Yeah. Right. That." He stared at the slice of velvet black where R'Bak was located. "Y'know, with all the rush to get spaceside for my wedding, I didn't stop to think that it would be the last time I'd see R'Bak for...well, years, maybe." He shook his head. "I never thought I'd say this, but it was starting to feel a little bit like home."

"More than a little, for some of us," Mara muttered.

Cutter glanced up. "What do you mean?"

Before Murphy could answer, Bo jutted his chin at the approximate location of the planet. "Harry has a wife and child down there. The tribe has adopted him—formally, if I understand what he told me."

Cutter's face was creased in confusion. "But his family—they were cleared to come up here, right?"

Murphy sighed. "They *were*. But there's been some unexpected push-back."

"Nothing's ever simple with SpinDogs," Bo muttered.

"Or RockHounds," Mara added.

Cutter raised an eyebrow. "Sounds like you're a lady who's in the know, Major."

Lee rolled her eyes. "Not so much. And yet, more than I'd like."

Bo murmured, "The real problem is that Harry doesn't want to come back at all."

Murphy shrugged. "Can't say I blame him. He's making a life for himself, over a hundred and fifty light-years from home." He glanced at Bo. "Not a lot of us can say that, yet."

Cutter was staring hard at the stars, as if they'd just affronted him. "Not like there's been a lot of time. Or opportunity."

"No, there hasn't," Murphy agreed, "but after a certain point, it really doesn't matter how good—how unavoidable—the reasons have been for not building a life. Times before, when soldiers were away for years, at least they always had something to go back to—a spouse, kids, a city, a town, even a war-ravaged country: some thing. But here?" Murphy gestured at the featureless gray bulkheads. "We've got none of that. And I'm not sure we'll ever really fit into life on these spins. Particularly since neither the SpinDogs nor the RockHounds think we're a good fit for their culture, and vice versa. Hell, that's about the only thing they can agree on."

Mara smiled, but her eyes drifted sideways toward Murphy, faint worry in them. "So... what was it you wanted to share with us?"

He smiled back at her with a slight shake of his head. Her gaze relaxed, which meant she'd read the reassurance buried in that gesture. *No, Mara, the MS hasn't gotten bad enough to reveal it to the other cadre—yet.* He returned to the crate he'd lugged into the compartment, moving its other contents out of the way until he could lift out a heavy, squarish object wrapped in cloth. He brought it over to the others, making sure they were all in front of the observation panel.

"What is it?" Mara asked. She sounded surprised and curious.

Probably because she always knows what's in the wind before anyone else, Murphy reflected with a private smile as he held it concealed for one more moment. "Makarov and I and a few others have been working on this for the better part of the year. We always kept hoping we were done, but sadly, there was always more to add. I just hope we really are finally finished."

He drew back the cloth. Bo was already in a position where he could look over Murphy's shoulder, and he expelled his breath in a long sigh when he saw what the object was: a square plaque with a long list of names etched into it. The metal's surface was almost granular instead of smooth, betraying its humble origins as a hull replacement plate.

As the others gathered close, they became as still as they were silent. Because each of them knew all those names. All the Lost Soldiers who, like the rest, had wanted so badly to go home, but instead, had permanently departed this battlefield in a fashion familiar to—and too common among—warriors since the beginning of time.

Cutter cleared his throat, sounded more grim than touched as he murmured, "It's a nice memorial, Colonel."

"Have you decided where you want to put it?" Bo asked, reaching out to run his fingers over a cluster of names. He'd been the CO for the Lost Soldiers' first real engagement and had yet to come to terms with the number who had fallen there.

Murphy sighed. "Finding the right place for it has been troubling me. If you have a country you call your own, then you set aside a town square, or a spot in a cemetery: a place where the names will remain across the years, so that they will not be forgotten. Hell, even if you're the crew of a ship without a home, you could put it at the foot of the binnacle, for all to see, for as long as the ship remained afloat."

He grimaced at the featureless walls of the compartment. "But this spinhab is never going to be any of those things, for us. We're just guests in a community of control-freak exiles hiding inside a long, rolling rock."

He stared down at the plaque. "We need a place of our own, a place where we can put this plaque so that it has some meaning to those who come after us. Assuming we last long enough for that to matter." He found a way to smile. "And on that cheerful note..."

Murphy returned to the crate and pulled out the remaining contents: a bottle of genuine Terran whiskey and glasses. As he poured out each measure, he said, as much to himself as them, "After every casualty we took, I wanted to do this: to mark their sacrifices with words and a drink and a permanent memorial that had their name on it."

He raised his glass. "So, for all the ones commemorated on this plaque, I say: here's to absent friends and comrades. Missed every day, and we'll never see their like again."

The others raised their glasses with a muted chorus of "Hear, hears," and sipped rather than threw back the shots. This real whiskey was not merely hard to come by; it wasn't to be found anywhere within a hundred light-years, let alone this system.

"God willing, we'll never have to do this again," Bo breathed. But his voice echoed what they all accepted: that such a happy outcome was very, very unlikely.

Mara cradled her glass in both hands. "How's the situation on the ground?"

Murphy glanced at Bo, who took up that tale. "Pretty much what we were aiming for before we had to pull out. The indigs are in control of the Hamain and most of the Fringelands along the Greens. The satraps are panicked because they've always been able to rely on one ironclad truth: that when the Searing comes, so do their Harvester allies. They only had to follow the Kulsians' orders to get their coffers filled. Now, they've got nothing to show their masters but empty hands, so they aren't sure how they're going to pay their troops and keep their power after the Harvesters leave. A few are wondering if they'll come at all, or whether that's good or bad—since their first order of business might be replacing the satraps. With extreme prejudice."

Cutter nodded. "Yeah, from the time the locals learned that the reavers—excuse me, 'coursers'—couldn't warn the Overlords about how things went sideways, they've started double-guessing everything. But they are all sure of one thing: if their bosses show up, they're gonna be pissed as hell."

Mara smiled coldly. "Sucks to be a satrap."

Murphy nodded, took a pull at his drink. "Yeah, but it could suck even worse to be us. It's not likely the inbound surveyor flotilla will have the time or resources to untangle what actually destroyed their coursers: namely, us. But, when the Harvesters arrive, they'll have ample time and reason to start a thorough investigation. Sooner rather than later, they're going to realize that the disruptions weren't random, despite all the confusion and contradictions we've sown in our wake. And if that happens, and they decide to cast a wider net that includes the whole system... well, we can forget surviving to the end of the year."

Bo nodded. "So far, we've been fighting a bunch of gun-waving whack-jobs. Any battles after this—on the ground or in space—will be against professionals with good equipment and decent training." He sipped at his whiskey. "Like you say, Colonel, it would suck to be *us*."

"Which has me wondering why you're going back at all, Colonel," Cutter said with a frown. "Kind of moving in the wrong direction, aren't you?"

Murphy smiled. "Along with a few other people, I'm taking the last transatmo planetside to wrap up some loose ends. Then we gather most everyone still on R'Bak and take the already on-station shuttle straight back here." When Mara stiffened at the qualifier "*most* everyone," Murphy shook his head at her. "That includes El—eh, Sergeant Frazier. Last word is that he's doing a lot better, thanks to the local, er, experts. But the last phase of his rehab requires the facilities up here."

"And the shuttle you took down?"

"That's truly the last boat out, mostly for the ground crew. The only people staying behind are Chalmers, his team, and a small group that will be setting up new landing fields in remote areas so that when we return, we can operate out of locations that the Kulsians have never visited. We're leaving them one small passenger transatmo for emergencies."

"That last boat out," Mara almost whispered, "that's the one Harry will be on?"

Murphy nodded. "I promised him he wouldn't have to return until the very last minute."

"I'm surprised he agreed to return at all," Bo murmured.

Murphy nodded. "In that matter, his sense of duty won a narrow victory over his personal inclinations." *This time.* He glanced at his G-shock. "If I don't get moving, I'm going to be late for a meeting with our hosts." He waved toward the observation panel. "According to the SpinDog techs, you can safely spend another few minutes here." He tossed back the last of the whiskey and strode out of the small observation compartment, the plaque secured tightly under his arm.

Chapter Two

"The situation is pretty much in line with what we projected," Murphy began with a nod at the wall-mounted situation map of 55 Tauri. "Our ongoing passive scans show that the surveyor ships continue to approach at an atypically high velocity. And, now that the enemy is closer, our sensors are giving us higher resolution results. They confirm that this flotilla has more stiffening elements than a typical surveyor force roster."

Korelon, a RockHound and by far the youngest of the three locals in the conference compartment, frowned. "This is worse than we had thought."

For a moment, Murphy found himself at a loss for words. *Worse than we had thought?* It had become axiomatic among both the Lost Soldier and local leadership that, once the jury-rigged intersystem transmitter on R'Bak had been destroyed, the overlords of Kulsis would respond to that ominous silence by accelerating the surveyors' timetable and increasing their security elements. Maybe Korelon hadn't been read in by the more senior RockHounds that he represented?

But Anseker, Primus of the Otlethes Family, simply stared at the younger man with something like a sneer. "Did Orgunz tell you to make those worried noises, Korelon? Even if they lacked substance?"

The RockHound flushed, eyes hard as he searched for words that would defend his statement yet remain sufficiently deferential to the most powerful SpinDog primus.

Murphy didn't envy the younger man's position. Korelon's rank was far beneath Anseker's and the other Primus at the table—Medrost of Family Erfrenzh. He was only present because he was already situated on *Spin One* as the RockHounds' official liaison to its powerful Families. He had held that position for several years, during which he had adopted many SpinDog ways...including their rarefied airs.

But after a moment, Korelon sat back and asked with admirable calm and high formality, "Primus Otlethes, shall I convey your inquiry about my instructions to Legate Orgunz himself? For I am sure you understand I am not at liberty to share them without his approval."

Before Anseker could bridle at Korelon's riposte to his purely rhetorical question, Murphy leaned forward across the table. "Gentlemen, this is neither the time nor place for such matters. As I made clear at the outset, there is a shuttle waiting to take me to R'Bak, so we must keep the meeting brief."

Anseker glared at the liaison, whose answering gaze was steady, if unreadable. "Very well, Sko'Belm Murphy...but only because *you* ask it."

"Thank you." Murphy suppressed a sigh of relief. They last thing any of them needed right now was yet another pissing match between the SpinDogs and RockHounds, particularly since the latter group's typically decentralized authority had recently been conferred upon a rarely appointed Legate. Consequently, slights and insults would no longer be perceived as general, but aimed at that one person. Awkward, but a Legate was necessary to coordinate the RockHounds' various contributions to the coming operations.

Primus Medrost had glanced warily between the two of them during the exchange. He was not Anseker's customary wingman. That role belonged to his most powerful, breedline-linked ally, the Primus of the Usrensekt Family. But the decision to bring Medrost on this occasion made sense in terms of Anseker's consolidation of power by strengthening alliances. The summons to accompany the preeminent Primus of all the Families to be the other SpinDog representative at such a crucial meeting underscored the importance of Medrost and his family, and so, amplified their prestige and influence.

Murphy nodded toward Korelon. "I will see that my chief of

staff, Captain Makarov, sends you the latest updates we have on the surveyors." *Which you've already been sent. Twice.*

Korelon's glance was initially wary, but then relieved as he realized that Murphy was offering him a way to save face. "I would appreciate that, Colonel."

Makarov made a note, might have been fighting not to smile.

After a final sideways smirk at Korelon, Anseker crossed his arms. "Perhaps it is too early to ask, but what is the final, er, 'sitrep' from the surface?"

"We've achieved all our nominal objectives." The blank looks on the faces of both Medrost and Korelon told Murphy that Anseker had not shared any details of the planetside campaign. *More reinforcement of his "dominance"; seeing he's already in the know shows them how closely he's working with the Lost Soldiers.* Murphy managed not to roll his eyes. "Since seizing Imsurmik, the satraps of the Hamain have pulled back from the wastes and from most of the Ashbands, right up to the border on the Greens. Even the dominant satrapy—the J'Stull—no longer sends out patrols or probes; they rarely venture outside the walls of their capital. No other towns attempt even that much."

"How long can they remain in such a state of siege?" Medrost asked, surprise in his voice.

Since the question did not come from Anseker, this was a moment when Murphy could invite Makarov to answer without risking insult. He nodded at Pyotr.

The Russian pointed to a map on the table, where red marks indicated the few self-isolating Fringeland and Ashband towns that remained in the hands of their original satraps. "Those that have survived this long have had the wisdom and the supplies to risk waiting for the surveyors to arrive. And they have just recently learned that they gambled correctly: our SIGINT—*prostite*; 'signal intelligence'—indicates that the approaching surveyor flotilla has communicated that their arrival is imminent, albeit without any details."

"That lack of detail is a tactical precaution," Anseker added for the benefit of the other two. "Kulsis does not know what destroyed their first wave of coursers, so the surveyors must presume that if it was some unknown force, it may now be preparing to pounce upon them as well."

Makarov nodded. "Exactly. And by messaging ahead, they

have reassured the remaining satraps that they will soon have allies in orbit."

Korelon crossed his arms, frowning. "Why did you leave *any* of these satraps in control? I am not familiar with planetary military strategies, but from the sound of it, you possess sufficient force to have eliminated all of them."

Anseker did not look at Korelon as he spoke. "We asked Sko'Belm Murphy the same thing. He explained that complete conquest was not only uncertain, but not worth the risks it would entail."

Medrost leaned in. "Such as?"

"Taking so many towns and small cities might involve long and costly street-to-street fighting. That could have inflicted demoralizing casualties upon his indigenous 'war bands' and might not have been fully resolved before the surveyors arrived. Besides," the Primus added with a smile toward the Lost Soldier, "he made a convincing case for leaving at least some satraps."

"Why?" Korelon was clearly intrigued.

Anseker gestured to Murphy, who pointed at the map. "Once the remaining satraps decided to bunker in behind their walls, they ceased to have any idea what was occurring on the other side of them. So as long as they saw an occasional vehicle or patrol, they knew we were still out there, waiting. What they couldn't know was that it was a charade. A few hundred indigs were able to keep all those towns not only under observation, but in a state of near-terror. In the meantime, we pulled our own forces off-planet and the indigs withdrew the majority of theirs. By now, even the few hundred that kept the towns in check have dispersed into the wastes."

Makarov added details. "This way, weeks before the surveyors arrive, all sign of them will be gone. All the vehicles have been hidden and all but a handful of the tribes have 'gone to ground.'" "Pistol Pete" smiled as he used the idiom; he was inordinately fond of American expressions and slang. "Before the satraps will dare to conjecture that the disappearance of their enemies is not simply a ruse to bring them back out beyond their walls, they shall be seeing surveyor shuttles and landers overhead."

"So," Korelon said, nodding despite his persistent frown, "it was a strategy to cover your withdrawal."

"It was a little more than that," amended Murphy. "Firstly, the weaker the satraps are when the surveyors finally arrive, the less likely they'll be to rush out in search of the indigs. They'll have a lot of rebuilding to do...just as the surveyors start demanding more than the usual amount of assistance to prepare for the arrivals of the Harvesters."

Medrost's smile was both appreciative and icy. "So they shall never have the time nor spare manpower to seek the indigs until they are long gone."

"Yes. And if any satraps start crying a river about how much they've suffered at the hands of 'wild tribes,' the Kulsians won't have the time or reason to give a damn. Besides, they won't find a lot of evidence to support the losses that the satraps will be claiming. Yeah, there's evidence that the indigs went on the warpath, but with what long-term effect? The ones that took over the towns will be gone, and either the original satraps or new ones will have returned. Similarly, there won't be any sign of the helicopters or armored vehicles that the satraps will claim beat them in battle after battle." Murphy shrugged. "My guess is that the already-overworked surveyors will dismiss the tales as wild exaggerations or just outright lies."

Even Korelon was smiling now.

Murphy paused for emphasis. "But all these outcomes were very much secondary objectives, compared to the primary reason for leaving the biggest satraps unconquered."

Medrost nodded, understanding. "You need to keep the surveyors unsuspecting of what actually occurred."

Murphy smiled and nodded back. "And as the Kulsians hear one wild story after another, they realize that they've got only one thing in common: no two are alike."

Anseker grinned like a shark at the other SpinDog and the RockHound. "So the surveyors conduct a search—more than perfunctory, yet less than determined—and when they find only scattered evidence and inconsistent accounts, they turn their backs and begin shouldering the double load of work that awaits."

He turned to Murphy. "My one reservation is that there will be nothing left of your indig army by the time we can return to R'Bak. Although the Ashbanders have less to fear from the satraps and the Harvester culling squads, they will have to remain hidden in the wastes during the Searing. That is an uncertain proposition."

Even if Anseker's concern for the Ashbanders was based strictly on their future utility, it was a decided step forward for a Primus who usually referred to them as "savages." Murphy shrugged. "That's why we prevailed upon you to stop replicating—er, autofabbing—weapons and ammunition during the last two months, and shift to simple, low-tech survival gear that they could not only maintain but copy." He saw perplexity on Korelon's face, shared the details. "Better pumps and water-drills, sun-stills, wind-powered lathes, small smelting furnaces, even crystal sets to monitor Harvester cull squads: because of those and a dozen other devices you replicated *en masse* for them, more of the tribes will survive this Searing than ever before." He nodded at all three of them. "From the very start of the campaign on R'Bak, your combined auto-fabrication capacities were the foundation of our victories. And that will be even truer as we begin the next phase of operations."

Anseker nodded back, but he was squinting. "And now we come to it."

Korelon's gaze went from the Primus to Murphy and back again. "Come to what?"

Anseker laughed lightly. "Ask him yourself. Ask him why he never misses an opportunity to speak about our autofabrication assets. Ask him why he has been inquiring which devices for the next mission can be produced most easily, in the greatest quantities, in the least amount of time."

Medrost looked confused. "But would that not be necessary even if he was simply attempting to balance his requests with our capabilities?"

Anseker nodded. "Of course...and in so doing, learn a great deal about them." Anseker stared at Murphy. "Is that not correct, Sko'Belm Murphy?"

Murphy smiled. "It is. And it was necessary, if we were to come to this day."

Korelon frowned. "So is that today's true agenda, Sko'Belm Murphy? To manipulate even us RockHounds into complying with your autofab demands?"

"In a manner of speaking," Murphy admitted.

"No, Colonel. Either it is your intent or it isn't."

Murphy laid one hand flat upon the table; it was less likely to quake, that way. "You are wrong, Korelon. There's a preliminary step that must be taken."

"Which is?" Medrost asked.

"To inform you that, at our next meeting, you must be prepared to have a frank and revealing discussion about your autofab capacities. There is no longer enough time, or enough margin for error, to accommodate vague estimates or Family secrets. I can't move forward with the coming missions unless I have precise and complete information about your replication assets."

As Korelon flinched back, Medrost shook his head. "This is utterly unacceptable." He glanced at Anseker—but that Primus's calm, resolved gaze revealed that he had been Murphy's collaborator in bringing them to this meeting. And for this express purpose.

Murphy put his other hand on the table and leaned forward. "I realize that every group's autofab capacity is a strategic secret. But everyone's in the same boat, now. We sail or sink together. Keep your other secrets if you must, but I need to ask frank questions—and get frank and accurate answers—about your replication resources."

Korelon's jaw was set like rock; he clearly did not trust himself to talk. It was Medrost who, looking from Murphy to Anseker in irritation, folded his arms and replied, "And if we do not agree to sharing that information?"

"Then we are just marking time until we die." Murphy pushed up from the table to his feet. "We can't finalize the only strategies that might save us until we know how deep your logistical and industrial pockets are." He saw Medrost's eyes shutter shrewdly. He pointed at him. "If you think that anything you might hold back now might save you later, you are utterly wrong. If we lose, the Kulsians aren't going to cut any side deals—not that you'd *ever* think of trying that."

They all flinched. Anseker's response was clearly the product of genuine surprise. The other two reminded him of how faces in church changed when a minister's homily grazed a guilty nerve.

"It's no different from what you've assumed for centuries: that if the Kulsians ever found you, they would exterminate you. Except now, it won't just be dispassionate genocide. It will be long, determined torture until they understand how their operations were derailed, and why, and by whom. And it won't just be to our bodies; they'll force us to choose between answering their questions or watching them inflict hours or days of agony upon our loved ones."

Murphy walked to his waiting rucksack. "This is war to the knife, gentlemen. There are no contingencies, no 'plan B's,' no reason to hold anything back or in reserve." He checked his G-shock. "I'll give you two weeks to get your grievances and suspicions squared away—at least enough so we can all work together the way we need to."

Medrost turned red. "You will give *us* two weeks? To whom do you think you're speaking, Mur—?"

Murphy pinned the Primus with a stare, continuing without a pause or change in tone. "I will set a time for the meeting. You will have the replication specs and data for presentation. You will come prepared to work together. And, if you choose not to, then here's my advice: stay home and take a pill, or open your veins, or do whatever it is you people do to commit suicide. Because if you're not at that meeting with the right data and the right frame of mind, the next best thing you can do is end it all now. For both yourselves and your Families."

He shouldered the rucksack, noticing that even Anseker had grown pale. "You may have the room for further discussion, if you wish."

"And you are leaving? Now?"

"Yes, now. To go dirtside and continue the work needed to stay alive. I suggest you clear your agendas and make that your sole task, also. Good day, gentlemen."

Murphy did not dare walk too quickly, even as he rounded the corner leading to the interface bay from which the dirtside-bound transatmo would launch.

He discovered that the shuttle wasn't the only thing waiting for him. Naliryiz was standing just outside the bay doors. Well, standing was the wrong word; it was more like she had posted herself there.

Before he could even wave or nod a greeting, she held him with her strange violet eyes and said, "So you are going to R'Bak again?" It had the structure of a question, but her tone was pure assertion.

He nodded as he closed the distance, noticing that she seemed to have gained weight. No, he revised: she had gained *mass*. She was more, rather than less, fit.

She put her hands on her hips as he stopped before her; she

was blocking the door. "Colonel Murphy, when you are on the surface, do not do anything..." She paused, as if searching for a word; her English was extremely good but there were still some gaps in her vocabulary. She started over. "Do not do anything—"

"Rash?" he supplied helpfully.

"I was trying to find a gentler word than 'foolish,' actually."

"Oh." He studied her face in an attempt to gain any clue as to why she had felt the need to wait at the bay to deliver this message. But within the first second, he realized that her perfectly straight nose and high cheekbones were going to distract him, ensuring that his reply would take one of two unfortunate forms: meaningless babble or entranced silence. "So," he said, looking away, "did Mara put you up to this?"

Naliryiz frowned. "My Family-sister knows better than that. No one 'puts me up to' any actions. But I know she shares my reservations, at least in part." Naliryiz stepped closer. "You have been doing research."

"I do a great deal of research."

"*Hssst.* You know what I mean." Her voice lowered to a murmur. "You have made many requests for the records and reports of our liaisons to the surface, even those that are centuries old. They can have no bearing on the current situation, so your interests are obviously not motivated by present or future operations." She nodded generally at his body. "You are trying to find the rumored cure before your access to the surface ends."

"Well," Murphy said with a sigh, "I won't lie; if I had enough time and information to go searching for it, I probably would." He shrugged. "But I don't."

Naliryiz crossed her arms as if she was suddenly chilly. Which made no more sense than the strange play of expressions on her face: relieved, but also crestfallen. "Then why have you been gathering so much research on R'Bak and its past?"

"Because we have only visited a very small portion of it, and, even there, we lack crucial data. For instance, if we had a better idea of where all the region-spanning tunnels are, we could assess how to use them when moving our forces from one salient to another when we return. And then there are all the ancient scrolls and tablets Cutter found in the archive beneath Imsurmik."

Naliryiz nodded knowingly. "Yes, many of which are related to healing and medicines. And so might contain clues to the cure."

"They very well might. But no one—not even your experts—can decipher most of those records. Old languages, guild scripts, forgotten words: translating it will take years, not weeks. If ever. But the more recent records have revealed a great deal about the Harvesters' pattern of activity on R'Bak: the places they've avoided, visited, what they prize the most, where they find it." He shrugged. "Besides, history furnishes the context in which to understand the present."

Naliryiz tilted her head quizzically. "Are you becoming a philosopher, now, Colonel Murphy?"

"No," he answered, "but I did major in history."

She frowned, bewildered. "'Majored'? How can you have a rank in history?"

He smiled. "No, no. 'Majored' means... well, what I studied while I was becoming an officer."

"Ah! So you are a historian!"

Huh: I wish. "No, just interested in it. Besides, since arriving here, all my research has been purely practical. I've had about as much time to delve into general history as I have had to chase mythical cures." He checked his G-shock—*Seems like I do nothing but that*—and smiled through his apology. "I'm five minutes late for the transatmo, and they're holding it for me."

She nodded, mouth slightly down at the corners. "Yes," she allowed, moving so that she no longer blocked the bay doors, "you must go."

Murphy qualified his statement: "Not that I *want* to." Her frown became puzzled rather than sad, prompting him to add, "I'd much rather keep standing here with you, talking. Or whatever." *"Or whatever?" Murphy, could you be any more lame?*

Maybe it was because she was not a native speaker, but Naliryiz apparently missed the awkward phrasing. She simply smiled. "Then return soon, so we may resume. And Colonel?"

"Yes?" he responded, moving toward the bay doors by walking backward—never a safe move for a man with MS.

"Do *not* do anything foolish. I would be very... aggravated if you did not return as you have promised."

"I'll be as careful as I can," he answered as the bay doors groaned open behind him. Turning and striding toward the waiting shuttle, he discovered that his step was lighter than it had been in weeks.

Chapter Three

Chalmers wilted as he stepped into the light of both suns. The temperature rose by twenty degrees in that single step. At least the cold worry-sweat he'd built up waiting in the hospital ward wouldn't be so out of place.

Much of the base was being pulled down around them. Word had just arrived from *Spin One* that the next wave of ships from Kulsis were decelerating out at the edge of the Shex system; the Lost Soldiers were being pulled out and any overt evidence of their presence—like the base—was being hastily wiped from the face of R'Bak.

"Why are you *such* a dick, Chalmers?" Jackson asked, shoving the door open and walking up the shallow, rammed-earth ramp to join his partner. Most buildings on R'Bak used the earth to help keep them cool, and the field hospital was no exception, despite its temporary nature.

"Am I?" Chalmers asked, hating the defensive tone that crept into his voice. He started walking toward the much-worn chassis of *Man-Eater*. They had orders to meet up with the Big Cheese before they bugged out. He wasn't sure what the meeting was for. It wasn't like they had a lot of time for a mission before the Kulsian surveyors were close enough to see what was going on in orbit, let alone on the ground.

Jackson caught up with Chalmers, hitting him in the chest with the back of one hand. "I thought you were done with this kind of shit, man."

"Look, it's not my fault Murphy is dragging us away from your new bestie while he's laid up in hospital." The "bestie" in question, Sergeant Elroy Frazier, had inadvertently OD'd on local stimulants toward the end of his last mission. Murphy and his staff had wanted to evac the big crew chief back to *Spin One*, but the locals pointed out that no one knew the effects—and treatment—of too much *ihey* better than they did: the SpinDog medicos agreed. There had been a lot of improvement, but El was still messed up, so he was heading back upstairs on Murphy's shuttle.

Jackson stopped walking and rounded on his partner. Chalmers expected his expression to be angry, but Jackson's face was suspicious. Not an angry *you screwed me again* suspicious, but the *I know what's going on, now* kind of suspicion that was generally a lot worse.

"That's what this shit is about, isn't it?" Jackson's voice had gone up an octave, another bad sign. "Why you were such a relentless dick on the radio every time El called in."

Chalmers didn't slow down. He didn't want to have this conversation. Not now, not ever.

Jackson followed after him, grabbed his shoulder, and forced Chalmers to look him in the face. "I was wondering why you were being such a relentless dick to El, and I just figured it out. You're jealous. You're fucking *jealous.*"

Chalmers raised his hands without quite knowing what to do with them. Wanting to say something witty, he came up short, and said, "Bullshit." The lie lacked conviction, even to his own ears.

"No, I think I'm on the money. It hurts your poor little ego that I'm buddies with El, and so you took it out on him."

Chalmers, as he had so often in his misspent life, scoffed at the truth. The truth hurt, so ignore it. The truth could wound, so dodge that shit like a bullet.

"You have friends. I only have you," he wanted to say, but couldn't. He'd promised to be the better man, but some situations made it a lot harder to live up to that promise than others.

"Look, man," he said aloud, "we got places to be." He turned and quick-marched the last few strides to the buggy.

Jackson muttered a string of expletives Chalmers could barely hear but followed after him. He was still shaking his head in disbelief as he climbed into the passenger seat.

Dropping into the battered vehicle, Chalmers kicked *Man-Eater*'s powerful engine over and put her in gear.

Murphy kicked the briefing room door closed behind his new adjutant-in-training. The kid—he couldn't have been more than eighteen—had reported that the colonel's shuttle was loaded and ready to head back upstairs. If he resented the interruption, it didn't show as he returned to the head of the long table that dominated the room.

"This operation will also be entirely clandestine: no uniforms, no copies of familiar weapons, and very little logistics other than what our groundside allies can furnish, though I have sureties from them that they will furnish everything necessary to ease your way into the local market. Comms will also be slow as well as intermittent, as we will not be able to risk transmitting in the vicinity of R'Bak Island. In short, Operation WORMWOOD is a go, gentlemen," Murphy said, bringing the informational portion of the briefing to an end. "Questions, comments, concerns?"

"Shit," Chalmers whispered, letting his chair fall to all four legs. "Where to begin?"

"A question, Chief?" Murphy leveled that cold stare at him.

"More a number of concerns, sir. We've barely heard of this couple, this Umaren and Vizzel, and you want us to turn them?"

"Two things. One: they already feel obligated to Sergeant Frazier for his aid. Two: I'd have thought they were your kind of people."

"*My* kind of people?" Chalmers asked, incredulous.

Beside him, Jackson covered a grin with one hand. He always seemed to enjoy it when Murphy—or any authority, for that matter—called "bullshit" on Chalmers's behavior.

Murphy raised his hands. "Smugglers, Chalmers. Not...not the other thing."

Chalmers didn't know whether to be more offended or less. He did know that if they'd been back on Earth, in the regular Army, and he'd not made a personal promise to be better, he might have considered threatening a complaint against Murphy under Don't Ask, Don't Tell. But none of those situations applied, so he said simply, "Left all that behind in the Mog, sir. Turned over a new leaf, sir."

Beside him, Jackson's arms wrapped around his chest as if

he was struggling to prevent a cough. Chalmers knew it for an attempt to stifle a chuckle. Every NCO worth his salt knew how "sir" rhymed with "cur," and when and where that mental translation should be applied. This being one such instance.

Murphy, never having been an NCO, missed it. In fact, his cold stare thawed slightly as it hung a moment on the fresh shrapnel scars on Chalmers's face. "Indeed you have. I simply want you to employ your considerable . . . powers for good, this time."

"Understood, sir," Chalmers said more easily. But because he couldn't entirely let it go, he added, "Not for nothing, but I'll have you know my people were bootleggers, Colonel."

"And that's different, how?" Murphy's eyes tightened with that cold look that made Chalmers nervous.

"For one, we wasn't crossing no borders, sir, just county lines." Chalmers continued in his thickest Southern drawl, "For 'nuther, my people never ran drugs nor evah carried guns. Just relied on speed an' knowin' t'back roads better'n t'revenuers."

Murphy cocked an eyebrow, the very set of his jaw radiating disbelief.

"My *people* never did," Chalmers repeated in a more understandable accent. "What *I* did in the Mog . . . and . . . elsewhere was not what my people were into."

His partner shifted uncomfortably in his seat. Chalmers avoided looking at him. They never talked openly about some of the more shady shit he'd been up to his neck in, not really. It wasn't necessary, not in the new universe they found themselves in, not after the things they'd been through together here.

Murphy shook his head. "While I enjoy hearing family histories as much as the next man, the need for your old skills—however acquired—persists. The nature of the ongoing threat the next wave of Kulsian ships poses to R'Bak dictates that we gather as much intelligence as quickly as we can on the island, its personnel, its security, and any and all vulnerabilities of the same."

"So you want someone to buddy up with the seaplane crew, set up a smuggling ring?" Jackson said.

Murphy nodded, shrugged. "From the report, the crew is already embedded in the black market, so it will be more a matter of 'making use of' than 'setting up.' I leave exactly how you do that up to you. I think that is the best route available, given your combined expertise."

"If I may, sir, I have additional concerns."

Murphy nodded permission.

"Will we be the only Lost Soldiers on R'Bak?"

"Eventually. And, after a time, you and the others with you will be on your own until we can safely return. We are almost finished pulling our conventional formations and cadre out to keep the incoming surveyors from learning the extent to which the R'Baku have had outside aid. We need the Kulsis survey guys fat and happy, or at least ignorant, so they don't go running back to their overlords for forces sufficient to hunt down the SpinDogs."

"Leaving aside questions of just how much of our presence here can be concealed, sir, I don't see how much a couple of investigators can reasonably expect to accomplish."

"As I informed you in the briefing, the expectations are not excessive, Chief," Murphy said. "We know your capabilities, and the SpinDogs are confident that the surveyors are, for the most part, unexceptional and incurious. People without much in the way of prospects on Kulsis who are here to collect the wealth of their superiors and return home with it."

Chalmers shook his head, deciding that particular subject was a dead issue. "What other assets will we have? The briefing was slim on details."

"In time, I'll be sending a couple of other specialists. Messina, first, I think."

"Who?" Chalmers and Jackson asked.

"A Vietnam-era security specialist. Due to recent events, we need him moved off the habitats, making him free to pull security for you and the crew."

And watchdog us, Chalmers thought.

"Very good, sir. Thank you, sir," Jackson said. "But I think the chief meant assets in terms of high-value items we can use to purchase cooperation from the indigs and, eventually, the Kulsians?"

"Ah, right. I'll arrange for our groundside allies to provide a selection of drugs, both recreational and medical, to trade with. We should also be able to arrange more specialized goods, given enough lead time and good reason."

"Makes sense, sir," Jackson said. Glancing at Chalmers to be sure he wasn't interrupting, he went on, "One question, sir: When can we expect Elroy to get healthy? I talked to the healers, but they weren't very forthcoming. I only ask because El—Sergeant Frazier—would be a big help in turning the crew our way." Chalmers could hear the concern for the other man in Jackson's voice.

A pained look flashed across the colonel's face before disappearing behind the cold mask of his habitual calm. "That is unknown. Sergeant Frazier did himself considerable damage. As I said, the healers have helped him improve quite a bit, but they remain less than optimistic about his return to full duty."

"Damn, sir," Chalmers said, glancing at Jackson. "I didn't think it was that serious."

"Does he know?" Jackson asked after a moment spent waiting for the colonel to continue.

"Know what?" Murphy asked.

"Does he know he might not make it back to Mar—Major Lee's crew?"

"I will make the appropriate notifications as and when necessary, Sergeant Jackson." He relented slightly, adding, "I'm told he needs to focus on getting better, just now."

Jackson opened his mouth to say something Chalmers knew he'd regret, so he spoke first. "The Clarthu are big on a good attitude leading to faster healing. A lot more than our docs were, back in the day."

"The SpinDog doctors also think in those terms," Murphy agreed, a strange expression Chalmers didn't recognize escaping his control for an instant.

Jackson gave a slow nod Chalmers chose to interpret as thanks for stepping in. He was still angry, though, so Chalmers changed the subject. "I assume we'll be using the plane trips to make our reports and pick up any contraband we'll be bringing in, Colonel?"

"Yes. We should be able to arrange a dead drop and commo bunker easily enough. And, when the time comes, we'll use the seaplane to connect other assets into your network as well."

"I bring it up, sir, because the indig crew is a critical failure point, and we don't know to what extent, if any, they'll buy in."

Colonel Murphy nodded. "Correct on all points, Chief. That's where we'll be forced to rely on their expressed debt of gratitude to Sergeant Frazier for saving the young crewman's life. We also plan to make them very wealthy and will rely on your ability to persuade both of them it is in their best self-interest."

"Didn't think you had this much faith in my ability as a salesman, Colonel."

A cold smile. "With Jackson's help, I'm sure you'll manage."

"And we'll be deployed on this op for a while, then?"

"Correct. You will be. Rest assured that I have someone in mind for ongoing intelligence operations once you've established a beachhead. Certain other dominoes have to fall before we can begin that phase, however."

Chalmers nodded, pulling his lip thoughtfully. "So, to summarize: We'll need to introduce ourselves, first, and that'll be harder to do without Sergeant Frazier, but we'll manage. Once we get a feel for where that relationship can take us, we start working our way up the food chain and into the more secure areas of the island. When we have a good idea of the lay of the land, we'll know better what we can accomplish. Is that correct?"

"Yes, Chief."

"Good. Then, I'd like some arms in addition to the drugs. Good to have on hand for bribes or other work—as needed?" He looked the question at Murphy.

"You'll have them."

"Good to know." He glanced again at Jackson, wondering if his only friend was still angry with him for treating El like shit. Taking a deep breath, he addressed Murphy again. "We'll be on our own for a couple months, right?"

"At least two months, as many as six or more." From Murphy's expression, it was clear he didn't want to go back over ground already trodden. "Consider it a vacation from military discipline and any requirement of wearing a uniform."

Chalmers shook his head. He was looking for an answer to a question he wasn't all that clear on himself. "This will be a long deployment without backup or extraction, on a mission we were never formally trained to do. It's not exactly what we"—he was about to say "signed up for," but settled on—"are used to."

Murphy's gaze wasn't *quite* as cold as it could get, but dropped to within a few degrees of its minimum possible temperature. "Just now joining the club, are we?"

Chalmers raised his hands in surrender. "Colonel, I'm not saying the rest of the Lost Soldiers ain't been handling rough business...God knows they have!" He looked at Jacks and rushed ahead. "But Sergeant Jackson here doesn't have to get saddled with another risky detail because I've got limited utility and a shitty record."

Jackson's surprised glance at Chalmers was missed by neither its subject nor Murphy.

Murphy's cold gaze warmed a few degrees. "Chief, Sergeant Jackson has made no request for reassignment."

Jackson nodded sharply.

"Until and *if* he should make such a request, I am not about to break up a proven team that I can rely on to adapt and fill the odd hole in my roster for those missions that require a high degree of adaptation to circumstances and spur-of-the-moment improvisation. This mission will not only rely a great deal on your extracurricular experience, but also draw on your investigative training and acumen."

Chalmers swallowed a lump in his throat, surprised at how much even an oblique compliment from Colonel Murphy meant to him. Or maybe it was the confirmation that Jackson wasn't trying to ditch his often troublesome partner. To cover for the sudden weird surge of pride, he asked, "When do you want to see results, sir?"

"Our best guess is a couple months or so to get the initial groundwork laid, make introductions, etcetera," Murphy said. "Then we start phase two."

"Phase two?"

Murphy nodded. "Once additional assets are in place, we start making moves. You'll understand if I do not go into specifics just now."

Jackson and Chalmers both nodded.

"That said," Murphy continued, "subsequent actions through the network may be on a much tighter timescale, given strategic considerations and the needs of the moment."

"Understood, sir," Chalmers said, looking at his partner for confirmation.

Jackson nodded.

"That will be all, then," Murphy muttered, turning away... but he turned back just as quickly. "One last thing, Chalmers. Not about the mission."

Now what did I do? "Yes, sir?"

"I've heard that you found a sound system on one of the Kulsian vehicles we shot up just after Imsurmik. Heard that you haven't been using the speakers for psyops as much as you have for entertaining the troops."

Always a snitch who can't wait to tattle to the CO like a little kindergarten shit. "Have there been a lot of those complaints, sir? I try to limit my use of it."

Murphy frowned. "I would characterize what I heard as comments rather than complaints. The only negative remark was that your playlist was...well, a bit repetitive."

Jacks rolled his eyes and exhaled like a man being saved from a shark tank. "'Bout time somebody said something, Colonel. The way he keeps playing them, it's like the songs are his anthems, sir. And, well, sir, I can't say I'm a fan of that cr—" He paused, went on, "Um, that kind of music."

Murphy raised an eyebrow as he turned toward Chalmers. "Would you care to elaborate, Chief?"

No, but I know a question that requires an answer when I hear one. Chalmers shrugged. "Guess you could say I've been going back to my roots, sir. Southern rock."

Jackson snorted. "Yeah, but only one band. And only one or two albums."

"Yeah, because they're the only tapes the Ktor threw in with the rest of the gear," Chalmers rebutted. But that wasn't entirely true; he did play one song more than the others. A lot, actually.

Murphy was nodding. "Lynyrd Skynyrd, if the reports are accurate."

"Guilty as charged, sir. Grew up to it. And, well, I guess some of it shaped me."

"Which songs?" Murphy asked. A sardonic grin: "'Call Me the Breeze,' maybe?"

Chalmers couldn't decide whether he was more surprised at Murphy's ready knowledge of the band, or injured by his choice of that particular song. "No, sir," he said, trying not to sound like he was sulking. "I mostly play that one to remind myself who I shouldn't be anymore."

"So, if that's not your new anthem, then what is?"

"'Simple Man,'" Chalmers said, surprised at the speed and eagerness of his response. It felt like a confession. Or, as his backwoods Baptist gramma had put it, like he was "shrivin' hisself."

Murphy's other eyebrow raised to join the first. "If I recall those lyrics correctly, that's quite a resolution you've adopted."

He stood, put out a hand. "Good luck, gentlemen. You are dismissed." Surprised, they shook his hand and left.

"You feel that tremor in his palm?" Jacks asked in a low voice when they had emerged back into the busy dust of the camp's breakdown.

Chalmers nodded. "Overworked, I guess."

"More like he was overcome by your choir-boy bullshit," Jackson muttered.

At a different time, on another planet, Chalmers would have told his partner to go fuck himself. But that was part of what he was trying to leave behind: part of his resolution, as Murphy had said with pleased surprise in his voice and eyes. "Yeah, Jacks," Chalmers eventually replied, "you're probably right."

Jackson stopped and stared.

But Chalmers just kept walking back to *Man-Eater*, his gramma's face in his mind's eye and the lyrics of "Simple Man" rolling through his head.

Chapter Four

"Easy with it," Major Kevin Bowden said. "Easy...come right a little..."

The pilot, Burg Hrensku, initiated a ten-degree angle of bank, keeping the laser from going into its gimbal stops. Bowden tweaked the joystick minutely, re-centering the crosshairs on the target—a guardhouse with two mounted .50 caliber machine guns. A similar facility on the other side of the road was already a smoking ruin.

The crosshairs flashed, indicating the bomb had three seconds time of flight left, then the guardhouse detonated as the weapon struck home.

"Shadow, this is Hornet," Bowden transmitted. "The gates are down. I say again: the gates are down."

"Roger," the ground commander replied. "The gates are down. We are en route."

Two miles away, from behind a low hill, a column of vehicles started forward.

Bowden smiled and looked across the cockpit of the interface craft at his SpinDog pilot. "That's two for two. Looks like the drinks are on you."

"It is not fair," his pilot said. "With the new lasers and laser receivers your Colonel Murphy had us autofab, it is almost too easy."

"This one is, because no one's shooting at us. It gets harder when there are missiles in the air."

"Maybe next time I need to arm the satrap's vassals," Hrensku grumbled.

"Thanks, but no," Bowden replied. "I've been shot at enough for two lifetimes, thank you very much."

Bowden watched as the convoy proceeded past the wrecked guard posts and into the small village in the ravine behind it. Several muzzle flashes winked from inside the cluster of huts. The trucks stopped and the men inside deployed, going to ground to return fire.

The assault was over in ten minutes. The villagers had relied too much on the nested machine guns to keep them safe; they were unprepared for the new way of war the Lost Soldiers had brought to the planet. Bowden and Hrensku provided cover until the assault was over—they still had three more bombs if they'd been needed—then they returned to base.

Major Bo Moorefield was waiting for them as they came out of the debriefing room. "How'd it go?" he asked.

"No problems," Bowden replied. "The new tech works well, and the indigs weren't expecting their guardhouses to spontaneously combust. Looked like Cutter's guys didn't have much resistance."

"Good," Moorefield said with a nod. "Another one for the good guys." He cocked his head. "Hey, they've started the quick turnaround on the jet you came in on." The interface craft—when they were used in an atmospheric role—had become "jets" over the last few months, even though the scramjet aircraft were definitely *not* like the jets the Lost Soldiers had left two hundred years and almost as many light-years behind them. "Murphy needs to talk to you upstairs."

"Ugh." Bowden shook his head. "Two RATOs in one day." The scramjets used rocket-assisted takeoff modules to get into the air for combat missions and trips to space to save fuel. Although the technology had improved recently, and they were less likely to malfunction, *less likely* didn't mean the modules didn't still fail spectacularly sometimes . . . making takeoffs far more dangerous than catapulting off an aircraft carrier, which Bowden had always thought was a crazy way to get into the air.

Bowden looked at Hrensku. "Want to take me upstairs?"

The SpinDog frowned, obviously not impressed with the idea of two RATO launches in a day, either, but then he sighed. "Sure. I need to get"—he paused, trying to recall the correct idiom—"some of *my stuff* from the hab." The amount of slang that the SpinDogs were picking up had gone from being impressive to downright scary.

Bowden nodded his thanks, tossed out a little more slang: "Cool." Although Bowden was fully qualified to pilot the interface craft in the atmosphere, he wasn't qualified in space and needed someone to shuttle him up to the habitat.

Hrensku frowned slightly at the word "cool," but nodded. "Let me grab a quick bite to eat," Hrensku added, "and then we can go."

"Would that work for Murphy?" Bowden asked.

"Yeah," Moorefield replied. "It was important, I think, but not urgent."

"You and Cutter coming along for the ride?"

Bo stared at the sky, then at the dying scrub of the Ashbands. "We'll take the last one." He smiled. "Not quite done saying goodbye to this shithole."

Bowden shook his head. Why Moorefield and Cutter had jumped on Murphy's downward-bound transatmo had been a mystery to him. Until, that is, he saw them staring at the sky and the desert and the barren hills; however much the place sucked, they were afraid they might never see it again.

Kevin shrugged. "Suit yourself. Just don't go and get shot."

"I'd better not," Bo scoffed, "or Liza will *kill* me."

Several days later, Bowden walked into the office of Colonel Rodger Murphy, aboard *Spin One*. Nothing had changed on the main rotational habitat of the SpinDogs, or in the CO's office... except that almost a quarter of the usually tidy desk was now occupied by a sizable slab of metal.

Bowden jutted his chin at it. "I heard about the memorial. I was sorry to miss it."

Murphy's nod had a hint of apology in it. "Wish we could have waited, Kevin, but it was getting to the point where if we didn't do it while we could—"

"—then it might never happen at all." Bowden smiled. "Been there, done that. Looks like you left some extra space on the far right-hand margin."

Murphy nodded. "I'd like to think we're done taking casualties, but..." He sighed and leaned back in his chair, motioning for Bowden to take a seat of his own. "So, as I hear it, you've had a busy time down on R'Bak, gathering the simulator data and finishing the last training cycle. How'd it go?"

"Fine, sir," Bowden replied. "The SpinDogs are getting pretty good at plinking targets with the new laser gear you got in the last download. Didn't get to finish gathering data for the simulators, though." He grinned. "Too much real work to do."

"Hopefully, they are up to finishing the pre-evac target list without you, because I need you up here, now. A very different assignment."

Bowden arched an eyebrow. "Oh?"

"I can't give you all the details now, but I need you to learn how to fly spacecraft."

"Okay . . . can you at least tell me what types of ships?"

Murphy smiled apologetically. "All of them, at least for now."

"And that's all the info I get?"

"That's all you *need* at this moment. We're taking a look at some . . . opportunities we may have, and I want you prepared if they come to pass. Go. Learn how to fly as well—or better—in space than you do in atmosphere. That's a big enough task for now. I don't know how things are going to shake out, but I need you ready for anything."

Bowden shrugged. "I always wanted to be able to pilot the interface craft back up to the habs; I guess now I get to learn. I'm good with that, sir." He looked around the office. "Where am I going for this training?"

"The training will start here, probably move to Outpost for a bit, and then will come back here for the final bits."

"Okay . . ."

Murphy sighed and cocked his head, obviously trying to decide how much to tell Bowden. He gave a brief nod—just a single jerk of his head—to show he'd come to a decision and explained, "You will start by training with one of the RockHounds."

"Not one of the SpinDogs?"

"No, a RockHound. You probably haven't had much to do with them because they don't have much to do with R'Bak."

Bowden shrugged. "No, not a lot of contact. I know they're scattered in small communities all over the outer system, and that they get pretty isolated during the Sear: minimal travel when the Harvesters come to town. Prospectors, miners, and salvage-monkeys, mostly."

Murphy nodded. "And because they spend all their time in space, they're the ones best able to teach you the tricks and traps of spaceflight. It was easier to have one come here to start the training since they don't really have 'cities' or big facilities to work out of.

"Once you generally know what you're doing, and your instructor pilot doesn't think you're too much of a hazard to people and equipment, he'll take you over to Outpost to run a few flights in a more austere environment. Once he's satisfied you can safely solo pilot in space, he'll bring you back here for the final portion of your training—flying to the planet and back. Since the Rock-Hounds almost never go to the planet, a SpinDog will instruct you on that portion.

"Does it all make sense now?"

Bowden nodded and sat back in his chair. "Yes, sir, it does. When do I get started?"

Murphy looked over Bowden's shoulder and out the door. "Seaman Lasko, is Karas'tan out there yet?"

"Yes, sir," a voice replied.

"Please send him in."

A rather tall and thin man with dark hair strode into the room. The one thing Bowden noticed immediately was that the man's eyes never stopped moving for more than a brief second. *Search. Spot Target. Identify. Repeat.*

"This is Karas'tan Kamara," Murphy said. "He's the Rock-Hound who will be teaching you spaceflight."

Bowden stood to shake the man's hand and met his scanning eyes. As they made contact, a corner of the man's lips dipped. Bowden chuckled to himself. *Already been measured and found wanting. Just like starting flight training in Pensacola all over again.* At least there weren't any drill sergeants yelling at him. *Not yet, anyway.*

"Good to meet you," Bowden said, suppressing a scowl of his own. "I'm looking forward to learning everything I can from you, although I'm sort of surprised to see you here."

"Why is that?"

"I would have thought we'd be meeting someplace, uh..."

"With less gravity? I've spent weeks preparing for the weight. It was not pleasant." He shrugged. "Are you ready to begin?" Kamara asked.

"Now?" Bowden asked. The RockHound's lips—both corners this time—dipped again, and he looked like he'd just eaten something sour. Bowden smiled. "Of course, I'm ready. Let's go!"

The man nodded once, said his goodbye to Murphy, and led Bowden through the habitat to a small room with a table, a couple chairs, and a marker board.

"Most of our training will be behind the controls of a ship," Kamara said. "There are, however, a few things we need to cover before we get into one of the craft and begin flinging yourself around the system, as I'm sure you're in a hurry to do."

"Well, I hadn't really given it a lot of thought," Bowden replied. "My flight time has pretty much been limited to in-atmo work." He chuckled. "In fact, I didn't find out that I was learning spaceflight until about one minute before I met you."

"But your people have flown in space, yes? You are familiar, I hope, with the concepts of spaceflight?"

"Some," Bowden acknowledged. "I wanted to be an astronaut back when I first got into the Navy. I was on track for the program...but things happened that led me in another direction, then I wound up here, and I've pretty much been flying attack and support flights on the planet. There hasn't really been a lot of time to think about flying in space."

"What do your people do for this 'astronaut' training?"

"There's a bunch of classroom work, I know. Studying what craft you'll fly and space station systems—stuff like that—along with a bunch of other things like Earth sciences, meteorology, space science, and engineering. The astronauts in training also learn land and water survival, aircraft operations, and scuba diving."

"Scuba diving? What is that?"

"It's when you dive deep into a body of water and stay down for a long time using a rebreather or tank system."

Kamara's brows knit. "But your people *have* space flight, correct?"

"Yes."

"And you start out by diving in water?"

"Correct. Then the trainees—depending on whether they are going to be pilots or mission specialists—learn the different skills they need for their positions. Pilots learn to fly the craft and mission specialists to conduct spacewalks, perform robotics tasks, and conduct scientific research."

Kamara laughed for a few seconds. "That is *not* how we're going to do it here. We're going to skip the majority of that and go right into space. After all, we're here, and there are no bodies of water in which to do your scuba thing. Also, we will be flying small craft, especially to start. You will be a pilot and a *mission specialist* at the same time. There is no division of duties, beyond what I tell you. Every RockHound can fly *and* conduct spacewalks."

"You asked how we did it, so I told you," Bowden said. "I'm prepared to learn the way you want to teach."

"Are you?"

"Am I what?"

"Are you really prepared to learn? Your people show up here and immediately change the way everything is done. We have been safe here for many centuries, yet now we are exposed because of your blundering. Then, afterward, you start telling us how things are now going to be done, and why we have to do it 'your way.'

"I have trained a number of SpinDogs in spaceflight, and the ones who have had the hardest times are those who were already familiar with flying in atmosphere. Spaceflight is different. Just because something works in atmosphere doesn't mean it works the same way here."

"Look," Bowden said. "You can tell me everything you want—everything you can, really—about how to fly in space. I'll gladly learn at your knee. It's my understanding, though, that you don't fly in atmosphere, so don't knock my piloting skills until you can land a plane on a ship. When you've done that, *then* we can talk."

His eyes got wide. "You've landed aircraft on ships? Like, the kind that operate on water? On purpose?"

"Yeah. Of course, the ships were a little bigger than the largest ones I've seen on R'Bak, and the aircraft were smaller than the interface craft I've been flying, but the principle is the same. Big ocean, little ship, and land the plane on it."

"In a hover, like I've heard your helicopters do?"

"No, landing on it like an aircraft does at the airfield. Except the airfield is on the water, moving in all three axes, and is a whole lot shorter."

"I don't think I'd want to do that." Kamara's eyes narrowed. "It would seem to take a certain kind of suicidal idiot to even attempt it."

Bowden chuckled. "Yeah, that's what we thought sometimes, too." He smiled. "Regardless, I've done that, and you haven't, so how about giving me at least a little respect for my piloting skills, all right?"

A smile ghosted across Kamara's face, then he gave a small twitch of a nod. "If you have rendezvoused with objects moving in all three axes, perhaps you will manage to earn my respect. I will tell you again, though, the people who have the hardest time with spaceflight are the ones who have a lot of atmospheric flight time."

✧   ✧   ✧

"This is what we'll be flying," Kamara said later as they approached a small packet-type craft in one of the habitat's docking bays.

"Really?" Bowden asked. "Doesn't look like much." He'd seen some of the smaller craft before but hadn't paid them much attention. They were fairly spindly-looking compared with in-atmo craft. "Where'd you get it from?"

Kamara frowned. "That's my ship."

Oops. Open mouth; insert foot. "Sorry," Bowden said. "I didn't mean anything bad by that. I just assumed you'd need something bigger, for umm...exploring things and bringing back ore and..." He tried to come up with something else to add but couldn't. He tried a different tack. "I expected we'd be flying one of the interface craft, since I'll have to learn liftoffs and reentries with it."

Kamara shrugged, looking away. From his tone, Bowden could tell he was only partially mollified. "Perhaps if we had your capabilities, where we could destroy anyone who wasn't our friends in the system, we might use bigger craft that are more noticeable. Then we also could fly wherever we wanted, whenever we wanted. As it is, though, we stay alive by staying hidden, and this craft is a lot easier to hide than the SpinDogs' interface craft."

"That makes sense," Bowden said. He chuckled ruefully. "With our friends no longer here in the system, it's probably a skill I need to learn, too. Maybe even more so than launches and reentries. Getting caught by a Kulsian military craft wouldn't have a very good ending."

"It would not." Kamara shrugged. "Besides, this craft is a lot better for prospecting. It's more maneuverable, which also makes it a better ship for you to learn on. There's less chance of you wrecking it. It's also smaller and less expensive so it will be cheaper to fix when you do ultimately wreck it."

"I thought that we already agreed I had flying skills."

"No, we agreed you had flying skills in atmosphere. *You* agreed that those skills translated into skills that were applicable to flying my ship. They are not. Almost everyone crashes spacecraft when they are learning, especially pilots with any significant in-atmo experience. Things don't work the same in space, and your eye—the way you view things—is going to tell you things that will be untrue in your new environment."

"Like what?"

"We'll get to that, but for the moment, you'll have to take it on faith." Kamara shrugged. "Let me show you the ship." He led Bowden around the craft, showing him the various systems. As a Navy Test Pilot School graduate and an applicant for the astronaut program, Bowden was able to understand the systems, even the ones he hadn't necessarily seen before, like the asteroid capture system.

As they went around, a new question formed as he looked at the systems bolted to the skin of the packet. While some looked to be permanent fixtures, others were obviously new and didn't look like a lot of thought had been put into where—or how—to hang them. "Are all these type of craft the same?" he finally asked.

"No," Kamara replied. "The main parts are generally interchangeable—motors, fuel tanks, and such—but every Rock-Hound has his or her own needs. Where they're going, what they're doing, and how they're going to do it once they get there. About the only thing in common is that you won't see any that are appreciably bigger than this ship."

"Because of the need to hide?"

Kamara nodded. "Exactly."

They started down the starboard side, and Bowden chuckled.

"What is it?" Kamara asked, sounding defensive.

"It's nothing." He pointed to a laser range finder. "If nothing else, I have experience with *that*. It's what we use to bomb with." He smiled. "It looks a lot better on your ship than the way they first wired it into the interface craft."

Kamara looked around the hangar bay. "Don't ever trust a SpinDog to wire anything into your craft. They are"—he thought for a moment—"sloppy."

"What do you mean?"

"They don't work on craft as if their lives depended on their repairs. Sure, *they do* ... but they never go very far from the habitats or the Outpost. Somebody can always go retrieve them if necessary. We go out on our ships for months, prospecting and salvaging, harvesting oxygen and hydrogen from ice, and we are often out of range of help. If you are two days away from the nearest ship or ice chunk and find out you have a day's worth of air remaining because there was a small leak..." His voice trailed off ominously.

"Yeah, that would be a bad place to be," Bowden agreed with a nod. "Got it; always check everything that's been done to your craft when someone else has been working on it."

Kamara nodded seriously. "You should always treat everything in this ship as if your life depended on it. It does."

Bowden took a deep breath and nodded. It wasn't something he'd really considered before. Sure, you preflight your aircraft before you accept it and take it airborne, but it was easy to dismiss small leaks or other minor problems. He'd once pointed out a puddle of hydraulic fluid under the aircraft next to his on the flight deck of the aircraft carrier. The Intruder guy had laughed and said that was normal. "If it ain't leaking, you better get it serviced 'cause it's empty," the bombardier had said at the time. Taking a ship into deep space for months at a time, though, would require a whole new level of detailed preflight.

You can't just eject out of a spacecraft if it stops working on you.

Kamara chuckled. "I can see from the look on your face you grasp the seriousness of knowing your systems are operational."

"Yeah. It's not a matter of life or death. It's more important than that."

"It is," Kamara said.

"Do you have the tac manuals for the equipment?"

"'Tac manuals'?"

"Yeah, the publications that tell you how to use the equipment. I'd like to study them before we get started. Learn the checklists."

"We do not have tac manuals. That is for SpinDogs. Some of the equipment comes with an installation or operating guide, but most do not. And we do not use checklists. Everything is too individualized with each craft. There is no standardization; you just learn what your craft needs and do it."

"How about a wiring guide so I know how things are powered?"

"Did I not say that most ships are individualized? The wiring will vary with the ship and how it's used. Not to mention everyone's ships have different electrical busses..."

"How do you learn all the systems, then, if you don't have the system specs for your gear?"

"You learn from one of the existing shipmasters." Kamara winked. "And you're one of the luckiest people on this hab."

"Why's that?"

"You've got *me* to show you not only the ship itself but also how to fly it." He smiled. "Let's step inside, and I will show you the interior."

Chapter Five

"You do not understand, Sko'Belm Murphy. I am not saying we cannot fashion these devices in the numbers you require. Rather, it is the number of *different objects* that exceeds our capacity."

Murphy might not have believed that assertion had it come from anyone but Anseker. The others at the table—his closest ally Primus Jedkom of Family Usrensekt, Medrost, and now Legate Orgunz in place of Korelon—were all nodding somberly. No, Murphy realized, none of them were holding back on this facet of their replication capacities; they were telling the truth. Which was sobering in two ways: firstly, their unanimous and grave admission meant they had put their pride and caution aside because they accepted that their survival was truly at stake; and secondly, they understood that this particular shortfall could be damning to the only plan that might save them.

He sighed. "Okay. But I need to understand why. I suspect that's going to be a central data point as we rearrange our priorities to accommodate this new"—he was going to say "limitation," but realized he'd better go with—"wrinkle in our production outline."

Primus Jedkom leaned forward, folding his hands. He was the elder statesman of the group, older than Orgunz and far more composed; therefore, a more significant ally—or opponent. "From what you have told us of the factories of your home-world, Sko'Belm Murphy, I would offer this analog: How many of the persons involved in the industries that create your goods are involved in the *design* of them versus the number that are involved in the fabrication of them?"

Murphy nodded, seeing where this was going. "I couldn't tell you exactly, but there are far more fabricators than designers."

"It is no different here." Seeing Murphy's dubious frown, Jedkom held up a hand. "I believe I foresee the nature of your misperception. You hear us refer to our machines being able to produce objects from merely scanning their blueprints. You understandably interpret that in terms of what that would mean in your world...but it means something very different in ours.

"Your people apparently possess a form of automation in which the great challenge is making the devices that fabricate individual parts and then assemble them into complete devices. For us, this is the simpler part of the process. The truly laborious part is creating the instructions that guide the machines in this process—which is apparently much easier for you.

"Our historic need has been to create many extremely reliable and accurate units of a finite number of designs. From smelting ore to parts production and then basic assembly, once an autofabricator is fully primed with instructions, it can maintain almost nonstop output with minimal human oversight. However, while it does scan and design the forms and molds for the new devices, they are usually large in scale and simple to assemble. This is why retooling to produce the guns and ammunition and tools you required was comparatively easy; they are comparatively relatively simple assemblies comprised of parts with comparatively forgiving tolerances. However, your helicopters—the Hueys?—were far more challenging."

Murphy nodded. Early on, one of Primus Kormak's liaisons had claimed that if the Hueys had not possessed such complicated wiring and electronics, they could have been assembled in a third the time. He'd always suspected that the scumbag in question, Bramath, had been exaggerating, and he probably had been. But now, Murphy wondered about his own eager readiness to dismiss the man's assertions. Of course, Bramath had been ready—and certainly eager—to kill him on two separate occasions. Which, Murphy allowed, might have led him to be less than perfectly objective in the matter.

Jedkom, running a hand through his thinning mane of white hair, might have been reading Murphy's mind. "I suspect many of you believed us to be exaggerating the time and difficulty of producing the Hueys, but we were not. As your own men—such as Major Bowden—shall soon learn, our spacecraft are designed to be simple, not only because it makes them easier to repair and modify, but because it makes them much easier to produce." He shook his head. "I remember when one of our autofab techs brought me to look at your helicopter's 'transmission' and its extraordinarily compact radio and avionics. We could not understand why anyone would create such intricate, fragile devices.

"However, as soon as our pilots began flying them, we understood. Whereas we need long-duration spaceships that are easy to operate and repair, you need machines that are light, compact, *and* strong in order to have the best possible performance—and so, survivability—in battle."

Murphy nodded. "I can only imagine your reaction when you reviewed our latest requests for command, control, and computing systems."

Usrensekt answered with a wry smile. "I wonder if you *can* imagine, actually. We will have to retool—not recalibrate, *retool*—any autofab tasked to produce them, due to the smallness and exacting tolerances of the parts.

"But that is not the greatest impediment. As I said, our system is automated but on a very simple level. It can assess the parts of a hand-built device, measure its components, and then turn raw materials into that finished product. However, even if it could scan your crowded blueprints, it would not be able to determine the most efficient sequence of molding, polishing, and combining the dozens of small components into a completed subassembly."

Murphy smiled. "Oh, is that all?"

"Actually, it is not." Either Usrensekt chose not to take the bait for a bit of sardonic banter or did not notice it. "Most of these new designs you have put before us—while marvels of sophistication—have subassemblies with *hundreds* of separate parts that should be handled by tweezers. For each of them, a separate autofab process has to be designed and optimized for mass production. This requires a human designer—who is also an experienced mechanic—to create and refine an entirely novel production line that produces each subassembly with at least reasonable efficiency." He leaned back. "And, of course, most of your devices depend not on one, simple integration of subassembly, but on large subassemblies that are built up from smaller subassemblies, which are in turn built up from even smaller ones."

Perhaps emboldened by Murphy's patient nodding, Orgunz leaned forward aggressively. "Then there is the matter of your electronics and computers," he added, making a warding sign as he uttered the last word. "Building a craft or other large construct which contains many such assemblies requires humans to install, test, and troubleshoot them. And the more there are in a given construct, the longer this process takes."

"So you see," Anseker said in a surprisingly reasonable tone, "when we produce especially complex machines, each one requires a specially-designed production process and significant amounts of manual retooling for the autofabs. For the vehicles you hope to create now, the challenge is exponentially greater. Whereas combining all our autofab resources barely increases our capacity by a single order of magnitude."

Murphy acceded with a nod. "I understand." And he did, but Jedkom was right; he'd failed to grasp how far beyond the SpinDogs' sophistication many of the new requirements would be. Murphy and his cadre had noticed the peculiar paucity of advanced logic elements from the outset and had even mentioned it to their hosts. The SpinDogs had haughtily explained that such devices were avoided because of ancient warnings, *not* lack of understanding.

And it had seemed an entirely reasonable explanation on the face of it, particularly given their obvious superiority in engineering. Propulsion systems, solar power, fuel cells, thermal recapture, composite materials, environmental processing: Murphy and his senior staff had been dazzled by the achievements—and so, accepted the SpinDog explanation for the lack of equally advanced IT—without ever realizing that they had done so.

And now, in between nods, Murphy realized how it had happened. It wasn't because he and the others had been stupid or unobservant; it was because they'd all been *trained* to expect and navigate cultural differences. They were confident they knew what to look for, what to expect. But that confidence had been their undoing, because neither their training nor experience had prepared them for the subtle yet bizarre interplay of social variables and equally bizarre social forms that were the norm in 55 Tauri.

Back in the Mog, they'd all learned—firsthand—the dangers

of cultural projection in the often grim and puzzling communities of that region. Even when you encountered what seemed like parallels in behavior and values, you learned not to trust that—because the cost of being wrong might not just be your own life, but those of your whole team.

But that hadn't prepared them for being equally alert when dealing with a culture that appeared to be technologically *superior.* After all, they were living among space-farers who cruised the star-strewn deep on a daily basis, lived in spinning asteroid habitats a mile long, blithely relied on environmental recirculation systems, and were able to replicate a wide variety of machines with ease. It was like living in the kind of society shown in science fiction movies—and the optimistic ones, no less.

So it had been all too easy to believe that, if it was really needed, the SpinDogs would be able to understand and churn out the information tech that Murphy's cadre took for granted and now desperately needed: comm hardware that could drive sophisticated encryption and decryption programs; electronic warfare suites that performed hundreds of tasks per second; algorithm-driven smart systems to support every shipboard role; and computer-generated projections of everything from bogey vector predictions to fuel-optimizing navigation plots. And that was the short list.

But the reality was that, just as the SpinDogs' twenty-first-century technology was slaved to 1960s control systems, their minds were, too. The techs who produced and worked on their rudimentary systems were certainly bright and glad for the sudden attention. They were becoming de facto engineers fairly quickly according to early reports, but it remained to be seen if that transition would occur quickly enough for what had to be done.

Murphy completed his third nod. "It seems we have some hard choices before us."

"I would say so," Medrost grumbled. He hadn't forgiven Murphy for interrupting him at their prior meeting. Probably never would, knowing SpinDogs in general and Primae in particular. At that moment, he would have given a lot to have the calming influence of the Otlethes' Breedmistress Shumrir at the table, but these meetings had been restricted to the senior leaders of each group.

"Where shall we begin trimming your list, Sko'Belm Murphy?"

Orgunz asked, not exactly pleased with the tasks before them, but clearly happy that even the commander of the Lost Soldiers would leave the conference table nursing disappointments.

But Murphy had come prepared to cut items; in his experience, no wish list or budget ever survived first contact with reality. "The new personal weapons—we can do without those."

The others at the table were surprised at the speed with which he made the decision, and there was no small amount of relief among them.

While they were still happily stunned, Murphy seized the initiative to both end on that high note and buy himself more time to consider the sharply revised—and depressing—calculus of the local autofabbing resources. "I'll need a little time to rebalance our requests to ensure they remain focused on the prime operational requirements. You'll have those revisions within twenty-four hours."

That produced unanimous nods, but opened the door for a new topic—which Jedkom put forth as soon as his head was still. "You have often stressed that the operations in question have as many fundamental intelligence requirements as technical. What is the status of that half of the equation?"

Murphy shrugged. "Pending. We have found no new persons of interest since we took Imsurmik. Frankly, we didn't expect to. The few coursers that are still alive have either gone into deep hiding or are dead. So, until the surveyors arrive, we won't have any new intel sources on the Kulsians' plans or forces."

"And what of the Kulsian *wa'hrektop* you captured in Imsurmik? He is named Yukannak, I think? Has he continued to share useful information?"

"He has, but we remain uncertain of his reliability. Until we have a second, comparably authoritative source that we can debrief separately, we have nothing against which to check what Yukannak has told us. And so, it is impossible to tease out any half- or un-truths that he may have blended into what he's shared thus far."

"But you feel confident in presuming that the balance of what he tells you is, in fact, reliable?"

"I do."

"That seems very optimistic."

"With respect, Primus Usrensekt, I feel it is the most likely situation. Naturally, we cannot expect him to be fully truthful and forthcoming. He is our enemy and no doubt still hopes to find a way to ingratiate himself with the Harvesters when they arrive.

"But he is also a professional, one of the few that were put in place to keep the coursers moving in the right direction. And, as a professional, he knows that our first priority will be to get a second source as a means of verifying the information he's given us. Which will naturally dictate how much his further cooperation is—or isn't—worth to us."

"And even if his information is all confirmed, still I would not trust him!" Orgunz exclaimed in a fast, harsh rush of words.

Murphy smiled. "I completely agree, Legate. You will note that I never said I'd trust him. My concern—for now—is determining how much we may rely upon the information we get from him."

Orgunz folded his arms, settled back. "Very well, Sko'Belm, but so long as he lives, we are carrying a poisoned knife against our chest."

"I agree." Murphy looked around the table. "Anything else that needs discussion? Legate? Primae?" He'd used the formal plural, which drew a squint of appreciation from leather-faced Usrensekt.

He was about to rise and bid them farewell when Medrost leaned forward. "Not a matter of discussion. Merely a final bit of business, Sko'Belm Murphy. It has been decided that Major Tapper may only bring one person up to the spins. Please communicate that to him with all haste." Medrost didn't quite smile. "From your updates, it seems he has little time to make his choice."

Makarov, who had been silently taking notes throughout the meeting, glanced at Murphy, who read the subtle cues of alarm in his eyes.

Murphy stood and nodded as the others rose to go, but kept his eyes on Medrost. "Thank you for that information, Primus Erfrenzh."

You petty son of a bitch.

Chapter Six

"A moment if I may, sir," Makarov called from over his shoulder. Murphy had forgotten his multiple sclerosis and his long, rapid strides had left the shorter Russian behind.

Murphy took the angry speed out of his walk. "What is it, Mack?"

The Muscovite had jogged to catch up with the American. "Sir, I apologize for making this request after such a . . . an unforeseen conclusion to the meeting, but if I do not bring it before you now, I fear—"

"Mack, it's okay. Just spit it out." Not the patient, hopefully avuncular tone for which he'd been aiming, but a lot better than biting poor Pyotr's head off.

"Yes, sir. To be brief—"

Please, oh please, be brief.

"—I wish to volunteer. For what is coming, that is."

Murphy almost missed a step when he glanced over at the Russian. "'For what is coming?' And just what would that be?"

Makarov somehow managed to fidget and keep walking at the same time. "Sir, just because you have not informed me of all your plans does not mean I cannot infer some of them. Particularly the final phase. And for what it is worth, I have been working on my movement in weightless environments. Of all kinds. Assiduously."

Well, well, "Pistol Pete" Makarov wants to come out from behind his desk. Which was, truth be told, not welcome news. "Behind

49

his desk" was just where Murphy wanted to keep the Russian's
skill set. Not because it was convenient—well, not *just* because of
that—but because Makarov's aptitudes made him what the strategy
and tactics manuals dubbed a "force-multiplier."

Still, his request was reasonable, and the least Murphy could
do was take it seriously. "I see you've given this some thought,
Mack. I will keep you in mind when and if we have to staff the
kind of team you're referring to." Murphy did not mention that he
not only knew about Pete's zero-gee practice regimen—including
combat movement—but that the linguistics professor–turned Red
Army translator had been making respectable progress.

But, still... "C'mon, Pete. Level with me—why the sudden itch
to jump into operations?" He smiled. "I mean, I know the same
four walls get dull and that I can be a bastard of a boss, but..."

As Murphy had suspected, that self-deprecating jibe opened a
conversational spigot that the voluble Russian usually kept sealed:
the one pertaining to personal matters. "No, no, sir!" he insisted
hastily. "You are actually one of the most fair and even-tempered
officers under which I have ever served!"

Ignoring Makarov's awkward insistence not to end a sentence
with a preposition, Murphy reflected that his adjutant's praise might
be genuine. It was equally likely that, assuming the scuttlebutt
about Soviet officers was true, that hadn't set his bar too high—

"But," Pete continued in a rush, "I am, to my knowledge,
the only Lost Soldier with combat training who has not been
called upon to use it." He hunched slightly as he muttered, "The
men—and the women—are beginning to make... well, unflatter-
ing conjectures about my bravery."

Murphy smiled. "You mean, the same ones they make about
me?"

"Sir! I was not suggesting—" He straightened. "Colonel Murphy,
nothing makes me as impatient with your countrymen as those
absurd smears! This is not a game. We cannot afford to lose you."

But you will, soon enough. Murphy controlled a tremor in
the hand with which he waved away Makarov's loyal indigna-
tion; random motions like that were gaps through which the
multiple sclerosis tried to slip through and betray him. "No one
is irreplaceable," Murphy asserted with conviction. He had been
repeating that mantra to everyone, every chance he got. That way,
when his time was up, whoever replaced him would be buttressed

against the superstitious fears that often followed the loss of a long-term CO, no matter how much grousing there'd been when he was alive. Death had the power to transmogrify the nastiest, hard-ass CO into the unit's lost lucky penny, without whom the whole sodding bunch might fall apart. Pure bullshit, but that didn't stop it from becoming belief in the barracks.

"I understand and share your feelings, Pete," Murphy added. "Sitting around while everyone else is risking life and limb dirtside?" He shook his head. "There's no way that can ever feel right." *Not even when you know that you'd be a danger to anyone who had to physically depend on you.*

He spotted a familiar figure with a familiar gait approaching. "Healer Naliryiz, is this a chance meeting or were you heading my way?"

"That depends. Where are you headed?"

"Where else? Lost Soldier country." Which was one of the many monikers—not all flattering—by which they referred to their tiny, tightly compartmentalized section of *Spin One*.

Her answer came along with a crooked smile. "I suppose I could be persuaded to make my journey a bit longer by going that way."

As they closed the last few yards between them, Makarov performed a quick bow in the direction of the First Healer of Family Otlethes. Before she could even utter a word of greeting, he turned to Murphy. "I must run ahead, Colonel. There is much to do."

Murphy nodded. "And here are two more things to put on the top of your list when you get back. First, have the cadre come see me before mess."

"An emergency, sir?"

"No, but I've got to get them up to speed on this afternoon's news. And second, please send word to Major Tapper. He'll need every minute, now."

Makarov did not move off with the alacrity he'd been poised to exhibit. "The major...he would want to hear it from you, sir."

Murphy felt like he'd swallowed a rock and said, "I know." *But I've got to stay here. Naliryiz might be able to explain why the Dogs are pulling this bullshit on Harry.* "Tell him I'm going to find out if there's any wiggle room. If the comms window is still open when I get back, I'll give him a shout."

"Very good, sir." And with another bow to Naliryiz, Makarov was off.

Naliryiz stared after him. "He is a strange person," she observed. "In some ways, he is more like a SpinDog than any of the rest of you. And yet, in other ways, he could not be more different." She turned back to Murphy, and, as they started strolling side by side, she asked, "Is Major Tapper in some kind of trouble?"

"I was hoping you might be able to shed some light on that very topic."

Her eyes widened slightly before shuttering as his meaning became clear. "I am sorry at the decision regarding allowing indigenous peoples to remain here during the Searing, Colonel—and I hope you will express that to Major Tapper for me. For many of us, in fact—but I cannot speak on this matter."

"You cannot or *must* not?"

She smiled. "The latter. However, Mara will no doubt have heard almost as much as I have."

Murphy smiled back. "Hmmm...and I wonder who the source of her information might be?"

"I suppose it could be anyone." Naliryiz smiled innocently.

"Present company excepted, of course."

"Of course," Naliryiz purred. Her eyes stayed on his, and she seemed to drift closer to him—but then hastily looked up at the overhead lighting. Some were lume panels, some were skylights that showed the hydroponic farms and other greenery that lined the inner walls of the asteroid, the slow spin holding it all in place. "Did you once again enjoy your time on R'Bak?" she wondered, her words suddenly clipped.

Murphy started at the change. "I can't remember ever saying whether I ever did or didn't. But it sounds like you certainly don't!"

She looked surprised. "Why do you say so?"

"Well, judging from your tone, it sounds like you must hate going!" Which made less than no sense: Naliryiz was one of the most frequent visitors to the pole-dwelling Skydreamers who were the SpinDogs' only dirtside contacts.

Naliryiz sighed. "What you hear is envy, Colonel. I had hoped to go down one more time."

He was about to warn her about spending too many hours in full gee, then remembered *she* was the doctor. He was just a concerned...friend. Which was the moment he noticed further subtle changes in her silhouette and wondered aloud, "Have you...have you been spending time in the spin gym? I mean, *a lot* of time?"

"Yes," she replied, but her tone said, *So you finally noticed? Harumph!* Her eyes sought the skylights that admitted the soft glow of the "sun beam," which was the bright spine that marked the long axis of *Spin One*'s hollow center.

"I wish I could have brought you down." The words were out of Murphy's mouth before he had any idea he was going to utter them. Completely impulsive, yes, but true. And maybe, just maybe, she'd . . .

Naliryiz looked sideways at him, her eyes intense but also regretful. "That would not have been a . . . wise choice."

Well, damn: what the—? "I don't understand. You just said that you wanted to go there one more time, and that you were, well, jealous that I did."

Her voice became clipped again, and she no longer met his eyes except for brief glances. "Jealous is too strong a word. But even if I was jealous, it would not do for us to go there together."

Murphy felt as though whatever internal compass guided his understanding of Naliryiz had just spun one hundred eighty degrees in the course of two sentences. "Together? You mean, as in 'with each other'?"

"Yes." Her eyes were wary, careful . . . just before she looked away.

"Look, I didn't mean to suggest—"

"I must be clear, Colonel Murphy. For us to be seen together in any fashion that would promote . . . speculation . . . could have serious repercussions."

Christ, is there anything that doesn't *have "serious repercussions" around here?* Aloud, he said, "What kind of repercussions?"

She looked at him, surprised. "You have not considered this yourself?"

Murphy suddenly felt very stupid. "Uh . . . no."

She looked both annoyed and hurt. "Consider what others might conjecture if they saw us together. Frequently."

"Others? You mean . . . your Family?"

"Well, yes, them, too—although *they* might be . . . But the other Families would be concerned. Likely alarmed. Possibly panicked."

"But Mara Lee's relationship with Ozendi . . ." And as those words came out of his mouth, he realized it wasn't about his being an outsider, or his still-secret affliction, or anything as negotiable as those issues. It was about a power that trumped and transcended any such personal issues.

Politics. It was all about politics.

A faint, sardonic smile wrinkled Naliryiz's lips. "*Now* you see."

"Of course. One of the leading Lost Soldiers is already... er, closely associated with the Otlethes Family. Has blood ties to them through her child. But if yet another high-ranking Lost Soldier became 'associated' with the Family, other SpinDogs might start wondering if those relationships arose spontaneously or were... well, calculated moves in a larger power play."

She frowned at the unfamiliar vernacular but nodded. "Exactly. And it would validate the misgivings of those who remain uncomfortable with how we, er, restructured the Kormak Family."

"*Restructured.*" *That sounds so much nicer than "gutted."* Murphy nodded—and felt gutted himself. A measure of relief arose also; even the most loving and compassionate partner wasn't going to react to multiple sclerosis as if it were an aphrodisiac—and particularly not among the dominance-driven SpinDog culture. But acknowledging that didn't make the sudden emotional hollowness go away. Although totally irrational and unreasonable, Murphy had harbored a hopeless hope that somehow, despite his prognosis and the cultural and political impediments, maybe he and Naliryiz might somehow...

No. Admit it, Murphy: it's better this way. Smarter, at the very least. "Thank you, Naliryiz. You are right; I completely overlooked this complication. But I assure you, I shall be cooperative and conscientious in helping you ensure that no politically dangerous misconceptions arise." He turned to take the shorter route back to his office, paused, risked looking in her eyes. "I *am* sorry you were not able to go to R'Bak one last time." He heard the edge of increased formality in his tone and instantly regretted the distance it reestablished. But it was the best way to remind himself not to fall back into his far-too-frequent daydreams about the woman before him.

Who was staring at Murphy as if suddenly dumbfounded, her lips slightly parted in surprise.

Okay: now *what have I done?* But he arrested that confused thought: *Best not to ask.* Because it was all too likely her answer would restart the conversation, which might then veer in an even more emotionally intimate direction...

Murphy, uncertain how best to take his leave, did so with a bow. It was a common parting gesture among SpinDogs, but still...

A goddamned bow? *Christ, now she'll think you're as strange as Makarov.*

Way to go, loser.

Mara "Bruce" Lee breezed past Murphy's new orderly/bodyguard—Polish submariner Janusz Lasko, who was almost as big as Max Messina—and fell rather than sat in a chair flanked by the two already occupied by Cutter and Bowden. Fifteen feet behind them, Makarov was head down and hard at work, but most definitely within earshot.

Lee's tone was as sardonic as it was droll. "I can hardly guess what *this* is about."

Murphy shrugged and sighed. "No reason not to give it a try; the guesses are free. Besides, just might hit on the right answer. By pure luck."

"How many guesses do I get?"

"Three." Murphy's smile was a bitter match for her own. "But I'm disallowing the first two." It was a near-certainty that Makarov's supposedly confidential relay of Tapper's decision was already known to the ranking members of the Otlethes Family. And therefore, to Mara as well.

She didn't disappoint. "Tapper is only being allowed to bring up one family member. Which is going to be his brother-in-law Grevorg."

Bowden started. "Didn't see that coming. Why the hell are they doing this to him?"

Murphy shrugged and uttered the hateful, one-word explanation: "Politics."

"What?"

"Welllll," Mara said, extending the syllable as she glanced toward Murphy, "it's like this..." Her eyes told him, *"No worries; I've got this."* He waved her on, glad to let someone else do the explaining for a change.

"So," Mara continued, "because I'm the momma of the first Terran-SpinDog child, I get to hear all of the dirt that flies around in my adoptive family. And this is what hit the fan today.

"When the Otlethes Family became the top dogs after taking our side against the Hardliners, a lot of other families went from being typically competitive to jealous. And wary."

"Wary about what?"

"Primus Anseker's potential to use his increased power to grab even *more* power. SpinDog culture may be a watered-down version of the Ktoran original, but its stability still depends upon having a lot of near-equals contending for 'dominion.' If any one family gets too powerful, the others go through a pretty predictable progression: resentful, then angry, and then—possibly—homicidal."

Bowden nodded. "And the one-sided outcome of a one-day war between the Expansionist and Hardliner factions probably makes it even worse. After the Otlethes and their pals broke apart the Kormaks, the families that refused to take a side don't have any ready allies if Anseker leans on them. That could make them worried enough to make common cause with those Hardliners who survived the purge."

"Yes," Mara said with a nod, "but only *if* Anseker gives them reason to fear him. So, right now, he's not going to do anything that could be perceived as aggressive or—worse still—autocratic."

"Got it," Cutter said, frowning as he fit the pieces together. He hadn't been part of the cadre when the multigenerational power struggle between the Expansionists and Hardliners had come to its brutal conclusion. "But what's all this have to do with Tapper and his Sarmatchani wife and relatives?"

Mara sighed. "Well, they became a lot more important since becoming our allies. Theirs was the first tribe in the Hamain to meet us, help us, and then join our fight against the satraps."

Bowden nodded. "Bo told me that when he captured Imsurmik, almost forty percent of the manpower in his indig battalions—er, 'war bands'—was Sarmatchani."

Cutter started nodding. "Okay, I'm starting to get the picture. One Lost Soldier"—he nodded at Mara—"is now a blood-connected member of the leading family up here. Another Lost Soldier is the war hero and favorite son-in-law of the biggest Sarmatchani chief down there. And through their connection to both groups, the Otlethes family has been the sole beneficiary of both of those Lost Soldier, er, bondings." He leaned back. "They're looking at this the same way old-time monarchs did on Earth: they built their power through marriages that not only linked their kids, but linked their lands, titles, and wealth. And, as they do, the already-little guys get comparatively smaller and smaller."

Bowden nodded, reading the last of the tea leaves that Mara had brought before them. "So now, seeing all the power that the Otlethes have through those two new connections, Anseker has to make sure that the smaller families out there don't start grumbling and gathering. So he throws them a bone: Harry can bring only one family member with him." He glanced from Murphy to Mara. "But why did he pick his brother-in-law rather than Stella?"

Mara took up the tale again. "First, Anseker didn't throw anyone a bone. The other families took the initiative by coming to him with a far more harsh resolution: that *no* dirtsiders be allowed on the spins. So the most pushback that Anseker could risk was to insist that at least one family member was allowed to accompany Harry."

"From there, it really wasn't much of a choice." She shrugged. "The Sarmatchani chief—Yannis—was out of the question; he's needed dirtside as both leader and figurehead. Bringing Stella would mean bringing their toddler, and that was a medical nonstarter: if that child is to return dirtside, he has to spend his developmental years in a full-gee environment.

"So that left Grevorg. Who, by being 'exclusively sequestered' on a single RockHound station at the ass-end of nowhere, assures the continuation of Yannis's line of succession. At least that's the fig leaf that Anseker put on it."

"All of which pretty much sucks for everyone in every conceivable way," Bowden spat.

Murphy nodded. "And there's probably worse in store, if the SpinDogs can't stop their endless jockeying for position and dominion."

"Like what?" Cutter asked with a frown.

As he did, Mara's glance slipped sideways toward Murphy. Although it had been only an hour ago, she'd probably already heard about his latest exchange with Naliryiz.

Murphy kept his eyes on Cutter's. "Every time we have to push the Dogs or Hounds to do something they feel is at odds with their social or political norms, they flex back at us."

Bowden nodded sharply, eyes bright. "Yeah, but Colonel, that's who they are. Whatever we want, they have to resist. Particularly because we've been right so often."

Murphy nodded back at him. "Yes, but look at *how* they've started pushing back."

Mara nodded, brow furrowed in frustration. "Social restrictions.

Who can see who; who can go where; who's allowed to live on their spins."

Bowden leaned back with a muted sigh. "I had hoped that Anseker would be above that, given how we've helped them." He sighed. "Of course, it's exactly because we *have* helped them that they had to cave about Harry's family coming up."

Murphy was careful to limit his reaction to a somber nod. He didn't want any of them to suspect that he himself was now caught in another situation caused by the endless political maneuvering.

But Mara's eyes confirmed she already knew he was. She asked the room, "I'm heading to the galley. Who's coming?" Cutter and Bowden rose. When Murphy didn't, she asked, "Colonel, what about dinner? You have plans?"

"Yes, Bruce; I plan to skip it. I seem to have lost my appetite. Dismissed."

Chapter Seven

"Hey there, Umaren," Chalmers said with a wave.

Umaren turned on his heel and stalked away, grumbling.

"Wait," Chalmers said, striding after the seaplane captain. He and Jackson quickly caught up with the shorter indig. "What did I say?"

"Maybe show some respect," Jackson offered, *sotto voce*. He continued more loudly, and with better, more polite R'Bakuun than Chalmers could summon, "Umaren, please wait. I apologize for my partner's flippant greeting. It was not proper, but I assure you we have nothing but respect for you, your crew, and your fine seaplane."

The man slowed, stopped. Not wishing to crowd him, Jackson and Chalmers stopped a few paces behind him as well.

"El wanted to thank you for getting him home," Jackson added.

Umaren turned, squinted at Jackson, then up at the taller Chalmers. His brown eyes softened. "He is well?"

"Not entirely. Yet he is far better than he would be had you not brought him into our care." You couldn't lie to an asset you were going to have to rely on for your own skin. Not if you wanted to create the necessary bonds of trust. You could avoid, downplay, even mislead, but outright and easily refutable lies were best avoided. "He told me to tell you that you and Vizzel were free of any debt to him."

Chalmers cast a worried glance at Jackson. There was telling the truth and then there was being unnecessarily open about the state of play.

Umaren looked down and scuffed the rocky beach with his boot. "The debt is not paid in full. Vizzel is fully recovered and both our lives were saved by El's quick action. I owe him service."

Chalmers had always admired his partner's ability to get a target talking, but this was entirely next level.

"*We* owe him service," another man said, emerging from behind a stretch of rocky shore not five paces from them with a compact and lethal-looking pump shotgun in hand. It wasn't aimed at either Jackson or Chalmers, but it was in hand, and the implicit threat wasn't lost on either Lost Soldier.

Chalmers flinched, showing his shitty startle response once again. He kept his hand from going for his pistol, but only barely.

"Greetings. Vizzel, I take it?" Jackson said, shifting gears without dropping a beat. Chalmers noted his hands hadn't even twitched.

Umaren looked at Vizzel and sighed. "You were to remain hidden."

"And you were to listen to their offer, not walk away like a sullen boy at the first opportunity," the younger man said.

Umaren's hands balled into fists, but he gritted his teeth and returned his attention to the Lost Soldiers.

Jackson smiled at both men. "Why don't we have a drink or two and discuss what might be?"

"What might be?" Umaren and Vizzel chorused with equally puzzled expressions.

"Indeed, what might be a very bright future for you and yours," Jackson said.

"There is only *us*, the crew of *Loklis*. No house, family, or clan; only us and the contract we have with our investors," Umaren said. "El might not have told you this."

Jackson's smile was broad and very, very white in the bright sunshine. "And if I were to tell you that's exactly what I meant?"

Both men looked puzzled.

"For one, we do not hold your relationship as other than normal. With us you could live openly, freely, *richly.*"

"I just want to fly," Umaren said. At least partially true, too. Chalmers didn't miss the desperate glance the older man cast at his lover, though.

Vizzel was less cautious than the older man, however. "What do you want from us?"

Jackson cocked his head. "First, let's get off the beach and have a few drinks. Get to know one another a little, then we can try and figure out what we can do for one another."

Chalmers sent yet another grateful prayer to the long-dead and nameless Army personnel clerk who'd condemned Jackson to working with him all those years ago.

Jackson shot a look at his partner that said, *I sold it, you close it.*

"He'll kill us rather than release us from our contract," Umaren said, brown eyes wide.

Chalmers followed the pilot's gaze. Umaren's primary investor was easily recognizable, if not by the haughty expression on his face, then by the stylized bird painted on his forehead as well as the bodyguard of, at a quick count, six thugs that surrounded him. He and his entourage had crossed the square, those few patrons of the cafés and bars not too intoxicated to know better quickly getting out of the way.

They'd set up the meet in public in hopes that Umaren's investor, Maktim, would be less inclined to violence with witnesses at hand. In retrospect, that might have been a mistake. From the look on Maktim's face, a public airing of this dispute might just drive him to greater violence.

"Hasn't killed anyone, yet," Chalmers said, hand unconsciously checking the holstered sidearm riding his hip under his light night robes.

"And won't if we have anything to say about it," Jackson added. Chalmers saw his partner already had his gun out under the table. Chalmers swallowed. Jackson ready for trouble was both good and bad: that he always knew *when* shit was about to pop off was good. That didn't mean Chalmers *liked* it when shit was popping off.

Maktim, owner-proprietor of Whikmari Global Transport—an appropriate name for a two-seaplane-and-a-couple-dozen-trucks operation—strode forward with a sneer on his painted lips. To be fair, he was a very big deal in these parts. For a private, non-Kulsian enterprise to keep and maintain so much technology on R'Bak when the overlords were not present was exceedingly rare.

Chalmers had been worried about displacing him, but Umaren had told them that hostile takeover attempts were not uncommon and would raise few alarms.

Chalmers stood, offered a half bow. "Wel—"

The man ignored him, slammed a hand down on their table. Fruit-and-drink-laden crockery shivered and bounced. "Get your ass to my office, Umaren."

"I-I—" Umaren stammered.

"Umaren is no longer in your employ, Maktim," Chalmers said, surprised at how reasonable his own voice sounded.

The man's eyes slid to Chalmers. "And who are you to speak to me?"

"One of his new partners," Chalmers said, gesturing with his off hand at Umaren. He added a friendly smile. The smile died as he realized the man's pupils were pinpricks despite the dim lantern light of the square.

Shit. Maktim was high as fuck.

"We have a contract." A finger jabbed at Umaren and the thumb of the same hand cocked back at his own chest. "You are not party to that contract."

"A fact we recognize. You will be compensated for his departure from your service."

"I am not selling my interest." Maktim sneered at Chalmers. "So you can crawl back to whatever whore spawned you and beg forgiveness for your failings."

Chalmers glanced past the would-be shipping magnate. His thugs were tense: white knuckles on belts, sweat streaking paint, dry lips licked by dry tongues.

Shit. This is just like the old days in the Mog, with the local militia chewing khat *until they were wound tight as a drum and had to let go.* He glanced at Jackson. His partner's face wore that almost-bored expression that told Chalmers he was ready for anything.

"Be reasonable, Maktim," Chalmers said, keeping his voice level and cool to avoid triggering anyone. "Things don't have to be this w—" Chalmers yelped as Jackson kicked him, hard, in the thigh. He lurched sideways just as a forearm-length blade whispered through the space where he'd been.

Chalmers felt his nuts draw up even as Jackson's hand appeared with his gun leveled. The local-made pistol barked twice, pushing needles into Chalmers's ears. The swordsman—Chalmers refused to call any weapon that long a knife—fell on that side of the table, the back of his skull made a mess by a ten-millimeter bullet. His weight half-flipped the table, as well. Crockery shattered on the pavers.

Umaren helped the table along, heaving their end up and over to provide some cover.

Chalmers stood gaping beside it, catching events in flashes: screams and shouts of alarm from bystanders, a general scramble as they fled or dove for cover, Maktim's angry painted face disappearing beyond the table.

One of the thugs standing to the side raised a big revolver and started to cock the hammer. Jackson turned and, without really seeming to aim, cracked off another pair of shots. The thug grunted, wheezed, and collapsed on his ass, pistol clattering on the pavers.

Finally diving behind the table, Chalmers struggled to pull his own pistol. He skidded on some fallen fruit but sat up behind the dubious cover of the café table. His hands were clumsy, refusing to pull the pistol free.

Jackson shot several more times.

Chalmers *still* couldn't get his pistol free.

"Red!" Jackson shouted. A faint clatter heard as his spent mag clattered on the pavement. A part of Chalmers was amazed he could hear anything after the gunfire.

An axe bit into the wood next to Chalmers's head.

A fucking *axe*!

A man's head appeared behind the weapon and pulled it free in a shower of splinters. The thug started to step over the table.

"Up!" Jackson shouted.

Hoping his partner could drill the man, Chalmers glanced that way but Jackson was already shooting at someone opposite his side of the impromptu barrier.

Chalmers threw himself backward, pistol finally coming free of the holster inside his robes. He fired from the hip. Bullets tore through light fabric, air, fabric once more, and found flesh and finally, bone, at the far end.

The axe-man stumbled but kept coming across the table at him.

Umaren appeared and threw himself against the thug, his arm traveling from his belt line up under his opponent's rib cage. His knife hand came away red. He repeated the motion three, four, five times in quick succession.

Shot at least once, stabbed multiple times, the dying man still dragged the pilot to the ground. Not wanting to hit Umaren, Chalmers got in close, pushing his muzzle, robes and all, against the man's skull. He pulled the trigger. The man stilled, the deformed bullet that killed him ricocheting off wet pavers and away with an evil whine.

Scrambling upright, Chalmers risked a look over the table.

Maktim was crawling away, a thick trail of blood glistening in the torchlight from the table to his belly. Another of the thugs was wailing while clutching a hand that appeared to be short a few fingers. The last two thugs had thought better of the fight and were hastily fleeing for the far end of the square.

A furious Chalmers finally extricated his pistol from his tattered, bloody robes.

"Decide to join the fight, did you?" Jackson said, eyes flicking to the gun in Chalmers's hand.

Chalmers shivered. "Couldn't let you have all the glory, could I?"

Jackson's smile was just the slightest bit crazy as he waved at the dead and wounded. "I don't think Maktim will have any more objections to Umaren breaking his contract, do you?"

"Probably not," Chalmers said, feeling a twinge of concern for his friend. Jacks was better than Chalmers at mayhem. Didn't make the sergeant easy with it. Not normally. "You all right?"

"Right enough. Street rules rule here, just like the South Side."

Chalmers let that ride and said: "You hurt?"

"No, you?"

"Nope. Umaren?"

The pilot spread his arms wide. "None of this is mine."

"Good. Looks like you're a free agent now."

Umaren walked over and spat on the now-still form of his former boss. "Good."

PART TWO

Chapter Eight

Show no fear, show no confidence, be the fucking expressionless Sphinx. Give your opponents nothing.

Harry knew all four of his remaining opponents were ruthless; he'd taught one himself, and his teaching hadn't stinted in the dirty tricks department. The rest were familiar with his wiles and traps; they'd watched him destroy two other challengers. Ruthlessly eliminated, the vanquished sat on the sidelines waiting to see who would fall next.

Harry Tapper, tribal warlord, ex–Navy SEAL, and ersatz time traveler, considered his cards and then glanced again at the large pile of poker chips, pharmaceutical ampules, and sparkling gems that represented the single largest pot so far that night.

Or even that month.

Maybe the past year.

Jesus, has it been that long?

The stakes lay on the improvised green felt tablecloth stretching between players, individual precious items glinting in the hard electric glare that was the trademark lighting of a RockHound habitat. The bright stainless steel, duraluminum, and composite structures making up the common areas provided even more reflective surfaces, bouncing the light about. With care, an astute player might even catch sight of a hole card.

To that end, Harry casually glanced around and caught his own reflection instead.

Shaggy, dark brown hair hung past his ears, gathered by a strip of supple whinnie-hide. Like most of the spacers, he kept his face smooth shaven, simplifying the fit of the oxygen masks required for many off-station maneuvers. His exposed skin was darkly tanned, courtesy of extended tours planetside. Black boots and the closed pouches on his equipment belt betrayed no additional information. His improvised utilities had started life as a SpinDog-issue dove-gray uniform. Devoid of rank or qualification badges, its sole decoration was a worn khaki breast patch that read TAPPER.

Not that there was much chance of mistaking Harry for anyone else, either seated or shuffling sideways through the press of the infamously tight confines of the comparatively tiny station. The uniform was drawn in tight lines across his broad shoulders, biceps, chest, and thighs. Nearly every RockHound enjoyed at least a ten-centimeter height advantage over Harry, but he'd yet to meet one he didn't out-mass by thirty kilos, often considerably more. The uniform fabric needed to accommodate the muscular frame of men raised at the bottom of a gravity well and shaped by hard service exceeded the capacity of a standard-issue Spin-Dog shipsuit. As a result, Harry had been forced to draw two suits for each set he wore, sacrificing one for the extra material.

And hadn't that pleased the SpinDog quartermaster assigned to support the Terran guests.

Harry appraisingly met the eyes of the next player in the betting order along the rectangular refectory table. This was an opportunity to eliminate another contestant in the traveling, never-ending, pointlessly high-stakes poker game that had begun shortly after the Terrans' arrival in the 55 Tauri system.

"See you," he said, and, keeping his voice even, Harry dropped an uncut blue stone onto the table. Then, carefully affecting an air of indifference, he dropped another. The second thumb-sized gemstone thunked into the pile, starting a twinkling mini-avalanche. "And raise you."

Harry took advantage of the lighting to watch the faces of his shipmates, fellow time travelers, and the one, mostly housebroken barbarian as they considered his addition to the pot. The stones, like much of the wealth in the space habitats, came from R'Bak. Harry had made several trips to the planet, which circled the same star as the dense asteroid belt that hid the RockHounds and their sometimes allies, the SpinDogs.

Sitting adjacent to him was Pilot Officer Volo "Crash" Zobulakos, a tall, spindly interface-craft skipper. He'd been along for Harry's first mission to the surface. Against the preferences of his Family's Elders, Volo had helped ensure the success of the mission and survival of the Terrans. Having burned his bridges, the young SpinDog joined the newcomers and cross-trained to fly the exoatmospheric craft under Terran leadership. His bright orange, space-rated flight suit was covered in patches, the largest of which was embroidered with a stylized golden leonine carnivore. The original, found in the grasslands that covered a fair bit of R'Bak, had a well-earned reputation for reckless ferocity and a taste for human flesh. It was also the unofficial symbol of the squadron reconstituted from the few survivors of the Terran-led air raid that destroyed the Kulsian interplanetary comm system under the leadership of Kevin Bowden. Volo had replaced one of the pilots from that op, which lost two-thirds of the attacking force. In a sane world, that kind of loss rate would mean a new CO.

This isn't such a world.

"I'll see you," the pilot said, frowning at his cards, "and raise you this." Volo withdrew a small, transparent sampling tube decorated with red and blue stripes from his zippered breast pocket and paused to consider it one last time. Then he delicately added it to the pot, drawing a collective murmur from the card players.

"Holy shit!" blurted the normally taciturn Frazier, who was next along the table. "That what I think it is?"

The six-foot-five-inch African American sergeant was another soldier abducted from Earth, though from an earlier time than Harry. Staff Sergeant Elroy Frazier, late of the Military Assistance Command—Vietnam/Special Operations Group, had been plucked by the Ktor from a hopeless firefight in the Vietnamese highlands. Like every Terran in the system, he'd been propelled forward almost two centuries and deposited in the middle of a rebellion between the planets of a binary star system, combining brutal, close infantry combat with spaceships and lasers. And, like everyone else, he'd participated in the repetitive briefings on the various drug precursors harvested from R'Bak.

In which regard, the markings on Volo's tube were particularly distinctive.

"As you like to say, Sergeant Frazier, the pure quill," Volo replied confidently. "Ten milliliters of distilled *londau'd*. Assayed and sealed. Diluted for use, it's enough for a hundred doses."

The sound of soft exclamations around the table was nearly universal. Harry's poker face might have wavered a trifle as he considered the bet.

Londau'd belonged to one of the rarest families of R'Bakuun pharmaceuticals, so scarce that their collective value and utility made the expense of interplanetary conflict worthwhile. Unlike most of the drugs already on the table, *londau'd* was so precious it was strictly controlled and centrally stored. Harry had never seen it in private hands. Until now.

"Hey, Ha-ree, are you planning on making another blood challenge?" asked Grevorg al-Caoimhip, laughing. Nonchalantly leaning against the refectory bulkhead as an observer, the tall, sandy-haired R'Baku warrior wore an outfit much like Harry's, complete with leather headband and Terran-style utilities made from SpinDog materials. "If you win the pot, you can ask Mother to patch you up again!"

Harry spared Grevorg a genuine smile. His presence was a rare concession by the RockHounds, who normally did not allow the surface-born on their hidden outposts.

"No table talk!" Major Korelon'va snapped.

This RockHound officer fit what was said to be the classic Ktoran mold of his distant ancestors: tall, chiseled, and arrogant. The carefully tailored midnight black shipsuit was set off by silver piping. Korelon's annoyingly heroic good looks were accentuated by pale amber eyes that were almost yellow and a shock of closely cropped blond hair over an aquiline nose and thin lips. The latter were pursed in distaste.

A pucker like a cat's asshole. And a very punchable face.

Harry thought Korelon a posturing, empty suit, but this evening was supposed to be a team-building exercise. In fact, when defending the gambling practices of the Lawless, Harry had won over his boss by extolling the cross-cultural benefits of gaming, highlighting the need to strengthen bonds by building personal relationships with the other factions in their alliance of convenience. In other words, the usual bullshit. Korelon, a RockHound salvage captain, was the perfect example of how impossible the Ktor castoffs were. He'd asked to play *socially*, which was ridiculous. You either played poker to win, or you were a patsy. Naturally, it had turned out to be a clumsy ploy, and he had proven to be anything but unknowledgeable about the game only recently introduced to the system. Korelon's remaining chips, stacked next to the half-full tumbler of mystery-root vodka, were a fraction of their original sum, most of which had gone to Volo, the lucky bastard.

Harry could tell, *social* player or not, Korelon was irritated. His features—no doubt perfected to some closely held ideal of the geneticists his Ktoran ancestors had fled—shifted to a sneer.

"Relax, Korelon." Harry kept his tone easy and relaxed as he used his elbow to point at Volo. "Way back when, the skinny git with all the winnings was supposed to help us make first contact with the R'Bakuun tribes who were fighting the satraps. It was my first trip down; in fact, it was *the* first time any of us Lost Soldiers set foot on R'Bak. Volo, being the youngest son of one of your own SpinDog Family leaders, had the bona fides that helped us build that first alliance."

Korelon had looked up sharply at Harry's contraction of his surname. Omitting the honorific was something that mattered only to another Ktoran has-been, and judging from Volo's stifled snort, not all of them. Korelon shot a murderous glance at the pilot. A moment later, he smoothed his features, presenting the same condescending expression he'd worn from the first hand.

"A SpinDog Family leader," he snorted derisively. "Never a Family and hardly a leader." There was no RockHound love lost for their richer cousins and Ktoran fugitives who had settled the rubble-strewn limits of the binary system of 55 Tauri.

"Am I telling this story, or are you?" Harry asked, quirking an eyebrow.

He paused, awaiting further editorial from the only Rock-Hound present. The RockHounds and SpinDogs were cordially antagonistic to each other at the best of times, both unable to confront the Kulsians directly, and consigned to hiding in the rubble of the system. That antagonism occasionally flared into something more serious. That they had common cause against a third, stronger faction had done little to endear one to the other.

Korelon glanced up, then back down, ostensibly studying his plastic cards.

"So, as I was saying," Harry drawled. "No shit, there I was, with the dubious honor of leading the first Terran mission to R'Bak. Almost blew it when our local contacts, the Sarmatchani, claimed an honor debt against Volo's older brother. I ended up having to fight that over-muscled, under-brained, broke-ass barb sitting over there."

He nodded to Grevorg, who grinned back.

"And he was a little overenthusiastic with his knife. Gave me this." Harry shifted on the built-in bench to turn his right side toward the table. He tugged up the folded sleeve of his utility blouse, displaying a fine white line that curved across his bicep, disappearing upward and out of sight.

"A scratch." Korelon looked at the scar, sniffing.

"Doesn't look like much now," Harry said, refuting the implied dismissal. "Grevorg carved me all the way up into my armpit, nicked the brachial artery. I damn near bled out. But thanks to Grevorg's mother—"

"She's yours, too!" Grevorg interjected. "Little brother!"

"—but thanks to my mother-in-law, the local field surgeon," Harry continued with some asperity, "and a generous dosing of pure *londau'd* extract, I woke up two days later with the wound well on its way to what you see now. A week later I was a hundred percent."

"No shit?" asked Frazier, lifting both eyebrows. "I've seen R'Bakuun drugs do amazing things, and I've heard the story, but I figured it was at least fifty percent exaggerated. You know, SEALs and their bullshit."

Harry used his free hand to offer Frazier a casual one-finger salute, softening the gesture with a tight smile. Frazier had seen the elephant, too. And *londau'd* was an amazing drug. Harry recalled perfectly the sight of his arm gaping all the way to the pinkish humerus. He'd seen enough battlefield trauma to recognize the deadly trifecta of septic shock, blood loss, and neurological damage. Harry had known, *known,* he'd lose the arm. On any other primitive battlefield, the loss of the limb would've been followed in short order with death from sepsis and shock. But between the miracle drug and a tribal shaman who knew her business, he'd lived. Instead of an infected wound leaking blood and lymph, his arm had been unwrapped to reveal a healed-over, red seam that led from his triceps deep into his armpit. Of course, it wasn't all down to the healer's skill or the powerful drug she'd made from a local plant.

It had more to do with the not-so-secret-anymore connection between the alien cold sleep process and every Terran's newly discovered biocompatibility with the R'Bakuun pharmacopia.

Harry didn't know how many other Terrans suspected a connection between the technology that had brought them forward two centuries and the uncanny drugs on this otherwise unremarkable planet. Naturally, the Terran mission commander had strictly forbidden further talk on that topic.

Then again, Colonel Murphy's grudging concession to allow gambling had also included a strict admonition to exclude the use of R'Bakuun drugs as stakes.

And yet, here we are.

"The point is, I know what *londau'd* is worth," Harry stated flatly, glancing toward the RockHound officer. "The bet is legit. Too rich for your blood? That's your problem. You in or not?"

"Personal possession of *londau'd* is prohibited," Korelon proclaimed, turning to glare at Volo. "It is strictly controlled and therefore the flight officer has made an improper bet and must forfeit."

The arrogant tone, the gall, the sheer weasel-dicked nature of Korelon's answer stung Harry hard as a slap. Already keyed up, he knew he was but a short nudge from fighting anger.

Stay cool, don't let this jackass screw up the night.

"Give it a rest, Korelon," Harry said, rapping the knuckles of his empty hand on the tabletop, perhaps a touch more briskly than intended. He put it in terms a RockHound understood: "And take the stick out of your ass. No rank in the mess. You wanted to play, fine. You follow the house rules. And the house rules are just like Family rules."

Harry waited a beat.

"And here, I'm the house."

Harry watched as Korelon's fine features reddened. Whatever Korelon's strengths might be, a consistent poker face wasn't among them. It wasn't hard to understand why. Technically, Korelon was the senior man present. He was also playing poker for money with a variety of lower ranks, a violation of the strictly enforced Rock-Hound hierarchy. A Terran enlisted man, a non-officer who could never hold honor in a RockHound's eyes, was seated at the table. Worse, a soft, degenerate SpinDog was daring to claim spoils from a RockHound 'ah. And, intolerably, a surface dweller, a member of the barbarian R'Baku, was breathing RockHound oxygen. And now, yet another Terran had just called him out in a manner that demanded a true RockHound issue an honor challenge.

Harry, tamp it down, you idiot. Breathe. Look at the pot. Remember the plan.

"Just a friendly game, Korelon," he breathed out through an underplayed yawn.

Harry watched Korelon surreptitiously glance around at the brief rumble of chuckles, gauging the lack of sympathy, before he schooled his face back into immobility, and laid his cards facedown on the green felt. Korelon selected a credit chip from his meager pile. The double gold chevron denoted a fixed denomination equivalent to a tenth of the salary that was digitally paid to Harry in a year, or perhaps as much as Korelon earned in a week. But its value wasn't equal to Volo's ampule. Not even close.

"I'll match the bet." He flipped the chip into the pot.

Korelon triumphantly met Harry's eyes and then Volo's as he slid his hands out of sight, presumably wiping sweaty palms on his immaculate uniform.

"Ante's a little light, Korelon," Harry said. "A hundred doses of *londau'd* are worth enough for a share in a salvage shuttle, not just a weekend in a pleasure hotel."

Harry was grateful that Volo kept his mouth shut, but there was more than one grumble of agreement.

Grevorg chuckled through a curse in Sarmatchani that Harry sincerely hoped remained untranslatable. Frazier might have muttered something about *fucking officers* as well.

Korelon glared about the table and locked gazes with Harry.

"Most of the salvage opportunities have been negotiated away, thanks to the alliance you Terrans have foisted upon us," Korelon said, anger lurking in his yellow eyes. "And *londau'd* is worth whatever you can sell it for, which is to say *nothing*, because no one is supposed to have it. If anything, my clear duty is to halt these proceedings. Indeed, my bet is generous. If you do not care for it, fold."

For a moment, silence reigned. Harry felt his adrenaline spike. He was old friends with rage.

No. I am not going to rise to this asshole's bait. He's not worth it. And...

Yes, he's worth it. What's the worst that can happen? Get shanghaied across a hundred and thirty years and a slightly greater number of light-years, losing my family in the process?

Grevorg began to laugh even louder from the sidelines. Volo, no doubt influenced by his origins in the SpinDog caste system, started to say he'd be happy to withdraw his bet. Korelon looked down his nose at them and made his play.

"Let us not forget that I am a RockHound'va," the RockHound said, proclaiming his blood lineage to the original Ktor founders that had led his family's wave of forced migration to R'Bak. "For generations, we have mined the system, endured the hardships incomprehensible to the planet-bound barbarians, refined the metals that made possible the comfortable life of the Spin-dwellers. We understand mercantile value. It is based on our blood and sacrifice, after all. It is not for a R'Baku surface-dweller, let alone a pampered SpinDog, to tell me the worth of a thing."

And he laid his right hand, holding a distinctive baton, on the felt.

Harry recognized the thumb-thick gleaming black cylinder, perhaps twenty centimeters long, from the early Dornaani-supplied intelligence briefings. It was the mark of RockHound aristocracy, among the smallest microminiaturized devices still permitted to the members of extirpated Ktoran houses, and then only to those of high rank. It was a personal data store, a recording device, a display of privilege, and a personal weapon. Traditionally, the batons were used to lightly chastise the lower castes among some Ktor houses. However, they were capable of a lethal discharge.

"Easy, sir," Sergeant Frazier said. "It's a friendly game, right?"

"So much for vaunted RockHound honor, eh, Korelon?" Harry asked. His own words sounded odd to him, as though they were somehow being uttered by someone far away. "No personal weapons on the station, isn't that right?"

"Fool!" Korelon spat, beginning to raise the baton. "A RockHound'va may carry what he wishes, where he wishes it. That is what it means to be domina—"

Well, shit, you already knew he was going to do something stupid.

Before Harry could process that unbidden thought, well before Korelon completed his proclamation, Harry dropped his cards. He drove his left hand downward and snatched the hem of his blouse upward as his right hand dipped just enough to snatch the hideout from his belt. He gave his wrist the slightest flick as he stood, thighs threatening to rupture trouser seams as he pushed his upper body across the table. He froze there, well short of full extension, the slender black leaf blade of his gravity knife laid backhand across the left side of Korelon's slender neck. Quivering.

Total elapsed time: seven-tenths of a second.

For about twice that duration, all motion froze. Then—

"Ho, ho, ho, ho!" Grevorg boomed. "Your faces! You should see your faces!"

Harry's eyes never left Korelon's. His focus was so intense he could distinguish the strands of color in the other man's perfect yellow-amber eyes.

"This is my table," he said calmly. "We may be guests on your station, but you are a guest at this table, in this space. Here, we don't make threats over money. Here, whoever you are out in the world is unimportant. There are only the *players* at this table. And *players* don't fuck each other over. The universe out there is ready to do that at any moment, so here, here *we* refrain."

Despite his focus, Harry maintained enough peripheral aware-ness to hear Grevorg's chuckles tailing off, to hear Volo's heartfelt if stuttered offers to forfeit abruptly end. He sensed Frazier subtly twist away, right hand carefully out of sight. Harry could *feel* Korelon's thumb tense ever so minutely on the baton's tiny stud.

Time stopped.

Don't do it. Please, don't do it.

Oh please, please yes; do it, please...

"AT EASE!"

The booming voice rebounded so loudly from the hard metal surfaces of the cafeteria that it almost didn't register on him as feminine. It did arrest all attention.

Major Mara Lee, aka "Bruce Lee," was like that.

"Major, withdraw that knife now."

Yeah, he knew that voice.

Harry hesitated, then gently lifted the knife away, automatically flicking it upward. The silver edges of the black blade seemed to flicker reluctantly as it slid back into the grip. The rictus smile he hadn't known he was wearing relaxed, his lips sticking minutely to his teeth.

"Put it down."

Instead, Harry pocketed the knife as he sank back into his seat and turned to face the door.

"And your baton, Major Korelon'va, if you please, sir," the voice continued.

As expected, he saw Major Lee standing a few meters away, hands on her hips, eyes slitted.

A few paces behind her, having just entered the large room, was his boss. In fact, the officer in question was everyone's boss, Colonel "I'm-In-Charge-And-Don't-You-Forget-It-Now-Let-Me-See-You-Smile" Rodger Murphy.

Well, shit.

Even knowing how much trouble he was probably in, Harry couldn't suppress the beginnings of a smile.

Murphy's Law. Every fucking time.

Chapter Nine

Harry found it easy to maintain his military bearing.

Standing in front of the colonel's desk, sustaining a much more rigorous form of attention than he had in a very long time, Harry carefully kept his eyes fixed on the gray bulkhead six inches above Murphy's head. They were alone in Murphy's small—and rarely used—personal office. The thin door panel maintained the fiction of privacy, but Harry was pretty sure the colonel's preceding dissertation on "Mister Tapper's" historical, current, and future shortcomings had been perfectly audible across the station. Certainly, the two Lost Soldiers waiting in the outer office had heard everything. Then again, Bruce Lee and Murphy's bean counter and hatchet man Makarov had heard worse.

Probably.

Murphy paused his diatribe and leaned back in his chair. The silver eagle of his rank—a competent local knockoff—shone from each collar point, and the subdued embroidery of a Combat Infantryman Badge and his name tape showed above opposite blouse pockets, partially obscured by the folded arms that Murphy seemed to periodically tense and relax. The multiple monitors that lined one edge of the desktop had all been locked, displaying only station time.

He's only been at this ten minutes? Feels like more.

"Tapper, you aren't just the sorriest excuse for an officer I've the misfortune to have assigned to this mission, you have evolved into the sorriest example of a soldier we've awakened." Murphy began again, delivering his points with the cadence normally associated with sustained, aimed rifle fire. "Self-control? None. Respect for command authority? None. Awareness of the tenuous quality of our alliance? None. Childish, absolute self-absorption and self-pity? Total."

Harry's boss hadn't really raised his voice once. Once he'd elicited the handful of answers to the initial yes or no questions used to confirm the particulars of the disastrous poker game tableau, he'd made Harry's position clear.

"Tapper, until I tell you different, I will send, and you will remain in receive mode only!"

His clear, penetrating delivery had therefore been completely one-sided and, so far, without repetition.

"Do you think you're irreplaceable? Hardly. Do you believe your performance and accomplishments somehow exempt you from the same rules that govern the rest of our team? Of course you do. Have you considered that perhaps, just maybe, the reason you were originally left in cryogenic suspension is something you should work on since we are all living on a razor's edge margin of survival?"

Harry stood mute.

"I would like to hear your response at this time, Tapper," Murphy said precisely, impatiently tapping one boot on the deck. "Your response might be all that stands between you and the void, if our hosts get their way."

"He drew first," Harry stated flatly. "And I didn't even mark him, let alone kill him. He needed to be reminded that his rank doesn't protect him from bad decisions. That the little people matter, that they can't be used and discarded."

"You think I don't know that, Tapper?" Murphy asked, momentarily raising his voice. "Korelon, the asshole with a direct link to the RockHounds' Legate, isn't the question. What's on the table is your poor—no, your utter lack of *good*—judgment as demonstrated by your threatening one of our allies. Small table stakes, you said. Build stronger relationships, you said. Somehow you left out the drug smuggling and knife fighting."

"Saying I didn't mean for it to happen would be meaningless, sir," Harry said, gaze still fixed above Murphy's head.

"The reason I was there, Major, is that I was coming to alert officers and key personnel for a situation update," Murphy said, clearly trying to jam his temper into the background. "I knew I'd find you at the game, and I was prepared to overlook minor irregularities in the interest of unit morale. However, your little display tore that strategy all to hell. So tell me: What. Is. Going. On?"

"Sir, I'm fully mission capable to return to the surface," Harry replied.

"I came to rely on you a very great deal and trusted you implicitly. But since your return, you've been a borderline insubordination case. Spill, Harry."

The silence stretched a bit.

"C'mon, Harry, it's me."

It stretched a bit further and then Harry took the plunge.

"When you recruited me for the first crazy op, I wasn't in love with the idea," he said. "In the end, it wasn't your appeal to SEAL pride that put me in motion, Murph. It was the realization that I had literally nothing left to lose. You pointed it out, and you were right: everything and everyone I loved was dead. But after the op, that wasn't true anymore."

Harry lowered his gaze to return Murphy's regard evenly. Neither man commented on Harry's familiarity.

"I was in love," Harry said. "Crazy, out of nowhere love, forged on the ragged edge of insanity, considering what we were doing, but real love, nonetheless. I also came to appreciate Stella's clan and their culture. And then, after giving the clans just enough rope to hang themselves by fighting and driving the satraps out of their own towns, we left. There's no guarantee we'll be back, either. Now, I have something to lose again, and I have to tell you, I'm more than a bit protective of it."

"I figured that was it, Harry." Murphy sighed, rubbing one hand across his face. "You aren't the only one this happened to. It's a routine risk when troops integrate tightly with indigenous personnel. But we aren't the same as the indigs, Harry, and they aren't the same as us."

"They're good enough to fight for us, though, aren't they?" Harry snapped. "Good enough to die for us?"

"Yes, they are," Murphy said, sitting straighter. "And you helped them get even better, specifically for that purpose. If you found a scrap of love or real affection while you were down there, that puts you ahead of the other ninety-five percent of us. Be thankful and get back on mission."

"My family is on R'Bak, *Colonel*," Harry said, dropping some iron into the words. "I walked away from my first family, including my kids, in order to advance some damn op that a long-dead politician thought was worth American lives. And what did our country get in trade? What difference did it make? Poke your finger in a glass of water, pull it out and wait for the water to calm. Take a good look at the water glass; that's how much difference we made in Somalia. And if my catch-up reading of history serves, in every American war since. Why would I ever sacrifice anything for that again, *sir*?"

Maybe that was a bit much.

No! Not even close to enough!

Harry returned to the position of attention.

"You're a member of a military outfit, Tapper," Murphy said, matching Harry's tone. "You go where you're told, support our allies as ordered, and destroy our enemies as required. You do not have the luxury of picking your battles—especially out here. None of us do. Period. Dot."

"I just want to get back to the surface," Harry replied, flicking his eyes down to meet his boss's flat gaze. "Send me back to what I'm good at. A long-term liaison slot on the surface makes sense. You could let me keep what I've regained, and I can make sure there's a bolt hole for all of us, if you need it. Win-win all around."

"We're a small team, Tapper," Murphy answered firmly. "We've taken casualties. I've had to spread the rest around to meet as many commitments to our hosts as possible. We aren't close to being finished yet. You were crucial to building our first alliance on the surface. You did good work seizing the ground vehicles, and you did great work following up during the other actions on the surface. You're a natural leader, respected by everyone who works alongside you. The convoy ambushes were spectacular. The R'Baku like you; they even admit to admiring you. The Sarmatchani think you're the hottest thing going save for the Searing. But you are a part of *this* team, and I need you to focus on that and nothing else!"

"Let me bottom line my position for you, Colonel," Harry said. "I know what the odds are, and I'm shocked we haven't lost more people. Sooner or later, my number will be up. And I'm not leaving another orphan or widow behind. Stella and our infant son mean more to me than the Dornaani or the SpinDogs. Or the rest of humanity! I laid everything on the line for an abstraction once already. We both know it cost me everything."

Harry tried to slow his respiration, tried to calm his pulse. He failed.

"What I don't get, sir, is why you're surprised I'm not excited about doing it again," he choked out.

"What the hell happened to you, Harry?" Murphy asked wonderingly. "You know I can't ignore direct defiance."

"This entire situation is crazy, sir," Harry answered as honestly as he could, if not as humbly. "It's driving me mad, and I'm only a symptom. All of us are screwed up in one way or another. Putting us in combat hasn't welded us into a proper team, and it hasn't healed the losses we took. In the field, we focus on the op and the enemy—there are things to absorb our attention. There are people to fight, someone tangible between us and our objective. But as soon as we're out of the field, we have too much time to think, and we think about Earth. Which you would understand if you spent more time on the sharp end and le..."

Harry stopped before completing the damning statement.

First time for everything.

The silence stretched uncomfortably.

Murphy put his hands down on the armrests of his chair and slowly, deliberately, smoothly stood. He was more lightly built than Harry, but everybody was. What he did have was sheer force of personality, like a glacier implacably pushing away every obstacle in its path.

Harry very carefully looked past his commanding officer's face, unwilling to meet Murphy's eyes.

"Go on," Murphy said. The boss's voice had become dangerously soft. "Finish what you were saying. If I spent less time where, exactly?"

Keep your mouth shut. First rule about being in a hole is to stop digging.

One menacing minute passed. A whole minute. Then another.

Murphy leaned on the desk, bracing himself with his knuckles.

"The better part of valor, eh?" he asked curtly, looking Harry up and down before calling out, "Major Lee."

The door slid open so quickly that Harry knew Lee must have had one hand on the manual latch.

"Major Tapper, you're confined to quarters," Murphy said briskly as he took his seat. "The Hounds have revoked your tribal kinsman's station visa and he is, as we speak, being repatriated to the surface. In light of that, I am certain that any attempt to resubmit your request to allow your dependents to join you on-station will be denied and so is an exercise in futility. If you break the habitat regulations regarding weapons or cause further disruptions, to include gambling, you will be remanded to RockHound custody under our Status of Forces agreement with the host nation. No further discussion will be entertained. Major Lee will escort you out. Dismissed."

Harry gaped, disbelieving.

He felt Lee tug on his elbow. "Let's go, Harry."

Chapter Ten

"What did you expect?" Harry's visitor asked sarcastically. "You threatened to cut the wrong throat. Uncle Sugar doesn't appreciate that. Only authorized throats are to be cut. Or have you forgotten how we both got here?"

"Not funny, Marco," Harry replied, grunting through another hundred push-ups. "Besides, it's only been a couple days."

"That's Sergeant First Class Marco Rodriguez to you, sir," Rodriguez said, flipping a sheathed Ka-Bar from blade to grip and back again, without looking. The experienced NCO perched on the edge of Harry's desk, casually swinging one foot while he scrolled through entertainment feeds. "By the way, do you always carry a holdout?"

"Always," Harry answered in the space between one push-up and the next. "What fool doesn't?"

"Huh. Well, here's something from a fool: if you watched your mouth and stopped playing barb, your promotion to major wouldn't be on the block. Right?"

Harry didn't answer until he finished his set and bounced to his feet, shoulders brushing against the room's fixtures. The single bed built into the ever-present gray bulkheads was made up with a dark blue whipcord cover, on top of which Harry's desk chair was laying. Above the bed, Harry had epoxied a series of plastic hooks to the bulkhead. Hanging from them was an eclectic collection of mementos and personal equipment. Around the rest of the space, every drawer and accessory tray was shut. Even the compartment's sink was folded up, leaving a narrow strip of deck from the door to the desk.

"Is there anything more useless than a promotion in this place and time?" Harry asked, watching Marco flip the knife. It seemed to hang forever as it tumbled in the low-gee field, which was less than half normal in station berthing. Despite months of experience in space, most of the Lawless still got a kick from experimenting with the low gravity. "You won't have much use for it if Murphy catches you with that pig sticker. No personal weapons allowed on-station."

"Officially maybe, but no one's looking too hard at little old me. I'm not the knifeman, part-time barbarian, and full-time notorious SEAL, Harry Tapper."

Rodriguez paused, studying the screen.

"Ah, here we go." Rodriguez tapped a key. Instantly, the room filled with the rhythmic clicking of drumsticks clicking on the edge of the drum, followed right away by the distinctive sound of a bongo. A few moments later, the singer begged the listeners' indulgence as he introduced himself as a man of wealth and taste.

"Ah, the classics," Harry said, cricking his neck left and right.

"Classics, hell," Marco said. "This is current events."

The singer went on to describe how he'd been around for a long, long year and stolen many men's souls and faith.

"You know, the longer I have this job, the more I understand that bastard," Harry said, briefly inclining his head toward the speakers before snatching up the desk chair and clicking it into the clamps set into the deck. "I didn't even get to say goodbye to Grevorg."

"He's lucky he didn't get searched," Rodriguez replied. "I happen to know he was carrying something bigger than your little blade."

"He's a good man," Harry said.

"Good man," the sergeant agreed affably.

The song continued; the singer was asking who killed the Kennedys. Harry was content to sit and listen. The Ka-Bar described its endless, irregular flip, flip, flip. The song wound down and the next started, the singer crooning about his brown-eyed girl. Naturally, Harry began thinking of Stella, who he hadn't seen since his last trip to R'Bak, several weeks ago.

He must have fidgeted.

"You miss your girl, right?" Rodriguez asked.

"Fucking Murphy denied my request to bring her back," Harry said, balling his fists. "He's just pissed I called him on his bullshit."

Harry hadn't thought about Stella for almost an hour and instantly began to seethe again.

"You know, I'm not often in a position to counsel an officer—"

"So don't."

"—but a few things occur to me," Rodriguez said, still moving his boot in time to the music. He gestured at the bulkhead over the bed. "Isn't that a claw off the godawful, meter-long poisonous land-lobster you had to eat at the Sarmatchani victory feast? The one after we shot down the airship and just before you hooked up with Stella?"

"Venomous, not poisonous," Harry answered, looking up for a moment before starting to pace in the short confines of the room. "Safe to eat, just don't get bit or stung. Actually tasted like chicken after you roasted it. Yannis was testing me. Checking my character. I think he wanted to know if I was worthy of his daughter. Guess he was wrong on that score: I can't even get back to the fucking planet! To my kid!"

"Well, then you need to hear this, Harry."

Harry glanced up at the unusual use of his first name. Rodriguez was no stickler for protocol, but neither was he familiar with officers. In fact, Harry knew Rodriguez usually only brought out more than one *sir* per hour if he was really pissed and wanted to get some dumbass officer's attention. He stopped pacing as Rodriguez held up one finger.

"First, Murphy was right. You're just feeling sorry for yourself. You gotta knock that off. Figure your shit out before you pop off again. Next time, Murphy might not be able to save your ass. And he did save your ass. The reason you're in here is as much because he's shielding you from the consequences of your actions as it is for any personal beef he may have with your whiny ass. Next time, he might not be able to protect you, because our survival depends on keeping the RockHound Legate onside. So, more likely than not, what the Legate wants, the Legate will damn well get."

Harry didn't answer, but dropped and started doing push-ups again, this time with his feet *on* the chair.

"Next, while you ain't exactly a paragon of military courtesy, you are a good operator with a pretty unique skill set." Rodriguez's endless speech was seriously interfering with Harry's count of repetitions. "I don't much care for shitty officers, but I haven't once had the urge to roll a frag into your tent, if you know what I mean."

Harry grunted, continuing to push them out. He knew every member of the Lawless had something seriously wrong with them, or the Ktor would have brought them out of suspended animation with the rest of their kidnap victims and used them for the one-way mission to implicate Earth in war crimes and break up the Accords.

How screwed up are you when a murderous alien race thinks you're too unreliable to be used, even as a criminal?

In Rodriguez's case, it was because he had a documented propensity for killing superior officers who made lethally bad decisions. For that matter, it might be why Harry was here, too. Of course, it begged the question about people like Murphy and Lee and the rest of the cadre.

Rodriguez continued, "While you've been in here cooling your heels for a few days, Makarov slid us some advance notice on the next phase of the op." The sergeant kept ticking off points on his fingers. "Frankly, it looks like another Death Star run."

When the Dornaani had dropped them off in the Shex system, they'd included a huge data packet. Buried in that were Terran history, education, and entertainment files. Digesting the last century of human history had been an unpleasant shock. The entertainment dump had been much, much more pleasant. Pretty much everyone had gone crazy for the same Star Wars movies Harry had loved as a kid, especially the World War II veterans. To his shock, they'd even made several more movies in the series, although he'd missed them in hibernation.

Small favors.

However, the original films were frequent reruns in the refectory; for an annoyingly long period, both the earlier Lost Soldiers and the SpinDogs had greeted one another with way too many "May the Force be with yous."

"Impossible odds, high casualty rates, and no medals for the enlisted?" Harry replied. "Chewbacca got screwed."

"Pretty much, pretty much." Rodriguez nodded. "Same old Saigon Puzzle Palace bullshit. Thing is, your current plan is even shittier. Winning is a much, much better plan. And, if you play your cards right and think like an old hand who's used to maneuvering inside the Big Green Machine, you're more likely to get your ass out of this crack *and* get what you want, all at the same time."

"You think I have a plan?" Harry gestured around the tiny room, letting his gesture end at the closed door. "You look at this and think, damn, that Harry Tapper is an absolute mastermind?"

"I didn't say it was a good plan," Rodriguez said, chuckling. "But sure. I've seen second looies land nav better than you're hiding your plan. Accumulate as much non-credit cash as you can. Maintain your ties to the surface and keep your barb battle buddies close. Wrangle a last trip down, just as we pull everybody out. Figure out a way to double some shuttle loadmaster, or a sympathetic interface-craft back seater, and once you're on the ground, go AWOL all the way back to the Sarmatchani."

That last was uncomfortably close, but Harry didn't so much as twitch.

Rodriguez laughed anyway.

"Then disappear and migrate to the poles during the Searing, living happily ever after with your barb girlfriend."

"She's more than my girlfriend," Harry growled, popping to his feet. He stared Rodriguez down. "And you know it."

"Easy, El-Tee, easy," Rodriguez said, relaxed as ever. With a final flip, he caught the Ka-Bar by the forte, and set it on the desk. "You know it, I know it, and anyone that gives your situation a think is going to know it. Do you think you're the first man who lost everything and then found a soldier's girl in the middle of the shit? Being in-country makes everything more intense. Higher highs, fucking shitastic lows. And everyone can see you're in it up to your thick-ass, highly tanned frogman neck."

Harry deflated, just a bit, and turned to sit heavily on the thin mattress.

Before he could formulate an answer, the door jumped to a heavy knock.

"Come," Harry called.

"Hello, Harry," Major Lee said, swinging the door open. "Got a moment?"

"I was just leaving," Rodriguez said, surreptitiously pushing the sheathed Ka-Bar a little more to the side of the desk, where it was obscured by Harry's oversize trunk and thick arms. He brushed past both officers, offering Lee a nod. "Major."

"Sergeant."

"Heya, Bruce," Harry said, once the door was closed. He leaned backward against the desk, so he could face the doorway squarely.

"You done fucked up good, Harry," Lee said, sighing as she folded her arms across her chest. A silver set of master aviator wings caught the light from the overhead lights. "Could you have done something less dramatic, like booby-trapping an airlock?"

"If I skipped a chance for drama, they'd pull my Trident, Bruce."

"Sure they would, dumbass. Except 'they' are several dozen light-years away and dead. Here, now, the Hounds want your head. You put Murphy in a real spot. And then you managed to piss him off even more. What did you say, right at the end?"

Lee was a thirtysomething helo pilot who'd done her share of hairy missions on the surface. She kept her dark hair short, noticeably shorter than Harry's own mop. Like most of the Terrans, she carried more muscle than her RockHound counterparts. Her forearms were bunched under the sleeves of her flight suit.

"I might have begun to point out we're the ones on the sharp end while he was mostly in the rear with the gear."

"Give me fucking strength, God," Lee said, tilting her head to address the pipes and bundles of wire overhead. "And I suppose the black-market drugs on the table were yours?"

"They were about to be," Harry replied, and then held up both hands in response to Lee's subsequent glare. "Don't blame me! All the old shit we used to play for is used up. I haven't seen a pack of gum or a cigarette in months." Harry started to think through what Lee's presence meant in the current context.

Lee was good people. She gave a shit about the Lost Soldiers *and* the R'Baku. She was also another Terran who'd fallen in love with a local. She'd lost her man but gained a daughter. If anyone would understand Harry, it would be her.

And she's still doing her job.

Thinking it through, Harry felt about three feet tall.

Of course, that's probably just why Murphy sent her. Can you trust her?

Before Harry could pursue that line of thought, Lee interrupted. "Well, you have Murphy as spun up as I've ever seen him."

"I fucked things up, Bruce." He tried for a look of dogged repentance. "What can I do to help unfuck it?"

"First, you get to grovel a bit," she said crisply, raising one eyebrow. "You're going to apologize to the annoying RockHound officer, and you are going to make him believe it."

"I can do that."

"Then, when you're done sitting here in this doghouse, you're going to come when they whistle for you and sit like a good boy at the formal briefing that's pending. And while there, you are going to help Colonel Murphy persuade some SpinDog and RockHound VIPs to do things his way."

"What's the op?"

"Right now, the job is to persuade our hosts our plan is sound, and you're our subject matter expert," Lee said, looking at Harry impatiently. "Later, the op is whatever Murphy says it is. Now, is that going to be a problem, or can you get it done?"

"A SME, eh?" Harry asked, pronouncing it "smee." He tried to keep the suspicion out of his tone. This was too easy. "I can be persuasive. What am I going to be persuasive about?"

"Whatever Murphy needs," Lee said, sweeping the door open and stepping through into the hallway, where she paused expectantly. "If he says hop, you jump and make ribbit noises. And you're going to start now."

"Imitating an amphibian is my specialty."

"Yes, but first," Lee said sourly, "there's the matter of apologizing to an asshole."

Harry shoved off the desk and moved into the companionway. "Let's go do this, Major."

Behind him, the desk blotter was empty.

Forewarned, Harry knew their next stop was the RockHounds' electronics fabrication area. He had to step out, since Major Lee was leading briskly, employing the low-gravity stride all the Lawless had learned was the best way to move without bouncing off the overhead. However, the extra hip action both sexes adopted for efficiency in minimum gee tightened her flight suit with each stride, prompting entirely inappropriate thoughts that made Harry feel vaguely incestuous.

Harry shook it off and instead began to silently compose a little speech for Korelon's benefit. Amity among allies and so on, no hard feelings among fellow warriors—Harry would baffle him with bullshit. He also took a preparatory round turn and a couple half hitches in his emotions, a prerequisite he surely needed before stress-testing his newly sworn self-control. Harry carefully didn't think about what he'd slipped into the small of his back.

Lee moved comfortably through passageways that were off-limits to most Terrans, moving far enough along the diameter of the station that Harry could feel the pull of increased gee. This part of the station reminded Harry of the petroleum plants in Texas and Oklahoma. They navigated a labyrinth of pipes, tanks, caution signs, stained floor tiles, and sharp smells. Fortunately, the tall RockHound officer was in the first workroom they checked, watching a few techs labor over a very old-fashioned circuitry test bench. Lee brought them to a halt, side by side.

Harry opened his mouth to begin his rote delivery, and then left it there when the RockHound raised one stiff hand, like a semaphore of arrogance. The RockHound muttered an order to the techs, dismissing them, before he turned to face the pair.

Hand still raised, he briefly eyed Harry before lowering it to his side and pointedly addressing himself only to Lee.

Like an elementary school crossing guard who only talks to grown-ups.

"Major, thank you for your visit," Korelon said, his teeth gritted so firmly he almost appeared to be smiling. "Having anticipated such a gesture was in the offing, I wish to assure you despite the...intensity of my sporting banter with Major Tapper, there is no need to meet or for him to seek me out at a future date."

Harry opened his mouth to try to apologize anyway but didn't get any further. The RockHound interrupted again, repeating himself. As far as he was concerned, the matter was forgotten. Any attempt for unneeded rapprochement would be inappropriate. Persistence would be ignored. Neither Terran was allowed a word. The techs were as far from the threesome as the limits of the compartment would allow.

There was a long pause, during which Korelon never once looked away from Lee. Harry began to take a step forward, to demand the RockHound's attention, but before he could do more than shift his weight, Lee spoke.

"I see," she said, her tone matching Korelon's icy composure.

"In the event the situation changes, I look forward to the opportunity for Major Tapper to present his points to you."

Without waiting for an answer, she turned on her heel and moved to the door. Harry waited a beat to see if Korelon would even look up. However, the RockHound turned away and immediately found something just *fascinating* on the work bench, so Harry turned to follow his escort. "Well, that certainly went well."

"That pure-blind conceited moron!" Lee hissed, eyes blazing. "That perfect specimen of inbred, ill-advised, self-important insolence!" It was the start of a modulated but highly descriptive diatribe. Lasting a scant minute, it wasn't as thorough an indictment as the chewing out Murphy had delivered to Harry, but it was easily as heartfelt. For his part, he merely watched the storm and enjoyed her command of prose. It much resembled a high priestess preparing a sacrifice to a thirsty god, and all she had to offer was the—as yet unspilled—blood of her enemies.

"Right," she finished. A long exhalation through her nose. "I'm done. He's an ass. You got off light, Harry. There's something more going on. More than his stupidity, I mean. Something I need to know? Why didn't he want to listen?"

"He's embarrassed," Harry replied. "The way a RockHound would see it, he got taken by an inferior opponent. Worse, his boss knows about it, so his pride is doubly bruised."

"Ahh, so the best outcome for Korelon is if we all pretend to forget it happened."

"Well, that's simpler than tossing him out the airlock, Bruce," Harry said, testing the depth of Lee's relief. "But not as funny."

"Do you see me laughing, Tapper?" she asked as they arrived back at his compartment. "Now get back in your doghouse."

"And how long until the briefing?"

"God only knows. Getting RockHound and SpinDog VIPs into the same room at the same time is about as easy as getting cats to walk in formation."

Harry put on his best crestfallen face.

"Yeah, yeah, I'll see if I can get you galley privileges, at least. Now get in there before someone sees you out here and convinces Murphy I'm being lax and undermining his orders. It wouldn't do to have him pissed at both of us."

Chapter Eleven

"Your controls," Kamara said to Bowden as he took his hands off the stick. He looked over and smiled.

Bowden forced himself not to wipe at the sweat pooling on his forehead as he took control of the spacecraft. Kamara had already shown him the intercept twice, and he'd made it look ridiculously simple both times. Before Bowden could even see what Kamara was doing, they'd been alongside the target, close enough to grab it with the packet's claw arm.

Bowden nodded once as he found the target outside the canopy. *All right, here's where you shut this bastard up by performing the best rendezvous you've ever flown.* He oriented the small craft with a puff of the control thruster, then another to null out the first one's thrust once he had the craft aligned the way he wanted. Bowden thrusted toward the target: a pod from a small rotational habitat the Dornaani had wrecked as they bulled their way through the system. Bowden kept a close eye on the target and gave two bursts from his thrusters, but—despite the thrust he'd given the packet— the pod seemed to move away from him and downward.

Bowden took a deep breath and released it slowly. *I've got this.* He lost sight of the target and pitched the spacecraft's nose down to find it again. As it came back into view, it now seemed to be traveling on a different track from what it had been, and he frowned at it in concentration. *You're not getting away that easily.* Satisfied with the orientation, he again thrusted toward it.

The pod—as if it had a mind of its own—again moved away from him and down. He tried the rendezvous a third time, but never got any closer than he had on the first run. All he succeeded in doing was moving higher and farther away.

"*Damnit!*" he exclaimed as it drifted off again.

He looked over to find Kamara chuckling. "I've got the controls," the RockHound said.

Bowden gratefully relinquished control of the craft, and his shoulders slumped. Before he could clear his head, the pod filled the front canopy, close enough to touch, its trajectory matched perfectly by the small packet.

"Okay, damn it, how did you do that? The more I drove toward it, the farther it moved away."

"It's all a matter of understanding orbital mechanics. The pod isn't moving away from us; you're taking us away from it."

"How so?"

"It's a matter of energy. You looked out the canopy at the pod, then you aimed and thrusted hard toward it. However, by giving the craft more power, you caused it to fly faster, which moved you higher in orbit."

Bowden looked out the canopy at the large moon below him, which orbited the fifth planet in the system, and shook his head, trying to understand.

"As you moved to a higher orbit," Kamara continued, "the pod seemed to fall away from you, but it was an optical illusion; it stayed in its same orbit and you moved away from it. Although it seems counterintuitive to your eyes, which are used to flying in atmosphere, you needed to slow down to catch up to it."

Bowden thought about that a little and held up his hands to simulate the two craft and how the rendezvous was supposed to occur. Finally, he shook his head. "Okay, I can see what you're saying, and I guess it makes sense. Faster pushes you out to a higher orbit. What I don't understand, though, is *how the hell you make rendezvousing with the pod look so damn easy!*"

Kamara's smile grew. "Practice, mostly," he said. He tapped the controls a few times, changed the packet's orientation, and the pod appeared again in the cockpit window, about a hundred meters away.

"The way you do it," Kamara said, "is that you have to visualize it backward. Instead of looking at the target and driving toward it, like you would in the atmosphere, what you really have to do is visualize the intercept point and work backward from it. The pod is in orbit, and we want to get the ship to it, so where do you have to put the ship so that as you slow down or speed up—either will work—the pod gets closer, and we meet it at the spot you visualized?"

Kamara cocked his head. "Does that make sense?"

"I think so...in some sort of twisted, bizarre logic. Basically what I need to do is not look at the target so much as fly the craft to where we intercept the target's orbit."

"Exactly," Kamara said, smiling. "Nothing could be easier."

Punching you in your self-satisfied face would be a hell of a lot easier, actually, Bowden thought, but instead he said, "Do I get another shot at it?"

"One more," Kamara said, looking at their plot. "It's going to burn a lot of fuel to get the pod back to the habitat from here."

"Fine."

"You've got the controls."

"I've got 'em," Bowden replied. *Just don't fuck this up. Just don't fuck this up. Just don't fuck this up.*

Understanding the concept, Bowden found, wasn't the same as understanding the course of action necessary to bring about the desired action, but at least he now understood the issue well enough to not approach the solution backward. Pursing his lips, he visualized where he wanted to meet up with the pod and applied a touch of the thruster that would slow him.

Nothing seemed to happen. It might have moved a little closer, but it was hard to tell. He goosed the thruster a bunch harder.

"Easy," Kamara said as the pod grew larger, quickly. "Going easier on the thrusters and being more patient will make things—shit!"

Bowden had tried to take out some of the closing velocity by hitting the retro thrusters; however, he had changed the orientation of the rendezvous, and the imparted energy drove them faster toward the orbiting pod.

"My controls!" Kamara yelled. He grabbed the stick and initiated a full burn.

Slam! Metal screamed and tore as the ship glanced off the pod.

"Put your helmet on!" Kamara said urgently. He got the ship under control, then fastened his own helmet.

"Are we losing air?" Bowden asked.

"I don't think so. But it's always a good precaution to put

your helmet back on until you're sure you're not. A slow leak is insidious. You feel yourself getting warm and happy as you asphyxiate, and then . . . nothing."

"So what do we do now?"

"We go back to the habitat and assess the damage."

"Without capturing the pod?"

"Yes, without capturing the pod. Hopefully, we didn't knock it out of orbit enough that it will reenter and burn up. There was probably a bunch of good stuff onboard, besides what I would have gotten for the pod itself."

Bowden winced. "Sorry."

Kamara shrugged. "It was my fault for trusting too much in your skills. Hopefully, we can go back after it tomorrow. If the ship isn't too badly damaged."

Ouch. Nothing like a midair collision on your first familiarization flight.

They flew the rest of the way to the habitat in silence, and Bowden could tell the RockHound was worried about the damage he'd done to the ship.

They landed, and Kamara shut down the ship and was out of his seat before Bowden could grab his stuff. Bowden found him looking at the bow of the ship, where three deep gouges ran for about four feet across the nose. A couple of wires also protruded from where something used to be mounted.

"Sorry," Bowden said. He pointed. "What used to be there?"

Kamara scoffed. "Auxiliary rangefinder."

"Why didn't we use it?" Bowden cocked his head. "Wait a minute, when we were going through the list of gear, you said your ship had a computer that let you calculate intercepts. I know it was rudimentary, but why weren't we using that?"

"Because technology breaks." Kamara shrugged. "And sometimes it leads you astray. It can't be trusted. You have to be able to do intercepts visually, so that you know when the technology is wrong. There might be times, like in an emergency, where you'd have to use it, but I would never actually want to *have* to use it."

Bowden chuckled.

"You think that is funny?" Kamara asked.

"No, not really, but when you first showed me this craft, you told me I was going to wreck it."

Kamara raised an eyebrow. "And?"

"At the time, I would have bet you that you were wrong."

Kamara waved toward the craft's nose. "It appears you would have lost."

"Yes, I would have."

Kamara looked at him for several seconds. "So?" he finally asked.

"So, I'm trying to work my way around to saying I'm sorry, but pilots have a hard time saying negative things about their skills in the first place, and then admitting they were wrong in the second."

"And?"

Bowden took a deep breath and let it out slowly. "And you were right. I was wrong. My in-atmo skills didn't translate into flying in space. And I *did* wreck your craft."

Kamara smiled warmly, the first time he'd done so. "Good. Now that you have admitted that, perhaps you will actually come to believe it, and then we can *really* make some progress."

Bowden gave him a half smile. "I do believe it. And I hate that Murphy is going to take the cost of repairs out of my paycheck. Well, we don't actually get a paycheck at the moment, but I'm sure it's going to cost me somehow."

Kamara shrugged. "The damage isn't that bad. I'm not sure we'll even need to mention it to your Murphy."

"No? You think those gouges will buff out?"

"I do not understand. 'Buff out'?"

Bowden explained the concept.

"Ah," Kamara said with a chuckle. "We would say, fill with dust." He shook his head. "I said it wasn't that bad, but it *will* need to be fixed before we can take it out again. And we'll want the rangefinder. One of the maintenance people here owes me a favor, though, and perhaps we can do him a favor the next time we go to Outpost. If you're willing to assist him in mounting the module—"

"I am," Bowden interjected with a nod.

"—then he probably won't charge us, and there'd be no reason to have to mention it to anyone."

"That's great."

"No, what would be great is if you were willing to listen to me."

"I am."

"Good, then let's talk about inertia while we wait for my friend to come on duty."

Chapter Twelve

Chalmers looked around the tarmac just beyond the perimeter fencing of R'Bak Island's downport, too keyed up to enjoy the play of cool air on his painted skin while they waited to be seen by the customs official. The terminal building of the airport was half underground but had all the modern conveniences—like air-conditioning—Chalmers hadn't seen anywhere but SpinDog habs since waking up. The facility also had a number of security and civilian officials in a variety of uniforms and face paint. At least the camera mounts for the surveillance system sat empty on the walls. The reavers were, according to Umaren, tasked with get-ting such tech up and running. But the destruction of all their space-side assets and the wide scattering of those on the planet had rendered such tasks not only impossible, but pointless.

Umaren had said the customs official they were required to meet with would be easy enough to get past, but Chalmers didn't like being this reliant on Umaren, let alone the seaplane captain's assessment of security.

The customs situation was unlike any he'd had to navigate, too. The downport required that any change in ownership or crew be reported to the authorities, but Umaren said they didn't bother to keep all that close a record of the comings and goings of the crews afterward. Indeed, they rarely checked incoming cargoes for contraband, which made sense in an odd sort of way. They had to be far more interested in outgoing traffic that might carry off some of the all-important drugs and medicines they were here to collect.

"Next!" the customs guy barked.

Umaren stepped forward and presented the customs officer with his documents, pretending a calm he didn't feel. Not from the sweat-slick fists he twined together behind his back, at any rate. Chalmers sidled closer, Jackson and Vizzel behind him.

"You never used to carry so many crew," the official said, thumbing through *Loklis'* manifest with one hand while he ran an eye over the men standing behind Umaren.

"The new owners wanted them aboard." Umaren leaned forward and added in a stage whisper meant to be heard by the crew, "I think to get rid of them. The owners have too many daughters who married men without other prospects." Chalmers and Jackson grumbled and tried to look more uncomfortable, playing their parts. Umaren continued, "They even said they're sending along another one in a few weeks."

"Well, if they want to cut down on the cargo you can carry, then that's their poor decision."

Umaren shrugged. "With the Searing nearly upon us, the new owners said they want to be sure we didn't look like an easy prize for pirates. Things are . . . not so stable as they usually are."

The official nodded. "Your new owners, what brokerage?"

Umaren pointed at the paperwork. "Twin Star Trading, out of Kanjoor."

The official nodded, noting the name. "We've had a few new operations appear recently, what with the takeover of Whikmari Global Transport."

Umaren shrugged. "As you say. I just want to fly, and they pay on time."

The officer's condescending smile eased the knot of worry in Chalmers's gut. No one looked down that way on someone they considered a credible threat. It eased even further as the officer reached into a desk drawer and withdrew a stamp, which he then brought down on several successive pages of Umaren's paperwork.

"Next!" the official shouted as he gave Umaren a dismissive wave.

R'Bak's star Shex had begun to send its last brass and orange rays wider across and above the horizon when Chalmers peered over the rim of an earthenware cup. He toasted the other three men lounging in the belly of the seaplane. "Well, the basics are in place."

Jackson was staring into his own watered-down drink with a scowl. "Yeah, but now comes the hard part: manipulating the manipulators of the local black market. That's certain to get hairy. Hairier than the bullshit with Umaren's old boss."

"Well, then tomorrow isn't a moment too soon to pick up our extra security." Chalmers resisted the urge to drain the cup. "It's crazy we had to wait this long. Sure could have used some professional muscle against Maktim."

"I agree with Chalmers," Umaren announced. "That battle was too narrowly won. As much by luck as by skill."

Chalmers tried not to hear the last sentence as a reminder of his fumbling during the combat.

Happily, Jacks kept the uncomfortable silence from lasting more than a second. "The new guy wasn't ready until now," he said with a shake of his head. "He's been acclimating—y'know, getting the feel of R'Bak—in an area *we* control."

"Where?"

Jackson frowned—probably weighing whether or not that information should be shared, Chalmers guessed. "Near the Ashbands. Getting the hang of their habits and dialects before he inserts with us. No one up there would ever take him for a native, but he'll pass here on the island."

"So," Vizzel prompted, "you have been told he is ready, now?"

"No," Jacks answered. "But we haven't been waved off, so we just pick him up at the appointed time and place."

Umaren's grumbling didn't become words, but he clearly was not happy with the arrangement.

Chalmers's own displeasure was focused on the thirty-hour flight the pickup would require. "Christ, Jacks, what the hell is the rush? The surveyors aren't even here yet."

"No, but we have to start acting as though they were. If we teach ourselves—and the new meat—the right habits now, then we won't fuck ourselves with slips later on. When the *real* players come to town."

Chambers shrugged, tossed back the rest of his drink anyway, and silently admitted that his friend was not just right; he was goddamned, mother*fucking* right.

✧   ✧   ✧

"You didn't tell me he'd be a giant. I'll need to off-load some cargo just to carry his vastness," Umaren said quietly into the night wind.

Chalmers peered up the dock. A large man had entered the pool of light shed by the lantern at the seaplane's cargo hatch. Jackson and Vizzel had left it hanging there while they crammed the last few legitimate packages into the hold.

Chalmers recognized the "security specialist" from the photo included in the redacted files Murphy had furnished. Maximiliano Messina was certainly larger than most men but moved with the easy confidence Chalmers associated with dangerous people.

"Not with the lightweight parts we've been swapping into your plane these last weeks," Chalmers said. The replacement parts, mostly manufactured of ultralight and durable alloys, had been furnished by the SpinDogs. An old bootlegger's trick, that: removing and replacing all parts that weren't essential to a vehicle's speed and endurance and then tricking out the engines for maximum performance. Chalmers had insisted they dirty up the parts to make them look locally built, but any experienced mechanic who held one of the fuel pumps would know something was up. The work had freed up something on the order of five percent of the bulky, over-built seaplane's weight. More free weight meant either more product or better range per kilo of fuel.

Messina must have fixed their location before stepping into the light, as he walked straight toward Chalmers and Umaren, who stood in the deep darkness beside the crew door of *Loklis.*

"Messina," Chalmers said, extending his hand.

"Call me Moose, brother," the big man said, engulfing Chalmers's hand in one large paw. "Sounds more like an indig name than my own."

"Sure, Moose," Chalmers said, wondering if he should have done something similar. Jackson easily got away with using his own name, as the locals took one look at him and assumed he was foreign to these parts.

Moose let his hand go without squeezing the life out of it and went to clasp Umaren's in turn.

There was a moment's fumbling as the local missed his first attempt at a grip, too busy looking up, and then up again, into Moose's eyes.

"Greetings, Captain Umaren. It is my honor to help protect you and your cargo on the ground."

"As I pledge to keep you safe in the air, Moose," Umaren said.

Umaren smiled and retreated into his beloved aircraft. He left the hatch open, the lights inside casting a wedge of light across the two Lost Soldiers.

"Damn," Chalmers said.

"What's that, Chief?" Moose asked, dropping into English for a moment.

"You sounded a lot more formal with the captain than I expected. According to your file, this is your first time on the surface. You do some research before coming down?"

"You bet. Pays to know your cultural cues. You know, in case someone wants to put a bullet in your—or my—head. Worked in-country, worked up there." He pointed skyward. "Should work here, too."

Chalmers started to laugh but was brought up short on recognizing the utter sincerity in the other man's eyes.

"Good point," he said. Looking for something to do to cover his awkwardness, he stooped to pick up the other man's bag. Or to try to. The thing was far heavier than Moose had made it seem.

Moose brushed his hand away without apparent effort. "I'll carry my weight and cover your six, Chalmers. You and the rest of the crew, that is."

"Good deal, Moose. I'll show you aboard. Not much elbow room, I'm afraid."

"Used to that after being up there," Moose said, following Chalmers through the hatch.

The plane dipped noticeably to the side as the big Lost Soldier climbed aboard.

"I do not like flying again so soon," Umaren groused. "And so close to the last place. It could look suspicious."

"Look suspicious to who?" Chalmers asked, suddenly regretting his decision to head for the cockpit. Moose was grabbing a meal, Jacks was sleeping, and someone had to put eyeballs on the destination before landing, so that meant him. But damned if Umaren hadn't started fussing like a wet hen as they neared the rendezvous coordinates. "Do you think anyone is watching us out here?" Chalmers tried to sound casual but was certain that some of his annoyance had bled through.

"Out here? No. But back at R'Bak Island?" Umaren shrugged. "It is always a possibility. And if they are any good at 'watching,' then we would never know it. And if they speak to the fuel merchants about how much we are purchasing after each of these two flights, they could begin asking awkward questions."

Chalmers had to allow that there was a certain inescapable logic in that.

"Besides, I do not like these rendezvous that are based solely on a time and map coordinates. Out here, we depend upon prior relationships as the assurance of our safety."

"You mean reliable relationships like the one you had with Maktim?" Chalmers had not meant to sound like a smart-ass, but it had come out that way, all the same.

"Yes," Umaren snapped with an undertone of self-recrimination, "who I betrayed at your bidding."

Oh, so we're to blame for the blood on your hands? "You could have said no. And stayed poor."

Umaren seemed to chew on his own teeth. "Even if he was a vicious bastard, he was at least a known quantity. Out here, we do not know anyone. So how can we determine if we might be flying into an ambush?"

"We can't, but it's a lot less likely than if we were sending signals all the time, maybe attracting attention we don't want. So a blind pickup is best." Chalmers almost sold himself on that claim. "Besides, no one has landed in this bay for a long time." At least that was what the locals had told the friendlies who had scouted it out. "And now it's being set up for our trade. *Just* ours."

That seemed to mollify Umaren. "And this fellow we are picking up, he is another, eh, Lost Soldier who went to the Hamain to become familiar with our ways?"

"No, he already knows the locals well enough. But he had some . . . er, old business to attend to. And while he was at it, he made the rounds in a few coastal cities where he had some contacts who could clue him in to how the local markets work."

Umaren sniffed. "We know the markets well enough."

Chalmers nodded, made noises of agreement, but thought, *You know the markets on the level of barter, buy, sell, smuggle. He's got the knowledge of the power players, the folks whose movements send out the ripples that keep little fish like you dancing and jumping. Movers and shakers, not fighters and traders.*

Chalmers peered out the cockpit windscreen over Umaren's shoulder. "Is that it?" He pointed toward the mostly brown horizon where the blue ocean was ruffled by white risers rolling in toward a greener patch of coast.

"I believe so," the pilot muttered. "Strap in. We will need to make several passes to assess the water."

"Worried about the chop?"

"I am worried about the depth—as in, possibly not enough for our floats. Now, sit down and let me fly the plane."

Chalmers stepped out of the waist-hatch of the seaplane onto a brand-new dock built expressly for *Loklis*. Made of fresh-sawn timbers that were already warping in the heat of the suns, it creaked in counterpoint to the gentle lapping of the waves on shore. Behind him, in no hurry to exit, Moose and Jackson were still arguing over the perfect BBQ technique: cut, spice, sugar, fat—the pair could argue for hours without coming close to a joint resolution. All they ever succeeded at was to either make Chalmers hungry or irritate him to no end. It was like the Student United Nations but less fun for Chalmers.

Chalmers stretched, enjoying the heat for a moment. What with the humidity off the sea, late afternoons at this latitude and with this wind were like a really, really hot day in Cabo. Finished stretching, he waved at the man reclining in the shade of a rather large pile of trade goods where the dock met the shore.

"Waiting long?" Chalmers called.

"Only since yesterday." The Lost Soldier's reply was in very, *very* good R'Bakuun. The coastal dialect Umaren and Vizzel had grown up speaking, no less. The man sat up, brushed sand from his robes, and waited for Chalmers to join him in the shade.

The protective face paint made it hard to lock down, but something about the man struck Chalmers as familiar. *Not since making planetfall, but something else. Somewhere else. No, that wasn't it, either.*

"You made good time, then," Chalmers said, extending his hand as he entered the shade.

The man took his hand in a firm, if slightly sweat-damp grip. "There are still a few technicals kicking around, even though most of them have been hidden away, now. Murphy saw to it my goods and I were given priority. Lots to do and not much time to do it in."

"Right." Chalmers released the hand and waved at the crates, which were marked with the brokerage's twin stars. "To the efficient worker bee, more work."

"You calling me a drone?" the man asked, smiling under his paint.

Chalmers chuckled, shaking his head. "What should I call you?"

"Vat will do."

A cold thrill of recognition went through Chalmers, like ice water on hot pavement. He shivered. This was the same fucker CID had tasked Jackson and him with investigating when things went sideways in the Mog. The same fucker who'd been on the ill-fated Blackhawk with them. He'd had a single, blurry photo to work from back then, and, to be honest, his own problems had kept him from recognizing the former lieutenant of the US Army turned international arms dealer.

Fuck. That's where I recognize you from. You were on my book.

"You all right?" Vat asked.

"Yeah, just a little strung out from the flight," Chalmers said, hearing Jackson's and Moose's heavier tread on the dock behind him.

"No, you ain't. You recognized my name." Vat's eyes glittered with reflected light off the shallow lagoon.

Chalmers slowly rolled his shoulders, then cracked his neck. Finally decided, he said, "I was two steps behind you, back in the Mog."

"Oh?" The man's lips thinned, but he otherwise appeared relaxed, ready for anything. *Butter wouldn't melt in this guy's mouth.*

"Made a fair bit of trouble for me, you did."

Jackson walked up, did a double take. Moose had stopped somewhere out of sight.

"FBI sent over a team to get you," Chalmers said. "While they were with us, they got wind of some…irregularities in certain cases I had worked in the past."

"No shit?" Vat said.

"No shit."

"Well, sounds like you fucked up and got caught."

Chalmers bristled. Then, thinking of promises made and of the mission at hand, he reconsidered. A short, barking laugh escaped his lips. The humor came a bit more honestly after that first braying sputter—so much so that he folded over, hands on knees, to catch his breath when it was over. It was only then he realized that one of Vat's hands was concealed behind his thigh, holding something dark and metallic.

"Do we have a problem, Chalmers?" Vat asked, a feral look in his eyes.

"No, Vat, we don't. Not at all." He raised one finger. "I can't think of anyone better suited to this than the guy who kept ahead of us"—he moved the finger in a circle to include Jackson and himself—"as well as the feebs for as long as you did."

The dangerous light dimmed. "Friend of mine stateside warned me they had me cold, were searching my home and business. That's why I was on the Blackhawk with you two. Trying to get out of Dodge before they caught me up. I had no idea the feds were already in Somalia."

"We good, Chalmers?" Moose asked.

Chalmers glanced at Jackson, who thought things through a moment, then nodded.

"We're good, Moose. Just discussing a bit of shared history with our new friend Vat."

"Good deal. When do we eat?"

"They've got something barbecuing. Smells amazing," Vat said, gesturing up the beach. "They've been smoking it all morning."

"Jesus, don't get them started on that," Chalmers said, smiling. He hadn't missed how, with the one hand distracting the viewer, Vat had used the other to make the pistol disappear into his clothing.

Jackson bought it, looked back from the cluster of low buildings on the foreshore only after Vat had empty hands.

"Nice pistol," Moose said.

"What pistol?" Vat asked, his hands as empty as his smile.

Chalmers snorted. "You're gonna fit right in, Vat."

Chapter Thirteen

"That's it?" Bowden asked. Having finally learned how to do orbital rendezvous, they'd moved on to the next stage in his training syllabus.

"Yes," Kamara confirmed, "that is Outpost."

"Shit," Bowden muttered. *Game time.*

Outpost was an oblong asteroid, just like the habitats. However, where the spins revolved around their long axes, like logs rolling in a pond, the eight-hundred-meter-long Outpost rotated end over end, tumbling along in its orbit. Located thirty million kilometers behind the cluster of rocks in R'Bak's spinward Lagrange point, the asteroid tumbled in a very "clean" spin—there was no roll or yaw to upset the centripetally generated gees that existed at the ends of the rock.

"I will take it in the first time," Kamara said after they had spoken with the station and gotten clearance to approach, "so watch and learn."

I learned so much watching him rendezvous with the pod, Bowden thought with a small sigh. *Hopefully, I can do better this time.*

"Okay," Kamara said. "What do we know about inertia?"

"Objects travel in a straight line unless a force acts on them to make them stop or change."

"And why do we care?"

"Because any force that I impart to the craft will require a nulling force. I won't automatically start slowing once I let off the throttles, like I do in atmosphere."

Kamara nodded. "It is far better to go slowly and be patient. If you hit the thrusters hard like you did when we were first at the pod, you had better be using them to break away from Outpost, rather than trying to recover from a shitty approach. If it looks like the rendezvous is going badly, break it off. As you said before—"

"Easy does it," Bowden chorused with him.

"And what's the most important thing about flying near Outpost?"

"Don't fly through the railgun launcher's firing path."

"Not just 'don't fly through its launch path,' but understand—and be aware of—where it is at all times. Other ships will be maneuvering to avoid it, and you need to watch for their movements, too."

Kamara's words proved prescient; as they approached Outpost, the railgun mounted in the center of the asteroid fired, launching a payload tub in the direction of *Spin One*. Bowden had shaken his head when the launcher had been explained to him; it was a massive railgun that was used for launching very small craft and drones from the station, as well as to send material—and, rarely, people—between Outpost and the habitats. The tubs weren't much larger than a person and required the receiving end to capture and bring the tub aboard the habitat. If they missed or forgot—or a thousand other failures—the person went flying past the habitat, heading out-system. It was a transfer method that wasn't used for people very often due to the dangers involved and the fact that they'd have to endure a five-second acceleration at over ten gees. Or thereabouts.

And one I am never getting in, Bowden thought as the tub flew past their craft.

Bowden watched as Kamara flew the packet past the launch path and then around to land on the asteroid; Bowden kept his hands above the controls, going through the motions as if landing the craft himself. He'd gotten better at rendezvousing with objects in space in the four weeks since he'd ripped the rangefinder off the nose of the craft. They'd gone back for the pod the next day and had actually found the device; it was imbedded in the pod. Unfortunately, it was smashed beyond use and had been turned in at *Spin One* as scrap/salvage, along with the rest of the salvage they'd obtained from the pod.

Kamara refused to use the craft's navigation system to assist with the approach, even though Kamara had told Bowden he was satisfied the Lost Soldier could perform a rendezvous manually. The nav system might have been helpful with this approach— Bowden had no way to know, since he hadn't used it—because the big asteroid was tumbling along at a rate of seventy seconds per revolution, so they needed to arrive at the precise location at exactly the instant necessary to capture the asteroid's docking collar. And at the matching radial velocity.

Bowden risked a quick glance over to his instructor. Although Kamara had said the approach was "no big thing," Bowden could see the intense concentration in the RockHound's eyes and the faint sheen of sweat on his forehead. It was obviously a much more difficult evolution than Kamara had let on.

Unlike chasing objects in orbit, there were some obvious parallels between this approach and landing an aircraft on the aircraft carrier. You were trying to meet an object at a certain point on its surface while it moved through three dimensions. There were plenty of differences, but the approach itself was straightforward in nature.

The one thing he noticed as Kamara flew the craft inbound was the way the RockHound kept a light touch on the thrusters. When landing on the aircraft carrier, the pilot flew a specific glideslope, which he referenced by keeping "the ball" centered between two reference datums. When the ball went high, you reduced power to bring your glideslope down; you added power when you were below glideslope to get back on it. The trick was to smoothly intercept the desired position and not go from a low to a high back to a low again. That was called "chasing the ball," and ended up with the pilot using increasingly larger throttle adjustments as he got in close. Bad juju.

Kamara, by keeping the thruster adjustments small, was able to keep the craft at the right velocity to arrive when the docking collar was in position to receive them.

Not sure I'm ready for this, Bowden thought as the locks clicked and the motion of the packet changed drastically as it took on the spin of the asteroid, with all the subtlety of a medium-velocity car crash. While he understood getting the right velocity to arrive when needed, there was also the side-to-side thrusters he needed to manage, as well as the up-and-down velocity needed to drop into the docking cradle in that incredibly short interval where you were in position to do so.

"Nothing to it," Kamara said, sitting back in his chair. Judging from his reaction, though, it was obviously not something even the experienced RockHound found "easy."

"Yeah, right," Bowden muttered.

"Do you need a break before you try it?"

"No," Bowden replied. "And there is no try."

"What?"

Bowden's voice took on an ominous tone. "Try not. Do, or do not. There is no try."

He looked over at Kamara, whose brows were knitting. "What are you talking about?" the RockHound asked.

"It's from . . . never mind. Too hard to explain. Yes, I'm ready." He took a deep breath and let it out heavily. "Let's do this."

Kamara touched the controls then made a show of taking his hands off them. "Your controls."

Bowden nodded. "I have the controls."

"As soon as you release from the docking collar, give the thrusters a boost away from the asteroid before you do anything else," Kamara instructed. "There are some bulges on it that stick out a little farther than where the collar is, and we don't want to have them hit us."

"No we don't," Bowden replied. He went over his new mantra as he thought through what he needed to do. *No more midairs. No more midairs. No more midairs.*

"Okay," Bowden said. "I'm ready."

"Very well, take us out a hundred meters from the asteroid."

Bowden nodded, then realized the motion was probably lost inside his helmet. "Got it." He released the docking collar clamps then gave a gentle boost away from the asteroid. The ship slid away from Outpost, its orbital motion different from the centripetal force it had imparted to the packet as Bowden let go of the clamps. He then took the craft away from the asteroid, careful to avoid the railgun launch path. There were no more launches scheduled, but, as Kamara had taught him, if you never flew through the launch path, you'd never get hit by something being shot out of the tube.

Kind of like walking beneath bombs hanging from the wings of aircraft on the flight deck—they will never fall on you if you don't walk under them.

He pushed that thought aside as he stabilized the craft in a position one hundred meters out from the asteroid and concentrated on finding the rhythm of the big rock's tumble. After a couple of revolutions, he realized it was like trying to time the waves in the ocean when you were about to run out into the water. *Except you could always dive into a wave if you miscalculated.*

"Any time you're ready," Kamara said as the rock began its third revolution.

"Next time around," Bowden muttered. He thought—but didn't add—*you asshole.*

As the docking collar reached the "bottom" of its tumble, Bowden nudged the craft forward. As the asteroid rotated, though, he realized his boost was going to get him to the asteroid before the collar was at the "top" where he could latch onto it. He gave the thrusters a little tap to slow the craft, careful not to "chase the ball." *Small adjustments over a longer time period are better than big power variations you have to null out.*

"Shit," he muttered as the craft started to drift to the left. He tapped the appropriate thruster, then tapped the opposite one to null the thrust. The craft still had a little velocity in the correct direction to bring them back into alignment, but he'd null that before capture.

In the Hornet, his scan on approach was "meatball, lineup, angle of attack," and he tried to work out something similar. After a few seconds, he settled on checking the arrival position of the asteroid and his lineup out the cockpit window, then checking the craft's velocities inside on the gauges.

As the ship reached the correct lineup, he nulled the drift, with another glance at the cockpit instruments. They showed him overcorrecting. He put in a correction for it. His eyes went outside the craft. *Damn that thing is big and close!* He fought the urge to shy away from it as the close end of the asteroid rose toward him. It looked like it was going to slam into his craft, but it was the same sight picture as when Kamara had done it—he wasn't screaming about their impending crash, either, which was a good sign—and Bowden knew he had to be close enough to grab the collar. If he shied away, he wouldn't be able to get back into position in time.

The ship slid to the left and he gave it a boost back to the right. Too hard. He tried to catch the momentum, but it overshot the collar as it rotated into alignment. He tried to boost the ship back into position for a second dive at it but clanked off the side of the collar as he went past. Kamara slapped the thrusters, hard, to boost away from the asteroid.

"What the hell?" Bowden asked.

"You were about to crash into the asteroid. I boosted us up and away from it." He paused and then added, "Get away from it and look at the tapes."

Bowden sighed and flew the craft back to the pre-approach position, then watched the tapes of the approach while Kamara piloted the craft. Everything was good until he got in close, then he overcorrected several times and made a big play to capture the docking collar. He winced. Kamara was right. He probably *would* have hit the asteroid if the RockHound hadn't boosted them away.

"You're right," Bowden said with a sigh. "As always."

"Of course I am," Kamara acknowledged with a smile. "What I want to know is, what happened? You had a nice approach going, then lost it—badly—at the end."

"I thought I saw a drift on the range-finding system. I over-corrected a couple of times, then made a play to grab the collar."

"When you saw the drift on the system, did you see the same thing visually?"

"Well, no. The lineup *looked* good."

Kamara shrugged. "Sometimes the rangefinder gets spurious inputs in close due to vagaries of the asteroid's surface and its spin. You know what doesn't get bogus inputs?"

"No, what?"

"Your eyes. If you look out and you're not drifting, *then you're not drifting*. There is a science to flying in space, but there is also an art to doing it well, too. You have to use your feelings and believe in what you *know* to be true."

"Go with your gut?"

"What does that mean?"

"It means I have to use my instincts."

Kamara nodded. "Exactly so." He shrugged. "Besides, you can't count on technology. If you become reliant on it, you are crippled when it doesn't work."

"Which is why you had me learn to rendezvous with objects in orbit without using the system."

Kamara nodded.

"So, why didn't you have me do this without using any of the technology, too?"

"This is different. There are more variables, and the chances of smashing the craft—as you showed—are a lot higher. I didn't want to destroy the ship and get stranded here."

Bowden thought about what Kamara said for a few seconds, then shook his head. "I'm sorry, but I don't see how this is any different. We're rendezvousing with an object, same as we were in orbit, but, this time, we don't have to fight the orbital mechanics as much. Sure, they're still there, but the effects are smaller. And if I hadn't fallen for an erroneous system indication—"

"You did fall for it, though," Kamara interrupted.

"I did, but I shouldn't have," Bowden said. "It's just a matter of learning the right things to watch and when to watch them." He shrugged. "There's also a different set of flight controls I'm still getting used to, too, which complicates things a little, but the better I get with the controls, the better I'll be able to rendezvous with things. Not having to actively search for where the controls are would give me more time to watch what I need to watch."

"That is true."

Bowden took a deep breath and let it out slowly. "I'm ready for another try."

"Very well." Kamara lifted his hands from the controls. "You've got the ship."

"I've got it." *This is going to be really smart, or the dumbest thing I've done since I woke up here.* Bowden reached forward and turned off the nav system.

"*What are you doing?*" Kamara exclaimed. "It will take ten minutes to realign the gyros!"

"I'm going to show you how we do things at the boat," Bowden said absently as he stared at the tumbling asteroid in front of him.

"The boat? I thought you said aircraft *crashed* on the boat!"

"They do, sometimes," Bowden acknowledged. He turned and looked at Kamara, whose eyes were huge. Bowden smiled. "But this isn't one of those times."

Kamara's jaw dropped, but he didn't say anything.

"Hold that thought, and keep your mouth shut," Bowden said with a wink. "I'll show you how we do things the Navy way."

A thought that perhaps his mouth was writing checks his body couldn't cash went through his mind, but he pushed it away as he refocused on the asteroid. *There!* The asteroid reached the right part of its revolution, and he boosted forward. Not having to look at the nav system simplified his scan. Revolution, altitude, closure, lineup. Just like landing on the carrier. *Sort of.*

He looked beyond the asteroid and visualized where he needed to be. Not only did he need to meet it at a certain spot, he needed to be going the right speed to minimize the shock of capture and then give it a pulse to minimize the torque of chasing the arc of rotation as he latched on. He started to drift a little to the left and put in a gentle correction. He fought the urge to flee as the end of the asteroid rotated up toward him like Thor's hammer, ready to smite his ship. Having already seen the sight picture once, though, he was sure he was high enough for it to pass underneath him.

Pretty sure, anyway.

He nulled the drift as he reached the "centerline" position of the "runway" in his mind. The fact that the asteroid didn't spin around its long axis cut down on one of the variables. He'd landed a Hornet on the boat in the North Sea in February, with the ship gyrating in all three axes...this was easier. He forced himself to keep breathing.

The end passed underneath him, and he did a gentle dive as he goosed the ship forward slightly to match the rotation. Lower...a touch faster, then he slapped the CAPTURE button as it illuminated. The magnetic locks grabbed hold, and Bowden had that "car crash" feeling again as the ship took on the rotation of the asteroid.

They were down.

Bowden turned to Kamara. "See? Nothing to it."

Sweat ran up Kamara's face due to centripetal force. It should have brought additional blood flow to his head, too, but the man was strangely white. After a couple of seconds, Kamara shook his head, scattering the beads of sweat, and released his safety belt. "Let's go get a drink," he said. "I need it."

Bowden looked at the starscape rotating in front of him, and the enormity of what he'd just done rushed in on him as the adrenaline left his system. *That wasn't the dumbest thing I've done since I got here; that was the dumbest thing I've ever done.* "Yeah," he said after a moment, a small tremor in his voice. "I need one, too."

Bowden cocked his head. "Here's what I don't understand, though. Why didn't you build a port at the axis of rotation—in the middle of the long dimension? That way, you'd only have to match rotation, and not chase an intercept vector with a constant curve built in."

Kamara grinned. "Who told you we do not have one there? In fact, that is the location of the primary bay."

"What? Then why are we—"

"To make sure you are the best possible pilot, of course."

Chapter Fourteen

"So," Kamara said three days later as they had lunch in Outpost before their flight, "we're not going to do any more landings on Outpost."

"We're not?" Although the statement should have made Bowden happy—he hated Outpost's capture sequence as it was more danger-ous than trapping aboard the carrier, where any landing could be your last—he found that he was truly enjoying the challenge of it. Just like coming aboard the carrier, you got better the more you did it, to the point where—even if you were never truly *comfort-able* with it—you accepted the fact that you could do it and lost the sense of fear that assailed you the first twenty or thirty times you willingly threw yourself at a moving deck.

"No, we are done," Kamara said. "You can rendezvous with objects in orbit and you can land on Outpost. Are you ready now for something *truly* challenging?"

"There's something more challenging than those things? What is it, landing on a comet or something?"

Kamara's face fell. "How did you know?"

"How did I know what?"

"That we were going to go to a comet today. Did someone tell you?"

Bowden felt his jaw fall open, and he had to consciously close it. "Seriously? I was just kidding around. Why would we want to go land on a comet?"

Kamara shrugged. "Sometimes they have minerals or ice that is needed at an outpost somewhere. Not at Outpost, but on a station out in the asteroids or beyond that."

"You spend time out beyond the asteroids?"

"Yes," Kamara said with a nod. "If you want to find hidden treasures, you have to look off the traveled path. If you go where no one else has gone, the opportunities there haven't already been picked through."

"That makes sense, I guess." Bowden cocked his head. "So we're really going to land on a comet?"

"Yes we are."

"Why is that harder than landing on Outpost?"

"What do you know about comets?"

"That they're big rocky snowballs left over from the formation of the system. They have tails that point away from the star."

"Why do they have those tails?"

"I'm not an astronomer, but, at a guess, it's because the ice starts heating as the comet approaches the star and the frozen stuff starts melting."

"Yes, but what you are missing from your description is the matter of *scale*. On its approach, the asteroid may be fifteen to twenty-five kilometers wide, but as its orbit brings it near the Sun, it heats up, spewing dust and gases, until it fills an area that is larger than most planets—sometimes up to *fifteen times the size of R'Bak.*

"The process of spewing all that material away is called outgassing and may also result in the comet having a tail one hundred million kilometers long, or longer, due to the effects of solar radiation and the solar wind."

"Do we have to fly through the tail?"

Kamara shook his head. "No, we don't have to fly through either of the tails, although we could if we needed to."

"*Two* tails?"

"Yes. Most comets—the ones that aren't dead because they've outgassed everything they have—actually have two tails: a longer ion tail that interacts with the solar wind and a shorter dust tail made up of smoke-sized dust particles caused by outgassing.

"As I said, we don't have to fly through the tails. We will, however, have to fly through the coma, which is the cloud of water, carbon dioxide, and other gases ejected from the nucleus as it nears the star. Once we are through the coma, we will have to land on the nucleus, and that is where things will get really challenging.

"This is because comet formation is not uniform, nor are the stresses they have been exposed to since their formation. Fracture lines accumulate over time, and heat-induced instability can cause them to give way at unpredictable times and in unpredictable directions. Trying to rendezvous with them is one of the most challenging and dangerous tasks in spaceflight. Imagine rendez-vousing with Outpost, but having it rotate in all three directions and not having a docking collar to attach to. Meanwhile, at any moment, it might outgas and spew rocks and debris at your ship, potentially damaging it."

Kamara smiled. "That is what landing on an asteroid is like."

"And you do that *on purpose*?" Bowden asked, horrified. "That sounds like an accident just waiting to happen."

"Well, it's not outgassing *all* the time," Kamara said. "The keys to landing on a comet are to get in and out quickly, and to disturb the surface as little as possible. Oh, and to watch out for any outgassing currently active. You especially don't want to use heavy thrusters near the comet, as you increase your chances of creating a plume exponentially." He shrugged. "Besides that, there's very little chance of anything bad happening. Usually."

"You're not filling me with confidence."

"Really, it's not *that* dangerous. I only know three people who've been hit by outgassing, and two of them survived."

"This doesn't sound like something we ought to be doing."

"Well, it *is* a little more dangerous here than out past the asteroid belt," Kamara said, "as the chances of an outgassing event are a lot higher here due to the proximity of the star." He shrugged again. "Also, Jrar is now close enough that it may cause its own outgassing. There could potentially be three tails—or more—or they could all be twisted into each other. We'll mini-mize the risk by trying to disturb the comet's nucleus as little as possible. Also, your Colonel Murphy told me you need to be as good a space pilot as possible. If you can land on a comet, you can land anywhere; however, the comet is in the best position today for us to launch and intercept it, so we need to get going."

He turned and started walking, then looked over his shoulder. "Are you coming, then?"

"Yeah," Bowden said as his feet started moving of their own accord. *Why do I feel like I'm about to set a new standard for the dumbest thing I've ever done?*

"Your controls," Kamara said three days later as they approached the comet's coma. It wasn't as big as it could have been—a lot of the volatiles had blown off the nucleus over the millennia—but there were still almost one thousand kilometers of ionized gasses and detritus to navigate through.

Still, it wasn't as bad as he'd been expecting. Having seen comets from Earth—and worse, the way they were portrayed by Hollywood—he'd expected the tail of the comet to be densely packed. It was anything but. From up close, it was unimpressive; low-density material flying in generally the same direction. *Kind of like a US Air Force flyby,* he thought with a chuckle.

Although they didn't, they could have flown through the tail. Yes, they would probably have been hit by a number of fast-moving particles, but it wouldn't have been that many, and the ship could have matched velocities with most of them, limiting their damage.

The coma was different.

"You want me to drive through that?" Bowden asked, looking out the canopy at the ball of gas. Although it wasn't *that* dense, it was still far more abundant than the material in the tails had been, blocking any view of the nucleus. "Aren't you going to do it the first time to show me how it's done?"

Kamara shook his head. "No, it is too dangerous to go through the coma more times than we have to, and you need the experience."

"Are you going to give me some sort of safety brief or anything? Do this? Don't do that?"

Kamara smiled. "Of course; I was just going to do that." He pointed to the coma out Bowden's canopy. "Approach the nucleus. If something gets in our way, avoid it. When we get to the nucleus, avoid any plumes being ejected from it. Fly to within five feet from the nucleus, and I will harpoon it and draw us in." He smiled. "As you say, easy peasy."

"How am I going to see something in our way?"

"Use your radar, of course."

"You make it sound like we've used the radar lots, and it's something I'm comfortable with." Bowden looked down his nose at Kamara. "We haven't, and I'm not."

"Well, now is a great time to get used to it," Kamara said with a smile. "This is what I mostly use it for."

"I just hope it fucking works," Bowden muttered as he flipped the radar on. Systems on Navy aircraft had a habit of breaking when they weren't used. The more you flew and used a system, the better it worked. Don't use it for a few flights in a row? It was unlikely to work when you turned it on.

But—wonder of wonders—the radar began powering up. *There's probably something to be said for not slamming the packet into the deck of a ship over and over that helps with system longevity.* Aside from the module Bowden had crashed the craft into early on, he hadn't really hit anything else "hard."

The radar had two screens: one that showed azimuth distance left or right, and another that showed elevation. In theory, he could do really basic radar nav through the coma when the gases got too dense. Assuming the radar didn't register all the debris as one giant target.

"Ready?" Kamara asked. "The longer we fly alongside the comet, the longer it will take for us to get back to Outpost."

"Yeah. Here we go." Bowden turned the packet toward the nucleus and boosted toward it, allowing the craft to continue tracking along with its forward velocity.

"You're going to have to go faster than that," Kamara said. For the first time since they'd been flying, he tapped one of the gauges to get Bowden's attention on it. "We're only overtaking it at a rate of about one hundred kilometers an hour," he noted. "It's going to take us ten hours to get there at this rate." He yawned theatrically. "I may have to go to the back and get—or is it *take?*—a nap."

"How fast is too fast?" Bowden asked. "I realize we didn't plan for this to be a two-week-long excursion"—*and maybe we should have*—"but I also don't want to get hit by a big rock fragment that damages the craft."

"The radar has a range of about one hundred kilometers in the average coma. If you go five hundred kilometers an hour, you still have twelve minutes to see and avoid particularly large rocks."

"What about smaller ones that won't be seen until we're in close—or ever? I doubt this radar sees anything fist-sized, but that would leave a large hole through the ship."

"There probably aren't many rocks—"

Clang!

Kamara winced as something hit the packet. "Okay, new plan. Continue inbound at one hundred kilometers per hour, and I'll get a nap. I'll spell you in a couple of hours."

Kamara peered out the canopy thirteen hours later. They'd had to slow several times as the rocks got larger and denser. "Got anything?"

"No," Bowden replied. "It should be just starboard of the nose, though." He was moving forward at ten kilometers an hour relative velocity, with the nucleus of the comet just over ten kilometers away. He glanced out but didn't see the nucleus, either. Kamara had said it was the densest coma he'd ever flown through.

Bowden shook his head. He didn't like flying through the mess; it reminded him too closely of flying near Mount St. Helens after it blew. The ash had stripped all the paint from the nose and leading edges of his aircraft, earning him a visit with the squadron's commanding officer and his opportunity to brief the squadron officers at the next All Officers Meeting about the dangers inherent to flying around erupting volcanoes.

He'd long ago lost the ability to see the stars, and his field of view was nothing more than a diffuse light, like what you'd see walking through a deep fog in the middle of the day. Six kilometers, and he still couldn't see the nucleus visually, although it was obvious on the radar, including a large return on it as if there was a concentration of metal.

Five and a half kilometers, and, if anything, the blasting the packet was getting was even worse. The coma wasn't thinning; the material was getting more dense.

"I don't like this," Bowden said. "I'm going down."

He nudged the thrusters and went "down" and "left" with respect to the comet's nucleus. Within a few seconds, the visibility cleared. It still wasn't great—it was like looking through a thick Los Angeles haze—but he could see the nucleus and the two bright jets spewing material from opposite sides of the vaguely dumbbell-shaped body. They'd been approaching into the ejecta coming from one of them. The nucleus was slowly rotating, so they would have been clear of it eventually; they'd just been unlucky to approach from the wrong direction at the wrong time.

"Good call," Kamara said. "I should have thought of that sooner."

"I wish you had." Bowden's brows knit as he realized the

nose kept walking off to the left of the nucleus. Trust your eyes, Kamara had said. *What do you do when your eyes are wrong?*

You have other issues, he realized suddenly and looked out at the port wing. The packet was never meant to fly in atmosphere so it wasn't a real "wing"; it was more of a place to attach things and store propellant. Which was currently leaking out the front of the wing through two small holes. He reached up and turned off the pressurization for the left-wing tank, and the leaks slowed.

"What did you do that for?" Kamara asked.

"I've got two leaks in the left-wing tank," Bowden replied. "Shit," he added as the nose started walking off to the right. "Looks like there may be one on the right, too."

Kamara looked out his window, then reached forward and turned off the pressurization to the right-wing tank. "Now I really wish I'd thought of that sooner."

"Still want to do this?"

"No. We need to get out of the coma and repair the tanks. I don't know how much propellant we've lost, but we didn't have a lot to spare."

"—tance, please help," a female voice said over the radio. "Any station—" A burst of static interrupted the voice. "... stuck on the comet's nucleus. My ship's damaged—" Another burst of static. "... assistance; please help if possible."

Bowden tapped the bright object on the radar. "That's a ship right there. Sounds like she's in trouble."

"You know radar mapping now?"

"Yeah, my plane had it where I came from, and that's something I *do* know. My plane's radar was a lot better than this one, but I trained on a radar something like this as a student." He shrugged. "What's the protocol here? Do we leave to fix our craft or try to render assistance?"

"If we leave, we won't have the fuel to return, and I doubt there's anyone who can get here and back. If we don't help her—whoever she is—she's going to die."

"So we help her."

"We do."

"All right," Bowden said. "Maybe we can make repairs to the tanks while we're down." He shook his head as a third plume of ejecta erupted from the nucleus and its rotation rate sped up. "Assuming we can make it down."

"You can do it," Kamara said. "I have faith in you."

"*Me? Are you kidding?* The ship is damaged, and we have a dangerous landing. Don't you want to land it? It's your ship, after all."

"Have you ever used the harpoon system? Ever tried to attach to a comet before?"

"Well, no."

"I have. You get us close, and I'll tie us in. Try to get us close to the other ship."

Bowden pointed out the canopy. "I can see it now. It's pretty close to one of the jets."

"Get us as close as you can."

"Did you hear what I said?"

"Yes. Stay out of the jet. We've already seen what happens when you fly through that shit. But land close to the other ship. Preferably on a patch of rock."

"Can I ask why?"

"The gravity is going to be minimal on a body that small. If you jump hard, you'll likely jump off it. It will take about two minutes for something to fall from here"—he held his hand at his chest—"to the ground. The less we have to walk around there—much less have a jet open underneath us if you park us on ice—the better."

Bowden felt his eyes open wide as everything hit him all at once. This approach was levels of magnitude harder than landing on Outpost, and yet infinitely more important. Three lives were counting on him flying a "rails" pass, the first time, to a body he'd never approached before.

He swallowed, his mouth suddenly dry. *No pressure there.*

"Got it," he said slowly. "I'll get us close. You bring us in."

"I will."

Kamara nodded and made a radio call while Bowden sized up the approach. The closer he got, the more he decided the asteroid looked like a peanut, with a narrow, elongated middle, than it did a dumbbell. The surface was pitted with huge indentations, although it was impossible to tell whether they were impact craters or cavities formed from the sublimation of material.

He slowed slightly as he got the rhythm of the nucleus's spin.

You can do this. It's a slower rotation than Outpost, and you don't have to hit an exact spot, just a close one. You can do this.

I hope.

Chapter Fifteen

And ... now.

Bowden gave the thrusters a gentle tap and started forward slowly as the nucleus rotated into position. With the body's weird shape, it seemed to wobble slightly as it rotated, and it had taken Bowden a couple of minutes to get the right sight picture on how to approach it.

He nodded his head as the other ship came into view. It was another RockHound packet, although it had a couple of different modules strapped on. Probably gas and prospecting gear, Kamara had said. What it didn't have was right-side thrusters, which had obviously been ripped off when the jet had erupted from underneath it. The right wing was a tangled mass of pulverized metal, and the starboard side of the craft showed impacts along its length. It also tilted down on that side.

Bowden gave it no more than a glance as he searched for the spot he'd seen on the previous rotation that was clear of ice. He lined up just to the left of the craft, and there it was—a little in-trail of the ship. He gave the thrusters another bump to match the spin of the nucleus and then a nudge to the left to make sure he was clear of the other craft. Within a foot or two of where he wanted to be, he didn't risk over-controlling the craft; he just gave it a tap "down" toward the nucleus.

"Now!" he exclaimed in a tense whisper, almost as if afraid his voice would cause the ship to go off target or open up a jet underneath him—anything to spoil what he'd done to get the craft where it needed to be.

"Standby," Kamara said in a harsh whisper back. "One's locked. Two's locked. Firing!"

He pressed the two buttons and the harpoons lanced out into the rock below them as the craft touched town on the nucleus. The lines retracted as the craft rebounded from the gentle impact and then gently snugged them into place.

"Fuck," Bowden said as he let out the breath he'd been unconsciously holding. "That's an approach I hope to never have to repeat."

"You need to fly with us RockHounds more," Kamara said with a half smile. "We do all the fun flying."

"You can keep it." Bowden's visor had been starting to fog, but now that he was breathing a bit more normally, it cleared quickly. "What now?"

"I talked to the woman on the radio while you ran the approach. Her name is Malanye Raptis. She landed on the nucleus without any problems, but a jet opened up next to her and destroyed her craft. She had just about given up when I called her.

"I don't want to stay here any longer than we have to; it's too unstable. Unfortunately, though, our trip here is going to necessitate some repairs, and we're going to need more fuel to get back. On the good side, I have a repair kit and Raptis has plenty of fuel she isn't going to be needing anymore. While I fix our ship, why don't you go to her ship and help her bring the fuel over? She said she would meet you at the boarding ladder."

"Sure thing." Bowden stood up slowly to keep from bouncing off the ceiling. There was indeed gravity on the nucleus, but, as Kamara had warned, it was extremely light. What Kamara hadn't mentioned was that "down" wasn't actually straight down. Due to the comet's shape, gravity actually pulled him down and to the side slightly. The pull wasn't strong, but it was enough to be a little disconcerting and disorienting.

Having gotten used to operating in zero-gee conditions over the last several weeks, though, having a little gravity made things marginally easier as there *was* a little "down" to help with momentum control. You didn't lose your mass with weightlessness, so stopping in zero-gee was difficult. On the ground, you used friction to stop, but if you tried to stop against the floor in space, you just bounced off it—there was nothing to hold you to it. He quickly found that the only way you stopped was by grabbing onto something, and he understood why the astronauts always seemed to move slowly on the space shuttle. Pushing off hard meant you had a significantly greater impact with whatever you were aiming at, and you ran the risk of breaking bones and dislocating joints when you tried to stop yourself.

Operating in heavy suits only increased your mass and made the resulting impact even more brutal. You had to move carefully or you ran the risk of killing yourself.

Bowden exited through the airlock and climbed carefully down the ladder to the surface. Heeding Kamara's warning, he moved cautiously across the intervening fifty meters to the other ship. His eyes wanted to focus on the erupting matter pouring from the comet and follow it up and away from the surface, until it was lost in the fog above them, and he had to focus his vision on the craft to keep from getting overwhelmed by the display.

The initial eruption had started next to her craft, but it had wandered down the seam and was now about twenty meters on the far side of the packet. He kept telling himself that, while the jet was close enough to be a distraction—and a real danger if the jet should move back closer again—it was not something he had to worry about. Be aware of, yes, but not worry about. Somehow simply knowing the distinction existed didn't make it believable in his mind.

He made it to the ship and climbed the ladder to find a space-suited woman waiting for him. She was dark-haired and considerably shorter than Bowden. After a couple of seconds staring at her, not knowing what to do, she tapped the side of her head and held up three fingers. Bowden turned his suit radio to channel three. "Hi," he said, unsure of how to continue. When she looked at him strangely, he smiled and added in the local SpinDog lingo, "I'm Kevin Bowden."

"Thank you for coming," the woman replied in SpinDog. "I'm Malanye Raptis." She cocked her head at him. "Wait. You are one of the... Terrans? What are you doing out here?" She craned her head to the side to look around him. "And what are you doing with a RockHound ship?"

"I was training with Kamara when we heard your distress call, and we came to help. He's fixing our ship—we took some damage on the way in here—and he sent me to see if you had fuel you could spare."

The woman laughed. "I do, and it isn't doing me much good

here. We can run hoses over to your ship. I will attach them. Meet me underneath the port wing."

"Okay," Bowden said, and he went back down the ladder and stood under the wing. Most of the area was ice, and he moved to the single rocky spot visible. Then he realized the rock might be like the cork in a pressurized bottle, just waiting to blow off, and he stepped back to the ice . . . which he realized was even more likely to blow off. He stepped back onto the rock and sighed, saying a quick prayer that the whole area would remain stable for a few minutes longer.

Waiting gave him a moment to study his surroundings, and he shook his head as the enormity was almost enough to overwhelm him. He was the first human to stand on a comet. Well, the first he knew of, anyway. No telling what the people on Earth had done in the couple of centuries since he'd been abducted.

Without warning, a ten-centimeter-diameter hose drifted down from above. He started to reach out and catch it, but then caught himself. Having no idea what it was made of—and therefore its mass—he let it drift to the ground. It made a big cloud of ice crystals when it hit; it had massed more than he'd originally thought.

After another minute, a second hose came down, followed by Raptis. Her suit gave a small braking jet just before she touched down, then she dropped the last few centimeters gracefully.

"Well, what are you waiting for?" she asked. "Grab a hose. We need to get the fuel out of my ship before the jet decides to come back over here and finish what it started." She picked up one of the hose ends and began trudging toward Kamara's ship.

Bowden grabbed the other one after a couple of seconds and followed in her footsteps, trying to mimic her flowing, slightly bouncing steps that allowed her to go a lot faster than Bowden's earlier cautious pace.

Kamara was on the starboard wing when they arrived. He tapped the side of his head and held his arms out to the side, palms up. Raptis held up three fingers, and Kamara joined them on the frequency. "Just finishing up here. What took you so long?"

"Your student is about as useful—and as space-acclimated—as a newborn," Raptis replied.

"You might want to speak a little nicer about him," Kamara replied. "He's the one who said we needed to come get you, and the one who piloted my ship to get us here."

"He did?" A new note of appreciation tempered her tone.
"Yes."

The woman sighed over the connection. "Well, it *was* a nice landing," she admitted.

"Ready," Kamara said. He stood at the wing's edge, holding out his hands.

Raptis coiled up some extra hose and then tossed up the end she was holding. Five meters above her, Kamara braced himself and caught the end. The hose snaked upward as he went to attach it to the fuselage. He returned a minute later and held out his hands again. "Ready for the other."

Knowing it was coming, Bowden had coiled it like Raptis had done, but his toss wasn't as accurate, and the slightly different gravity pulled it away from the craft. Kamara leaned out but wasn't able to reach it.

"Want me to do it?" Raptis asked.

"No," Bowden replied, unwilling to admit he wasn't up to the task. He coiled it again, looked up to see that Kamara was in position, and tossed it up again. This time, he adjusted for the altered gravity by aiming at the tip of the wing. It drifted away—missing it by a centimeter or two—and rose to where Kamara could grab it. He went to attach it to the craft.

Bowden turned to Raptis, satisfaction in his eyes, only to receive a vision of her backside as she walk-bounced back toward her ship. Bowden shook his head then chuckled. *Leave it to an aviator to turn hose tossing into a macho competition.*

"What else do you need me to do?" Bowden asked.

"Get back to the cockpit and be ready to flip the switches when I tell you to."

"You got it." Bowden went back through the airlock and sat in the pilot's seat. He'd never done a refueling before—normally, the station's ground crew handled it—but he was able to follow along and flip the switches for Kamara when he called for them. Fifteen minutes later, they were almost finished. Raptis had brought extra fuel with her, expecting to return from much farther away, and it was enough to completely fill Kamara's ship. During that time, Raptis had made two trips between the ships.

"Emergency breakaway!" Kamara yelled. "Emergency breakaway. Turn off all switches!"

Bowden's hand flew across the panel. "They're off!" he called back.

"Disconnecting!" he shouted.

Bowden hurried to the starboard window and looked back. His eyes widened, and his mouth dropped open in horror. The ejecta jet had returned to Raptis's craft and blown it upward off the comet. Kamara had disconnected one hose, and it snaked back toward the ship while Kamara wrestled with the other, held taut as Raptis's ship pulled away from them.

Kamara's ship shifted, and it creaked as the wires held it in place. Bowden stared, unable to figure out anything he could do to help. Which would break first? The wires holding Kamara's ship? The hose? Something in Kamara's ship? Bowden had no idea.

Finally, Kamara succeeded in detaching the hose, but it snapped up, smashed into his faceplate, and hurled him up off the wing. Motion from the ground caught his eye as Raptis launched herself up after the cartwheeling Kamara.

"Kamara, come in!" Bowden called. No response. "Kamara, are you okay?" Still no response.

"I'm tracking him," Raptis said, "but I don't have much fuel in my suit. I can get him, but you're going to have to come get us. I don't have enough to return."

"Shit," Bowden said. "Shit, shit, shit." *Kamara gone; maybe dead. Raptis gone Dutchman in space after him. What do I do?*

"First things first," he muttered. "Gotta go after them. Start ship."

He ran through the ship's start-up sequence, once again wishing for a checklist to ensure he didn't forget anything. He got two steps reversed and had to go back and redo them. *If I get out of this, I am by God putting together a checklist.*

Bowden finally got the motors going but the ship wouldn't lift off. *Damn it, the harpoons!* He shuffled over to the other seat and looked at the harpoon panel. The button with the cover caught his eye. Emergency Release. *Perfect.* He flipped up the cage over it and mashed the button. He felt two *pops!*, then the ship started drifting away from the comet...heading toward the eruption that had already claimed Raptis's ship. He pushed off toward the other side of the cockpit, harder than he'd intended, and crashed into the port window, bruising his left forearm. As he rebounded, he snagged his seat and pulled himself into it.

He tried to attach his straps, but his left arm burned like fire every time he moved it. He settled for only latching the lap belt, which would at least hold him in place, and concentrated on flying.

Chapter Sixteen

Bowden realized he'd damaged his left arm more than he'd thought as he steered the packet up and away from the jet blowing debris from the comet. Every movement hurt, but he couldn't think about it—he had to find Kamara and Raptis.

Which was probably going to be impossible since the stupid RockHounds were too worried about staying unseen to have handy little things like a Blue Force Tracker or some other locator he could have used to zero in on them.

He visually searched the coma, looking for them in the haze, but they were nowhere in sight. Belatedly, he realized they'd been ejected off in a different trajectory than he'd lifted off in, and he spun the craft around to an approximate heading of where he'd thought they'd gone.

Still nothing.

I could wander around in the coma forever and never find them, he realized. Would they still remain caught in the comet's gravity, or did they have enough escape velocity to break free? He had no idea. What did he have that could find them?

The radar. He'd found the nucleus with it; maybe he could find the two suits with it. Sure, the radar was shit, but he could differentiate the metal of their thruster packs from the generic bits of rock flying around, and they weren't in the debris being spewed out, so they ought to stand out a little more clearly. He flipped the radar on and waited impatiently as it warmed up.

After a subjective eternity waiting, the picture finally formed on the screen. Nothing. Some small, fuzzy returns that were probably rocks, but nothing that looked like refined metal.

Think, Bowden, think. Why don't you see them?

They're not there, obviously.

Why not?

They're somewhere else.

But where?

He opened up the scope to scan the most volume possible. Still nothing.

You need to set up a scan pattern, just as if you were looking for enemy fighters.

As soon as he had the thought, he realized the problem—he wasn't looking in three dimensions. He was certain—well, *mostly* certain—he was on the right general azimuth; he might just not be looking high or low enough. Space was big—too big for one small radar to look everywhere. He needed a better scan pattern. He hadn't flown very far above the comet, so he gently pitched the nose of the craft up and panned it from side to side.

Still nothing.

A little more pitch, and re-scan.

This time he got two blips.

Gotcha.

He tapped the thrusters, wanting to get there immediately, but also knowing he'd have to match velocities with them when he found them. As he approached, the smaller of the blips resolved into two blips, very close together. *That's them!*

As he got closer, the coma thinned a little, and he could see them. One was holding onto the other. As carefully as he could, he slid into position next to them. One of the figures waved, then pointed at the packet, then pointed back at the two figures.

That must be Raptis, and she wants me to come get them.

Oh, hell.

Bowden snuggled the craft up to the two figures and saw one of them holding up three fingers.

He looked at his suit; somehow the controls had gotten switched to channel four. He switched it back to three. "Hi y'all. Need a ride?"

"Yes," Raptis said. "Kamara is unconscious, and I'm out of thruster fuel. Get out here and get us."

"On my way." He unstrapped and went to the airlock, trying to ignore the pain in his arm. As he cycled it open, he searched for the suited figures, but didn't immediately see them. Panic started to set in, but then he caught motion from the corner of his eye. *They were holding onto the wing!*

Whether it was the coma blocking the blackness of space or his haste to get out to them, he forgot to feel overwhelmed—like he usually did—and released his hold on the airlock and jetted away from the ship.

Every motion he made set his left arm on fire, reminding him to keep his approach slow and under control. Raptis pushed off gently from the wing so he'd have a bigger target to aim for, and he intercepted the pair. Pushing the group of them with his thrusters took a good bit of experimentation and flailing around—which wasn't helped by Raptis's biting comments on thruster control—but eventually, he got them back to the airlock and inside.

"Glad you found us," Raptis said once they had Kamara inside the packet and strapped down. She took off his helmet and held it up to show it had several pieces of tape across it. "He wouldn't have lasted much longer. I did my best to seal the holes in his helmet and suit, but he was still losing air."

"Sorry it took me so long to find you," Bowden replied. "You had spun off into the coma before I could get the ship fired up, and I had to use the radar to find you."

"You used the radar?" she asked. "And you were able to find us..."

"Yeah." Bowden gave her a wry smile. "Sorry if there was a better way; it was all I could think of."

Raptis shook her head. "No. That was a great way to do it; I'm not sure I would have thought to do it that way." She cocked her head. "That's the second time you've saved my life today. You know, you're not too bad...for a Terran."

"Well, thanks." He chuckled. "I think."

"Why don't you go fly us home now?" she asked. Raptis was all business again; the moment was over. "I will do what I can for Kamara."

"Uh, yeah, sure." Bowden stood in the hatchway a moment, not sure he should leave Kamara in case there was something he needed to do for him.

Raptis looked up after a moment. "He will need competent medical treatment. The sooner you get us back to Outpost, the sooner he'll get it."

"Oh, yeah." Bowden turned toward the cockpit. He was half-way there before he realized he had no idea how he was going to find Outpost again without Kamara.

Chapter Seventeen

Lee knocked on the open hatch's coaming as Tapper finished straightening his regulation shirt. "Ready?"

"To get out of hack or to go to the briefing?"

"Both."

"Well, then: yes...and no." He smiled. "But it doesn't really matter if I'm ready, does it?"

"No, particularly since you'd plead lack of preparation even if the briefing was a year from now. You'd make any excuse known to man, woman, or fish if it would save you from having to sit in the same room as Murphy."

Which wasn't quite true, Tapper amended silently as he followed Lee out into the companionway. But he wasn't about to disabuse any assumption that added to his already considerable reputation for buried ferocity, even if it went wide of the actual mark. He didn't hate Murphy, but that didn't mean he liked him—not anymore. He'd been a good enough guy, for a commander. Until, that is, he'd insisted that Tapper head back spaceside, even after the SpinDogs turned away his family. Harry didn't often examine his consequent change of opinion regarding Murphy; too much thinking might problematize keeping the colonel as the complete—and satisfyingly convenient—focus of his resentment and anger.

"What's up?" Lee asked her atypically silent friend.

"Uh...just taking a moment to think. Got a little distracted."

"I didn't think SEALs did that."

"Get distracted?"

"No, think. C'mon. We'll be late."

The briefing was in progress by the time they arrived. After first extracting a promise from Harry he would neither disrupt nor leave prematurely, Lee slipped up the side aisle and sat well behind the small audience, Harry in tow.

Up front, Makarov had just ceded the podium to Murphy. Both men were wearing the familiar gray coveralls provided by the SpinDogs. Murphy thanked the short Russian as Makarov lifted the cover on a black plastic easel supporting a large paper flip chart before joining Harry and Lee in the rear of the room. The colonel took up a matching black pointer.

"Nice to see you out of your cage, Tapper," Makarov said, sotto voce. "You know, I never did hear how it went when you apologized to Korelon. Did you use lots of lipstick before you kissed his ass?"

"I used your favorite brand," Harry said, twisting in his briefing seat. "Industrial strength." He managed to bang his knee on the folded desktop as he sought a more comfortable position. Fortunately, they were far enough back to avoid interrupting Murphy's preliminary comments. The rows of seats were packed together tightly, arranged much like an old-school Navy squadron ready room. Rows of tightly nested metal seats were clipped to the deck, leaving just enough room to squeeze between them. Each seat had an upholstered green plastic seatback and matching headrest. The ubiquitous gray paint covered the seat frames, even though bright stainless peeked between the cracks in the sound deadening tiles glued across the bulkheads. Harry's last SEAL platoon had periodically borrowed one whenever they'd embarked on an aircraft carrier, much to the chagrin of the squadron involved. Maintenance, training, and the hab's systems' status displays further blanketed the walls, their monochromatic screens reflecting the overhead lights.

They build these things for midgets! Why aren't we more spread out? Most of the seats are empty. Oh right, I need a babysitter.

Squirming to get comfortable, Harry had to choose whether to brush shoulders with Bruce or the next seat. It wasn't really a choice, so he leaned over the empty chair, his elbow making an even louder bang, drawing a look from the colonel.

Up front, a pair of senior SpinDog officers sat adjacent to each other. Separated from them by a few empty seats was a lone RockHound, marked by his blacks and the family crest on his collar points as the Legate to the conference, representing all RockHound Families. None of the senior officers had their usual retinue of aides and secretaries.

"You ask us to risk much, Colonel Murphy," the RockHound said. "Is this degree of secrecy truly necessary? It complicates planning, and alert members of our Family will perceive a lack of trust and respect. We operate from tightly controlled outposts and our enemies are from out-system. Surely you don't expect a traitor?"

"Honored Legate Orgunz, I don't know what to expect," Murphy answered politely. "I didn't expect the assassination attempts on my person, one of which occurred in a similar station. We'll have but a single opportunity to act from a position of surprise, and surprise is our best chance for victory."

"Bah!" Orgunz said, waving one hand. "That was a SpinDog habitat. Our security is tighter. Our personnel more loyal. They can be trusted, and their early understanding and support assures our success, more so than secrecy."

"SpinDog security is—" began one of the SpinDogs heatedly before Murphy smoothly interrupted.

"Even so, Elder J'axon," Murphy said. "I believe our prior operations have demonstrated the value of surprise. If you'll allow me to continue to present the entire concept first, then we can address individual objections."

"Ooh, things sound tense up there," Harry whispered at Makarov. "Hope your presentation is convincing! You could earn a cluster to go on your Combat Administration ribbon."

Makarov's look spoke volumes.

He was one of several Russians whose abduction dated to the days of the former Soviet Union's ill-fated adventure in Afghanistan. Harry had been shocked to learn that even after that example, a few decades later, his own country had elected to try its hand among the rocky mountains and hostile Afghans who had broken more than one empire.

Makarov wore a clean uniform, which was nearly as undecorated as Harry's own, but where Harry's was modified and worn, the Russian's was as crisp as the day it was first issued. Like the other Terrans, Makarov's right chest was bare, erasing his identity for OPSEC.

"Didn't you earn a wound badge for papercuts?" Harry might not be able to backtalk Murphy with impunity, but the aide was fair game, especially since Harry suspected Makarov got to read everything that crossed Murphy's desk, including the dirty secrets in everyone's personnel files. "With a bronze cluster in place of a second award?"

"*Potselui mou zhopy*," Makarov finally replied in a very low tone. "Kiss my Russian ass."

"Not if you were the last Terran goat in this part of the galaxy," Harry said equally quietly, letting his grin stretch wide enough the Russian couldn't miss it.

"If you two are done with the length and girth comparisons, shut the fuck up," Lee whispered urgently. "Unless you want to trade spots with him, Harry?"

"Run the Dornaani equivalent of Harvard Graphics and make coffee?" Harry asked, feigning shock. "Risking death is one thing, but I'd sooner suck-start a shotgun than be a staff puke, shuffling overhead transparencies."

"Shut it!" Lee's forehead vein was pulsing.

If he intended to keep his part of the bargain, step one was keeping a low profile. He subsided. Up front, the grown-ups were still talking.

"...I want to emphasize; we have in fact successfully implemented Terran tactics and strategy," Murphy was saying. "In turn, this has assured victory during a difficult campaign on R'Bak," he added, sweeping his eyes back and forth across the three men. As he spoke, he slowly increased the volume of each phrase. "The results have launched our joint effort to throw off the shackles of Kulsis."

The SpinDogs nodded. The set of the RockHound's shoulders suggested he wasn't impressed.

"Further, despite a few hiccups here and there..."

Harry might have imagined Murphy paused ever so slightly to seek out Harry in the room. Harry carefully didn't glance about or make any other motion.

"...our alliance with you is stronger than ever. The J'Stull and associated satraps are completely disrupted. Further, we've isolated R'Bak by eliminating their interplanetary comms."

These guys know that. What's Murphy up to?

"We've retrieved an industrial amount of critically needed pharmaceuticals from the surface, including the *tra* necessary to assure the safety of pregnancies for the next generation of your Families."

He's in full-on hard-sell mode, that's certain.

"We also extracted a Kulsian agent from R'Bak, generating very useful intelligence, which will allow us to move forward with the next phase of our plan. Meanwhile, Kulsis nears its closest point of approach."

The RockHounds and SpinDogs in the front row bared their teeth. Both groups had been trapped in a perpetual state of need, denied the higher tech needed to flourish in space. The Kulsian threat enforced terms even more harsh than those of their original banishment.

"Survey teams from Kulsis continue their approach to facilitate the eventual Harvester extraction operations," Murphy said, gesturing at the easel. This page showed the likely orbits that would be used by the approaching marauders. "We expect they'll be within range to detect our movement within thirty to sixty days, depending upon the level of caution they've adopted in response to the coursers' disappearance. While we're refining our plan, an important first step will be to sharply reduce the amount of traffic between R'Bak and our space-based forces. We'll soon cease all transits to and from the planet shortly, for obvious reasons."

Harry's chest tightened.

Stella and their son were on R'Bak. Under the protection of the Sarmatchani, they should be safe. But still. While one couldn't ever completely relax in space, Harry wasn't really worried about getting drafted to participate in space combat. Air Force eggheads and go-fast pilot types were needed. No one had ever accused the SEAL of being a rocket scientist, after all.

"Next, our alliance must complete three closely linked missions," Murphy continued. "Because of the lead time required to prepare these missions, I've dispatched joint forces so they will be in position and trained in time. We've tightly compartmentalized the missions to mitigate the threat of espionage and sabotage. To that end, I'm respectfully requesting you acknowledge this information will remain only within this group until I or Major Lee otherwise inform you."

Murphy paused, and Harry watched all three members of the audience fractionally incline their heads, making the briefest acquiescence possible.

"As most of you know, this plan capitalizes on the data packets left by the Dornaani more than a year ago but only released and decrypted over the last few weeks. Some only dropped within the last few days," Murphy said with a meaningful glance at the surprised VIPs as he advanced to the next chart. "For those of you who haven't already been read in, these intermittent data drops disclose sets of blueprints and automation enhancements that, when applied to the extant replication capabilities, will enable us to construct superior system-level craft in numbers sufficient to directly challenge Kulsis. They also include a number of comparatively advanced systems that fall broadly within the realm of C3I improvements."

Left and right of Harry, neither Lee nor Makarov reacted. So, not newsflash to them, then. Up front, the other three members of the audience sat a little straighter. The Dornaani data, released in a steady if unpredictable trickle, had been simultaneously resented and anticipated by the SpinDogs and RockHounds both. It was an important part of the Terran safety net that kept their allies of convenience... well, as allies.

Harry was about to make another comment, but he caught Lee's steely glance.

"This enhancement to our replication technology?" the Rock-Hound Legate demanded from the front row, from which he was reading the fine print on the newest chart. "Will it enable my people to finally duplicate entire Kulsian ships?"

"The alliance will have the ability to replicate much larger spacecraft, with greater speed and a much lower fault rate than currently available technology permits," Murphy answered carefully.

Harry, habitually alert to Murphy's nuances, smiled. The colonel was known for asking questions, not answering them. However, Murphy was a past master of precisely worded evasions.

"To return to pending operations: denying the Kulsians any opportunity to react as we execute the steps of our plan is non-negotiable. Specifically, no Kulsian can be left alive or uncaptured to warn the rest. No leaks can be tolerated. And our *own* unit closure must be absolute."

Harry noted there was no reaction to Murphy's not-so-veiled threat.

I wonder if the Kulsians recognize the code for "none of our team may be taken alive"?

"Step one will be to seize a Kulsian lighter, one of those always brought by their survey teams. It serves as a midsized transatmospheric cargo ferry with moderate operating range." Murphy nodded to Makarov, who uncovered the relevant image. It was a surprisingly bulky craft, with four variable attitude thrust nacelles that appeared to be the creations of a designer who had refused to streamline them for planetfalls. "In a theme that will persist for all three stages, the Kulsian lighter must be seized intact, preferably shortly before or after leaving R'Bak Downport."

Harry nodded. Several other of the Lawless had traipsed through the primary spaceport on R'Bak. Both Chalmers, that slippery bastard, and his conscience, Sergeant Jackson, had much more useful and relevant knowledge on it than Harry.

Harry relaxed a bit more, shifting in his seat, trying to find a comfortable position for the sheath in the small of his back. No one was going to ask Harry to fly a ship or fake an emergency, and if they did, what was he going to do with a holdout knife?

Just another stupid, melodramatic reflex. I've been cooped up too long.

"After reaching the second planet, our insertion team will need to make a far orbital rendezvous with the lighter, and your forces will be required to make any needed hasty repairs. A joint force will fly the lighter to the optimum orbital track for controlling the terms of engagement. There, we'll manufacture what appears to be a critical accident and broadcast a correspondingly urgent distress call. This will require an experienced pilot."

Bowden had been missing from the poker game for quite a long time. Now, Harry supposed he knew where the Navy pilot had disappeared to.

The three men up front started a rumble of sidebar conversation, forcing Murphy to pause. Harry was sympathetic. To a space-based community where safety is king, the deliberate creation of an emergency was akin to blasphemy.

"Create an in-space emergency and then abuse an emergency call?" Legate Orgunz asked, frowning. "This breaks all SpinDog and RockHound norms. It is...highly irregular."

Murphy raised his hand to dispel the chatter.

"Good. I'm counting on the Kulsians agreeing with you. We

must create a critical emergency, something quite severe. Simply put, we must hasten our adversary to investigate and save one of the few lighters they have in-system to prepare for the arrival of the actual Harvesters. Bringing them close to the lighter is critical, because the final step is the most dangerous. Our intelligence is clear that the Kulsian lighters operate in concert with larger ships, mostly corvettes and frigates capable of protracted deep-space operations. The surveyor flotilla has arrived with multiple corvettes, which is helpful, because we need one. In order to get it, we must lure it within reach of a small team and perform a contested boarding to take the ship intact. Once in our hands, our prize will become the template to build a squadron of ships."

The hands of both SpinDogs flew upward; Orgunz didn't bother.

"Your plan is suicide!" he barked, a sweep of his arm cutting off the questions the others were poised to ask. Then he continued, standing and adopting a condescending tone. His black shipboard coverall was tightly fitted, and, unlike the heavily decorated uniforms of the aides who usually orbited SpinDog VIPs, only the Legate insignia shone from his collar points. "Suicide, I say again, and overoptimism at many levels, reflecting your race's . . . foundational level of understanding. Space combat is nearly impossible, unless all parties agree to fight, or one side can achieve perfect surprise. Kulsian corvettes have sensors, delta-v, and weaponry superior not only to their own lighter, but to everything in our fleet. They will be on their guard. Any manned and powered ship will be detected at a considerable distance. You are relying on Kulsian pirates deigning to fight on your terms, instead of standing off and safely obliterating any suspicious small craft. The size of any assault force large enough to overcome resistance before the corvette is scuttled by her crew requires a correspondingly larger boarding craft, thus it becomes even more difficult to conceal. Again, they will stand off and blast you into junk too small to salvage. At their leisure."

Harry sat back, folded his arms and relaxed a bit. The mission parameters Murphy had outlined were tough, all right. The RockHound wasn't wrong. Murphy expected him to persuade these guys, who lived in *space*, that a boarding action was viable? Well, Harry would give it the old college try.

Pity the poor bastard who gets to run this op. And I thought assaulting an oil platform from a submarine was bad.

"Those are important points, Legate Orgunz," Murphy said encouragingly. "I'm confident we can plan around them."

The RockHound was unimpressed at the vague reassurance. "What's more, if your plan to lure them within reach of a boarding team is successful, and the assaulting element gains the safety of the target hull instead of merely entering a long duration orbit that inevitably ends in fiery death or asphyxiation, you will have to overpower a Kulsian crew, on their own decks, without damaging the ship." The RockHound wasn't finished. "We have always survived by our discretion. For good reason, we have never had the need to board a hostile ship. This is not a plan. It is madness! Not one among us has ever done such a thing."

Harry had been listening carefully. The RockHound had made more valid points. But Harry realized he knew something Orgunz didn't. And Colonel Murphy did.

Oh shit. Shitshitshit.

"Honored Orgunz, you see the problem very clearly," Murphy replied over the heads of the intervening audience, as a smile slowly slid onto his face. He turned, quite deliberately, to look directly at Harry.

The Legate turned to see what was capturing Murphy's attention and, recognizing Harry, scowled in anger.

Before the RockHound could raise an objection to Harry's presence, Murphy continued speaking. "Fortunately for us, Legate Orgunz, the obstacles are not so insurmountable. We happen to have a ship-boarding specialist, and he is, I'm assured, perfectly mad."

Since Makarov would be busy for a while yet, Murphy ushered Anseker past Seaman Lasko and into his office. When they were comfortably seated, Murphy turned on the white-noise generator that Makarov had cobbled together and reflected that with the briefing behind them, a minor celebration was in order. "May I offer you a drink, Primus?"

The head of Family Otlethes waved away the offer. "Some other time, perhaps. I am needed elsewhere, shortly."

Murphy nodded, folded his hands. "What did you want to talk about, Primus?"

Anseker shook his head. "Let us leave titles aside, Murphy. Here I wish to speak freely, as men first and leaders of our respective peoples second."

Hmm... "Very well, Prim—Anseker." *That's going to take some getting used to.*

"These plans of yours—they are bold, even by the standards of my people. Many beside those present today have also called them rash."

"I'm not surprised."

"And so you should not be. Each of the three missions relies upon unprecedented strategies and tactics, to say nothing of the other requirements you put forth: the secrecy, the resources, the training, the compartmentalization of information, and the unique autofab initiatives. And yet, I have been an ally to you in all of this."

"Thank you." *Where are you taking this, Anseker?* "I have noted, and deeply appreciated, your unswerving support."

Anseker smiled indulgently. "You have noticed the support in the gatherings where you have been present. That was the least of it."

Murphy smiled back. "Legate Orgunz?"

"His is but the most recent voice of concern and doubt. But he speaks for more persons than any single Primus. And his worries go beyond failure."

"What do you mean?"

Anseker frowned. "RockHounds have a latent fear that they are descended from lesser beings. In part or in whole."

"Do you believe that?"

Anseker's answering glance was sly. "It has been convenient to let them believe we do." Seeing Murphy's confusion, he expanded. "It plays upon fears that existed among them from the very beginning of our exile. They are descended from the less educated among us. It is said some had soiled their breedlines with R'Bakuun blood." He waved his hand as if to push it all into the past where it belonged. "In short, they were consigned to the tasks that required less sophisticated skills."

"They seem to be excellent pilots and prospectors."

"They have become so, but not without costs, both past and present. Their labors are dangerous and their exposure to radiation much greater than those of us who live in the spins."

Murphy had become accustomed to hear SpinDogs—particularly Primae—refer to oppression and deadly inequities with chilling indifference. Still, it took a moment of focus before he could be sure of responding in a tone as calm as the Primus's. "I am unsure how this bears upon the present-day RockHounds and our plans."

Anseker nodded. "Despite violently opposing such low opinions of their origins and abilities, they have nonetheless internalized them. They struggle with shades of self-doubt that they assert are groundless and were inculcated in them by the early SpinDogs to ensure obedience."

"And are they right?"

"Who can say what happened in those chaotic, early days? But as I intimated, we find their self-doubt a useful lever of social control." He frowned, stared at his balled fists.

"And now?"

"And now all of us may reap what we SpinDogs have sown. You see, the RockHounds are not merely worried that your plans will fail; their more primal, reflexive fear is that *they* will fail. And believing that makes them more susceptible to doing so."

Well, that would almost be an amusingly just end for you SpinDogs—except for the fact that we'd all go down together. "I presume you are telling me this because you would like our help in, er, reassuring the RockHounds?"

"I merely bring it to your attention that you may share it with your officers, so they may act accordingly, when and where appropriate." Seeing Murphy's reaction to such impossibly vague guidance, he raised a palm. "I have no better suggestion, since my insight can be no greater than my understanding of your ways. Which is almost nonexistent.

"Before working alongside you Lost Soldiers, I would have averred that the casual fluidity of your social status—both one's own and among different ranks—would inevitably lead to atomization and anarchy. But I have seen that this is not the case. So although I may—indeed, I *must*—share this insight into the RockHounds, I cannot tell you how to incorporate it into your plans to optimize our odds of success."

Murphy considered not only the problem Anseker had revealed, but also how much pride he'd put aside in order to explain his own ancestors' role in creating it. "I appreciate the faith you place in us."

Anseker put a broad hand on either arm of the chair; his tone became sardonically jocular. "As if we have any choice? Besides, it is but a small step after having to accept your insanely ambitious plans." He pushed himself out of the chair, already in motion toward the hatchway. "We will speak soon again, Sko'Belm Murphy."

PART THREE

Chapter Eighteen

Kevin Bowden never thought he would miss the food aboard *Spin One*... until, that is, he encountered the bland, chunks-and-gruel meals that were the norm on Outpost. So he was doubly happy when he strode into one of the two galleys in Lost Soldier country and discovered it empty. Lack of privacy was one of Outpost's other undesirable features. He grabbed a tray, piled on the entrees he'd missed most, and sat down to the serious business of eating.

About halfway through his meal, Bowden was startled by a cheery "Welcome back!" from the entry. He didn't recognize the voice at first, turned, and discovered Murphy almost halfway to his table. *Since when has Murphy ever been "cheery"?* he wondered—at the same moment he realized that he had never seen the galley entirely empty. *Well played, Colonel,* Kevin thought as Murphy sat down across from him.

But even if the CO was here on business—what else?—his smile seemed genuine. "How'd it go, Major?"

"Good, sir," Kevin replied, "even if it wasn't without some challenges." He explained the trip to the comet and how he had—eventually and with some coaching—returned to Outpost. They'd spent a couple days there while they got treatment for their injuries, then he'd flown them back to *Spin One*.

"Speaking of challenges," Murphy said with a smile, "I heard you had fun during your first rendezvous with an orbiting object."

"That was one of them." Bowden chuckled ruefully. "How did

you hear about that? Kamara said he wasn't going to mention that to you."

"Nothing travels through the hab like a good rumor." Murphy winked. "The fact that you destroyed his rangefinder was quite the topic of conversation for a few days." Murphy chuckled like Bowden had. "He didn't tell me, by the way. I had a bet with one of the SpinDogs that you'd ace it on your first approach. That's how the rumors got started. He'd never won a bet from me before."

"Oops, sorry, sir." Bowden winced. "I hope it didn't cost you much."

"Nope." Murphy smiled. "I bet him twice as much that you'd be able to land on Outpost within your first two tries."

Bowden shook his head. "You had a lot of confidence in me. I'm not sure I'd have made that bet." He smiled. "I'm also glad I wasn't aware of the bet until afterward. I had enough pressure on me at the time."

"I knew you'd come through." He nodded. "By the way, Kamara said you're the best student he's ever had."

Bowden's eyes opened wide. "Really? He said that?"

"Yeah. Apparently, he was pretty impressed with your skills. Finding his floating body with your radar, then rendezvousing with it and saving him may have had something to do with it."

"Huh." Bowden shrugged. "Raptis saved him—she dove off the comet after him and sealed his suit, or he never would have made it." He shook his head. "Based on how he treated me, I never would have guessed I was better than a RockHound five-year-old. That's what he said, anyway."

"It's true." Murphy's face got serious, and he rubbed his left hand absently. "Would you be ready for more? Launches to space and reentries?"

"Absolutely, just as soon as we can resume flying. I can't be a full-up astronaut unless I can do launches and reentries."

Murphy's sweeping hand took in the habitat beyond the empty galley's bulkheads. "Some people would say you're already an astronaut. You *are* in space, after all."

Bowden shrugged. "I'll consider myself an astronaut after I've been at the controls for a round trip. Every other time I've been down to the planet and back, I've just been baggage, and while I've been here, I was more of a tourist. Astronauts *do* things in space."

Murphy smiled. "Like land ships on tumbling asteroids like Outpost?"

"Exactly. You don't have to tell Kamara how scared I was the first time I did it."

"I won't." He winked. "Based on what he told me, he was a lot more scared than you were."

Bowden shrugged. "I was in the zone. Sometimes, when you're behind the ship, everything just works as if you're on rails. Airspeed, angle of attack, lineup... they're all 'on,' and it's as if you didn't have to put any conscious thought into keeping them there. There was never a doubt in my mind."

"Is that pilot bravado or do you think you can do it again without anyone there to hold your hand?"

"It's not just pilot bravado." Bowden chuckled. "Well, not much, anyway. I did another ten landings on Outpost after that pass. Only took me thirteen attempts to get ten landings, which Kamara did say was better than most of the RockHounds can do. I nailed the one coming back from the comet, too, even with a hairline fracture in my left arm."

"Ten out of thirteen makes you better than most?" Murphy asked. "It must be hard."

"It is, but then again, so is landing on an aircraft carrier in heavy seas, and Navy pilots have gotten... well, when we got snatched, we were pretty good at it. No telling what they're doing now back home."

"Maybe we'll find out," Murphy said. "But before we can..."

"You have a new mission for me?"

"I will. For now, though, you still have more training to do."

"Still can't tell me what the mission is?"

"No, I can't share it yet as the walls here have ears, but things are in motion, and I need you trained ASAP. Maybe sooner than that. I need you to concentrate on becoming the best astronaut you can be, as quickly as you can do it."

"Well, I've had worse jobs," Bowden said. He smiled. "This is better than flying for the Navy."

"How so?"

"Back on the ship, when you got back from flying, you had a ground job you had to put hours into. Here? All I have to do is fly and get better at it. I love my job." He frowned. "But sir, I thought there were no more flights to or from R'Bak."

Murphy nodded, leaned across the table. "The surveyors haven't followed their usual game plan. They've only sent a handful of lighters ahead to R'Bak. The rest of their smaller craft are snooping around above and below the ecliptic."

"That doesn't add up," Kevin muttered, mostly to himself. "They've got no reason to look for us." Then the realization hit: "They're looking for their missing coursers. Or their remains."

Murphy nodded. "That's the only thing that makes sense. Either searching for wreckage or potential mutineers lurking in the lee of an out-of-the-way rock. But whatever the reason, it gives you an unexpected opportunity to complete your training and for us to make one last supply run to the surface. The volunteers who are staying behind to set up our isolated landing fields need a few more tools and an extra water purification unit; theirs crapped out."

"These are the guys you stranded on an island south of the equator?"

Murphy grimaced. "Well, they volunteered, actually—but yeah, more or less. And the work they're doing will make it a lot easier—and safer—for us when the time comes to return. It's one of the few locations where our birds can deorbit safety. No locals to see the spiral descent contrails, and no terminal glide-path that takes you right over R'Bak Island and then the satraps north of the Hamain."

Bowden nodded. "And no more VTOL-assisted acute angle descents. Those burn so much fuel that you frequently can't make it back upstairs without a RATO."

"Said the guy who's *not* an astronaut?"

"I'm still just making noises like one."

"Whatever you say, spaceman. Now, in addition to the supplies for the runway team, I've got a little biofreight for you to haul."

Kevin raised an eyebrow. "So, you're still going to send Yukannak dirtside?"

Murphy nodded.

"And how does he get anywhere useful if this island is so remote?"

"You are his ride, but he's getting off before you land."

Kevin stared, then understood, smiling. "So he gets to land via drop pod. Fitting. But won't the surveyors be more likely to see us if we're loitering to make a drop?"

"If your mission profile was to ferry him to a drop zone, then yes. But you're just going to dump his pod out of your bay. Then we remote-operate the pod's thrusters and push it into a descent sleeve that will drop him into the laps of the Sarmatchani. More or less."

Kevin smiled. "A meteoritic descent, huh? That should make Yukannak sweat some more."

"You bet. And test his loyalty, too."

"How so?"

"Because the Sarmatchani are not actually going to be *in* the drop zone. They're going to hold back a few hours. That gives us a chance to see what Yukannak chooses to do if he believes he's a free agent."

Kevin nodded. "Does he wait or bug out to look for someone who can take him to his own kind?"

"That's the concept. We need to give him every chance to betray us before Chalmers's team has to depend upon him."

Bowden frowned. "Yeah, but even if he doesn't run, that's not proof positive that he can be trusted. He's probably levelheaded and smart enough to realize that it could be a test. Anyhow, if he really means to betray us, he won't show he's a turncoat until it really counts."

"Agreed. It might boost him pretty far up the Kulsian social ladder if he can deliver our collective heads on a platter. But so far, he's provided us with pretty useful information."

"Does that include confirming your conjectures about the surveyors staying close to the downport at first?"

"It does. Although the current situation is unprecedented, he's guessing that they won't start trying to show the flag or investigate what happened to the coursers until the bulk of their flotilla joins them."

Bowden heard the hanging tone. "But ... ?"

"But he also shared a less encouraging projection: that the Harvesters will follow the surveyors as soon as they can."

"He likes making ominous pronouncements, doesn't he?"

Murphy nodded. "His take on the dominant Kulsian Overlords— Family Syfartha—is that they don't like uncertainty and they like failure even less. And even though the Syfarthans don't have much to do with sending the first two flotillas, as far as the rest of Kulsis is concerned, whatever happened to the coursers is their fault."

Bowden smirked. "Guess their 'succeed-or-die' standard cuts

both ways, after all." He sat straighter, very conscious his food was getting cold. "So are there any shuttles already at the landing field? Because if there aren't, and we have a major malfunction, we'll be stuck dirtside with the surveyors soon to arrive in orbit."

"By the time you get there, there will be two craft on site. You take one back up; they'll keep the one you took down." He broke off and waved to someone behind Bowden. "And here's the person who'll take you on your next flying adventure."

Bowden turned to find Burg Hrensku walking toward him. "Hi, Burg. What are you doing here?"

"Hello," the SpinDog said. "Apparently, I am to be your next instructor—at Primus Anseker's direct request." He shrugged. "When the Primus asks..."

"You say yes."

"Well, I'll leave you two to get on with it," Murphy said, standing. He glanced down at Bowden and held the gaze for an extra second, giving it significance. "As quickly as possible." He nodded once, a sharp jerk of his head. "I've got a lot of new sewage to stir through back in my office." He left and Hrensku sat down in Murphy's spot.

"So," Hrensku said, "I know you've been on a number of runs to the planet and back. What is most important about performing a reentry?"

Bowden chuckled. "I was riding in the back for all but the last trip up, so I wouldn't say I've got a lot of experience doing it." He pondered the question a moment. "Slowing down and landing in one piece?"

Hrensku smiled. "You're not wrong, but that was not what I was asking. How do we get from space safely through the atmosphere so that we *can* land in one piece?"

"I'm sorry, but I never went through astronaut training. I can modify and fly aircraft, and now I know how to fly spacecraft *in space*, but I don't know how to transition a spacecraft into an aircraft." He gave Hrensku a wry grin. "I was kind of hoping you'd teach me that."

"I will, but I wanted to see what you knew, first."

"Well, based on the spacecraft piloting I've done, I know you need to slow down to go lower, so I imagine it starts with going slower."

"Correct. Besides, if you go too fast, you'll bounce off the atmosphere and go flying off into space, never to return."

"I will?" Bowden asked, horrified at the thought.

Hrensku laughed. "No, you won't go flying off into space. We always tell the new trainees that, though, to see their reactions."

Bowden chuckled self-deprecatingly. "Okay, you got me. So you can't skip off the atmosphere."

"Oh, no, you totally *can* skip off the atmosphere," Hrensku said.

"But wait—"

"You just don't keep going into space," Hrensku finished. "If you don't slow down enough for atmospheric penetration, you can bounce off, but you are still in orbit. You will go back up partway toward where you started, and it may take you a while to get back down to the atmosphere again, but you don't fly off into space. You just end up at a lower orbit than where you started.

"If you are performing a reentry, the two most important things to doing it successfully are your velocity and the entry angle with respect to the local horizon. These two things need to be within the limits of your craft or bad things happen.

"We'll talk about velocity first. As you already mentioned, it's a major factor. If you are going too fast, the thermal loads and braking forces will overwhelm your heat shield. Once the heat shield fails..."

"You burn up," Bowden said with a nod. "How fast are you talking?"

"Typically, from a low orbit, the velocity is around eight kilometers per second, but you also need to have the correct entry angle. If the entry angle is too steep, the braking effect due to atmospheric friction will become too large and the spacecraft can break up. Additionally, the steeper the entry angle, the higher the heat. Once again, if the heat exceeds what the shield can take, you will either get burn-throughs or the heat shield will fail entirely."

Bowden nodded. "And your crispy remains will fall to Earth. I mean the planet's surface."

"Correct."

"And, let me guess, based on your earlier comment, it can't be too shallow either, or other bad things happen."

"You are correct again," Hrensku said. "At a shallower angle, the deceleration won't be enough, and the spacecraft will travel much farther than it is supposed to. You might not be able to make it back to where you intended to land... or even find a spot where you are *able* to land. Additionally, even though the heat shield will be exposed to a lower amount of heat, it will be exposed for a much longer time, which may result in a larger total heat load. No matter how good the shield, at some point, you're going to burn away all the protective insulation. Whether that results in burn-throughs or heat seeping through the shield, making the temperatures inside the spacecraft too high, neither is pleasant."

"And both are probably fatal," Bowden opined.

"Correct. Also, if the entry angle is really shallow, you again run the risk of bouncing off the atmosphere and continuing with your orbit. This results in an elliptical orbit, and when you come back down, you'll be in a different place than you'd planned, probably nowhere near your intended reentry corridor."

Bowden nodded. "So we end up landing somewhere far, far away."

"Probably." He shrugged. "For reentry, accurate guidance and control is extremely important."

Bowden took a deep breath and let it out slowly. "I see." He shrugged. "So how do we figure all that out?"

Hrensku stood. "Come with me, and I will show you."

Murphy checked the video feed from the small compartment on the other side of the double-locked bulkhead door.

As always, the asset was in constant yet moderate motion. Yesterday, he had been meticulously packing the gear he would take down to R'Bak. Today he was binding them with straps; tightly wrapped gear had the best chance of withstanding the brutal buffeting of a meteoric descent from orbit.

Murphy nodded to Janusz Lasko. The submariner brought his Thompson level with his belt and toggled open the door. "Just about ready?" Murphy snapped from his side of the coaming.

"Very nearly," the asset answered. He showed neither surprise nor the faintest hint of anxiety. "It seems rather early to be sending me down, though."

Murphy smiled. "I have to hand it to you, Yukannak. After all this time, you still think you're going to get me to respond to your leading comment, to reveal information by irritating me into showing that I know more than you do?"

Yukannak shrugged. "There's nothing I could do with that information, even if it was my intent to gather it."

Murphy wondered if any part of that reply was true. "Yet, you know that's what we will always assume. Just as you know that if you give us any reason to doubt your loyalty—"

Yukannak held up a hand. "I quite understand, Colonel. The SpinDogs have made it quite clear that if I betray your trust, it is *they* who will decide how I am to be dealt with. And I have seen what is in their eyes."

"Your death?" Murphy asked.

"Much worse than mere death. Regardless of the many ways in which this system's exiles have departed from the original path of their Exodate progenitors, it is clear they remember that terror is one of the pillars upon which dominion is built." Yukannak's lip creased in what might have been a smile. "Of course, the SpinDogs' dominion over me would last only so long as they felt themselves adequately entertained by my suffering."

Murphy shrugged. "An outcome that is entirely up to you. In seventy-two hours, you'll be in position. Twelve hours after that, if you survive the drop, you will be in the hands of Sarmatchani tribesmen. Many are relatives of the ones who died as a result of the advice you gave to the satrap of Imsurmik."

"I was simply playing a role that would enable me to survive long enough to escape," Yukannak amended.

"And in the course of that," Murphy retorted, "you lied to or killed whoever stood in your way. Including relatives of the people who'll be waiting for you, and who crave an excuse—any excuse—to gut you like a fish. So it behooves you to be, as we would put it, on your best behavior."

"Another of your strange idioms," he commented, leaning away from the tightly packed kits on the bunk before him. "I am ready."

"Before you go," Murphy said, stepping into the tiny compartment. "I've been entertained, even interested, in what you've had to say about Kulsis. But I wonder how much of it will prove true."

Yukannak shrugged. "As you have pointed out before, once the surveyors arrive it will not be long before you capture some Kulsian and use his statements to assess the veracity of mine. So I would be a fool to deceive you."

"So it would seem to me," Murphy replied, crossing his arms. "But you may have reasons that I cannot foresee, because my knowledge of you and your people is incomplete."

"I have often thought the same about you and your people," Yukannak answered. "But there is certainly at least one great difference between us."

"You mean that we're the ones with the guns this time?"

Yukannak smiled. "Yes. That is the determining variable, isn't it?"

"We'll see," Murphy said. "But before you depart, there's a term I've heard among the SpinDogs that I suspect may mean something different on Kulsis. While it's not relevant to your specific mission, I am seeking clarity about that difference. As a matter of curiosity."

"Yes, a matter of *such* curiosity that you came to seek an answer now...in the event that my drop capsule has a 'suboptimal' descent."

Murphy shrugged, turned to leave. "As I said, it is not urgent."

"What is this term?" Yukannak asked quickly. "I will provide what information I can."

Still facing away so the Kulsian could not see his small smile, Murphy said, "Tell me what you know about 'Reification.'"

Chapter Nineteen

I can't believe this is how we do it, Bowden said to himself for at least the tenth time as they prepared to de-orbit. Hrensku had shown him that they had a computer in the craft that *could* calculate the navigational data for the return trip. For some reason, though—and Hrensku didn't want to talk about it any more than Kamara had—they weren't big on autonomous programs and didn't use them unless some sort of emergency required them to do so.

Not that it was much of a computer in any event. If Bowden had to compare it to something from his time, it was most like the computer in the A-6E Intruders from his airwing. Their computers operated at four hertz. The Intruder guys had joked, somewhat sarcastically, that it updated four times a second, "whether it needed to or not." The programming in the interface craft's computers might have helped NASA in the sixties and early seventies, but operating it would have been a lot like the first round of computer games he had played—uncomplicated and not entirely satisfying.

But that would have been better than the actual method the SpinDogs used. He'd been fairly horrified when he'd found out what was going to determine whether he lived or died on reentry. Hrensku was going to "eyeball it in."

Too bad we can't use the technology the Dornaani left us to do it better and smarter. He'd asked Murphy about it and was told the cultural backlash for using the technology they had access

163

to would probably have led to several hundred of the SpinDogs dead and all the Lost Soldiers on a forever stroll beyond the airlocks—without benefit of vac suits.

"The 1960s called," Bowden muttered. "They want their computers back. Sad thing is, I do, too."

"What was that?" Hrensku asked.

"Nothing," Bowden said louder. "I'm ready for the checklist."

"Checklist?"

"Yeah. Don't you have a checklist to make sure you don't forget anything?"

"Of course there's one, but I have it memorized. I know what I'm supposed to do."

"How do you know you won't forget a step?"

Hrensku tapped his forehead. "It is all here. Papers can be forgotten."

"It would be easier on a slate."

"And what if you had your list on a computer and it suddenly malfunctioned or ran out of power? You wouldn't know what to do. *I will.*"

"But what if—?" Bowden stopped himself. Approaching reentry was the wrong time to argue the merits of having written checklists. Certainly, Hrensku had already shown he wasn't interested in having the checklist on a tablet computer—an electronic flight bag—and he wouldn't permit Bowden to even have one in *his* interface craft. "Never mind," Bowden said. "So what do we do?"

"First we close all the doors and hatches." Hrensku flipped a couple of switches and pointed to a section of the control panel where six lights glowed dimly. One was red, but after a couple of seconds, it went green. "All set."

Hrensku pointed. "Flip the switch over there that says 'toilet.'"

"Toilet?"

"Yes. It shuts the toilet and seals all the contents."

"Got it," Bowden said. *Also added to the checklist I'm going to make.*

Hrensku flipped the switch that brought up the craft's gyro display. Typically, the SpinDog pilot had no use for it—and said repeatedly that it was better to not use it as a crutch—but it was marginally acceptable to use it for getting the right attitude for reentry. A small picture of the interface craft and a tunnel-like image filled the center screen. The display looked like something out of *Star Wars*, but designed by a five-year-old who had little concept of what he was trying to depict.

Hrensku pointed to the left screen—the one with the image of the craft—which now showed two different outlines of it. "The red image shows the current attitude," Hrensku noted, "while the green one shows the attitude we need to be in for reentry. I must maneuver until I have superimposed the red or 'actual' craft onto the one representing the optimal attitude for reentry."

Would it have been child's play to design a computer program to accomplish the maneuver?

Yes.

Was doing so somehow anathema to the SpinDogs?

Also yes.

Bowden sighed to himself as Hrensku manipulated the controls and brought the craft into alignment with the desired attitude at almost the same time an image of the craft appeared at the end of the tunnel on the right half of the screen. It was shown above the tunnel.

"See?" Hrensku asked. "As expected, we are above our projected velocity. We must slow down." He fired the main thrusters. After a couple of seconds, the image on the display began to drop into the tunnel. When it got to the center of the tunnel, Hrensku shut down the thrusters. Immediately, the green image on the left flipped around.

"Braking is complete," Hrensku advised. "Now we adopt our reentry attitude."

"How long do you have to do it?"

"It is not a race. We have about twenty minutes until we reach the edge of the atmosphere." He shrugged. "You should do it this time." He removed his hands from the controls. "Your craft."

A little warning would have been nice. "My craft," Bowden said, taking the stick. He then manipulated the thrusters until the two images on the left screen superimposed. The bottom of the craft was now aligned nose-first with respect to their orbit, with the nose pitched upward. The view out the side of the craft showed they were on the opposite side of the planet from where they were headed.

"Oh, I forgot," Hrensku said. "You need to burn off the gas in the forward reaction control system."

"Oh?"

"Yes. It is a safety precaution because that area experiences the highest heat of reentry."

"A checklist could be used to remember this," Bowden muttered.

"What was that?"

"I said, 'Won't firing the thrusters mess up our flight path and our attitude?'"

"Yes, it will. You will need to counter it with the aft thrusters."

"Wonderful," Bowden muttered. "Dumbest system ever."

"What was that?"

"Nothing. I'm concentrating. What powers the thrusters?"

"Nitrogen tetroxide is the oxidizer, and monomethyl hydrazine is the fuel. The propellants are hypergolic—they ignite when they come into contact with each other."

"I know what hypergolic is."

"Oh, good. Well, they are fed into the engines, where they atomize, ignite, and produce gas and thrust."

"And we'd be a lot better off without a bunch of them somewhere that is about to get really hot."

"Correct."

"That's a stupid system," Bowden muttered.

"What was that?"

"I can see why we'd want to get rid of them," Bowden replied as he worked the controls to burn off the propellants, while still keeping the craft's attitude relatively stable. Dust started falling slowly past his face. "Is that gravity returning?"

"Yes, we are starting to feel it more. I've got the controls."

"You've got the controls," Bowden replied.

A glow to his left caused Bowden to look out the window again. The sky had become a light pink, and, as he watched, it became a deeper pinkish red. He glanced at the display; Hrensku had the craft centered in the display. The glow from the window brightened visibly, going from red to orange.

"Looks like we're in the atmosphere," Bowden noted. He hadn't felt nervous before, but now there was a whole swarm of butterflies in his stomach. *Or is that gravity returning with more force?* It felt more like butterflies.

"Yes," Hrensku said, his voice a little louder. "Compression and friction are heating the air around us. Right now you're in the middle of a three-thousand-degree fireball."

Yep. Definitely butterflies.

"Even if we wanted to, we couldn't call anyone; the radios will be out for another ten minutes due to the ionization effects."

Unlike the movies he'd seen, there was very little feeling—no shaking or vibration, just the glow of the massive amounts of heat being generated by the interface craft's atmospheric entry. He should have known Hollywood would make it worse than it was. He'd pictured the shuttle almost falling apart; the reality was much less scary...until he thought about the massive amounts of heat being held at bay only a few meters away, and the butterflies returned.

Eventually, the glow faded, and Hrensku waggled the wings. "I have atmospheric control," he reported as he initiated the series of S-turns shown on the screen.

"Are we going to light the engines?" Bowden asked.

"You don't want to fly a glider?" Hrensku asked with a smile.

"Not if I don't have do."

Hrensku sighed theatrically. "If you insist." He flipped the switches and relit the motors, although he kept them at idle. "Still have a lot of velocity to bleed off." He pointed out the window. "There's the field. Want to land it?"

"Me?"

"Sure. You can land it, right?"

"Well, yeah, sure. I've done it lots of times. Just never after a flight to space."

"Unless you land like a glider—which we're not—it's the same thing."

"I've got the controls," Bowden said.

"You have the controls."

Bowden continued to do S-turns to slow the craft and then brought the throttles up slowly to bring the craft into the powered flight regime. Although he felt like it should have been different, the craft flew just like it had the last time he'd flown it in atmosphere. He brought it in to land, taxied to the makeshift base operations building, then powered it down and started the fifteen-minute wait while the craft cooled and the gases created on reentry dissipated.

Bowden released his seat belt and tried to stand, but only made it about halfway up before falling back into the seat.

"That is one of the hardest things about returning to the

planet," Hrensku said. "Readapting from zero gravity is difficult, especially if you've been gone a while."

"Which I have."

"Just go slowly, and it will come back to you."

"Ready to go?" Hrensku asked as they walked out to the interface craft for Bowden's first launch to space at the controls.

"Yeah," Bowden said with a chuckle. "I finally just got readjusted to gravity again; must be time to leave."

"Just so. Such is the life of an interface pilot." He glanced at Bowden out of the corner of his eye. "Is that what they have planned for you? To be the Lost Soldiers' interface pilot?"

Bowden shrugged. "I don't know what they have in store for me." Except "they" was Murphy, and he'd never kept anything this close before, not from his senior staff. Bowden did not find that particularly comforting.

"There must be something you Terrans are planning. To need these qualifications all of a sudden speaks to there being something going on."

"Maybe." Bowden shrugged. "If there is, though, I don't know what it is."

They put their gear in the craft and did the aircraft's preflight while the loadmasters finished stowing the cargo. Although there wasn't going to be anyone else on the craft with them, they were going back fully loaded with medicinals, food, and other stores for the habitats.

The preflight was fairly normal—a small leak to be fixed and a couple of bolts to be tightened—until they got to the cockpit. The landing gear lever was missing the round ball-like attachment on the end that was used to grip it, leaving just a metal post sticking out of the instrument panel.

Bowden got down on his hands and knees and searched the cockpit but couldn't find it.

"It's not necessary," Hrensku said after five minutes of searching. "We'll get a replacement at the spin when we get there."

"That isn't what we'd do back home," Bowden replied. "If something was missing from the cockpit, the aircraft would be down until they found the missing item."

He looked up to find Hrensku looking at him funny. "Down?" Hrensku asked. "Where would it go down to?"

Bowden chuckled. "Not physically down. The word in that case means 'not flyable' until they found the missing piece. We didn't want it to get into the controls and bind something."

"In this case, it is all right," Hrensku replied. "The piece is big enough that it couldn't have gotten into anything."

"Where did it go, then?"

"Who knows? Maybe someone took it as a souvenir."

"A souvenir? Why would someone take that?"

"Who is to say?" Hrensku shrugged. "This is the only craft, though, so we either take it or we don't go flying today. And, if we don't hurry, we're going to miss our launch window."

"Okay," Bowden said slowly, not feeling entirely comfortable with it. Navy procedures were typically written in blood. If there was a procedure that *had* to be followed, that usually meant the reason for implementing the procedure was because someone had died. He shook off his misgivings—there really was no place for the knob to go in the cockpit; perhaps it had gotten loose and someone had taken it before it fell off.

They strapped in, fired up the craft, and taxied to the runway. They stopped just short of it so the maintenance crew could arm the RATO—the rocket-assisted takeoff—bottles. As conventional takeoff consumed a great deal of their dual-phase engines' fuel— limiting cargo capacity to twenty percent of what could be lifted with RATOs—the interface craft usually used the rockets to get airborne and on their way to space.

"Your controls," Hrensku said as the maintenance guys moved away from the craft. The leader held up two pins to show both bottles had been armed.

"My controls," Bowden replied. Sweat prickled across his skin. Although he'd done RATO takeoffs before, usually the SpinDogs supplied the pilot for any RATO takeoffs. While they were fairly common, they were also dangerous, and there were a lot of opportunities for things to go wrong.

Bowden took a deep breath and visualized what he needed to do. In some respects, the RATO takeoff was similar to launching from a carrier. Once the button was pushed, there was no stopping until the assist was over. With a RATO, though, you actually rotated the aircraft while still boosting, so you had to make sure your seat was close enough to the instrument panel to reach everything. It was somewhat worrisome that the landing gear lever in front of him didn't have the ball on the end of it, but once the gear was up, it wouldn't be pointed at him anymore.

"Well?" Burg asked. "We're going to miss our launch window."

"Keep your pants on," Bowden muttered.

"Why would I remove them?" Burg asked.

"It's just an expression...never mind."

He checked the runway and taxied out onto it. Bowden shrugged his shoulders, making sure the straps were set. "Ready?"

"I have been," Hrensku grumbled. "Can we go now?"

"Sure." Bowden put his finger over the RATO button. "Three, two, one." He mashed the button and was pushed back into his seat. The force, however, wasn't what it should have been. As the craft roared down the runway, it pushed against his control, trying to go to the right. The right rocket bottle had failed.

"Bad rocket!" Hrensku called.

"No shit," Bowden muttered. He pulled back the throttles and fought to keep the aircraft on the runway. "Keep your damn hands off!" Bowden yelled as Hrensku's hands moved toward the controls. "My plane."

The craft streaked down the runway, and he had to keep forward pressure on the stick and pop the spoilers as their speed increased past the point where the craft was going fast enough to fly, and it tried to get airborne. As they passed the halfway marker—six thousand feet remaining—the operational bottle went out. It would be close, but Bowden knew he could still stop the aircraft.

He pressed the brakes while keeping the spoilers up. Nothing happened. He released the brakes, then jumped on them as hard as he could. The right one grabbed for a second, then it blew. The strut slammed into the ground and then ripped off, dropping the wing into contact with the dirt.

Bowden was thrown out of his seat and into the port window. There was an instant of pain, then everything went black.

Chapter Twenty

Bowden opened his eyes to see Captain Dave Fiezel, a former F-105F pilot in another time and place, walking into his room. Bowden's eyes widened; this wasn't his room—*Where am I?*

Everything snapped back. The takeoff. Rockets failing and brakes squealing. Going off the runway. Pain. Lots of pain. Blackness.

"Where—where am I?"

"You're in the infirmary," Fiezel said. "Don't you remember?"

"The crash? Yeah, I remember the crash. I hurt all over."

"You're lucky to still be here to feel pain."

"Why's that?"

Fiezel looked around and his brows knit. "Hasn't anyone told you?"

"Just woke up...I think. Told me what?"

"Uh..."

"Out with it," Bowden said. He was obviously on pain meds of some sort; his thoughts were mushy and thinking was hard. The act of concentrating, though, brought things more into focus. "Told me what?"

"The only reason you're alive is that the tire blew. The landing gear knob was missing. If you hadn't been thrown to the side—up against the window—the sudden stop when you went off the runway would have impaled you on the lever. It would have gone right through your chest. As it was, it went into the meat of your arm. It still nicked your brachial artery, though, which almost killed you. They had to bring in one of the local witch doctors to use some of their magic weeds on you. Your recovery is nothing short of miraculous, according to our medic types."

Bowden looked down; his right arm was a mass of bandages.

"You'll be fine. It'll hurt a while, and you'll have to work it back into shape, but you're going to be all right." He took a breath as if he were going to add something else but then sighed.

"What?" Bowden asked.

"Not sure it's my place to say..."

"To say what, dammit? What are you trying to avoid saying?"

"No one's told you?" Fiezel temporized.

"Told me *what*?"

"I'm sorry to be the one to have to tell you, but your seat belt was cut."

"What—" Bowden did his best to focus. "What do you mean? It looked fine on preflight."

Fiezel shook his head. "The part where you latch it was fine. It was cut most of the way through, underneath the seat where it goes into the latching mechanism. You wouldn't have seen it unless you crawled up under the seat and pulled it out. It held under normal usage, but couldn't take the deceleration of a crash."

"How... Why would someone do that?"

Fiezel looked at the floor. "Well, I'm no safety inspector, but it looked like sabotage to me."

"And I ask again: Why would someone do that?"

Fiezel winced as he looked up. "You weren't supposed to survive that crash." He shrugged. "Like I said, I'm no safety inspector or whatever you called them in your time, but that whole crash appeared to be an elaborate trap with one sole purpose: to kill you."

Bowden lay back on the bed and chuckled. "A seat belt breaks, and you see murder plots? Are you still seeing VC inside the wires?"

"I wish it were as simple as that," Fiezel said. He cocked his head. "It would make it a whole lot easier." He paused and met Bowden's eyes. "It's not, though."

"What do you mean?"

"Well, after they pulled you from the aircraft, I went and looked at everything, inside and out. Once I saw the seat belt—which there's no doubt in my mind was cut—I followed the chain of events from start to finish, and there it was."

"There *what* was?"

"The plot to kill you."

"Why don't you start from the beginning? Perhaps the drugs or whatever the local shaman gave me has addled my brain, but I'm not seeing it."

"Okay, from the beginning. You launch, but immediately your starboard rocket fails. I looked at it; the wire to the rocket was disconnected."

"That could happen on its own. Strange that we didn't see it on preflight or that the ground crew missed it when they were pulling the pin from it."

"We'll come back to that. Next, I looked at the brakes. There were pinhole leaks in the hydraulics to both of the brakes. The leaks wouldn't have manifested until the system was pressurized, but then the hydraulics would have bled out."

"But the right brake worked. At least I think it did."

"It did, but I don't think it was supposed to. I found the hydraulic line still attached to the strut, which came off when the tire blew. The line was holed, but the holes weren't big enough for them to drain the system immediately. Whoever did this messed up. I think you were supposed to drive off the runway and hit something that resulted in a sudden stop, catapulting you—when your seat belt failed—into the landing gear handle, which would have impaled you right about here." He pointed to his heart. "If not for the fact that the starboard brake still had enough fluid to throw you to the side, you'd be dead right now."

"But why? Who would..."

"Good questions." He shrugged. "It was meant to look like an accident. If I hadn't happened to see the cut seat belt, I would have thought it was just a series of unfortunate accidents. Why did it happen? I don't know. The 'who,' though, that's a lot easier to figure out. Have you pissed off any of the ground guys? Someone that might want to frag you?"

Bowden shook his head, overwhelmed. "Not that I'm aware of. Who even *does* that?"

Fiezel gave a wry chuckle. "Happened in my era a couple of times. One time a ground maintenance guy got extended when he thought he was going back to The World. Got pissed off and, under the influence of drugs, messed up some of the planes' systems. He wasn't trying to kill anyone; he just wanted to take his frustrations out on the planes and break some stuff. Didn't matter to the guy who did a shitty preflight and took one of those jets flying. He crashed and died. When we found other planes had been sabotaged, we tracked it back to the maintainer. He was sad—and even sadder when he went to Leavenworth for his crimes—but that didn't bring back the pilot who died, who was a friend of mine." He shrugged. "Like I said, it happened sometimes."

"No, I'm not aware that I pissed off anyone or that any of the maintenance guys were mad at anyone or anything. And we *did* a good preflight. We knew about the missing ball from the landing gear handle, but we figured we'd just get a new one when we got up to the habitat."

"That's just it. Whoever did this *knew* the systems. Some of the stuff was insidious. You wouldn't have spotted it—the seat belt was cut underneath the seat where you wouldn't have been able to see it, and the brake lines wouldn't have failed until right when you needed them. Not sure how you would have missed the rocket, though..." He pursed his lips. "Who followed who around the plane?"

"What do you mean?"

"Were you following Hrensku around, or did he follow you?"

"As the qualified guy, he followed me."

"So he could have loosened the wire after you checked it."

"But why?"

"No idea. The fact remains, though, that someone—someone who knows the systems in the aircraft really well—took a lot of time and effort to crash that plane, and to do it in a manner that would kill you without being obvious about it."

"But the cut seat belt was obvious."

"It sure was." Fiezel nodded. "Here's the thing, though. When I took Sam Hirst out to the bird to get his opinion on if whether or not it was repairable, the seat belt was missing and the rocket motor wire had been reconnected."

Bowden's jaw dropped as everything became real to him for the first time. "Any chance you were wrong?"

Fiezel shook his head. "I don't think so. I know I saw the wire hanging, and I know the seat belt was cut. I guess it's possible that all those things just happened to line up...but I doubt it."

"Had Hrensku been out to the plane before you came back with Hirst?"

"I asked around and one of the maintenance guys said he saw Hrensku coming back from the aircraft. Apparently, he left some of his stuff out there when they brought you in."

"Anyone else go out to the wreck?"

"A few of the maintenance types, but none of them remember seeing the seat belt in the cockpit. Hrensku said the same thing when I asked him."

"So he knows you may be onto him."

Fiezel winced. "Yeah, I wish I hadn't asked him, but I did. I'm not much at police work, I guess. If it's him that did it, he at least knows I'm looking into it."

"Well, until we get this figured out, I wouldn't get into an aircraft that he's been around."

"That thought had crossed my mind." Fiezel coughed theatrically. "I think I'm coming down with the R'Bak crud. May not be able to fly." He shrugged and coughed again. "Could take me a few days to get over it, too. Depending on how things turn out."

Hrensku looked up from the schematics he was going over as Bowden walked into the base operations building. "My friend! It is good to see you mobile again."

"Am I?" Bowden asked.

"Mobile? It certainly appears so. You are walking around, which is better than the last time I saw you."

"I wasn't talking about mobility; I was talking about friendship. Am I really your friend, Burg?"

"Yes. Of course you are. Why would you ask that?"

"Because friends don't try to kill friends."

"What do you mean? I didn't try to kill you. You were the one at the controls when we crashed. In fact, it was *you* who told *me* to keep my hands off the controls."

"I did...but I didn't know you had sabotaged the aircraft."

Hrensku's cheeks turned bright red. "I did not sabotage the aircraft! You will want to take that back right now!"

Bowden walked up to Hrensku and looked him in the eyes. "You didn't sabotage it? Because it sure looks like you did."

"That is madness! Why do you even think it was sabotage? This isn't the first time you've seen a rocket bottle fail."

"No, it isn't. It's the first time I've seen pinholes in brake lines and cut seat belts, though."

"I don't know what you're talking about."

"Really? How about the missing knob on the landing gear handle? Without it, it makes a great stake to impale myself on."

"We both saw it. We both looked for it and couldn't find it."

"I'm wondering if we couldn't find it because it was in your pocket. You're the one who wanted to go even though we hadn't found it."

"Because we were going to miss our launch window. You haven't done many launches, but even *you* have to know that."

"It's all very convenient, isn't it?"

"What is convenient? I didn't try to kill you! I was in the same craft with you!"

"Investigators always talk about looking for someone with motive and opportunity. You certainly had the opportunity to cause all the problems... what I don't understand is why? Why would you do that, Burg? What do you have to gain from killing me?"

"That's just it—I don't have *anything* to gain from killing you, especially when I'd be putting my life at risk to do so."

"That might be the best alibi I've ever heard."

"It's not an alibi; *it is the truth*! You ask me why, Bowden, and I ask you the same thing. *Why* would I try to kill you?"

"I don't know."

"Because there *is* no reason. This is all ludicrous. I didn't try to kill you."

Bowden stared into his eyes for a long time, but he couldn't find deceit in them. "Fine," he finally said. "I believe you."

"Good," Hrensku said. "Because you should." He indicated the chart on the table. "Now, can I get back to this? I have a meeting with the mechanics in fifteen minutes; that shuttle will not fix itself."

Bowden nodded, turned, and left.

"Did you believe him?" Fiezel asked as he walked out the door. Fiezel had been waiting around the corner, "just in case."

"Yeah," Bowden said. "But that scares me even more than if I didn't believe him."

"Why's that?"

"Because if it *wasn't* Hrensku who sabotaged the plane, who did? And when will he or she strike next?"

Chapter Twenty-One

Timmy Uggs, Murphy's new and very young adjutant, was typing on Makarov's computer at the arduous and tortured pace of a beginner. A high school sophomore in Brooklyn when the bombs fell in Pearl Harbor, he'd had little to no experience with a typewriter, so his relationship with a computer keyboard was uncertain, to say the least. But he didn't lack determination.

Still, with so many operations under way and coordination between various Hound and Dog leaders especially delicate, Murphy felt Makarov's absence keenly. And not just on a professional level. For all his formality and often dour pessimism, the Russian had been someone Murphy could actually talk to: a peer in terms of age, epoch, and even experience. Now, with Max Messina gone, too, Murphy felt more alone than ever. Ironic, considering that he had already been convinced he was as isolated as a CO could be.

That was arguably your stupidest assumption yet, Murphy: thinking the universe lacked an infinite capacity to make things worse than they are—including your loneliness. Which brought Naliryiz's face to mind.

He brushed away the image as quickly as possible. "Timmy, is the drop mission still on track and on time?"

"Uhh..."

And once again, the sixty-four-thousand-dollar question is: will he find the right program and menu this time?

Happily, Timmy did. "Aye, aye, sir: numbers are right. Major Bowden is, uh, five-by-five, sir."

Despite a hit-and-miss relationship with post–World War II military slang, Timmy Uggs was still doing pretty well for a kid who'd been sitting in Makarov's chair for less than two weeks. But, unfortunately, "pretty well" didn't even come close to filling the gap left when Murphy had approved Major Pyotr Makarov's request to be the Lost Soldier CO of the boarding team. No one besides Tapper had the zero-gee qualifications, and neither the Hounds nor the Dogs had the experience or mindset for running the op—despite being ruthless and vicious when prosecuting their highly polished equivalents of gang wars.

Unfortunately, it was equally true that no one else had Pete's facility for juggling a wide array of diverse activities, data streams, and comm threads. Part adjutant and part master data manager, Makarov hadn't merely understood how the various facts and figures fit together, but more importantly, how they blended into a whole picture that was much greater than the sum of its disparate parts. Perhaps one day Uggs would develop similar capabilities, but the chance of that day ever coming was a long shot.

As was the chance that anyone would ever address him by his actual name: Timothy Uguex. Bored and overworked officials at Ellis Island had Anglicized without caring—or possibly even noticing—the brutally comic result. His father had legally changed it back years later but died while waiting for confirmation that never arrived. So, when his son enlisted in the Navy, the only surname on record was the bastardized one and, inasmuch as it matched the one on his birth certificate, Timothy Uguex was once again Timmy Uggs.

Happily, Timothy was the opposite of his dull and plodding moniker. Small and clever, he was a natural for assignment to submarines. There, he quickly confirmed what his incomplete high school transcript promised: a marked aptitude for math and machines. To the initial delight and eventual envy of the warrant officers who determined the prelaunch setting for torpedoes, Timmy was always the first to finish the calculations.

However, Apprentice Seaman Uggs's reputation went beyond having a head for numbers; he gained notoriety for having the temperament most commonly associated with his shock of bright red hair. Before he ever saw combat, he'd racked up so many drunk and disorderly charges that he'd not only lost any chance of promotion, but had forfeited more pay than he was likely to earn in the course of his enlistment. Bitter and largely unrepentant, Timmy underwent a transition from hot-tempered extrovert into sullen loner who preferred the company of books to that of his crewmates.

As it so happened, Timothy was an avid science fiction reader. So while one part of him was just as dismayed and depressed as the rest of the Lost Soldiers when they awakened in the twenty-second century instead of the twentieth, another part was fascinated by the world of wonders in which he found himself. A great number of the changes that he'd encountered between the often lurid covers of his favorite books and magazines were now reality. However, he confessed to two related disappointments: the unchanged dullness of both duties and uniforms. He had very much liked the thought of wearing capes while on ever-changing adventures across the cosmos. So it seemed unfair to him that, 150 years later and 150 light-years from Earth, living in this brave new world of technological miracles still entailed wearing dull clothes and doing dull paperwork—even if there was now a great deal less actual paper involved.

The brisk opening of the hatch swept away Murphy's reflections upon his hapless new adjutant. "Sir?" inquired Uggs.

"Yes, Timmy?"

"Major Lee has arrived. She says she is here on your orders."

"She is. Please show her in."

Mara "Bruce" Lee breezed past him. Her clipped gait not only told Murphy there was business to discuss, but that it had to remain private. "Timmy?"

"Sir?"

"Before that hatch closes, make sure you're on the other side of it."

"Sir!" Uggs said as he snapped a salute on the move.

When the hatch had sealed behind him, Lee came to attention. "Permission to speak freely, Colonel?"

Oh, for the love of... Murphy waved a weary affirmative.

"Sir, what the hell did you say to Naliryiz?"

"What did *I* say to *her*? Don't you have that a little backward?"

Lee's answering frown was puzzled. "Maybe so, sir. She's extremely upset, but is also being really vague."

"And how's that last part any different from usual?"

"She may be indirect with you, sir, but she is direct with me. *Very* direct. But this time, all I can tell is that she's distracted, irritable—which I've never even seen before!—and was determined not to let me become involved. But I'm . . . well, persistent."

Murphy chose to ignore Bruce's staggering understatement. "Well, I understand a whole hell of a lot less than you do, Major. Last time I saw Naliryiz, I thought I'd be friendly and express how nice it would have been if she, too, had been able to come to R'Bak during my last planetfall. Her reaction was a wary look and a solemn warning."

"A warning? About what?"

"About what I was suggesting. Specifically, that it would have been a very bad idea, politically."

"And then?"

"And then I resolved to accommodate her judgment on the matter."

Lee frowned. "That doesn't make sense. I'm going to get to the bottom of this."

"Thank you, Mara. I'd appreciate that."

Lee blinked—whether at his use of her first name or his frankly personal tone, he could not tell. "Don't think twice about it, sir. Adoptive sister or not, if her behavior is being constrained or coerced for political reasons, getting clarity on that is job one—as is anything that might complicate our strategic relationship with the SpinDogs."

Murphy managed not to reveal his surprise at Mara's crisply professional tone. But her always powerful emotions were coursing behind her regulation exterior. He shook his head, smiled. "Not sure I've ever heard you so damn serious, Lee."

She shrugged. "I *am* serious, sir. Given the stakes we're playing for up here, you might say I'm deadly serious."

A faint knock on the hatch "Sir," Tim's muffled voice reminded from the other side, "coming up on the comms window."

"Thanks, Timmy. Return to your post."

"Aye, sir," his young adjutant responded. The hatch opened and he almost ran back to the computer. "Monitoring the prearranged wavelength via the, uh, alien satellites." He sounded like he was on the verge of giggling every time he uttered the word "alien."

"Very good. Watch the clock closely. Seconds matter."

"Sir?"

Mara looked over her shoulder at him. "Sometimes, the precise clock-time when a signal is sent *is* the signal."

Uggs frowned, then brightened. "Sure, I get it! We just listen for a . . . a squelch break. There's no code for an enemy to crack, because the clock-time of the empty send is tied to a preset message." His smile disappeared as he realized what he'd forgotten to add: "Ma'am!" He flushed. "I mean, sir." The last word was uttered like a question; like others of his era, Tim was still becoming accustomed to the practical and formal realities of having women in the ranks.

Lee smiled. "Either works." She turned back to Murphy and moved to where she could look at his computer screen. On the left side was a list of one-minute clock intervals: the "signals." Each such signal was separated on either side by two minutes of "dead time." In the right column were the messages associated with each interval. They were already thirty seconds into the first "signal" minute.

When it had elapsed, Mara leaned back with a relieved sigh. "Well, no deal breakers. Still 'mission go.'"

Murphy only nodded. His deepest concern was not in connection with any particular message, not even the first one, which was "MISSION ABORT." Murphy's nightmare scenario was if, at the end of the comms window, there had been no signal at all. The explanation could be anything from equipment malfunction to the elimination of Chalmers's entire team. And worst of all, they'd never know, because now comms windows were becoming very rare and carefully scheduled events. Within days, there would be too many surveyors on site who'd be listening for their own—and the possibility of any unidentified—radio traffic.

They waited through two more silent intervals before a squelch break came out of the speakers as a squawk of static. As Murphy released a very slow and silent sigh of relief, Mara leaned over to look at the message associate with that "signal minute."

"NO EVIDENCE OF ACTIVE ENEMY SIGINT MONITORING. NO DETECTION OF NEW CYPHERS IN ENEMY COMMS."

Another minute, another squawk: "FURTHER VOX COMM SUSPENDED INDEFINITELY."

Mara frowned. "They worried that the surveyors could get lucky and hear us?"

Murphy shrugged. "Possibly, but I'm guessing they're just being cautious regarding bandwidth and signal density. Sending Morse code at irregular intervals is darn close to background noise. But voice communication is a constant 'here I am' notification to anyone who happens to be spinning around the dial."

Another squawk emerged: "WILL USE PRESET TIMES TO NOTIFY OF UPCOMING SAFE COMMO WINDOWS."

Mara nodded. "Sounds like the surveyors are already getting into a predictable pattern of check-ins and updates." She turned to him. "I'm glad you asked me to be here for this, but you didn't need to, Murph." She glanced at the way his hands were resting on his desk, palms flat. "Not yet."

Murphy shook his head, kept his voice beneath the level of the static. "I agree; my 'condition' hasn't reached the stage where I have to worry about...about something occurring suddenly. I wanted you here because someone else in the chain of command should be present. That way, no matter what happens to one of us, the other can still confirm the comms and carry the operations forward."

"Yes, sir," she murmured. At that moment, her gentle tone reminded him of how his younger sister had said good night—at least, before puberty caught up with her.

The timer in the right-hand corner of the computer screen ticked down and reached the final interval.

The last squawk went on for twice as long as the others, as if insisting that everyone should stop what they were doing to hear it.

They leaned back with relieved sighs, knowing the associated message by heart:

"FINAL PLANS SET. MISSION IS A GO."

Chapter Twenty-Two

"Didn't think they'd go in so hard for bloodsport," Chalmers said, taking in the ranked tiers of stone seats rising from the walls of the arena pit. The place could seat a *lot* of people.

"You're kidding, right?" Jackson said. "This kind of competition is just the kind of shit supremacists are into." He gestured at the arena as they walked down the aisle from the locker rooms the fighters used.

"Jackson's right," Vat said. "Given the way they are trained to think, it's quite natural to do this sort of thing. It ain't as popular out in the back country 'cause the satraps can't afford the wasted personnel and medical assets, but it turns out the lesser houses here are constantly looking for ways to prove themselves better than their neighbors without resorting to out-and-out warfare. Thus, the popularity of hand-fighting here among the brokerage personnel." He gestured at the stone ring at the middle of the building. Stretches of the sandy floor of the arena were still damp with blood from the evening before.

The group of Lost Soldiers made their way down onto the sands and stood looking up at the stands and private boxes. Both were empty.

"Looks expensive," Chalmers said, spinning on one heel to take it all in.

"It was," Vat said, outlining some blood with the toe of one sandal.

"Was?"

"Bought it last night," Vat said, looking him in the eye.

"I thought you said the owner refused your initial offer," Chalmers said.

Vat shrugged. "He did. And the second. I then made him an offer he couldn't refuse."

"Wake up with a horse head in his bed?" Moose asked.

Everyone turned to look at Moose, but it was Chalmers who blurted, "How do you know that reference?"

"What, just because I'm a big fella, I don't read?" the Vietnam-era Lost Soldier asked.

"Read?" Chalmers said, shaking his head. "It's a movie."

Vat started laughing first, then Jackson.

At last understanding dawned for Chalmers. "Right, the full title of the flick is *Mario Puzo's The Godfather*!"

Moose blinked. "They made a movie out of the novel? Like *Gone with the Wind*?"

"*Gone with th—*" Jackson started.

"More 'sleeps with the fishes' than 'gone with the wind'!" Chalmers cracked.

"Puzo co-authored the screenplay, even," Vat said, smiling at Moose.

Chalmers looked a question at him. The former arms dealer didn't seem the type to be a movie aficionado, but neither did he seem the type to be a mob boss.

Vat shrugged. "I watched that film a *lot*. Young James Caan was...very watchable."

Chalmers grinned and shook his head.

"I bet the book was better," Moose muttered in R'Bakuun, eyes roaming the stands.

"Must be an amazing novel..." Chalmers trailed off as he realized the big soldier's eyes were searching for threats. The exchange had been in English, and while they were supposed to be alone in here, there was always a risk someone was listening, and they were standing in an amphitheater designed to carry sound.

"Damn it," Chalmers said, in R'Bakuun. "We need to be careful."

The light mood of before was replaced by a moment's steady watchfulness from all of them. When no sounds or movement came from the cheap seats or the boxes, they all relaxed, if only marginally.

"But should you be pushing in on someone else's business like this?" Jackson asked quietly, breaking the watchful silence. "Won't it attract attention?"

Vat winced, half-shrugging. "The nature of this society makes some notice desirable, especially power plays that are carried out with smooth authority. If it breaks no taboos or jeopardizes no one higher up the food chain, it gets me noticed. Notice means more access to power players and the opportunities they can provide. Combine this with my rapid rise to prominence on the merchant front, and people will start coming to me with information and for opportunities I might provide them. Besides, we needed to get this done before the rest of the surveyors got here. Can't be more than a few days, now."

Chalmers shook his head, toeing a darker patch of sand without thinking. His lip twitched in disgust as he realized it was blood.

Jackson was nodding, though. "All makes a sick kind of sense."

"Who brought the owner the offer he couldn't refuse?" Chalmers asked, careful not to look at Moose. He'd heard the security specialist had smoked a number of assassins bent on killing Murphy without breaking a sweat.

Vat met his gaze, held it. "Did it myself."

Uneasy, Chalmers changed the subject. "So, what's next?"

"I start playing for contracts serving the downport."

"We can do that?"

Vat smiled. "Brokers are *relied* on for that. The brokers here are considered more trustworthy than the individual members of the surveyors on some things. In their view, the humble R'Baku are without Houses in the true Kulsian sense of the word, without a serious technological base of their own, and are therefore not considered any kind of *real* security threat. The brokers earn a living by facilitating the gathering of the biologicals before the Searing and then selling off whatever comparatively high-tech devices and goods the Kulsians leave behind as not valuable enough to freight back to Kulsis, give to their satraps here, or keep mothballed. Indeed, selling any real technology is more a black-market activity than legitimate trade."

"All right, so how do we use that?" Chalmers asked, resenting the other man's easy confidence.

"Why, we make nice with a broker or his minions, of course," Vat said, smiling.

✧   ✧   ✧

"Another delivery? I had thought Twin Stars had no more to give after being squeezed by Fangat," the clerk said, standing in the door of the Fangat warehouse. House Fangat held the Chair of the Broker Principle and wielded a *lot* of power. So much so their lowest employees seemed to think they could speak openly about Fangat's role in robbing a lesser brokerage like Twin Stars, even when they were only a warehouse manager, and about as far from the wealthy inner circle as Chalmers was from Earth.

"Yes, Daroz, another delivery of heavy, valuable goods from our good patron to yours," Jackson said, glancing at Chalmers as he and Moose wrestled the crate from the back of the truck.

Chalmers caught the look and stepped between the truck and the clerk. "Daroz, I have the thing you wanted."

"Not now, there is work to be done, you filth," Daroz said. The clerk was a waddling little punk with an inflated ego who felt that everyone should bow before his specialness. Unless, of course, someone of greater station appeared, at which point he behaved as if there were no more loyal or hardworking servants to be had in all the world. He was...thirsty, always looking to suck up to his betters or lord it over others. Of course the disappointment when his expectations met reality had proven a fine avenue to corrupting him.

Sweating in the incredible heat, Jackson and Moose set the crate down just inside the warehouse.

"My friend, you sure you don't want...?" Holding the manifest in the same hand, Chalmers pulled a box the size of a cigarette pack from his breast pocket and shook a dull rattle from within as he handed both to the clerk.

"Well, I'll just check the manifest," the warehouse clerk said, licking his painted lips and taking the box from Chalmers. "I'll, umm, be back in a few minutes to sign off on everything."

Jackson shook his head as the guy hurried out of the warehouse, nearly salivating over his prize. A moment later Chalmers heard the faint clack of the latrine door closing behind the clerk. If previous experience was any judge, they had about fifteen minutes.

"Hope his need for the junk you're pushing doesn't get him removed or, worse yet, make him OD," Moose said, his bulk barely shadowing one corner of the vast warehouse door.

"Fuck Daroz," Jackson said, coming up behind the other man. "You didn't see him flog the shit out of a couple guys whose only crime was to drop a box. Didn't even break the contents, just dented the crate. That fucker had 'em whipped till they bled. Like that scene in *Roots*, man. I had flashbacks and shit."

"*Roots?*"

"Never mind. After your time. Probably not your jam anyway."

The sound of Moose's knuckles popping was like a sequence of slow, wet gunshots. "I suppose I prefer a more direct approach. Saw too many legs in-country get hooked on H to be comfortable with this kind of thing."

"Focus," Chalmers said, uneasy with it himself. It was all too easy—far too easy—to fall back into old habits. Shaking his head, he hiked a thumb at the crate sitting just inside the warehouse. "Get that in place, and I'll keep watch for our thirsty friend."

Jackson and Messina picked up the crate and carried it farther into the darkened interior of the warehouse. The office was at the receiving end of the huge building. At the far end of the place the goods were transferred to cargo containers newly sent down by the surveyors. They were similar to CONEX boxes back on Earth: built to a regulation size, weight, and volume. The containers didn't leave the island but were commonly filled at warehouses outside the downport, so they had access to plenty of exemplars.

Chalmers did his part, lounging against the warehouse's office door and watching for the clerk's return. It had taken months of careful work to get to this point. If his pride in the job done thus far was wounded by the methods he had to use to accomplish the mission, it was a dull ache rather than the open sore he used to contend with. He shook his head. It still surprised him how much being honest to the people around him mattered. Yes, he had to lie like a rug, cheat, push drugs, do all manner of nasty shit, but doing it for the mission, for the Lost Soldiers' collective survival rather than for himself, made it somehow right. Like Murphy had said, "Using your dark powers for good." He'd spent too much time like a rat, killing other rats just to get two more breaths on the sinking ship that was life. It was time to plug the hole that was sinking the ship, even if that meant swimming in some of the same old shit.

He started to pull at his lip but stopped with his hand halfway to his mouth. The sunblock paint jobs were a pain in the ass, but they did allow a certain amount of built-in disguise.

That, and they were supposed to prevent skin cancer, an illness he wasn't eager to try on for shits and giggles. Not after watching his grandfather's nose get cut and recut to remove a tumor.

At least the paint, unlike so many sunscreens from his time, didn't smell like coconuts, which smelled like Malibu—the rum, not the place, which always summoned to mind a certain night puking his guts out in a Cabo gutter.

A rumble in the western sky announced a lighter on final approach. He resisted the urge to look at a watch he didn't wear while on the island and pretended a disinterested squint at the heavy security gate that kept the riffraff out of the downport proper.

The huge, angular craft thundered by high above the gates, held aloft by nacelles that rotated its vastly powerful engine into a VTOL attitude as it slowed for landing and eased out of view below the fence line.

Chalmers suppressed the urge to gape. Since arriving just days ago, the so-called surveyors had been flying in and out of Downport at one hell of a tempo, dropping off personnel and their gear—all of which made him feel like he was in the middle of some sci-fi flick. He dragged his gaze from what was definitely some Star Wars–level shit back to the gate. None of the security contingent had even looked up. He'd have to look elsewhere for distracting the guards, some of whom were Kulsians who'd been on the first wave of landers. And those who weren't from off-world didn't want to get caught gawking.

Port traffic had steadily increased since his first visit with the crew of the *Loklis*, but, unlike his previous experience with smuggling, that increase in traffic had made security tighter, not more lax. He'd run the questionable behavior by Murphy, who'd asked their allies. The SpinDogs had a ready, if unwelcome, answer: the increased security measures were motivated more by the internal conflicts that so plagued Kulsian-style rule than by any real concern over threats posed by a given satrap or, more laughable still, the barbaric nomads. That was the reason they'd placed their downport here, so far from the mainland. It certainly wasn't convenient, but it was safe. An entire town of brokers and traders had grown up around the inner port. Not Kulsian, not satraps—they were a class unto themselves, sourcing and shipping those goods not seized outright by the reavers in the long lead-up to the Searing and then living off the proceeds in between.

Still, that they were so meticulous in guarding against internal threats meant problems for the operation. Penetrating the downport—he wanted to call it a starport, even though actual starships didn't land there—would be a lot harder than getting past security on the seaport. He'd tried to imagine how cutthroat Kulsian politics must be to generate such paranoia, but even films like *The Godfather* left him wondering if the mafia was paranoid *enough*.

The rumble of the lighter's drives eased back to a heavy drone and then ceased altogether. The security detail on the gate, a squad of painted men wearing what he'd been told was the gray of survey security uniforms, passed a small convoy of trucks onto the port property. Probably preparing to load the ship with cargo. The lighters usually took a day or two to refuel and prep, but they could speed that up in an emergency. It was pretty amazing when Chalmers thought about it. It had taken months for NASA to plan and execute shuttle launches into Earth's orbit, and here these assholes could turn a truly *interplanetary* ship around in a matter of hours. Probably less if they were in a real hurry.

"A hive of scum and villainy, indeed," he muttered.

"Just your kind of place, Obi-Wan," Jackson said from behind him.

"Who?" Moose asked emerging from the shadows behind Jackson.

"Never mind," the partners chorused as the latrine door flew open. Daroz staggered when the door's rebound clipped his shoulder as he walked out into the light of both suns.

"Must be scratching that itch pretty good, Chalmers," Jackson murmured, nodding at the clerk, who had a dope-happy smile pasted across his face.

"Maybe too good," Moose said, equally quietly.

"He's where I want him," Chalmers muttered.

Coming to an unsteady halt, Daroz thrust the manifest back at Chalmers.

Seeing the signature crawled across the bottom, Chalmers bowed over it. "All is in readiness, Daroz," he said aloud, silently adding, *You thirsty fuck.*

"Then why are you still in my sight?" Daroz asked, dismissing them. He wheeled away to walk, loose-legged, back into his office.

"Mount up," Chalmers said, reflecting that some assets served best by being burned sooner rather than later.

Chapter Twenty-Three

"That's a bad sign," Jackson said, looking down from the balcony that ran around the upper stories of the Twin Star offices.

Chalmers nodded. Another crash sounded from below.

"Is it, though?" Vat said.

Jackson waved his hand. "That's like the third raid in the last two nights."

"Fifth, actually," Vat corrected. "The market is adjusting."

"The market?" Chalmers said.

Vat smiled. "We ... well, *I* upset a few apple carts. No one likes price fixing, so they're regulating the market."

"But haven't *we* been price fixing?" Jackson said.

"If anything, we've been undercutting the local market," Chalmers said.

"And we haven't been hit since the deliveries in the first week," Jackson added, looking thoughtful.

"You mean the deliveries I had—" Vat began.

"You had *me* on a roundabout path through the docks," Jackson interrupted.

"And made sure no one but locals were with it when it got robbed," Chalmers added. Suspicion in full flame, he added, "And discussed at length with me at the fights."

"Yeah, those," Vat said. For some reason, the grin splitting his face reminded Chalmers of a shark.

"What was in the crates, Vat?" Jackson asked, his tone telling Chalmers he had his suspicions.

"Oh, nothing much, just clear evidence that two of the most powerful brokerages have been engaged in artificial price-fixing to shore up their profits."

"But those were our shipments, with Twin Star markings."

"Were they?" Vat asked, his grin becoming positively shit-eating. "Yes, they were marked for our warehouse, but the contents and the shipping manifests uniformly declared we were acting solely as shipping agents for Masok and Sons. What's more, all records indicate we were the middlemen for shipments between their mainland offices and Fangat Trading."

"I was wondering why we made a payoff to Masok and Sons," Chalmers said. When Jackson sent an old-fashioned look his way, he shrugged defensively. "I thought we were just kicking up a bribe to keep them off our backs."

"As far as anyone at Masok and Sons knew, it was," Jackson said, an edge of admiration creeping into his voice. "But to everyone else it looked like we were making good on their financial losses, confirming the evidence you gave them."

"Evidence of what?"

"Of collusion, naturally. Price-fixing, more specifically. The only sin that counts here on the island." Vat's smile was no longer simply feral; it was positively beaming with pride. It somehow made his expression that much more malevolent.

"Jesus, man," Chalmers breathed. "That's some dangerous fire you're playing with."

"Not so dangerous, really." Vat shrugged, grin vanishing. "At least, not as dangerous as facing a motorized battalion of angry satrap goons."

Chalmers and Jacks shared a look at the apparent non sequitur.

Guess we all have our share of bad memories, Chalmers thought.

"But won't Twin Stars get spattered with the fallout?" Jackson said.

"Yes, but only in the sense that we will come out of this with some prize, some 'fallout ass,' I believe you breeder boys call it?" He grinned again. "Indeed, we should expect some representatives of the second-tier brokerages to come by tonight or tomorrow, latest."

"What?" the partners chorused.

"I'm going to assume you understand what fallout is, and are wondering what the rest meant." Vat chuckled and gestured out beyond the balcony. "The middle and lower-tier brokerages are the ones pulling the raids on the primary houses. The ones who show up here tonight will likely know my play for a ruse, but also know it for a *very* useful ruse, one that allowed them to take direct action against the biggest brokerages without fear of reprisal from either the brokerages or the surveyors."

"Because they're all doing it, 'for the good of our collective reputation with the surveyors,'" Jackson breathed.

Chalmers glanced at his partner, stunned. Vat had done wonders to establish Twin Star Trading as *the* up-and-coming brokerage, to the extent the business was actually generating a profit, even without the regular influx of free goods from their allies on the mainland or the SpinDogs. The brokerage was now so large as to require a headquarters big and impressive enough to house the offices and critical employees of the organization, but this was an entirely different level of crazy.

"Jesus."

The doorbell rang. An old-fashioned thing, it was an actual bell. On a rope.

Vat leaned back in his seat, his eyes glittering in the lamp-light. "Someone want to get that for me?"

Chalmers and Jackson looked at each other. Neither one moved.

The bell clanged again.

"Moose!" Chalmers called.

"I got it, you lazy fucks," Moose stage-whispered from the hallway.

"Still, would have been nice for you to tell us your plans," Chalmers insisted.

Vat shrugged. "If you couldn't figure it out, from your position next to me, then I was sure the opposition couldn't follow the shell game I played."

"If I didn't know any better, I'd think you were enjoying this," Chalmers said.

"Oh, I *am* enjoying it. I mean, the more I'm here, the more I dig it. Cutthroat, sure, but everyone is so busy watching their opponents, they fail to see the board. I've earned—and spent—a king's ransom or two since we got to this island, and I'm getting ahead in a game I was not born to. All while being appreciated for my skills. What's not to like?"

"That and there's no one to keep you in line."

A murmur of voices from downstairs.

"No one?" Vat sniffed. "Shit, there's no *law*, just custom and power," Vat said. The erstwhile arms dealer's expression said he loved that lack.

"Just so long as you remember who your friends are, Vat," Jackson said, smiling to take the sting out.

Vat looked at him, did not smile back. "For all the bullshit, it's still straightforward to me: we're alone among enemies. Makes things very easy on the conscience."

Moose made some noise at the bottom of the stairs, said something apologetic and loud enough they were warned of his approach.

"I still think there's gonna be some violent pushback on this shit," Jackson said.

"And you didn't tell us the nuts and bolts of your plan. Kinda like a certain person we all know and love," Chalmers said, pointing skyward.

Vat frowned. "I'll ignore that aspersion for the moment to concentrate on my real reasons for keeping you all in the dark: When our shipment got hit on its way from the docks, would you have been able to *act* like you were as pissed as you really were?"

"Maybe," Chalmers said.

"Well, I wanted to be sure. We can't very well rely on maybes..." Vat said, trailing off as Moose escorted the broker's messenger into the room.

Chalmers bit back a retort. Knowing the logic backward and forward didn't make it feel any better to be the one duped.

The messenger bowed.

Vat's eyes flickered over the man's elaborate face paint. He must be reading it far faster than Chalmers could, because he immediately said, "Greetings, servant of Broker Thilokmes. What brings you here at this late hour?"

"Matters of import meant for your ears alone, Lead Broker Vat." The messenger looked at the others, haughty and dismissive.

Vat sat straighter, stared at the messenger. "You are not here to tell me who in my brokerage is worthy of trust, servant of Thilokmes. I will have you removed if you continue to behave so presumptuously."

Moose put a hand on one of the man's narrow shoulders and squeezed.

An audible swallow. "Apologies, Broker Vat."

Vat nodded acceptance of the apology and waited. Moose removed his hand from the man's shoulder.

"Thilokmes requests your backing in Council tomorrow. It is time the Fangat were ousted from the Chair of the Broker Principle. In return—" The doorbell rang again.

Moose glanced at Chalmers and smiled. The message was clear.

"In return?" Vat prompted.

Chalmers got up and started for the door.

"In return, he offers a waiver of fees to the amount of five percent of annual dues and duties."

"Five percent, eh?" Vat shook his head. "What Twin Stars requires is that five percent you mentioned in addition to preference for certain labor contracts—" Chalmers closed the door on the conversation and started down the stairs. The doorbell rang again before he'd made the landing. He sighed and wondered when they'd all become Vat's servants.

Chapter Twenty-Four

"Don't get mad, get even!" Harry said reprovingly, offering a gauntleted hand to the RockHound. The man was floating just out of reach of the handholds projecting from the impact mat. Originally white, the stained and scuffed ad hoc padding covered all the heavy equipment and most of the surfaces of the mining and salvage skiff hangar. Here and there, yellow-painted maintenance carts and ramps were chained to the deck, peeking from beneath improvised protection. Under the goad of a lucky hit or painful joint lock, sparring routinely accelerated into full speed fighting, but the EVA suits and padding generally sufficed to turn potential broken bones and contusions into bruises and deflated egos. There was a surfeit of both, especially among the host station personnel, who were getting their first taste of Terran aggression.

"Let's go again. This time try to escape faster. Fight near the bulkheads and deck. A man without an anchor has no leverage in micro."

"This is an unfair test!" the RockHound insisted, ignoring Harry's hand. He grabbed a handhold, levering himself to an "up" position unassisted. As he spoke, he tugged his twisted and bunched black EVA suit into a more comfortable position. "How can I win, when there are two of you attacking me? You shame me to justify a plan to use inferior Terrans in your mission!"

There was a stir as two men grabbed for a third as he prepared to challenge the angry RockHound.

"Inferior my ass!" shouted Rico Grave de Peralto, a compact and intense Cuban American. Furious Flea, as he was called by his buddies, had been a Navy gunner's mate before he was blown over the side of his ship during a fire support mission in Vietnam. The Flea had a short man's readiness to charge any hill and a temper that made every knoll a good hill to charge. Fortunately, this particular mountain would remain out of reach. Another American caught Harry's eye and received a nod in reply.

A ham-sized fist snagged Flea's ankle, aborting the mad Cuban's attempt to push off a wall toward the angry RockHound. The fist belonged to Brent Roeder, a mild-mannered man whose World War II submarine had vanished on patrol. He'd been left in stasis due to undiagnosed terminal cancer, which Dornaani medicine had easily resolved. He was also the size of a medium-large bear, and what he grabbed tended to stop as though anchored in concrete. He ignored the minor violences Rico tried to inflict on him and merely raised his eyebrows in mild amusement.

The incipient brawl successfully nipped in the bud, Harry calmly wiped his sweaty forehead with a scratchy but absorbent chem wipe. The RockHound facing him, a normally polite noncom named Markaz, visibly relaxed while Harry took his time deliberately drying all the skin he could reach. The rough recyclable paper towels were found everywhere in the station, including both the heads and the refectory, inspiring several jokes among the Lawless. Harry had specified full EVA gear for the exercise, and, given the soaked state of his own unitard, he imagined the others were swimming in their suits, too. His one concession to comfort thus far was to let them leave their helms open. Not only did drilling with open faceplates ease communications in the hangar they were using for training, but it was also much easier to scratch your face.

Harry looked over at his assistant and made a little "go ahead" motion with his hand.

"We don't try to disqualify anyone, Markaz," Senior Sergeant Pham Kai said stolidly, his Ktoran nearly perfect, if heavily accented. Ironically, his command of the alien language was much better than his choppy English, courtesy of the Dornaani language programs. He was another Vietnam War–era abductee. Pham had been detached from his North Vietnamese regiment, advising Viet Cong allies in Cambodia, when an American Arc

Light strike wiped out nearly everyone he'd been training. If coaching RockHounds in close combat techniques was a stretch for the wiry, shaven-headed Terran, Harry couldn't detect it. "Every remaining candidate possesses basic and intermediate freefall skills. The point of this exercise is to determine the best method to render Kulsian opponents mission-incapable in freefall, in the shortest possible time. You RockHounds are most likely to have skills and experience similar to the opposition we will face, so we use you, as Americans say, as practice dummies."

"Is this an insult?" Markaz stiffened. He was among the relatively few RockHound volunteers who combined a willingness to work under the Terrans and had accepted the vague mission information shared thus far. Markaz was also somewhat mentally flexible—for a RockHound. In Harry's experience, that meant he only questioned every third order, placing Markaz well ahead of the rest of his people.

"I do not understand this word, 'dummy,'" Markaz added.

The loud, prolonged exchange was attracting attention, and Harry's assistant instructor, Volo, floated over to listen in. The other candidates were close behind, Harry's favorite RockHound among them: Korelon's inclusion in the training had been a concession upon which the Legate had insisted. As far as Harry could see, Korelon was as excited to be involved as Harry was to have him. Like the others, Korelon turned as he approached, automatically orienting to the natural up and down of the compartment. Harry had requisitioned the hangar at the hub portion of the station, taking advantage of the microgravity environment found there, earning the ire of every RockHound captain now forced to use less convenient approaches to their berths.

"And the incessant training in full suits!" Korelon picked up the thread, ready to air his own grievances. "Are we unproven novitiates, owed no respect? Nay, I am a fully qualified salvage captain. Is it necessary to maintain discomfort to demonstrate my resolve, already proven in twenty thousand hours of ship duty? No Terran can handle himself in micro as well as we can, and yet here you are, teaching us?"

Harry had known this was coming. He stared at Korelon in his fancy-pants black captain's suit and then exhaled. He shrugged a bit, like a man settling the weight of a heavy pack. Might as well address it now.

"All right, everybody, rally up." Harry raised his voice and waved a forefinger above his head, describing a circle. He waited a moment while the nearly two dozen men making up the training cohort came within easy speaking distance. He spotted Murphy's hapless aide about to drift beyond reach of a handhold. "Grab something, Makarov, before you float away.

"We've got a tough mission, and the success of all our clans— sorry, Families—depends upon it," Harry began, maintaining his own position. "I don't know all the details yet. I can't share everything I know, either. However, the terms of our call for volunteers included extended EVA time. You volunteers know we're preparing for direct action at close quarters with a hostile force of unknown size. We don't have much time to master several important skills. We need to be ready to work in microgravity, and yes, under acceleration as well."

Acceleration, ha! These poor fuckers have no idea.

Better them than Momma Tapper's boy.

Harry had agreed to train the assault force contingent on learning more about the mission, and Murphy had reluctantly acquiesced. The operational profile was as ugly as anything Harry had ever heard of, and he'd been on the Panama airfield op.

"The ability to handle yourself in zero gee and under heavy accel is important, but it's not everything. The team will need to work very fast indeed, under severe pressure, and while in direct infantry combat. That means clear and precise communications, instinctive teamwork, and split-second timing. But, above all, one thing is required when you invade another man's space and take it from him: violence of action. Fast, brutal fighting at very close quarters. Close enough to feel his breath on your face when you run your knife into his belly. And that's the kind of fighting at which we Terrans excel."

Some Ktoran muttering was audible.

"Yes, the training is uncomfortable. It's intended to be. We Terrans have a saying: The more you sweat in peace, the less you bleed in war. Training when you're uncomfortable, tired, and aggravated is good training. When the time comes to fight, you won't depend on ideal conditions and those Kulsian pussi—fools with their fancy technology and complacent attitude will be meat on our table!"

This time the muttering was tinged with approval.

Inspired, Harry looked for someone he'd worked with who the Hounds would find a credible source.

"Volo has worked with us in several operations," Harry said, motioning to the SpinDog who'd been listening avidly. "Volo, can you explain why I assigned two attackers to Markaz?"

"His training is sufficiently high that two attackers are required to rapidly subdue him," Volo said, assuaging the ever-touchy RockHound honor. "Therefore, his skill is not a deficiency, but a point of honor—is it not?"

With an audience of his peers present, keeping RockHound honor unruffled required a soft touch, and Harry appreciated the assistance.

"Indeed," the man said, unbending a touch. "I thank you."

Of course, Volo couldn't stop there.

"Further, Major Tapper made certain all are tired, sweaty, and thirsty when we fight. We are learning just how fast we can subdue our enemies, evaluating both attack and defense, even when we are uncomfortable. Perhaps *especially* when we're uncomfortable. This is good training. My first exposure to Terran ideas of good training involved attaching somewhat unreliable chemical rockets to an orbital interface craft to improve the craft's maneuvering characteristics in atmosphere."

A few of the RockHounds winced.

"It cost most of our ships to do it, and no one was ever comfortable or happy, but the mission was subsequently completed. Good training, you see."

"Thanks, Volo," Harry said, hoping his grudging thanks weren't too obvious. He could've done without the recitation of historical losses.

"You're welcome," Volo replied nonchalantly, before turning back to Markaz. "I suggest, fellow spacer, you work closely with the Terran sergeants Rodriguez and Pham. They are experienced with no-limits, *to-the-death* combat. They have thousands of hours in that environment, quite different from honor duels and arena competition. That may be the edge that helps you succeed."

Harry took the opportunity to look at the Vietnamese sergeant, catching the carefully blank look on Pham's face, which was creased like old leather. Recommended by Makarov, the lightly built, phlegmatic noncom had formed an unlikely friendship with Rodriguez, another veteran of the same conflict. Both men had crystal-clear memories of the lessons the US invasion of Vietnam had taught the respective combatants and shared a passionate hatred for incompetent leaders. Had they been talking with Volo?

Transitioning to another convenient handhold, Harry scanned the group of volunteers, some of whom were dispersing back to their own corners of the hangar. Beyond them, a distinctive white EVA suit, marked with the four gold rings of a Terran colonel, was perched high on the bulkhead just inside the main doors. There was only one suit like that on the station, and the occupant was no doubt taking advantage of the sensitive binaural exterior microphones on his helmet to listen in and evaluate Harry's performance.

"All right, Sergeant, they're all yours," Harry said to Pham, speaking loudly for the benefit of the group. "Run the drills for another fifteen, rotating through roles. Then we'll take a break and do it again with the faceplates closed."

The group gave a low, collective groan.

"Good training, remember!" Having delivered that gem, Harry oriented and pushed off to go see what the good colonel wanted.

Approaching the main doors, Harry lightly touched down on the deck and gently pushed off. Terrans had a tendency to overcontrol body movements in micro, but he timed it just right, reaching the bulkhead at a speed that let him grab a handy bracket and come to a stop without ricocheting off.

"Sir."

"I don't want to interrupt, Harry," Murphy said, clearing his opaque visor and raising it. "How are they shaping up?"

They both watched the action in the hangar. Spread out in clusters of three and four, every group included Terrans and RockHounds. Harry could easily distinguish between students by suit color. Command deck black, miner red, and the whitish-gray of station maintenance personnel made for a kaleidoscope of colors just from the RockHounds. The Terrans used a slightly different design, borrowed from the SpinDogs. The dirty white of the uniform contrasted nicely with the oversize rank insignia on the suit sleeves. Regardless of color, pairs of attackers were trying to immobilize the singleton defenders, applying various submission and compliance holds. Defenders fished about, writhing to break the attackers' grip while maintaining a position that allowed them to strike more effectively. Harry and his instructors had again encouraged all hands to move at half speed to avoid injury, but the innate competitiveness found among men-at-arms eroded that admonition in nothing flat.

"They're coming along pretty well. They have plenty of fire. Add in the competition between the Terrans and the RockHounds, and I'm a bit surprised no one's been seriously injured yet," Harry said, studying one group in particular. They had ignored the basic principle of fighting in micro and drifted away from any possible hold or surface, reducing them to a spasming, cursing ball. Harry recognized Mike Zymanski, a burly, red-nosed submarine man. Harry couldn't be certain, but judging from the unscientific punches the chief was throwing, he might be drinking the product of his own still again. Another, steadier and quieter Navy submariner, McPherson, attempted to use recently acquired skills to stop the fight, but merely added to the ball of angry humanity floating farther and farther from the bulkhead. Finally, Harry watched Pham push off from the nearest bulkhead, blowing a small tin whistle to break up the wrestlers before pushing them to the deck for a debrief.

"Have you decided on the assault group?" Murphy asked. "Chalmers's team planetside is building intelligence on the lighter schedule and building their contacts so he can make the snatch in the next month or two. Bowden's training with the RockHounds, flying approaches—to comets of all things—and getting familiar with their ships. You'll have to be ready to move soon."

"Tonight I'm asking the hangar boss to pump this space down to vacuum, and we'll keep sparring. Tomorrow, we'll do the same thing in the black," Harry said, disregarding Murphy's use of *you'll*. He focused on watching Pham work. A few individuals were still having trouble remembering the core lessons they'd reviewed earlier. Pham demonstrated the technique again, swarming his target, almost as though he was swimming, rapidly achieving a back mount before simulating a knife hand to the hapless RockHound's Adam's apple. The Hound wisely and quickly tapped the sergeant's forearm, acknowledging the strike. "The specs on the habitat modules mean we can have up to six people in each for up to three weeks. It's going to be very, very hard on the men. The habs aren't much larger than an old-school CONEX box, Murph."

"Astronauts lived in Spacelab for months at a time, Harry," Murphy answered, although his wince ceded Harry's point. "It had about as much volume as a shipping container, too. None of the old-school astronauts thought it was a picnic, but it was the mission, and they accomplished it. This team will, too. Also, we solved the shielding issues. We can use the railgun system to send care packages along the team's trajectory for resupply, but it's a work in progress. The teams will have to EVA frequently, but the exposure to ionizing radiation from the primary is within healthy limits. We're lucky this system's primary is less energetic than Sol or Barnard's Star. There are stars that reduce maximum EVA time to only a few minutes in total."

"The mission profile is already miserable, and additional EVAs will make it worse, particularly since the habs will have limited facilities for showering and such," Harry replied, recalling his own experiences with intense discomfort during a mission. "There's an upside, sort of. The unavoidable side effect of an unpleasant insert is to aggravate the hell out of your assault force. The more shit we had to eat on the way in, the more we had stored up to take out on the target once we engaged. Given what you're going to subject the teams to, I wouldn't expect any Kulsian survivors, sir."

It's going to be a shit show. Your shit show.

"I'm not counting on any," Murphy said flatly.

No one ever said Murphy wasn't ruthless.

Yeah, but to his own side, too?

"About our secrecy, Colonel. Between the specialized weapons and the tactics I'm going to teach them, the assault team is going to figure out what we're doing, regardless of how much I'm forced to leave out of your mission profile, sir. So, as soon as we finish the basics and finalize teams, they'll need to go into isolation, which is yet another pain in the ass, if you don't mind me saying so again."

"I know we have leaks," Murphy said flatly, his eyes narrowing as a figure was thrown heavily into a lumpy, if padded, tractor unit, eliciting a yell of pain. "We might even have an active saboteur somewhere in this station. Or more than one. Segregating the mission teams reduces the information risk until you are isolated and prepped for insertion."

"You mean, until *they* are prepped, right?"

Below them, a RockHound medtech approached and began examining the injured man's leg. When he attempted to straighten it, the student yelled again and batted the medtech's hands away from his knee.

"Is that man all right?" Murphy asked, ignoring Harry's question. "And why are you so focused on the hand-to-hand skills? Everyone should be armed to the teeth."

"The RockHounds move very well in micro, don't get dropsick, and the suits are familiar to them," Harry said, throttling the defensive tone he knew would piss Murphy off. "Our guys have plenty of aggression and readiness to work in-close. Additionally, the Lawless are much stronger physically, a nice side benefit to living under acceleration your whole entire life. Normally, the way space battles go, physical strength wouldn't matter. They're not fighting a space battle, though. The performance I can assess during sparring lets me pick a crew with the best mix of everything. They'll be ready. All Makarov will have to do is introduce them to the Kulsians and let the lads do their stuff."

"And the weapons?"

"We'll bring gas guns, of course," Harry replied, using the Terran term for the variable-velocity, low-recoil pistols that were produced by both space-based factions. "And shaped charges for cutting hulls, bulkheads, and hatches, if need be. The new items are already prototyped, and Makarov tells me the SpinDogs promised delivery by the weekend."

"I'm worried about Makarov, Harry." Murphy was still looking at the students. "I know he volunteered to lead the op. I really can't spare him, but he insisted. He feels he has to prove himself, but he doesn't have your experience. I've read your reports, and Makarov's consistently in the bottom half of the group. He would learn much from working under you during the mission, and I would gain another combat-experienced veteran."

"Both Rodriguez and Pham are going," Harry said, with a sidelong glance at the colonel. "You requested I help plan the operation and train the teams. You called for volunteers and then stated you would respect my decision to decline participation in the op. That's where I'm at, sir."

Murphy was relentless; Harry had to give him that.

Pham's whistle blew again, and the sergeant ordered the men to take a break. The last trio continued fighting and had to be untangled by several men. Harry watched Rodriguez use an expertly applied arm bar, adapted for micro, to force another Lost Soldier out of the scrum. He couldn't be sure, but the black-clad figure in mid-tangle was the right height to be Korelon. Accompanied by a few more whistle blasts, the remainder reluctantly allowed themselves to be pulled apart, exchanging angry comments about parentage, martial prowess, and body odor. The chest tabards of a few were stained with telltale red smears. When all combatants were untangled, most gratefully unlocked helmets from their EVA collars and used wipes to sop their necks, faces, and as much of their chests as they could reach. Others beelined for the cooler of chilled, sweetened electrolytes. Harry saw Rodriguez and Pham hanging together near the overhead, comparing notes. He swore under his breath. The class had self-segregated again; Terrans were congregating about the cooler, and the RockHounds were seeking the company of their own faction, circling Korelon, who held a red-stained chem wipe to his lip.

Split lips burned like fire. *Pity, that.*

"You know what's riding on this mission, Harry." Murphy's voice interrupted Harry's reverie. He pivoted in place to see Murphy watching him through his open faceplate. "If we don't snatch the corvette and reproduce it in numbers, the Kulsians will run rough-shod over this system. A failure in any mission will alert them to a threat they cannot ignore. They'll know where to look and what to look for, and our allies will be lucky to avoid being wiped out. Even if some survive, their resources will be insufficient for our larger mission to proceed, and most of us will die."

Harry just looked at his CO.

Show no fear, be the fucking expressionless Sphinx. Give him nothing.

"Once the RockHounds and SpinDogs are dealt with, the Kulsians will purge the planet of anyone they suspect to have fought the satraps." Murphy's arm twitched as though to lay a hand on Harry's shoulder but stopped mid-motion. "Everyone, Harry. They can't afford not to. They'll have plenty of time, not to mention an overwhelming degree of overmatch. Just because you sit this out doesn't mean R'Bak will be there the way you left it." Murphy nodded and left with an unusually weary gait. His posture wasn't the best Harry had ever seen, either.

Heavy is the head and all that shit. But driving that silent rhetorical dagger into his CO's receding back didn't slay the core truth of the man's assertion: if this plan didn't work, there would be nowhere to hide, and nowhere to run.

Just lots of places to die.

Chapter Twenty-Five

"This is Ivan," Harry broadcast via suit radio, patting the suit-clad dummy on the shoulder. Some wag—probably Rodriguez, if Harry had to guess—had used a red paintstick to draw angry eyes and fangs on the closed faceplate. The nylon tabard bore the mottos ALL TERRANS MUST DIE! and THE ONLY GOOD ROCKHOUND IS A DEAD ROCKHOUND! In the front row of Harry's audience, Makarov read the script and visibly rolled his eyes. "And I've got bad news. Ivan is a death-dealing, planet-raping, two-gun mojo motherhumper, and he's utterly unimpressed with the low-bred, knuckle-dragging scum on and around R'Bak. Fortunately for you, I've got some new equalizers, and if you promise to kick Kulsian ass, I'll share."

He turned around and unclipped the first new weapon from the table set up next to the target and held it in both hands to show it to the assembled class. Three squads of six men attentively watched his every move. One was entirely RockHounds, led by Korelon, but the other two were a mix. Makarov and Rodriguez each headed a squad. Pham had phlegmatically accepted his assignment to back up Makarov.

"That thing looks like the love child of an oversize box wrench and a tire jack!" Zymanski yelled across the all-hands channel. "But it ain't no gun!"

"Chief, you are so right," Harry said, smiling big for the benefit of the people in back. "A gun is of questionable utility in this kind of fight. This is a combat grappler. It's better than a gun. What you do is grab this by the grip, and push the safety like so..."

Suiting actions to words, Harry depressed a green plastic knob that stood proud of the black plastic handle, forcing the other end through the slightly thinner than normal pistol grip. On the opposite side, a corresponding red knob emerged. Riding the grip was a black metal frame along which two rear-folding, spike-tipped crescent arms lay. Between them, where the muzzle of a gun would be, was an actuator plate embossed with the words FRONT TOWARD ENEMY.

"When the red button is showing, Mr. Grabby is not your friend," Harry said, turning the unit to show the students the safety mechanism. "Red, you're dead. Do not play with this or try to test fit it on yourself. I'm not going to warn you again. Observe."

Then, moving quickly, he twisted and shoved the business end of the weapon against the thigh of the dummy's suit, actuating the pressure plate. The crescent arms snapped forward, spikes engaging the suit material. A previously hidden link snapped from the end of the first jaw to lock against the one opposite. Harry let go, and the unit began to vibrate and shake, although the vacuum of the practice hangar prevented anyone from hearing the ratcheting sounds of a one-way carbide bit forging its way into the dummy's leg, impelled by a high-torque electric motor. The spiked collar constricted, and the drill burrowed, causing the suit to off-gas. A white mist of frozen water vapor was instantly visible, jetting from the edges of the biting clamp. When the bit punched through the opposite side of the target's leg, the suit sagged a bit, losing pressure in moments.

"You apply this weapon to your opponent and let go. As long as you give it a good bite on a leg or an arm, it will adjust for the limb diameter, and the rest is automatic. Your enemy will suffer incapacitating bleeding and broken bones, and believe me, this thing *hurts*! As an added bonus, if you are fighting in vacuum, your enemy will be further distracted by managing an unexpected case of explosive decompression. Either way, they're out of the fight."

The comments on the radio link were predictable and largely positive. It was easy to tell the RockHounds from their Terran guests.

"Interesting concept."

"Mr. Grabby for president!"

"Is this truly practical? It seems clumsy."

"Sheeeit! Let me have one!"

"Radio silence, please," Harry overrode the channel, then held up a white metal brick from which nylon straps and buckles dangled. "This is your primary contact distance weapon, a pneumatic punch. It features a captive, sharpened tungsten spike projecting twenty centimeters from the weapon face. It can be used in both micro and under acceleration. The rear of the weapon has a balance rod that projects to the rear. It is three times the mass of the spike, so it requires only six or so centimeters of clearance to keep the user safe. Regardless, you don't want to actuate this weapon when anything you care about is adjacent to either end. It's worn under your forearm, like this."

Harry put the brick back on the table and, fighting the resistance of his suit, laid his forearm along the top. The upper surface of the box was slightly concave and the straps cinched down, wrapping securely around the cuff of his suit gauntlet and just below the crease of his elbow.

"To use it, you simply palm-strike your target, like this." Harry punched the dummy on the faceplate with the heel of his hand, his fingers tilted upward. There was no sound, but when Harry withdrew his hand, a neat one-centimeter circular hole surrounded by starry cracks was revealed. "The spike auto-deploys and retracts faster than you can see. Make sure you cock your wrist up, just like a cobra strike to the nose. This is a three-shot weapon, powered by a replaceable gas canister."

Harry punched again, this time on the aluminum neck ring of the dummy helmet. He felt the crunch of the spike as it perforated the softer metal of the ring.

"First you get the Grabby, next you get the Stabby!" Zymanski crowed.

"It will defeat aluminum and thin sheet steel," Harry added. "To reload, you have to take it off, so make each strike count."

"Hey!" one of the gray-suited volunteers, who was also a tech, said in scandalized tones. "Who's going to fix these suits? They're valuable resources!"

"Great question," Harry answered in a reasonable tone. "During this mission, we will be operating with constrained resources.

We'll have to maintain our own suits, and, since the assault will almost certainly occur in vacuum, suit maintenance is a top priority. So, for training purposes, we'll repair the suits. And by 'we,' I mean all of you."

A general groan arose.

"I hate good training," someone muttered from the rear of second squad. Harry didn't bother to look up.

"Will we be issued projectile weapons, Major?" Markaz asked. For once, he sounded genuinely polite.

"Yes." Harry unbuckled the large flap of his thigh holster, exposing the angular, yet familiar, shape of a SpinDog handgun. He withdrew it. With the ease of long practice, he operated the action to expose an empty chamber, which he tilted toward the nearest student, allowing them to verify the weapon was safe. "We'll be using a standard SpinDog caseless design featuring a replaceable magazine, an oversize trigger assembly for use with EVA gauntlets, and a holographic sight. Note the large compensator baffles."

Harry rotated the weapon to highlight the small spade-like baffles at the muzzle. "These offset what little recoil is present. Because of the low chamber pressure, there is no reciprocating mechanism. The weapon is nearly without recoil, because the rounds are fired at a low velocity, and ignite solid rocket motors after departing the muzzle. They require three meters to achieve full velocity, so this is not a contact weapon."

He replaced the pistol in the holster. For once he still had the rapt attention of every member of the class. Harry chuckled inwardly. Soldiers and weapons.

"All right, Pham, you take Alpha team and conduct a familiarization and handling drill. Sergeant Rodriguez, you get Bravo. Charlies, form on me. Once we make sure you knuckleheads won't accidently amputate any limbs or make any new and unwelcome holes in each other, we'll start live-fire training. Remember, shooting yourself or your buddy is not good training."

The combined scrounging capabilities of the notoriously independent-minded soldiers under Murphy's command had to be seen to be believed. Or in this case, very carefully *not seen*. Two large digital display screens, crudely affixed to the appropriated RockHound outpost wall and connected with temporary wiring, were replaying an ancient American professional football game. Harry didn't even want to know where the Terran-style equipment had been before it was scrounged. It was enough that there was a sports-bar ambiance to the place. However, that ambiance was spoiled when Harry consulted the drink in hand. Even at the outside diameter of the slowly spinning trading outpost the gravity was minimal, so every drink was served in a closed container. Thus, the abomination he held in hand: pouch beer.

Harry scanned the faces in the small, communal gaming space that served the diminutive RockHound outpost as an informal bar.

The whole gang was celebrating the end of training.

Or lamenting the loss of their freedom. Isolation would begin tomorrow.

Could be both, Harry realized. Loud conversations, red faces, and serious drinking were common around the small, waist-high tables bolted to the deck. The bulkheads weren't bare rock exactly, but the uneven contours under the white polyfoam sealant clearly showed the mining origins of the little base.

Drinking beer from a straw stuck into a partially silvered pouch reminded Harry of middle school football practices, not his time doing bar crawls in Coronado. The incongruity added to the sense of dislocation, the feeling of being "elsewhere" that had been the ever-present companion of every member of the Lawless Harry knew well enough to ask. One of Harry's favorite things about R'Bak and fighting alongside the Sarmatchani was the certainty of knowing his place and being accepted in it. Then again, it could have been as simple as being in a gravity well and having dirt under his feet.

The much lighter gravity of their current base was definitely a factor, Harry admitted.

After the weapons familiarization and some limited live-fire testing on the preceding larger RockHound outpost, the group had exhausted every training opportunity possible under the secrecy restrictions there. Compelled by the ever-shortening timeline, Murphy had ordered the teams and their trainer to a smaller base where relative isolation would permit mission-specific scenario preparation. A significant portion of the station had been set aside, and the team was confined within its boundaries. No one else was allowed inside, and all logistics, from food to medical, were self-contained. It also meant no one in the "bar" was likely to complain about the unauthorized modifications to the outpost's information net or the oversize, purloined Terran flat-screen displays.

"Tomorrow's the big day, boss," Rodriguez said, addressing Harry in perfect Ktor and closing the distance to Harry's table. Like Harry, he was drinking the fermented RockHound beverage to which the Terrans assigned the label "beer," but which had seen neither hops nor malt in its life. "You promised to reveal the mysteries of the universe to us. Any chance of a sneak peek?"

"Maybe I'll trade you, Marco," Harry replied, eyeing his pouch with suspicion. "First you have to tell me what the hell this is. It's not beer."

"Well, sir," Rodriguez studied his own pouch for a moment before swigging a bit more through his straw. "This here drink is amber-colored, carbonated, and very cold. It's also got a bit of kick."

"Not answering the question."

"It's also free." Rodriguez dropped his empty and fished in a cargo pocket for another. "Free is good."

"I think I hate it," Harry said decisively, and finished his pouch. "I still want to know what it's made from, Marco."

"Actually, I've seen what passes for a *brewery* here," Pham said, joining them. He held another pouch, this one with the blue label that universally designated fresh water. "I respectfully suggest ignorance is the better part of . . . happiness?"

"You're mixing your metaphors, Pham," Rodriguez said, waving an unopened pouch at the shorter man. He dropped it in front of Harry when Pham shook his head no. "Ask the college boy here if I'm right, or if I'm right."

"Sergeant Rodriguez, more important than what's in the beer tonight is how you feel tomorrow, eh, *Dai Uy*?" Pham asked his teammate. He turned and smiled approvingly at Harry when the SEAL declined another beer. "You know what the men who drink too much will find tomorrow morning?"

"No rank in the mess, Pham," Harry answered, taking another pull at the pouch. "I appreciate the honor, but lay off the Vietnamese. It could confuse the Hounds. But what the drinkers will find tomorrow is a big head, unless they drink plenty of water or have something handy from the R'Bak pharmacopeia. Doesn't matter to me. They're all big boys and can make their own decisions. I'm their trainer, not their babysitter."

"And who do you think they regard as their leader, Dai Uy?"

Pham asked, pointedly ignoring Harry's request to skip the rank honorific. "Who do they look to?"

"The mission OIC is Makarov," Harry said with a grunt. "I'm pretty sure the RockHounds have their own idea of who's in charge. Oh, nearly forgot, but I'll be announcing it tomorrow. I was able to get another concession from Murphy. Major Korelon will keep the third squad and run it during the operation—under Makarov, of course."

"The RockHounds remind me a bit of home," Pham said. "This is not a recommendation, you understand."

"These guys remind you of NVA cadre, Pham?" Rodriguez asked incredulously. "That's a stretch."

"They are bound by process and regulation," Pham explained. "Like the Vietnamese army, they are trained to work inside a formal hierarchy. Questioning an order is simply not done, or at least is unlikely to be survivable. Men may reliably follow Makarov or obey Korelon's orders. They won't be inspired by either. Those two are officers, but they are not leaders."

"Your army wasn't inspired by their leaders?" Rodriguez asked. "I find that hard to believe. I saw VC do crazy things, endure impossible hardships."

"Quite the opposite, Sergeant. The most important thing the Viet Cong and the regular Vietnamese army had was inspiration. Certainly, we didn't enjoy the same strengths as the Americans. The American way of war was incomprehensible to us. You questioned everything, continuously changed your ways of fighting, and enjoyed infinitely more supply and greater firepower than we did. The thing that kept us alive was inspiration. It was the one thing we had more of than you. We didn't have to win. We just had to never give up."

Harry didn't respond, even though the last barb had been planted uncomfortably close to home.

"As long as everyone fights, you can pull this off," Harry said, straightening up from the table as he sensed another person approaching.

A slightly boozy RockHound didn't quite stagger into the table. He recovered and slapped a fistful of pouches on the tabletop, where they sloshed gently.

"Markaz, haven't you had enough?" Rodriguez asked, helping the man capture a stray pouch.

"No, I have not," Markaz replied, taking perceptible care to articulate with precision. Using a bit too much concentration, he pushed a beer in front of each man. "Wanted to toast the new leader of our squad!"

Harry shot Rodriguez a meaningful look. Taking the hint, the American sergeant put his arm around Markaz's shoulders and gently steered him to another table.

"And if flexibility is needed?" Pham asked, ignoring the interruption. "What if the plan changes in response to an unforeseen event? Something outside their experience? Who will lead us then?"

"The plan is solid," Harry replied. Hedging only a little, he jerked his head toward the retreating RockHound. "Markaz is solid. The training is solid. Nothing fancy is required. There aren't any hostages to complicate the op. No pesky rules of engagement about escalation of force. No camera crews embedded in the team, getting underfoot and asking distracting questions. Just get onboard, kill the Kulsians, hog-tie any who inconveniently surrender, and break the minimum amount of stuff."

"I see," Pham said, resuming the blank-faced expression that Harry had come to recognize as the shorter man's face of judgment. Noncoms were the same the world over. Any world. Pham's probing questions weren't nearly as subtle as he probably thought they were.

"It's an early morning tomorrow," Harry said, seizing on a reason to escape Pham's Miyagi-san treatment. He stood and genially slapped the smaller man on the back. "Don't stay up too late. I'm going to go get rid of some of this rented beer and call it a night."

A few people hollered glad hellos and waved more pouches as he made his way to the door, but Harry just returned a wave to the entire room and slipped out. Once outside the club, however, he made his way to the circular corridor that ran along the widest circumference of the base.

What he needed was a good stretch of the legs.

A brisk walk wasn't really feasible. Space was one factor. The outpost was small enough that cubic was valuable, so even the main corridor served as a storage area. Racks of tanks and stacked, standardized shipping containers were cabled to the bulkheads, leaving a space that wove from the center and side to side to make room for the supplies that consumed floor space.

Besides, exerting the amount of muscular effort required to speed walk or run would've sent Harry rebounding from the overhead. However, even if he had to remain vigilant, carefully walking in the sharply reduced gee, Harry's nervous tension welcomed the sensation of motion.

That lasted only a few minutes.

They caught sight of each other simultaneously.

Korelon had been out for a stroll, too, walking in the opposite direction. They paused, and Harry warily eyed his counterpart. Apart from brief, uninspired exchanges in training, they hadn't exchanged any words since Harry's belated attempt at an apology, which seemed like ages ago.

"Good evening, Major Tapper," Korelon said. Was there a hint of sincere warmth there?

"Hi, Major," Harry said, affably. If the RockHound could make nice, he could too. "It's a little crowded in the lounge so I decided to try a short stroll. Care to accompany me?"

He gestured broadly along the corridor, as if it were a grand promenade and not a twisted, claustrophobic, low-gee tube with a raised plastic floor and uneven walls.

A heartbeat later, Korelon offered a curt nod and turned sideways, indicating with a hand he would adopt Harry's direction of march.

After a half circuit of the station, Harry had become sufficiently accustomed to Korelon's presence to try a question. "What do you think of the training so far?"

"It is quite unlike our own," Korelon answered promptly. "There is a different rhythm to our methods."

"Oh?"

"I adhere to the SpinDog approach to employ checklists, rather than relying upon memory," the RockHound said. "If there is an emergency, there is a procedure to respond. The Terran training varies considerably. Your emphasis on action over deliberation or acting according to preexisting plans can make an emergency worse. If one is tired, injured, or there is an equipment failure, one can withdraw and prepare again. The Terran method requires we resolve chaos on its own terms. This seems as likely to amplify the chaos as resolve it."

Harry thought for the space of several steps before replying. "I don't know if it's true or not, but back on Earth, long ago, my country was known for our unusual way of making war. For a long period, America was militarily supreme on the planet."

"That is when you established planetary hegemony and ruled?"

"No, no, not at all," Harry said, shaking his head. "Whole different conversation. What I was saying was, at the start of our ascendancy, the established powers had been intermittently fighting for a long time. They were quite accustomed to each other's strengths and weaknesses. A very high-level enemy officer, what you would call a *K'Seps'bel*, made the comment that planning to fight the Americans was difficult because we didn't follow our own doctrine or procedures, and to fight us was to fight chaos. His army, his military, wasn't designed to be as flexible. His side lost. Decisively."

"You ignore your procedures and regard this as a strength?" Korelon sounded incredulous. "When resources are scarce and the margin for survival is narrow, risking so much is dangerous."

"Less dangerous than doing nothing," Harry answered. "Or being too slow. Your turn."

Korelon looked the question at Harry by raising one eyebrow.

"Your turn to ask a question," Harry explained. "Anything."

They paced together for a few minutes. Korelon was quiet. Ahead, the corridor visibly curved upward, following the physical limits of the station. The Hound suddenly stopped, and Harry turned to see what the matter was, putting a hand on a pallet of racked gas cylinders to arrest his momentum.

Korelon was looking at him intently.

"Since my assignment, I have learned much," he finally said, placing his hands behind his back. "Weapons, tactics—those I expected. But I have spent more time and in closer proximity with other ranks in the last weeks than I have since I was posted to the spins as a very young man. I know more about them than ever before. At the intersection of completing this mission successfully and reducing our casualties lies the need to have the best leader for the operation. I flatter myself that I have improved. But—and it is difficult for me to admit this—I believe *you* are the right person, not I. So, why are you not leading this mission, Major Tapper?"

Oof. It was the question Harry really didn't want to discuss with anyone, especially Korelon. He knew his only answer was a tangled mess of rationalizations, anger, resentment, and loss.

It will only complicate things to be open with anyone. Defer any answer.

Screw this guy, tell him it's none of his damn business!

"That's a complicated question, Major Korelon."

"Not so complicated, Major," the RockHound said, acknowledging a salute from a technician, who hurried past. "My Legate shared a record of your time on the surface of R'Bak. Clearly you are no coward. You belonged to an elite group on your home planet, so it is clear you should be accustomed to the pressure and stress of command."

Harry didn't answer and resumed walking. Korelon kept pace as they continued their circumnavigation.

"There is an additional point," Korelon said after a few more minutes. "I think you may not be aware of it. I did not purely volunteer for this mission, Major. It was suggested—strongly suggested—to me that I do so."

"Then why did you come at all, Major?" Harry asked, both glad the earlier question had been left behind and surprised at this level of candor from someone who had previously cultivated an air of superiority and a barrier of silence.

"You are aware we RockHounds are considered insular, yes?" Korelon asked with a narrow glance at Harry. "We do not permit many visitors to our stations, and we treat others differently from how we treat each other. Our senior ranks appear to enjoy privileges inaccessible to the lower ranks."

"Yes," Harry answered, turning a bit to fit his shoulders through a now familiar narrow bit in the corridor. Everyone knew about the RockHounds and their stiff attitudes. It was part of the reason it was so easy to both dislike and distrust them as new and unproven allies.

"The reason is trust."

Almost like he can read my fricking mind.

"Our senior ranks are different. We take an oath to be responsible not just for ourselves or our caste, but for the entirety of the Family. We make the survival of the Family our personal responsibility. This means all 'va, all of the Hounds who are born to the blood, are ready to place themselves between the heart of the Family and vacuum, and do so willingly, in order that the Family survive. I trust other 'va to do this, and they trust me, regardless of whether I agree with a particular strategy or a tactic. Legate Orgunz has decided to accept your colonel's mad scheme, and so my disagreement is no longer relevant. I was shamed when I understood I had somehow forgotten this. My Legate, representing all the RockHound Families, reminded me. *That* is why I am here. There is only the Family. So, I ask you, Major Tapper, where is *your* Family?"

PART FOUR

Chapter Twenty-Six

"Down!" Moose hissed.

For once, Chalmers did what he was told. Of course, some of his compliance was the result of Moose's off-hand wrapping itself around the nape of his neck and shoving him into a shambling, hunched run across the tiles of the market square.

Gunfire rattled from behind them, punctuated by the sound of rounds crackling against stone.

Jackson was already well ahead of Chalmers, sliding the last few steps to halt in the dubious shelter of the large fountain dominating the center of the square.

Chalmers glimpsed Moose aiming the fifteen-millimeter pistol he preferred back the way they'd come. Despite being aware it was coming, Chalmers still jumped as Moose's weapon barked, then barked again.

Chalmers fled in a crouch that, within a few panicked strides, fetched him up next to Jackson in the lee of the fountain's basin. Moose followed after, slow and precise with each shot, letting the big pistol fall back on target before squeezing off the next round as he marched in their wake.

He looked from the big shooter to his partner. Jackson's light pistol, a local-made job he and Chalmers carried to better fit in, had appeared in his hand.

Chalmers pulled his own pistol, wishing he'd spent more time with it at the range.

"Fucking Vat! 'Fangat won't dare strike at us,' he says!" Jackson snarled, firing at the men on the east side of the square. Men whose faces were painted in the gray-barred blue of the Fangat Brokerage.

At least no bystanders were going to get plugged. No one who did not absolutely have to be was out and about at noon on R'Bak during the Searing. Chalmers wouldn't have been, either, if there hadn't been a minor emergency at the arena. They'd been on their way home from putting out that fire when Moose had seen the armed men approaching. Which was, on reflection, probably part of the trap that had been laid for them.

Chalmers discarded thoughts of how the trap had been set up in favor of getting free of it. He looked around, assessing their situation. They were just over two blocks west of the Twin Stars offices. Things would be over long before any help could arrive from that quarter. The square was about thirty meters on a side, with the fountain sheltering them in the middle. The ambusher's plan appeared to have been well timed to isolate the Lost Soldiers, but they appeared to have traded isolating their victims for allowing their prey access to cover. Unless... He glanced over the rim of the fountain. The men who had triggered the ambush were no longer advancing; they were now either trying to find cover along the edges of the square or already in it. Chalmers turned, put his back to the fountain, and looked up just as a pair of armed men rose from the roofline.

"Fuck! Six, high!" he shouted, raising his pistol. It was a long, shitty shot at this range, one Chalmers didn't think he could make on a good day. He banged a couple rounds that way anyway, just to keep them honest.

One figure ducked, overbalanced, slid on the tile rooftop, and fell, arms windmilling. A brief, wordless scream was cut short when his head made its inevitable, heavy, wet crunch into hot stone tiles. The dead man's gun hit the tiles stock-first an instant later. Something must have broken in the firing mechanism on impact, because the gun discharged uselessly into the white-hot sky.

"Nice!" Moose thumped down against the wall of the fountain next to him, reloading. "Keep 'em thinking about their skin, snake!"

Unsure why Moose was calling him a snake, Chalmers nodded and squeezed two more rounds at the remaining guy above them. He didn't hit a damn thing. The ten-millimeter light pistols carried more rounds than the bigger fifteen-millimeter that Moose carried, but the barrel length of both weapons made for shit accuracy at this range.

Jackson's pistol crack-cracked, hammering his eardrums. Wincing, a distracted Chalmers couldn't help but grin as Moose moved. The big man looked a little ridiculous crab-walking below Chalmers's extended arms and around Jackson's back to take up a position opposite where he'd taken cover.

"When I pop up and fire, move to the plants over there, copy?" Moose's shouted English was accompanied by a gesture of his free hand toward the narrow road that entered the west side of the square.

Chalmers looked and saw a big planter box about a third of the way between their present position and the road that let off the square. Part of a border for the nighttime seating area of a café in that side of the square, the plants rising from it had definitely seen better days.

"Copy!" the partners shouted.

Water splashed on Chalmers's shoulder as bullets were swallowed in the basin behind him. He looked up to see the guy on the rooftop standing to get a better angle on the three Lost Soldiers below. Chalmers aimed, fired. The shooter flinched behind some ornamental stonework.

"Red!" Jackson shouted, dropping into full cover to reload.

Chalmers shot again at the man above, turned on his shoulder, and, not even bothering to aim, sent a few rounds in the general direction of the men on the far side of the square.

"Up!" Jackson shouted, shooting again as Chalmers's slide racked back and stayed there.

"Red!" Chalmers yelled, fumbling for the magazine next to his holster.

"Go! Go! Go!" Moose said in nearly the same instant, rising from his position and resuming his almost metronomic fire.

Someone screamed at the other end of the square.

Jackson popped a few off at the man on the roof and started toward the dubious safety of the planter.

"Fuck!" Chalmers gasped, staggering to his feet. He stumbled along in Jackson's wake, trying to jam the fresh magazine home in his weapon and screaming silently at the device, wondering why *the fuck* it wouldn't succumb to the desperate power of his need. Belatedly realizing he wasn't using the Beretta he'd trained on for years, he finally found the magazine release a finger's breadth up from where it should be. He dumped the spent mag with a metallic clatter and slapped the fresh one home. He was just looking up when something slewed him around by his belt and tossed him into the cover of the planter box.

"Scratch one," Moose growled as another scream sounded.

Chalmers looked up, saw Moose standing over him, firing again. The man had somehow seen Chalmers was out of it, dragged him back and pushed him to cover, all without losing track of—or missing—his target.

Jackson was shooting back the way they'd come, too. "One mag left."

"One here," Moose said. "And then my holdout."

"I've got...the one in my gun," Chalmers said, watching the roofline. The Lost Soldiers had moved closer to that side of the square. With any luck, it would force the shooter up there to stand and expose more of himself to get an angle on them.

"Cover me," Moose said, taking a knee to reload.

Chalmers turned and, seeing movement, cracked a few shots at a man charging toward the fountain they'd abandoned. The guy went down with an angry cry, though Chalmers didn't think he'd scored a hit. He wasn't happy with that result. The charging man meant that group was advancing again. Probably because the rooftop men had failed to put rounds in Chalmers and friends and end the fight.

Chalmers's shots must have gotten the attention of the man's companions, because the desiccated growths rising from the planter above it started shivering as bullets whickered through dried-out fronds and whacked into trunks. Pottery shattered as bullets clattered into, and through, the far side of the planter.

Chalmers cowered lower behind the planter and gave a silent but fervent prayer of thanks for the potter, the gardener, and every other person who might have played a part in causing the planter to be here, protecting his sinner's carcass in this moment of peril. He turned, wide-eyed, to tell Moose the good news, but he'd dropped so low that Moose's pistol, held at his own knee, was at his eye level for what happened next.

Moose's huge hand finished seating a fresh magazine and let the slide forward into battery. Looking up from the gun and hands, Chalmers saw the big veteran wasn't looking his way. Instead, Moose was looking up over one round shoulder. He followed the line of Moose's gaze and saw the rooftop shooter come into view again.

The man leaned out to draw a bead on Chalmers.

Everything slowed down. He blinked, tried to raise his own gun. It was heavier than worlds, and dragged against Chalmers's every effort to bring it into line.

Chalmers watched in slow motion as, still on one knee, still looking up at the shooter over his shoulder, Moose calmly pushed his pistol under his free arm and, muzzle barely protruding from beneath the armpit, pulled the trigger. The pistol barked, hot brass tinkling off the planter to sizzle painfully against Chalmers's cheek.

The man on the rooftop stood straight, a red strain spreading from the center of his torso. He fell, only to end up hanging by the scarf he wore as the thick fabric caught on something. His blood didn't so much drip as click, almost entirely dry before it hit the seared ground.

Moose snorted. "Never in a million years."

Late, Chalmers's own pistol barked, bullets sparking against the wall beside the swinging body.

Time seemed to unlock, wind out faster and faster, almost to normal speed again. Jackson was shooting again, the sound driving more pain into his skull.

Moose yanked Chalmers to his feet, pushed him toward the road again. The deeper bark of his pistol sounded a few more times as the partners staggered into the shade of the buildings framing the road off the square.

"Keep going," Moose panted. "They're done, for now."

They crossed the few blocks in a paranoid, blurred, sweaty rush. It was only when he cramped up in the relative shelter of the office that Chalmers realized not a one of them had complained about the heat since the shooting started.

Chapter Twenty-Seven

Exceedingly bored and a little warm, Chalmers leaned back and yawned. Things had been pretty calm since the attempted assassination a few weeks back, and he'd never found paperwork exciting. Awareness had faded into a light doze when the office door slammed open. Jackson entered and winged a message packet across the desk at him. Chalmers ducked. The packet bounced from the wall behind him and to the ground.

"What the hell?" Chalmers said.

Jackson snorted.

"Seriously, you sick bastard. What do you think it is?" Chalmers bent to pick up the packet.

"I suspect we're getting fresh orders," Jackson said. He was grinning as Chalmers sat upright from collecting the packet from the floor.

Ignoring the letter opener lost somewhere under the papers scattered on his desk, Chalmers pried the packet open with his thumbnail.

He flipped through several pages, then sorted them into the proper order. He removed the codebook—a very real technical manual on aircraft engines—from the desk and flipped it open. It took a minute and some absentminded cursing, but Chalmers eventually had the headline deciphered.

"Operation BUCKET," he read aloud. "What the hell is BUCKET?"

"Won't know till you decrypt the rest, genius."

Chalmers sat back. "I freely admit you're better at this than I am, Jacks."

"Damn straight I am, but it's your turn." He looked thoughtful a moment. "Bucket like an old car, maybe?"

"We won't know until the resident genius decodes it," Chalmers said, but he was grinning as he picked up the manual.

The grin died a quick death as he dove into decoding the rest of the message. Dimly, he noted that Jackson sat still and silent while he worked, giving his partner both time and quiet in which to work. A quiet only broken by his own occasional expletive as the new orders were slowly, painfully revealed.

"Fuck me," he breathed once he'd finished.

"What?" Jackson asked, leaning forward and trying to read upside down.

"Murphy wants us to play *Ice Pirates!*"

"What?" Jackson said.

Chalmers looked at his partner. "An SF flick. Eighty-three or f—"

"'Why'd you make him black?'" Jackson interrupted, doing a fair impression of Robert Urich.

Chalmers sat back in his chair, surprised his partner knew the movie.

"'B'cause I wanted him to be perfect,'" Jackson quoted, as if reading from a film script. "It's an immortal line for black SF fans. Roscoe was the shit. And the black robot made the movie. So, yeah, I know the fucking flick, Chalmers." He shook his head and flipped the decoded message around to read for himself. "I meant, what, specifically, does Murphy want us to do?"

"He wants us to capture a lighter intact. Preferably without alerting the rest of the port that it's been taken."

Still reading, Jackson sat back in his chair and muttered, "Not asking for much, is he?"

Chalmers grinned. "Never."

"Says here we're to rendezvous for further instruction. There's also a schedule for delivery of additional assets beginning next month . . ." Jackson let his voice trail off, shaking his head.

"And he adds that we should prepare preliminary plans for review," Chalmers finished for his partner.

Jackson let the hand holding the orders fall into his lap. "The guys are not going to be happy, being forced to leave after all the work they've put in."

"Unless we can pull it off without revealing our hand," Chalmers said, pulling his lip.

"We need Vat's thoughts on this. Where is he?" Jackson asked. He'd already forgiven Vat for underestimating the violent response of Fangat.

"Meeting with the Ghnzi," Chalmers said, lip curling. He, on the other hand, had yet to forgive the former arms dealer for underestimating the backlash from Fangat over the Broker Principle position.

"Moose with him?"

"Yeah."

"Send a messenger to ask him to come back to the office?"

"No." Chalmers shook his head. "Not that time critical, really. We can get started without him."

Jackson was looking across the papers at him, his expression showing he saw right through Chalmers's bullshit.

"I'll just send someone to make sure he comes straight here instead of the baths or his club," Jackson said in the tone that told Chalmers it wasn't up for discussion. Setting the papers on the desk, Jackson stood up and left the office.

Wanting to distract himself, Chalmers set about clearing the desk for action. That done, he bent and uncovered the floor safe containing sensitive documents. Entering the combination, he withdrew a bundle of files containing hand-drawn maps and hastily written patrol schedules. Each had been cajoled out of compromised personnel—confirmed by firsthand observation by a Lost Soldier where possible—then collated and constantly updated over months of painstaking surveillance work. He pinned each piece of the puzzle to the local version of a corkboard, and had to set up another one to take all the material. He was just finished laying it all out when Jackson returned.

Seeing their work in plain view, Jackson quickly closed the door behind himself. The brokerage employed a substantial number of local hires, and, while they were as loyal as could be expected, that particular bar was set at about knee height.

"Security is tight," Chalmers muttered, examining the most recent guard schedule for the main gate.

"And we were focused on sabotage—getting access to fuel lines and the parts depot—thinking that's what Murphy would want," Jackson said, leaning on the desk with both hands.

"Vat was right, though," Chalmers admitted grudgingly. "The Kulsians are focused on internal competition, not infiltration by outsiders hostile to their presence."

"Can you blame them? What back-country R'Baku madman could get across the ocean, then past their security—and then, what could such a relative primitive accomplish if, by some miracle, they managed a breach?"

Chalmers cocked his head. "Terror attacks?"

"And not much more."

"Yeah, this mission might be more easily accomplished than it sounds."

Jackson snorted. "You been smoking that shit you give Daroz? Last I checked, we barely qualified with space suits. I sure as hell don't know the first fucking thing about piloting a spacecraft."

"Me neither, but I gotta believe Murphy has something planned," Chalmers said.

"A SpinDog pilot?"

"Could be. Or maybe one of us Lost Soldiers underwent some special hypno-training by the Doorknobs before they bounced?"

"They're called *Dornaani*, you dick," Jackson said.

"I know that. Not like any of those assholes are around to correct me. They took off, so I figure we don't owe 'em shit." Chalmers shook his head. "What I was trying to say, before you so rudely interrupted me, was that the mission might be both easier and harder than it looks."

"How so?"

"The perimeter security is hard, sure, but once past the gates and fences almost everything is focused on keeping their own side from stealing cargo. Their measures against outsiders are almost laughable in comparison."

Jackson slowly nodded, understanding dawning in his eyes. "So they won't be on the lookout for someone trying to stow away."

Chalmers felt the hair on his arms stand up, a sure sign they were either onto something big or his thinking was entirely, even idiotically, wrong.

Only time would tell which was correct.

"Everything all right?" Vat asked upon entering the office.

Chalmers was glad to see Moose shadowing the smaller man. He waved him in as well.

"Sort of," Chalmers said, closing the door behind Moose.

"What's up?" Vat asked, glancing from Jackson's pensive expression to Chalmers's poker face as he stepped across the icebox set in the wall. There wasn't any ice in it, but rather the broken branches of a particular plant that had an intense endothermic reaction when submerged in a particular solution of water and a honey-analogue of all things.

"New orders," Chalmers said.

"So?" Vat pulled a pitcher of blespa juice from the fridge and poured himself a drink. Keeping hydrated in the growing heat was a stone bitch, even if you were only outdoors for a short while.

"So, the objective is so high-value it—or the aftermath of acquiring it—might require us to cease all other operations on the island. Indefinitely."

Vat's knuckles whitened as he clenched his fist around the glass. "What?"

Moose had to turn sideways to get by Chalmers and take the pitcher from Vat. He poured himself a glass. "Anyone else?" he offered.

"No, thanks," the partners chorused.

"Answer the question, Chief," Vat said tightly.

"I heard you," Chalmers said, intentionally omitting the other man's rank. Vat was, ostensibly, his superior, but this op was so far off the regs as to be undetectable to the naked eye. Besides, using ranks was a dead giveaway to eavesdroppers that they weren't who they appeared to be, so he was covered.

"So." Vat set his glass down on the sideboard with a dull thunk and crossed his arms. "You gonna keep us in suspense?"

Chalmers shook his head. "First, I want to tell you I want to keep going as we have almost as much as you do. I enjoy the trappings of power here, too."

"What the fuck is the target?" Vat growled.

"It's just that I know you're a little too happy here, enjoying your wealth and whatnot," Chalmers said, knowing he was winding the other man up but unable to help himself. "The challenge, that kind of thing, to your skills."

"I don't need this shit," Vat said, turning to leave.

"This about stealing the lighter?" Moose asked, looking at Jackson.

"Sure is," Jackson said, then he looked at Moose, eyes wide.

Everyone in the room turned to look at Moose, who chose that moment to chug his drink.

"You knew?" the partners chorused.

"Steal a lighter?" Vat sputtered at the same time.

"I did," Moose said to Jackson and Chalmers. "And," he continued, looking across at Vat, "yeah, it was part of the plan from the first sign of the surveyors approaching."

"Wait," Chalmers said. "Why tell you and not us?"

"Because you and Jackson might have been caught and tortured in the early days of the operation. So. Here's to that not happening." Moose lifted his glass and pretended clinking it with another. "And, if we were cut off from reaching higher, I was to inform you of the mission if a month passed absent fresh orders from on high."

"But why keep it from *me*, then?" Vat said.

Chalmers almost sneered, hearing the incredulity in Vat's voice.

"I'm not sure, but I do have a lengthy record of keeping my mouth shut and my nose clean while I *follow* orders." He looked meaningfully from Chalmers to Vat, the silent subtext clear to both: *And I don't dick around on a mission. Ever.*

Jackson shook his head. "Shit."

"Well," Vat said, "I ain't playing this go-round. Not if it means sacrificing everything I built, again."

"I?" Chalmers said. "There's no 'I' in team, buddy."

"Like you could've done this without me, you redneck fuck."

Chalmers came off the door. "Who you callin' redneck, yo—?"

"Murphy plays a damn deep game," Jackson said, loud enough that his voice cut across Chalmers's retort.

"*Has* to," Moose said, nodding.

"What's that?" Chalmers snarled.

"Murphy *has* to play hardball." Moose looked at each of the other men in turn. His normally placid expression was displeased, even angry.

"Look, the shit I did up in orbit? The stuff that made it politically expedient to send me down here? Well, it wouldn't have been necessary if the political situation up there weren't clear as mud. Right when everything was going well for us planetside, when we had the J'Stull satraps on the run, that's when the factionalism among the SpinDogs started getting murderous." He sighed. "No, that's not right. The factions became even *more* murderous then."

He shook his head. "But that's not really my point." He jabbed a finger at Chalmers and then Vat. "You two take every command in light of how it affects you, personally. Makes you feel like the decisions Murphy is making are meant to dick with you, personally. I'm here to tell you that attitude is complete bullshit, and a product of your misapprehension that the fucking universe revolves around you, gives a fucking *shit* about you, about any one of *us*. Thinking it's personal in any way is wrong. So fucking *wrong*.

"I had the opportunity to watch Murphy work up there. Every *single* decision he makes is intended to increase our collective chances of survival. Not his personal power or individual odds of survival, mind you. He could have easily secured a position of relative security for himself with the SpinDogs by using up the Lost Soldiers like so many bullets in his sidearm. He hasn't—*he won't*—do that because he's trying to ensure our survival. Not his, not mine, not any single one of us, but our *collective* survival. And in deciding to do that, he's been repeatedly forced to bet on our skills and our will to win to even the odds in a brutal, zero-sum game that we either persevere in or perish from."

A thoughtful silence fell as the big man stopped speaking.

Vat looked at his hands, face twisted as if he were in pain.

Chalmers had never been one to feel much shame, but he felt his cheeks burning under Moose's accurate assessment of his shitty attitude. What made it even more painful was that Chalmers was sure that if he were to add together the word count of every conversation Moose had taken part in since the big guy had joined them, the sum wouldn't equal half the words he'd just spoken. More than that, he'd never heard Moose express an opinion, positive or negative, on anyone in their little ersatz unit. He'd consistently presented a uniformly solid workman's attitude to getting the job before him done and a sly sense of humor that was fun, if not as edged as Chalmers's and Jackson's could be.

For the first time in a long time he thought about his vow to do better, to be better, and how he might have fallen short of that in front of his peers, especially recently.

"Still waters run deep," Jackson breathed, breaking the silence.

"That they do," Vat said, looking at Moose first and then Chalmers.

"Look, man, I shouldn't have been trying to push your buttons," Chalmers said, recognizing the moment.

"And I shouldn't have called you a redneck," Vat said.

Chalmers shrugged. "Shoe fits and all..."

"Damn, brother, you know how to cut through the bullshit." Jackson reached out and offered his hand to Moose, who clasped it, then drew the smaller man in for a rib-thumping pat on the back.

"Now we got all the bitching, moaning, hugging, and groaning out of the way, can we get on with the business at hand?" Moose asked, gesturing past Jackson at the map-and-report-littered boards.

Chapter Twenty-Eight

"Don't forget to use the code words for everyone," Jackson reminded Chalmers for what seemed like the tenth time since they landed.

"I won't, thanks." He shook his head. "The time delay'll make this a stone pain in the ass." Chalmers gestured at the communications unit's readout, which listed the current delay at thirteen minutes, thirty-seven seconds, and some change. One thing about the universe Chalmers and the other Lost Soldiers had found themselves in: some laws of physics were a lot more in the realm of *2001: A Space Odyssey* rather than *Star Wars: A New Hope*.

"It's still quicker than what we have in town. We could be filling out codes and shit back on the island and waiting weeks on the communications loop to close," Jackson said. He smiled, added quickly, "Then again, we're gonna have to inform the rest of the crew what's expected of us. I'm sure that'll be *tons* of fun."

The communications unit was SpinDog manufactured and used a tight beam antenna set in a cleft up the draw from where the bunker was sited.

Chalmers nodded, girded his loins with his robes, and sat down on one long side of the table the mic sat on. The spartan communications bunker they occupied was buried well up in the hills above the beach, concealed in a crease in the rock that would be subject to flash floods when the Searing was over, but remained dry as a bone as the Searing approached. While spartan, it was far cooler inside than out. It reminded him of trips to Vegas, the way the temperature dropped thirty degrees on entering a building. He didn't know if they kept the place cool for the people who used it or the communications gear itself. Probably the latter.

"Five gets you twenty he says 'bottom line' in the first five minutes," Chalmers said as the countdown went into single digits.

"With or without the delay?"

"Shit, wi—no, without!"

Jackson grinned. "That's a bet, Chalmers."

The comm chirped, the light indicating a connection started to glow.

Chalmers clicked the mic on. "PRIMARY is present. Coded assessment of capabilities of WORMWOOD transmitting. Parameters for BUCKET received and verified by SECONDARY. TERTIARY believes there is a window of opportunity to accomplish the mission. TERTIARY convinced PRIMARY and SECONDARY of same, but all of us agree that the mission objective is undeliverable barring additional assets." Which was an understatement. None of them had suddenly developed the skills necessary to fly—was it fly? No, operate—a damn lighter.

The comm panel chirped, additional lights indicating both the verbal and written messages had been sent.

Chalmers clicked the mic off. He kicked back, putting his thick-soled sandals up on the table while they waited for a response. Jackson did the same on the other side of the table.

Chalmers hadn't been a fan of sandals before R'Bak. Seemed they were a recipe for sunburn on some really sensitive skin. Or, worse yet, bug bites. But near the tropics of R'Bak, where the sun seemed to delight in making leather boots an oven, he'd been happy enough to ditch the uniform and don the sandals, especially since the local equivalent of walking-about clothes was either body paint for a laborer or thick, stifling robes for the merchant-gentry. The latter at least kept the feet from being exposed, and let some air circulate on them.

"Think he'll update us on Elroy?" Jacks asked, drawing Chalmers from his contemplation of footwear and proper dress codes.

Chalmers shook his head. "Doubt it. Murphy's not one to gossip, especially on a mission."

"Can you ask?"

"Of course," Chalmers said, lacing his fingers behind his head.

Jackson fixed him with a glare made less venomous by coming between their sandals across the table.

"What?" Chalmers said, hating the defensive note his voice held.

"Man, you don't get to say it like that—all cool and shit. Not with the way you were on the radio when he was on mission."

Chalmers dropped his hands, was about to defend himself when the comm went live. "PRIMARY, we applaud your team's achievements thus far. Operation BUCKET's last remaining piece, MENDACITY, will be arriving in three weeks, coordinates coded in the accompanying transmission. Bottom line, MENDACITY will make BUCKET deliverable. Caution in employment of MENDACITY advised. Please stand by as we integrate your most recent reports with other operational data and advise."

"Jesus," Jackson breathed, letting his chair thump back on four legs.

"What, pissed you lost the bet?" Chalmers said.

"No, of course not. 'Mendacity' not mean anything to you?"

"Should it?" Chalmers said, flogging his vocabulary for the term.

Jackson shook his head, wonder writ large on his features. "How you crackers ever came to rule the world, I'll never understand. Can't even be bothered to read a goddamn dictionary. Your *own* goddamn dictionary, at that."

"It's just a code word," Chalmers said, wishing Jackson would let slip what the word actually meant.

"Sure, buddy. You would think that. Mark my words, man: this bodes ill."

"Since when did you start dropping words like 'bodes'?" Chalmers asked.

"What, don't know what that one means, either?"

"Fuck you, Jacks," Chalmers said, grinning. "Sounds like whoever MENDACITY is, they'll require watching, but have the skills necessary for BUCKET?" He could see several ways that could go horribly wrong, up to and including acting like they were with the program right up until the lighter was taken, then betraying the whole operation to the surveyors.

"Right . . . a SpinDog?"

"Can't think of anyone else with the necessary skills."

"Someone from the wrong side of the recent unpleasantness Moose was talking about?"

"Must be . . . shit, we don't know, and won't even have a chance to formulate our opinion until the fucker arrives." He glanced over at the coordinates the tech had up on his screen. "At least we'll be picking them up at Fibberzs Bay on the way to Kanjoor. Convenient, if long, flight path."

"That's great. Just great," Jackson groused.

"What?"

Jackson shook his head. "Crack a goddamn dictionary, would you?"

"What?"

"We'll be picking up a guy code-named 'lying' at a place that translates into English, phonetically, as 'Little Liar's Bay'!"

"Shit," Chalmers said, connecting the dots between the words now that Jackson had painted the lines clearly. "When you put it that way, it really does sound bad. Think Murph is trying to tell us something?"

"Ya think?"

Chalmers thought about that and his obligation to promises already made. Deciding on how to word what he was about to say, he set his sandals on the floor and keyed the mic.

"We will pay close attention to MENDACITY to ensure success of BUCKET. While we wait for you to digest reports regarding BUCKET, PRIMARY wants to know if THE KING has recovered."

"THE KING?" Jackson said.

"Now who's showing his ignorance?"

Jackson grimaced, flipped Chalmers the bird.

"Pretty sure Elroy means 'the king' in French. Creole or something."

"No shit?"

"No shit," Chalmers said. After a minute staring at the comm, he got up, made himself a drink, and spent a few minutes watching the readout as the data Murphy was sending trickled in. Unable to make sense of it without more and better context, he took his sweet time returning to his seat, just to find that only a couple minutes had passed. He sighed and mumbled, "This is the worst."

"Nope. Still better than manually coding shit," Jackson said, leaning back in his chair again.

Chalmers pretended to toss that idea in the shitter, even flushed after.

Jackson grinned. "Thanks for asking, Chalmers."

"No sweat, man. I hope he's better."

They waited in a more comfortable silence. The large fan that served the bunker's heat pump kicked on. The air grew noticeably cooler. Chalmers savored the sweet cool air across his toes.

The comm clicked on. "THE KING is doing better than expected, but still has to defeat a few rebels," Murphy said. "We will reestablish contact in eighteen hours with further direction in light of WORMWOOD success and possible targets for BUCKET. End transmission."

"Since we're here another day, want to get the rods out? See if we can't catch something edible for dinner?"

"Probably won't be able to eat most of what we might catch, but sure." Chalmers shrugged, dreading the heat, but content to be doing anything other than stressing over what was to come.

"He doesn't look special," Umaren said, voice pitched to carry over the roar of the engines as the seaplane turned to shore and the dock.

Chalmers, crammed into the space between the pilot and copilot, and trying not to hit anything important, squinted at the figure emerging from the trees on the foreshore. Unable to make out dick for details and unwilling to admit it, he simply nodded at the pilot and stepped back into the small gangway between cockpit and cargo bay.

Now that the plane was plowing through the water, the late afternoon suns began to heat her interior faster than the cooling system could rid the hull of heat. Chalmers was sheathed in sweat by the time he'd eased his way past some of the goods they'd picked up in Kanjoor and made it to the water cargo hatch. He plugged his headset into the intercom system and opened the small porthole set in the cargo hatch. Hot, humid air began to puff into the seaplane. It didn't do much to cool him off, even standing in front of the opening.

"Man, it's fucking hot! Crack a window, Umaren!" Chalmers barked.

"Wouldn't have to if you hadn't insisted on stripping her biggest cooling units to make room for your contraband!" Umaren snapped.

"Contraband that's made you wealthy beyond your wildest dreams," he said, sweating. The words were Umaren's own, or close enough. The pilot and his partner had appeared at a Twin

Stars soirée in Liberace-level outfits. When asked to tone it down
a bit, Umaren had claimed such conspicuous display was necessary to convey their undreamed-of level of success.

He felt a strong draft of—if not cool, then at least fast-
moving—air as the pilot opened one of the cockpit windows.

"Thank you, Umaren," he said with heartfelt sincerity.

Chalmers spent the next few minutes twisting and turning to
cool various body parts in the artificial breeze. That had to stop
when Umaren slowed the seaplane even further for the final few
yards to the docks. The heat quickly rose to sweltering again, but,
not wanting to flood the plane with an errant wave, Chalmers
waited for the command from Umaren to unbutton.

"Make secure," Umaren said a sweaty minute later.

Chalmers undogged the hatch and pushed the upper half up
just as they pulled alongside the dock. He reached out and cast
a line across a convenient bollard, making the toss the first time,
despite the prop wash. He smiled. He'd never have been so good
with a rope just six months past. Hell, he'd not known a tenth of
the nautical and aviation vocabulary—in English or R'Bakuun—he
used on a weekly basis when they'd started this op.

"Starboard roped," he said.

"Bow roped," Vizzel reported from the bow hatch, just forward of the cockpit.

"Secure," Umaren said. A moment later the engines died,
props slowly spinning to a halt.

In the relative silence that descended, heat expansion summoned the occasional ping from the upper hull, a counterpoint
to the gentle lapping of wavelets on the lower hull.

Chalmers looked at the shore. The vegetation that ringed the
lagoon had thinned, grown ragged and dry, offering far less foliage
than just a few weeks ago. It looked a little like some Vietnam-era
photos he'd seen of stretches of jungle hit with Agent Orange.

Taking a long pull of water from his canteen, Chalmers dropped
the lower half of the hatch to rest on the dock. He returned the canteen to his belt. The blaze of snow-white paint covering the interior
of the hatch was blinding in the light. He blinked and walked off
the seaplane onto the dock. Standing still in direct sunlight was
brutal, but it was so hot he might pass out if he exerted himself more
than maintaining a slow walk. He looked longingly at the lagoon,
but knew it wouldn't be much of a relief, either. The shallow water

wasn't that much cooler than the air here along the border of the
tropics. Besides, seawater would melt the paint protecting his skin
faster than sweat and he couldn't afford the sunburn two minutes
of direct sunlight would give him if his protective coating thinned,
let alone washed off completely. He had a growing hotfoot going
by the time he cleared the dock and approached the man standing
among the native vegetation.

As instructed, the paint on Mendacity was plain white, ready
for Umaren to embellish with crew markings. The paint also
made it hard to tell what the guy looked like beyond the even
facial features and hard golden eyes. That took Chalmers aback
a moment. Upon reading the section of Murphy's file describing
the man's eye color, Chalmers had assumed an error. But no, the
man's eyes were really gold. They also had that hard edge Chalmers had learned to associate with people who'd been in the shit
a little too often and left there a little too long for safety's sake.

Chalmers came to a stop a few feet from the other man. He
did not extend a hand, and waited for Mendacity to speak first,
reflecting that the mind games these people played on meeting
one another for the first time were far less "sniff the other dog's
ass" as "must show them who's boss from the get-go."

A brief hesitation, then the man spoke. "I am Yukannak. You
are Chalmers?"

"I am."

A deep bow. "I am at your service."

"I have your word on that?" Chalmers said, watching the other
man's painted face very closely. According to his file, he was a
renegade Kulsian who had played both ends against the middle
quite smoothly in the recent past, and, while Chalmers admired
a good player as much as the next guy, it was his ass if Yukannak decided he could score a better deal with the opposition in
the next few weeks.

"I have given my word to your Colonel Murphy," the man
said. "I give it to you."

Good poker face, Chalmers thought.

"You have sworn on your House," he said, sticking to the
script Murphy had given him and Moose had vetted, "but I find
I must wonder aloud whether that oath is binding on one so
distant from the wellspring of his honor..."

The man's lip curled slightly before he got it under control. "I have no House. I have no other path to a life than that which you and yours offer. I am entirely at your mercy. I live only because your Murphy wills it. The . . . others we were with would have executed me once they were done interrogating me."

Chalmers noted the care with which the man spoke. Mentioning the SpinDogs by name was a tell he'd been told to watch for.

"And still might do, if you show the least sign of betraying us." Chalmers could play the heavy. Hell, he might even carry through on the threat if his life or Jackson's were threatened.

Yukannak's expression didn't change one iota as he bowed once more.

It made Chalmers nervous, not knowing what the hell the man was thinking. Murphy's file said the guy was *fully* vetted. Murphy's file said Yukannak could probably be relied on for the duration of the mission. Every instinct Chalmers had screamed Yukannak was anything but reliable. But he'd learned from recent misadventures that his instincts could be less than perfect.

Shit, the Mog had taught him that much.

"You have more baggage?" Chalmers asked, putting his misgivings away for the time being.

"Only a few items deemed necessary for the mission." Yukannak gestured at a duffel a few paces deeper in the shadows of the native vegetation.

Chalmers gestured at the additional bag resting at the man's feet. "Drop pod must have been cramped."

A slight smile. "Very. Very cramped."

Chalmers bent to pick up the duffel at their feet, nearly colliding with Yukannak when the man reached for it as well.

A tiny grunt of pain issued from the other man's lips, despite a lack of contact between them.

"You all right?" Chalmers asked.

Yukannak snatched the bag up. "Some bruising from the drop, but nothing to worry about."

Chalmers shrugged and went to get the other duffel. "You can tell me about it on the flight. The sooner we're airborne, the sooner we're out of this hot hell."

Chapter Twenty-Nine

"There you are," Chalmers said, examining the surveillance records tracking the shift sergeant's movement. Every other guy on the downport's security shift had been relatively easy to bribe or blackmail. Not Sergeant Siggun. He was simply not going along with the program, and it had to be third shift. The other shifts were either not in the proper places or would leave the team too exposed to observation from other patrols and checkpoints.

"Options?" he said, stepping back from the notice boards they used to display the various notes and surveillance records for collective review and planning. It was a security risk, but Chalmers wanted input, and this was the best way to get it. They'd lock everything up once they were done, and the staff had already been sent home.

"Liquidate him?" Moose asked, pinning Yukannak's assessment of the survey lighter crew schedule to the board in front of him. He nearly bumped into Jackson as he stood up. The meeting room was crowded between the notice boards, the Lost Soldiers, and Yukannak.

"Jesus," Jackson said, shaking his head. "This ain't the 'Nam, man."

"What, it's an opti—" Moose started.

Chalmers interrupted, "I'd like to do this without smoking too many people. That kind of mayhem will leave a trail we don't want."

"What do we know about him?" Vat asked.

"He doesn't gamble, doesn't visit the happy houses, and isn't in debt to anyone on R'Bak. He does two things aside from eat, sleep, and work: read and hit the gym."

Vat looked thoughtful. "What kind of gym?"

"Not sure," Chalmers said. He glanced at the record again but caught Yukannak's puzzled expression.

"What is it, Yukannak?"

"The question is strange to me."

"What question?"

"There is only one kind of gymnasium on Kulsis."

"Oh?"

"Thega-Tak."

"And what's that when it's at home?" Chalmers asked.

"Their premiere school of unarmed and melee close quarters combat," Vat explained before Yukannak could answer. "From what I've heard at the fights, it's similar to the fighting style we see in the arenas here on the island, but focused on disarming, disabling, and ending resistance as quickly as possible."

"What, you don't lift weights, run, jazzercise?" Chalmers asked.

"What is 'jazzercise'?" Yukannak asked.

Chalmers shook his head and smiled. "An ancient form of exercise."

"We do other things than this jazzercise in order to build strength and endurance for military operations or Thega-Tak rites."

"Can we pay someone to put him down for a while in the gym, then?" Jackson asked. "Break an arm or something? Engineer some kind of training accident?"

"Hell, get him into the arena and see how he fares?" Chalmers queried, looking at Vat.

"No one from the survey crew fights in the arena," Vat said, looking at Yukannak. "Something about 'pretend fights' being beneath them."

Yukannak nodded. "We do not expose to those beneath us those techniques we may someday be called on to deploy against them. This is especially true of those entrusted with command of those outside their own houses."

"How very... *Übermensch* of your people," Jackson said.

Moose and Chalmers both snorted.

Yukannak must have decided he didn't want to know, because

he went on without addressing the comment, "Also, not every survey member is ... fully proficient in the techniques, and their participation in such fights might prove an embarrassment to the leadership. I have only recently begun rebuilding my strength, and not every Kulsian has the drive to improve their skill as I do."

Chalmers let that go, thinking that gym rats were the same everywhere and everywhen.

"Do they spar?" Jackson asked. He'd always been more into martial arts than Chalmers.

"Of course."

"So we can set up something where he gets hurt in training?" Jackson insisted.

Yukannak cocked his head. "Perhaps. This man seems very serious in his training regimen, however. That could make it hard to find someone to accomplish your ends."

"Still, it's a better option than attempting to cover up his killing, no?"

A slow nod. "I believe so, given mission parameters. But I think it will be hard to accomplish with local talent. These people are not exactly the best representatives of strong breeding. They are ... inferior."

Chalmers saw the quickly hidden disgust in Jackson's expression as the Lost Soldier asked, "Right, so what do you suggest?"

A small shrug. "I have no suggestions. Only cautions."

"Why not just put something in his drink?" Moose asked.

"They all carry canteens around," Chalmers mused, liking the idea.

"Canteens they do not bring onto the fighting floor," Yukannak added, nodding.

Jackson was smiling. "One problem down?"

Chalmers looked at the others. Seeing no objections, he nodded.

"All right. So let's assume everything else worked, and we've made it onboard. How do we take control without busting up the place?" Jackson said.

"That's the sixty-four-thousand-dollar question," Moose said, nodding.

Jackson and Chalmers both looked at Moose, but it was Chalmers who said, "I've heard of the million-dollar question, but that's an oddly specific amount."

Moose shrugged. "A game show from when I was a kid."

Chalmers smiled. "I keep forgetting we're all time travelers here."

Yukannak frowned. "I am not. I may not know what a dollar is, but we have to avoid shooting on the bridge or anywhere aboard. Gunfire in any pressurized environment is suicide. You are not trained to fight in microgravity. You will get in each other's way and injure yourselves. And that is assuming you can get to the crew without being detected and then murdered in whatever spot you manage to stow away in. If the crew are the least bit competent and conscious—"

"It's a shit show, we know," Chalmers interrupted, barely keeping his anger in check. He didn't need reminding, the guys didn't need reminding, and he didn't like Yukannak doing the reminding. Not one bit.

"I don't understand your anger. I merely point out facts relevant to your plan of actions."

"Thanks, Captain Obvious," Jackson said.

Chalmers bit his lip to keep from piling on. He really did not like the Kulsian.

"I am not a captain," Yukannak said, gold eyes slitted as he stared back at Jackson.

"No, you're not. You're our pilot," Moose said with a meaningful glance at Chalmers.

Intercede, man! the look begged.

"Moose is right, Yukannak," Chalmers said, careful to keep the reluctance from his voice. "You're our best bet." Chalmers could see Jackson swallowing against gut-level dislike. He continued to speak to Yukannak, looking for the words that would mollify the new man. "And we need your help planning this. Forgive us, as we're very informal in our speech, and find it easy to misunderstand your words just as you find it easy to misunderstand ours. No offense is intended."

Yukannak blinked cold gold eyes. "None taken."

And if I believe that, smack my papa for raisin' a sucker, Chalmers thought, but, very carefully, did not say.

The heat pump kicked on again, even though it was well after sunsdown. It was still well into the hundreds outside the climate-controlled homes and businesses of the island. A grateful Chalmers made another blespa and rum-analogue. He and Vat had been drinking hard for—he squinted at the office clock—a couple of hours, now. Everyone else had gone off to bed as the nightly skull session wound down, but Chalmers had been banging his head against the problem for so long he felt the need to get a little fucked up and forget for a moment how much was riding on their success or failure.

Also, late at night was the only time he felt comfortable enough to really think, now that the fast-approaching Searing was making the equator a sunbaked hell. Even the evenings were hot enough to broil the brains, given that the humidity off the water retained a lot of the day's heat when the winds didn't blow.

But the approach of the Searing wasn't his problem. The problems he had were hard enough as it was: how to stow away aboard a lighter, then take that same lighter's crew down in a cramped, pressurized environment—in microgravity, no less— and without giving them a chance to radio for help or breaking important shit like the ship's controls.

"No matter how many firewalls and cutouts I use to hide my involvement with you guys, I'm still not sure I'll be able to stay here after you've gone," Vat said, drawing Chalmers from yet another go-round with the problems the mission posed.

Glad of the distraction, Chalmers nodded. "I'm sorry about that." He offered Vat his freshly made drink. "I wasn't clear on why—aside from the money and position—you wanted to stay."

Vat accepted the glass with a wry smile. "I've got a kid."

Chalmers was so surprised he spilled some rum-analogue as he poured a fresh glass for himself. He set the bottle down and picked up the pitcher of iced juice. It held enough ice-cold blespa for maybe one more round.

"But..." he mumbled.

Vat pointed at the floor with one hand. "Here, not back when."

"But..." Chalmers repeated. Vat's answer hadn't exactly clarified matters.

"But I'm gay?" Vat finished.

Chalmers nodded, then drank off a good portion of his glass.

"I am." Vat's smile grew mischievous. "I like men. But desperate times and all that..."

"Desperate ti—" Chalmers snorted.

"Not like that." Vat interrupted. "Not me that was desperate. Just that the local ladies are pretty damn insistent when it comes to making babies with successful fighters . . . one of 'em, she made it clear I was the donor she wanted." He shook his head. "Not that my reputation ain't a bit overblown." He took a long drink. "Besides, I'm young enough that if you stimulate the equipment in the right way things happen, regardless of where the mind wants to go . . ."

Chalmers snorted into his drink. He'd enjoyed the advances of a few women since Clarthu, and they'd all been quite clear about what they wanted—and didn't—from him.

"Regardless, the kid exists. And you know the fucked-up thing?" Vat's words were quite slurred now.

"No?"

"The fucked-up thing is, I want to see him grow up. I want to be there for it. Teach him the shit he needs to know 'bout life."

"Makes s—"

Vat interrupted him again, slurring through another realization, "Christ on a crutch, I want to be a dad, not a daddy."

"Right, man," Chalmers said, uncomfortable. "Jesus, I didn't need to know *that.*"

"What, that I'm a daddy, or that I used to want to be a *daddy*?" Vat said. Chalmers saw the man's grin had grown a bit green around the gills.

"Either? Both?"

"Ah, fuck you, Chalmers," Vat said without heat.

Chalmers chuckled, took another drink.

Vat hiccupped, belched wetly, and scratched under his robe. "Hell, why not both daddy *and* dad?"

Chalmers looked at Vat, decided the other man was definitely not getting another drink.

A brief silence fell. Chalmers started thinking about how to take advantage of the firsthand knowledge Yukannak had shared. It might not prove useful, but Chalmers thought it over anyway. None of them had known, for instance, that whatever space was left over in a given lighter crew's supply container, was, by tradition, open to freight whatever cargo the crew saw fit to carry. Not on every run, but on missions marked "survey" they were.

He looked through the paperwork, stopping at the shipping schedule they'd bought yesterday. Two weeks of lighter shipping. One "survey" lighter scheduled for the end of next week. Flight 1517B. The crew consumables container for it would not be ready yet.

"I-I think I might have had too much to drink..."

Hooking it with one leg, Chalmers pushed the trash can across the floor.

Vat turned his head, threw up in the can.

Mostly in the can.

"This is awesome. So. Damn. Awesome," Chalmers said, toasting God, the gods, the Holy Spirit, aliens, humans-who-looked-like-us, whatever. They sure knew how to dick with one Warrant Officer Chalmers.

It wasn't until he was helping the other man into bed that things started clicking into place behind his eyes. One thought led to another to another and then *bang!*

At first Chalmers sat in the high, narrow hall outside Vat's room, thinking. After an hour or so, he believed he might have figured out how to disable the flight crew. He got up, unsteady at first, and tried the idea out as he paced the halls. He tried to run down all the angles, searching for flaws, playing devil's advocate. Only when he was reasonably sure he had a plan that might work did he wake Jackson and run it by him.

Jackson wiped sleep from his eyes, shook his head. "I'll want you to run all that by me again, once I've had something to wake my ass up."

"Fuck you, I haven't even slept."

Jackson stretched. "And that's my fault, how?"

"It ain't," Chalmers said, tired in his bones. And not just because of the long night. He was tired of the constant tension. Of the not knowing—no, that wasn't accurate; it was the actual *caring* about—who would get hurt. And not just by his actions, but by his failures.

Say one thing about old Chalmers: he'd always felt he had so few options, so little room to maneuver, such limited time between crises, and so much on the line that giving a shit about what his actions might do to other people never really entered into his calculations.

That wasn't the case anymore. Not by a long shot.

"I need you to tell me it's okay. That I ain't fucking up. Again."

Jackson was quiet for what seemed like a long time after that.

"I'm fucked, right?" Chalmers said when he couldn't take the suspense any longer.

"Shit, no," Jackson said, holding Chalmers's gaze. "Best I could come up with was to put a bullet in the head of each crewman. In microgravity. With—much as I hate admitting it—a bunch of vital electronics we can't afford the least bit of damage to as the backdrop for our shooting."

Chalmers looked away. "Might still have to, something goes wrong."

"Yeah, but none of us are what you'd call a cold-blooded assassin."

"Right, but still . . ."

Jackson cocked his head. "It'll be a lot easier on my conscience knowing we tried to avoid killing noncombatants."

"Are they really noncombatants, though?"

Jackson sniffed. "These supremacist fucks still look at everyone else as their inferiors. Subhumans. Not people. That sort gets what's coming to 'em in my book."

"Couple of ferry pilots hardly constitute the Waffen SS, though."

"No, but all that is required for evil to prevail—"

"—is for good men to do nothing," Chalmers finished.

"And these assholes have been doing a lot more than nothing to ensure the continuance of Kulsis' dominion over R'Bak. So, yeah, push comes to shove, I'll do what's necessary." He looked at Chalmers again. "We all will."

Chapter Thirty

"Now you've heard the full reason for this operation and understand just how many moving parts are already in motion, the following briefing will outline the full mission profile rehearsal for this team's primary responsibility: the seizure of the Kulsian corvette," Harry said, addressing the packed equipment locker. Much space was taken up by a large rectangular habitat module. "This will be our final rehearsal at this scale. Our timetable has accelerated. The seizure of a Kulsian lighter at the downport could be happening even as we speak.

"That lighter's your ride to the briefed target. We've spent weeks rehearsing each part of the operation, mastering the steps individually. The technicians who rode the pressurized mock-up of the target corvette were still busting their hump working through last night, making last-minute changes in order to conform as closely as possible to what is known of the actual target. Now, for the first time, you'll assemble everything you've practiced, using live weapons and demolitions on the best target we can provide."

In front of him, the three squads stood in groups of six. All suits had been modified to be the same color of mottled gray-white. There had been some argument about the color selection. While black might blend better against an empty background during EVA, two of the teams would be hiding on the hull of the lighter during the final approach, and darker colors provided an unhelpful—which was to say, a potentially unsurvivable—amount of contrast against the background of the reflective hull. Some of the spray-on elastomer used to re-tint the equipment was peeling, giving the suits a leprous appearance. Harry hoped the color would remain uniform. In the confused mess of a boarding action, the assault team had to be able to distinguish between a Kulsian and a comrade at a glance.

"You've heard me preach this over and over," he continued, "so I'll say it again: Surprise is our biggest advantage. The Kulsian crew will believe they're on a rescue mission, so we expect them to match vectors with our ship and affix an umbilical to the lighter. Once that is done, Bravo will assault from inside the captured lighter, charging across the docking tube. Simultaneously, Alpha and Charlie will EVA to the enemy hull, force an exterior lock, and storm the ship before they can escape. If they jettison the umbilical, you'll still have overwhelming force already on their hull. Soon thereafter, Alpha and Charlie will be stealing their ship out from under them."

Harry put his hands on his hips and let the smile slide off his face.

"This isn't a safe evolution," he said, staring hard at each man in turn. "Space is a hard, unforgiving bitch. We don't have time to waste. We've been informed of our launch window, and if this rehearsal is successful, the next step will be to board ship and move toward our rendezvous point. We've got one shot at this rehearsal. There's a fine line between good training that embraces a certain amount of risk and lethal stupidity born of mistakes."

A few suits creaked as their owners imperceptibly shifted their weight in an otherwise quiet space.

"Major Makarov, what's the best way to take a ship that is already performing a boarding action itself?" Harry asked the Alpha squad leader and overall mission commander. Makarov had caught a promotion while in isolation. Harry wasn't sure what Murphy had been thinking by providing that level of distraction, but it had seemed to perk up the Russian.

"Simultaneously, from two directions," Makarov answered crisply. "And from two environments, both pressure and vacuum."

"Correct," Harry said. "You'll need to split the attention of the defenders and avoid fighting your way into a single chokepoint." He turned to his next victim. "What's the most critical action of the first step of the boarding, Sergeant Rodriguez?"

"To gain access to the inside of the target hull with all dispatch, sir!" the sergeant barked loudly.

"Also correct," Harry said, eyeing the Bravo team leader to see if he was cracking wise. The man wasn't known for his military courtesy, after all. "Once inside their hull, we can move to the next priority action. Major Korelon, what would that be?"

"Render the crew incapable of either scuttling the ship or making emergency communications," Korelon replied neutrally.

"You're on a roll, gentlemen," Harry said. "Once inside, the top priority must be the neutralization of the crew. There're too many ways they can damage or destroy their own ship once they understand what's happening. For that matter, you'll exercise the strictest fire discipline and avoid all unnecessary damage to the corvette."

Harry looked at the class, then at the diminutive bald sergeant in the front row. "Final question, Sergeant Pham. What's the key to a successful boarding?"

"Speed and violence of action, Major Tapper," Pham answered steadily. "No hesitation. Get inside the span of their arms, grab them by the belt, and don't let go. Kill from touching distance. Leave none alive to tell the tale."

"Exactly right, Sergeant Pham. All right, you know the drill. Seal your helmets, stand by to pump down, and let's do this!" Harry ordered. He turned to the intercom panel and detached the corded mic. "All hands, this is Trainer Six. We're starting the full mission profile at this time."

It would've been much more dramatic if they could have actually begun as soon as the briefing was over. However, just like every other exercise Harry had experienced in the bad old days, there were a seemingly interminable number of steps, most of which were safety-checklist related. Over the howling objections of the outpost commander, Harry's teams were carrying live weapons and demolitions inside the base. More unthinkable still, the Lost Soldiers had been cleared to use them in the final, free-space drill to be conducted within spitting distance of his precious station. The remaining outpost crew plus the team's own techs were sequestered as far from the exercise areas as possible. Harry had actually considered evacuating the entire station, but the dislocated personnel would've had to go somewhere, and the conjecture so generated would have been far worse than angering a single station CO.

Finally, after more than forty minutes of radio calls and checklists, the final all clear was given. "All teams, green light," Harry announced over the radio channel. "Major Makarov, you may start when ready."

"Roger," Makarov quickly answered. "Alpha, initiate as briefed. Confirm when engaged."

Harry leaned back in his seat to watch the screens. Everything should, *should* go like clockwork.

Of course, this was training, so several trade-offs had been necessary. They didn't actually have a ship to board, only the shell of a hull that could barely retain atmosphere. It was lightly tethered to the station's rocky exterior by the battered remains of a conventional ship-to-ship umbilical. Worse, the intelligence on the configuration of the corvette was incomplete. Among the many sticking points Harry had listed during his sessions with Colonel Murphy was the lack of solid intel. To say the lack of deck schematics was suboptimal when practicing a boarding action was akin to describing the RockHound beer-analogue as a bit unpleasant.

Still, the Dogs had made some educated guesses. The target simulated the Kulsian corvette as closely as could be estimated and included such details as corridors, locks, and tankage, but the key components of the ship were pure guesswork. Many empty, blocky objects were scattered inside the hull and covered in oversize signs with cheery legends such as DRIVE: MAY DETONATE IF FIRED UPON!, ARMORY, WILL DEFINITELY DETONATE!, and RAD HAZARD, DO NOT APPROACH! The cost in metal to build the shape had been considerable, and both the SpinDogs and RockHounds had impressed on Harry the need to recycle everything.

Harry was reasonably content with the personnel situation. Maintaining tight tactical command during a quick-and-dirty close quarters fight was unrealistic. He'd really meant it when he'd said all Makarov had to do was get the teams aboard and let them do their thing. Surprise, speed, and numbers would overcome any reasonable defense the crew could muster once the boarders got inside the ship.

All Harry had signed up for was to get them ready. And now it was done. Easy peasy.

Makarov understood the constraints of the exercise. In charge of the main effort to seize the corvette, he and Alpha were already outside the station, staying in close proximity to Korelon's Charlie squad. Rodriguez, leading—or as he liked to call it, *herding*—Bravo, was waiting to assault the umbilicus from the open training bay, simulating the interval while the "enemy" extended the boarding tube.

"Contact," Rodriguez reported.

"Alpha, Charlie, commence transit," Makarov ordered.

The two external teams began to cross the distance from the side of the station to the uneven shape of the notional Kulsian corvette.

"Enemy in view!" Rodriguez transmitted thirty seconds later. "Initiating."

One of an array of small screens Harry was monitoring showed a small cloud of suits flitting onto the enemy "hull." Another showed a pair of assaulters swarming the empty suit that had been positioned to "contest" their approach.

"Charlie to command. Soft key failure, going mechanical," Harry heard Korelon report. Harry didn't know if the devices loaded with access software stolen from the downport would work more than once, or for that matter, *at all*, so the teams would use physical breaching methods for practice, regardless. In order to vary the attack, the exercise would flex both mechanical and explosive methods. Korelon's team had been selected for the exciting bit. "Mechanical failure, going explosive."

Harry had supervised the design and initial testing of certain special purpose devices. Copper sheeting had been cut into multiple two-meter-by-three-centimeter strips. Flexible explosive putty, not unlike the composition plastic explosives from Harry's misspent youth, was molded onto one side and the entire thing arranged in a circle about two meters square. In turn, the assembly was stapled to a stiff sheet of plastic. To use, slap the entire thing against the hull plate or lock to be cut, using vacuum-rated adhesive. Not unreasonably, several men had wanted proof the glue would work, preventing the cutting charge from floating free once primed. Nothing was simpler: the two-part epoxy created its own intense curing heat in seconds and required substantial effort to remove. Once the charge went, the absence of an atmosphere also meant a negligible blast wave. Of course, blazing hot fragments were still an issue, but you couldn't have everything.

On screen, Harry saw the brief flash of light from Korelon's charge. On the hangar display, the lone "Kulsian" was spouting atmosphere from both an arm and a leg, and the Alphas were simulating their own forced entry against the closed airlock, which meant opening not one, but two armored doors.

Harry heard a garbled call from the second exterior team, but the transmission was stepped on by Korelon reporting a successful breach of the shape's thin plating. He almost requested clarification, but remembered Makarov was in charge, and he wouldn't be on hand to help when they did this for real. Makarov had to do it himself. There could be only one OIC.

"—repeat, going explosive," Harry heard Makarov report.

That didn't make sense. One team was supposed to use the demolitions, the second was to employ the mechanicals, which were nothing more than simple, if extremely strong, cutting and expanding tools. Jam the carbide teeth into the lock seam and let the low-geared motors do the work. Harry shook his head and looked at the screens, and then at the target's layout of corridors, locks, and tanks. Makarov's team was at hull lock three, and there wasn't anything either potentially or actually dangerous nearby. Yet...

Harry reached for the mic but registered the distinctive flash of the second breaching charge on the display and, a moment later, an even brighter flash that washed out the screen.

Harry felt a horrible prickle spread across his skin.

"Check fire, check fire, the range is cold!" he yelled futilely, watching the monitor as the image resolution improved. "All personnel discontinue exercise and report!"

"Lost the umbilical," Harry heard Rodriguez report, his laconic tone unmistakable. "Doors auto-deployed. What the hell? Over."

"Teams report status," Harry ordered again.

It took but moments, but that short wait was agonizing. The first thing Harry noted was the movement of the simulated Kulsian corvette. It was rolling on its axis, and very slightly pitching downward from the station. The radio came alive as Bravo and Charlie acknowledged his call.

"Alpha, report," Harry ordered.

On a secondary monitor, first one, then a second, and finally four emergency suit beacons lit.

"It wasn't as bad as I thought at first, Colonel," Harry said, rubbing his forehead. He looked up and faced the video pickup, meeting Murphy's image squarely. "But it's still pretty bad. Rodriguez's entry team in the bay had only one significant casualty, and he swears he'll be all right. He got a hand badly pinched when the umbilical broke apart. The RockHounds also had one injured. Caught a small amount of frag when the propellant tank went up. He'll recover, but the Hound surgeon is offering no better than one chance in two his condition will improve fast enough to make the op. Makarov's squad, they're pretty much out altogether."

Harry paused and waited for Murphy to get the entire message. After a year of managing the delay over a radio link spanning several hundred thousand kilometers, the Terrans had adopted the SpinDog protocol of keeping your side of the conversation about as long as the light-speed lag between speakers. This allowed the speaker to finish talking just as their audience began to hear the first thing previously said. However, over the slightly grainy black-and-white video link Murphy didn't react much. He appeared to be reading a compilation of quicklook reports Harry had immediately begun transmitting as soon as the accident occurred.

Finally, Murphy looked up.

"And the men who were blown clear of the training platform?" he asked, grim-faced.

"Zymanski was killed outright. It took the RockHounds almost half an hour to chase him down; they had to use visual enhancement to spot the reflection changes from his tumble. He took the brunt of the blast," Harry said, rubbing his forehead. "His beacon was shredded, as was his suit. Between that and a cracked faceplate, it's unlikely he ever knew what hit him.

"But the remaining five in Alpha squad have all been retrieved. Three are hurt badly enough they can't put a suit on, let alone recover in time to make the op. They just brought in Makarov. He did a Dutchman, and his suit's electronics were damaged, which meant no beacon. Which in turn meant the Hounds having to retrieve him by visuals, too."

"What's his condition?" Murphy asked, his face tight with concern. "Can you get him on the line?"

"He didn't take a scratch physically, but he caught a pretty heavy dose of rads and his life support was almost gone. The suit's O_2 feed hose got nicked by a sliver and the dead electronics meant that the warning system never activated. But, Colonel, he's still in shock and only marginally responsive. He couldn't answer questions, and the surgeon decided to sedate him."

Harry watched Murphy sag, just a little, before his posture firmed up, and he resumed speaking in his customary "give me answers now!" tone. "What's your preliminary finding on the accident, Harry? How did you get an explosion of that magnitude?"

"Sir, I'm an interested party, and it was my responsibility," Harry said, straightening all the way up in his seat. "The right thing to do is to convene an independent board of inquiry to determine causality and confirm responsibility."

This time, there was no mistaking when Murphy heard Harry's answer. The obvious expression of concern over the casualties changed in a blink, and Murphy's brow wrinkled as he leaned further into the camera pickup.

"No time for that, Harry," Murphy said, biting off each word precisely. "If and when this operation is complete, I may exercise my responsibility in overall command to conduct an inquiry into this entire damned campaign. What I have to know, Major, is why... *You*. Think. It. Blew."

"Sir, the root cause of the accident was pure haste," Harry replied. "In our hurry to get ready, we demanded the fastest possible fabrication time, and we accelerated the training schedule to accommodate operational demands."

"Expand."

"We asked the SpinDogs to simulate a bigger ship, and they did their best," Harry answered. "They used whatever they had lying around, pulled conveniently shaped parts out of their recycling, including what we thought was an empty spun-fiber pressure tank. It could just as easily have blown when they torched the donor wreck apart, or when they welded the mock-up together. The survivors report the missing man, Zymanski, was anxious to breach the lock quickly. He broke one of the carbide teeth on his expander jack on his first try. Then it kept slipping out of the lock jamb. He decided to use the frame charge in order to maintain the realism and quick pace of the rehearsal. The frame charge was a little larger than the personnel lock that was his target, and the tankage appears to have been immediately adjacent to the lock. The linear shaped charge we used functioned exactly as intended. It did a number on the thin hull plating, but it also ignited whatever residue was in the tank: a breath of propellant, maybe. We're lucky the amount was so low. If it had been full, we would have lost everything, and we'd be talking about replacing all three squads and a good part of the station.

"Even so, the explosion was still significant. One really large hull section lifted entirely away, sending a bunch of fragments into the team. The big piece hit Makarov broadside and gave him a helluva push. The others in Alpha were also blown outward, but at lesser velocities. Ironically, they were hurt much worse."

"What's your assessment of the operational impact?" Murphy asked, his face impassive once again.

"Sir, the training target is toast," Harry reported. "No further large-scale exercises are possible in the time remaining. We have enough functional men to assault the target and retain a degree of overmatch to ensure success."

"Very well." Murphy looked away from camera for a moment, nodding to someone off-screen. When the exchange persisted more than a few seconds, he raised his right hand to shut the speaker down before returning his attention to Harry. "We don't have a lot of options. The mission needs an experienced commander. I need you to step up."

"You're right, sir," Harry answered. He'd begun thinking about the implications of the accident nearly as soon as it happened. He disciplined himself, concealing his surging emotion, the conflicting anger, resignation, and guilt. "We don't have a lot of time or options."

Give him nothing. Be the expressionless Sphinx, Harry.

Fuck that, let him know how pissed you are! Are you seriously saying yes to this guy?

Harry waited to allow the transmission lag to catch up.

"I need two things, Murph," Harry continued when it became obvious Colonel Murphy was waiting for the other shoe to drop. He omitted the usual honorific on purpose and had gotten Murphy's attention, at least. "One right away, for me. And another for everyone, later."

"Less cryptic bullshit, Harry," Murphy growled impatiently as the transmission reached him. His balled fists were visible at the bottom of edge of pickup. "What do you think you can demand of me? What do you require to do your duty?" The rest of what he was likely aching to say was written on Murphy's face in neon letters a meter high: *"You fucking prima donna."*

"I want your personal word that when we leave this system Stella can come with us if she wants," Harry stated firmly, suppressing his instinct to meet anger with anger. "I want it in writing, whether I live or die, she gets a ride out, if one exists."

"Of *course* you want it in writing," Murphy said disgustedly. "An officer who disregards his oath and negotiates for extras instead of doing his clear duty might think my signature is somehow more binding than my word. Done, Tapper. What else do you want?"

"You've waved my oath in my face before, Colonel," Harry said, hiding his elation. "It doesn't work. And it's not just me, either. One way or another, you've used every trick of patriotism, jingoism, and persuasion to get all of us two-time losers to do what needs doing. To lay our asses on the line. It works on some. Doesn't work on me or people like me. Even the ones who've grudgingly done what you asked really *need* something more. I want you to think about it and come up with a new reason for us to work together. And I don't mean because we've got a debt to little gray men, or because of our oaths to support and defend a Constitution, or whatever passed for a government where and when each of us got snatched. And especially not to save some bureaucratic United Nations surrogate back on Earth. Everyone who went into cold sleep effectively died, Murph. *Died.* Died and lost everything they had. You said it yourself: no more family, and even our countries are unrecognizable, if they still exist."

Harry paused for a breath. He had to make Murphy understand, so he mastered the strain that was about to make his voice break. It was time for the most important point, the thing that fueled Harry's desperation and anger. It was the difference between the Lawless remaining borderline ungovernable or becoming something new, something stronger.

"Dying fulfills our old oaths, Murph. Fulfills our oaths to the full measure of devotion. You can't ask that of us twice. We need a new reason, a better reason, to fight together, a new cause. Something that matters to every single one of us. Come up with an education plan, some kind of shared cultural literacy we can understand, and then give each of us an option to make a new oath. Or not. If you want real teamwork and sacrifice, you're going to have to give us something real to fight for."

It was a long speech, longer than it had seemed when Harry

had rehearsed. He got to watch Murphy's expression change from angry to confused, and from confused to . . . something Harry didn't immediately recognize.

This time the pause on Murphy's side of the conversation was even more prolonged.

"You surprise me, Harry," Murphy finally said. "As long as I've been in command of squirrely-ass soldiers—and the odd sailor—I've developed the conceit they can't surprise me anymore. Clearly, I was wrong. I agree to your codicil, Harry. But—and this includes my equally nonnegotiable terms—you will help me answer your second question. If you can come up with something that will convince yourself, then maybe we have a chance at creating something worthy of this new allegiance you're describing. Deal?"

Harry exhaled, emptying out a reservoir of frustration and releasing accumulated resentment.

"Deal, sir."

Chapter Thirty-One

"So you're now a fully qualified space pilot?" Murphy asked as soon as Bowden's butt hit the chair on the other side of the colonel's desk.

"I'm not certified by anyone or anything...but yeah," Bowden said. "I can do launches, fly anywhere you need me to go, and then do a reentry to a touchdown."

"Good. I was a little worried after your first launch..."

"That wasn't my failure; that was sabotage."

"I know, but I was worried. Anything I need to know about?"

"Like what?"

"Were there any other incidents after that?"

"None. I did three launches, including one with Burg Hrensku; all were nominal. Launches are actually pretty easy if you survive the RATO takeoff. After that, it's just 'keep flying up.' Then the sky gets black, and you go where you need."

Murphy looked toward the hatch. "Janusz?"

The large, expressionless submariner appeared in the hatchway, filling it in every dimension. How he'd ever moved through the tight spaces of the Polish submarine *Orzel* was a mystery to Bowden. Equally mysterious was the disappearance of Murphy's first bodyguard, Max Messina. Until the last couple of meetings on *Spin One*, Bowden had rarely seen Murphy without Max nearby. He wanted to ask about the big Vietnam vet's absence, but doubted Murphy would provide any information if he did.

"Yes, Colonel?" Janusz asked.

"Could you see that we're not disturbed?"

"Yes, sir. I'll take care of it." He closed the hatch.

Bowden smiled. "Is it game time?"

"Yes, as a matter of fact, it is." He sighed. "Past game time, actually. I would have liked to have given you a few extra days for another launch and reentry, but the surveyors were getting too close, and we need you now. Needed you yesterday, if you want to know the truth."

"Is that a figure of speech or did you really need me yesterday?"

"I really needed you yesterday. Certain opportunities presented themselves that we needed to grab hold of. Now we're going to be playing catch-up."

Murphy's eyes bored into Bowden's. "Before we go any further, I'm sure you realize this is all strictly classified; I'm the only person with whom you can discuss any of these details."

Bowden nodded. "Based on your earlier comments, I figured it was something like that. I won't say a word."

"Good, because—as you've seen—there are entities in this system who are not onboard with what we're doing."

"Besides the Kulsians."

"Yes. People closer to home. People who would sabotage an interface craft full of supplies to prevent what we're intending. They'd like to stop our daily operations. If they knew the mission on which I was about to send you..."

"There'd be conflict?"

"They would certainly do their utmost to stop us, even more so than they have thus far. Hopefully, by presenting them with a *fait accompli*, they will have no choice but to join with us."

"Do you have any more information about who's organizing this?"

"People among the SpinDogs and RockHounds who are far more comfortable hiding from the Kulsians than they are taking the fight to them. They are unhappy with the way we've upset their apple carts."

"Isn't it a little late to try to hide this time around? We've already made our presence known on the planet."

Murphy nodded. "We have, and yes, it's too late to try to hide. That doesn't mean they don't wish it was otherwise."

"Got it. So what's the mission?"

"There is a lighter—a small freighter—going from R'Bak to the second planet in this system where the Kulsians are already harvesting. We have put people in place to capture it. You and a small team of SpinDogs and RockHounds will rendezvous with the lighter—which is already on its way to the second planet, in accordance with its normal profile. I need you to figure out a way to catch up to it, then, once you do, you'll load the two modules of commandos you're carrying onto it."

"Modules?"

"They're transfer boxes, but they look a lot like the CONEX boxes we had back home."

"Who's in charge of the commandos?" Bowden asked.

"It doesn't matter, and you don't need to know. You'll load the transfer boxes—with their cargo—onto the lighter, then you'll do whatever is required to get intercepted by the corvette operating above the second planet. At that point, the commando team you're carrying will capture the corvette for future operations."

"A corvette, eh? That kind of ship would be able to make it to the other system, wouldn't it?" Bowden smiled broadly. "I can see a whole host of future operations that would be possible if we had one of those..."

The smile was lost on Murphy, who frowned. "I would appreciate it if you kept any suppositions of what might be possible in the future to yourself and concentrated on the original mission—getting your team into place."

Bowden's smile faded. "Yes, sir. I understand. Take the lighter to the second planet and get close to the corvette so we can grab it. Who else am I supposed to coordinate with for this?"

"You're coordinating with me. It isn't necessary or desired for you to know or interact with the people you'll be transporting. This is strictly a need-to-know operation, and you don't need to know who the cargo is. The SpinDogs and RockHounds on your team will need to know even less. The commandos are in their own modules, and the only time you'll need to talk to them is when you give them the 'go' code to begin their part of the operation."

"Okay, got it. Don't talk to the commandos." Bowden pursed his lips as he thought, then he shook his head. "I'm sorry, sir, but that's not going to work."

Murphy's eyes hardened. "It's going to work because you're going to make it work."

"Sir, you were involved in a lot of joint operations, right?"

"I was, which is why I know how important doing this under blackout conditions is. We can't give them any indication we're coming. More importantly, if there is a double agent in one of those modules, we need to deprive them of any information they could use to craft a tailor-made sabotage scheme."

"Sir, a complete comms blackout imposes greater dangers than any possible sabotage, because the most important part of this operation occurs when the *cargo* streams out to capture the corvette. How am I supposed to orient them so that when they come out, they know where to go and what to do? If I don't have a method of communicating with them, their odds of success are going to go way down. Ever have a mission where the recon elements couldn't talk to the operators? And what if we have a critical malfunction? Bottom line: we need the ability to talk to them if required, or at least let them know what's happening."

Murphy cocked his head and was silent for a few moments, then he sighed. "There's a comm panel on one of the transfer boxes. You can jack in there and give them a one-way message."

"What about the guys in the second module?"

Murphy smiled. "Don't worry about it. They can handle their own internal communications. And they are the sabotage risk, anyway."

"Fine," Bowden said, happy to have gotten at least a small concession. "Is there any other information you can give me on the turnover of the lighter?"

"A different team will secure the craft; that's not your problem. You just need to catch up to the craft as soon as you can, and hopefully before it gets to the second planet. At that point, the Kulsians are likely to see it and anyone operating around it. The corvette is armed with ship-to-ship missiles, so you don't want to do anything that will make them shoot first and ask questions later."

"Has any planning gone into how to get them close to us, then?"

"Yes. You will have the proper codes, and you will make it look like there is a problem with your spaceship. The best way is probably to send out a mayday saying you had an impact with something that has put you into a three-axis tumble, and then kill your radio signal.

"Hopefully, that will get them close enough for the commando team to storm across and capture their ship."

"You know that hope isn't a strategy, right, sir?"

"I do, but I have you to fill in all the other operational data to make this happen. We've invested a huge amount of assets in setting this up; I need you to bring it to fruition."

"A three-axis tumble, eh? That's probably something the cargo might want to be aware of before we do it."

"They were briefed to expect that."

"Fair enough." Bowden shrugged. "What happens if we get caught?"

"Don't get caught. I doubt you'd be treated very well by the Kulsians."

"I see." Bowden thought for a moment. "So, failure isn't an option. We either succeed..."

"Or you won't be coming back."

"Got it. The lives of my team, plus the lives of the commandos, are all riding on the success of this mission."

Murphy shook his head. "No, Major Bowden. This mission is much more important than that. If you fail, the Kulsians will become aware of our presence here in the Shex system, and it will provoke a response beyond our ability to stop. The lives of everyone on R'Bak, as well as the spins and everywhere else, will be in jeopardy. If you fail, we stand to lose it all."

"So," mused Bowden, "just like taking out the transmitter last year."

"Yes," Murphy agreed with a very long sigh, "just like that."

Chapter Thirty-Two

Bowden walked into the hangar bay Murphy had mentioned, and his eyes widened to find Burg Hrensku and Malanye Raptis talking to Karas'tan Kamara in front of Kamara's ship, which had two boxy structures—that *did* look very much like CONEX boxes—mounted on top of it. The RockHound nodded to him as he approached, and the others turned to gaze expectantly at him.

"Hi, umm...everyone." When they continued to look at him, he turned to Kamara. "Uh, can I talk to you?"

"It's okay," Kamara replied. "This is the rest of the team."

"Seriously?" Bowden asked, a little louder than was necessary. "Seriously?" he asked in a more conspiratorial tone. "This is just like old home week."

Raptis's brows knit. "What does that mean?"

Bowden smiled. "Nothing. It's just a way of saying everyone's back together again. I've spent more time in space with the three of you than anyone else. Other than Kamara, I didn't know you'd all be part of this, and it surprised me to see you all here."

"It appears that your Murphy called in a number of favors," Raptis said. "With the loss of my ship, I didn't have anything better to do, but Kamara and Hrensku had trips that had to be canceled so they could be part of this."

Bowden scanned the hangar bay; a number of SpinDogs were walking around. "Why don't we go inside the ship to talk?"

The others nodded and followed him into Kamara's ship.

"So, how much do you know about what we're supposed to do?" Bowden asked once they crowded into the ship's small galley area.

"Only that my ship was completely repaired and refurbished for it, at no cost to me, and two modules were brought and attached to it," Kamara said. "What can you tell us?"

"At the moment, I'm not at liberty to tell you anything other than this mission is incredibly dangerous and extremely important, and that I need your assistance to accomplish it. You can read into that whatever you'd like. Once we get to where we're going—or at least are on our way there—I can give you more of the details."

Kamara shook his head. "They want us to follow your directions— to do something you admit is extremely dangerous—and you won't tell us what it is?"

"Sorry," Bowden replied, "I've been sworn to secrecy." His eyes swept across the group. "You can back out now, I guess, if you don't want to be part of this, but I can't give you any more information at this time."

"I, for one, can't back out," Hrensku said. "The Primus asked me to do this as a favor; if I drop out, he will be greatly displeased with me."

"Wouldn't want that," Bowden said with a chuckle.

Hrensku didn't join in the mirth but looked Bowden in the eyes. "No, I wouldn't," he said after a moment. "You have no idea."

"Well, I was told I'd get a new ship of my own at the end of this mission," Raptis said with a bit more humor. "I figured it was going to be something dangerous, but everything I owned was on my old ship. When the comet ate it, it took away my life. This is my chance to start over again."

"If you survive," Kamara said darkly.

Raptis nodded. "If I survive."

Bowden shrugged, and his eyes met Kamara's. "I'm in because Murphy gave me an order, and I believe in this mission. Seems like you're the only one with a choice. Are you in or out?"

Kamara's eyes dropped to the table. He didn't move for a few seconds, but then he sighed and looked back up. "Yes," he said finally. "I am in."

Bowden checked the hydraulic fluid level and shut the access hatch. After the accident on the planet, his preflight inspections had become *very* thorough. A smiling Dave Fiezel stood waiting when he turned around.

"Any problems?" the former Air Force officer asked.

"No," Bowden replied. "I haven't found anything that looked like sabotage since that one flight."

"Good." Fiezel winked and nodded to the space suit and gear he carried. "Because I'm coming with you."

"You are? Since when did you get qualled to fly in space?"

Fiezel chuckled. "About the same time as you, apparently, but my training was a little more...under the radar, shall we say? I didn't blow up any interface craft or rescue maidens from comets or anything like that." He smiled. "Little did either of us know, but I was your backup for this...whatever it is."

Bowden felt the blood rush to his cheeks. "In case I got killed? Was I nothing more than bait? Or was it because Murphy didn't think I could cut it?"

"I don't think so," Fiezel said, shaking his head slowly. "I think my training was nothing more than Murphy being cautious. Bad things happen in space, and your trip to the comet could easily have gone horribly wrong. I think I was nothing more than Murphy wanting a backup option. And with everyone looking at you, I could get my training under the radar."

"Okay," Bowden said, a little mollified. "So why are you here? I've got this."

"Yes, you do, and I wouldn't want to take your place." He held up a hand. "Before you ask, I don't know any more than you do about it; in fact, I probably know even less than you do. All I know is that I'm just here to pilot the packet once you get to...wherever it is we're going."

Bowden nodded. "We better get at it, then. We're already behind schedule."

The packet launched from the habitat, and Bowden had Kamara put it on a flight path to Outpost, then everyone met in the galley.

"Are you finally going to tell us what we're doing?" Kamara asked.

"Well, I'm going to tell you what I can for now, anyway," Bowden said. "We're trying to catch up with a package that launched from R'Bak yesterday for the second planet."

Amazement—and a little shock—flew across the SpinDog's and RockHounds' faces. Fiezel's remained a neutral mask. Raptis was the first to speak. "A package?" she asked. She cocked her head. "I take it this package is valuable."

Bowden nodded. "Very valuable. And we need its contents."

Hrensku shook his head. "If they see us, either before or after we catch up with the package, the Kulsians will kill us."

"They will," Bowden agreed. "Our first priority is to remain unseen."

Kamara shook his head. "There is nothing in that package important enough for us to risk ourselves and this ship."

"It's more important than that," Hrensku said. "If the Kulsians see us, it is possible they will come search us out and destroy everyone on the spins."

Bowden nodded again. "That's why it's imperative we remain undetected."

"Still," Raptis said, "this is a near-suicide mission."

Bowden shrugged. "And yet, I tell you that it's necessary for not just us Terrans, but the well-being of everyone in the system." He paused and then added, "Anyone that wants to get out at Outpost is welcome to do so."

"I don't have anywhere else to be at the moment," Raptis said. "I'm still in."

"Nothing has changed for me," Hrensku noted. "I imagine the Primus was aware of what this mission entailed when he asked me to come. I doubt he would have done so if this mission wasn't vital."

Kamara nodded slowly. "True...at least to a point, I guess."

"What does that mean?" Fiezel asked.

Kamara raised an eyebrow. "It means you have no idea of how things work here." He shrugged. "As Burg said, though, nothing has changed. I am still in." He shifted to look at Bowden. "If we need to go in-system, though, why are we headed to Outpost?"

Bowden smiled, happy to have at least their partial buy-in. *That's probably going to change, though, once they see what we're really doing.* "Some of you are aware of what I did back before I came here, right?"

"You flew atmospheric fighters from ships on your planet," Hrensku said.

"Correct. On takeoff, though, we only had a hundred meters to achieve flight speed."

"How did you do it? You certainly didn't use RATO on a ship. Or did you?"

Bowden chuckled. "No, we didn't. That would have made things...interesting, to say the least. No, what we used was a catapult system to get us up to speed in the shortest amount of space possible, and that got me thinking..."

"The railgun," Kamara said, catching on. "You want to use Outpost's railgun to get us up to speed."

"Well, I'm not saying I *want* to do it that way, but that's the only way I can think of to give us the velocity we need."

"It won't work," Kamara said.

"Why's that?"

"It's never been done before."

"That doesn't mean it *can't* be done. It just means no one's *needed* to do it before."

"Or been stupid enough to try it," Hrensku noted.

"Or that," Bowden acknowledged. "Having said that, though, I looked at the design of the gun and this ship, and I think it can be done."

Raptis shook her head. "I don't think it will give us enough velocity."

"Especially with whatever those modules that were added have in them," Kamara said. "What's in them?"

"I'm not at liberty to say," Bowden replied. "Not yet, anyway."

"Can you tell me what their mass is, then?"

"Five thousand kilograms."

Kamara shook his head. "The railgun won't give us enough velocity to catch up to your package."

"Well, no," Bowden admitted. "Not on the initial stroke anyway. And not in its current configuration." *Not from what I did with back-of-the-napkin math. A supercomputer would figure this all out easily...if we could use any of the ones we have.* "Let me tell you about baseball."

"What's that?" Raptis asked.

"It's a sport we play back on Earth," Fiezel said. "What's that got to do with it?"

Bowden smiled. "I'm glad you asked. One of the positions is called 'the catcher,' and his job it to catch a ball that's thrown as hard as the person called 'the pitcher' can throw it."

"I don't understand," Raptis said.

"Well, I was thinking about the glove he wears to keep from breaking his hand. It's nice and padded to absorb the force of the ball."

"I still do not understand."

"What would you say if we built something similar on the back of the packet and then, after launch, had the railgun fire several heavy slugs into it, giving us additional velocity?"

"I would say you are doing your best to destroy my ship," Kamara said.

"I don't think so," Bowden replied. "Not if we add a shock absorber system to mitigate the instantaneous shock to the structure of the craft from catching the slugs." *And besides, it's far more likely that the force of the catapult is going to destroy the ship by ripping off your landing gear, Bowden thought. Especially since the craft's never been stressed—or intended—for something as stupid as that.*

"That might work," Kamara admitted. "Maybe. It would be better, though, if you used smaller slugs. It would reduce the kinetic shock from each impact and would be easier on both the ship and the crew."

"You're probably right," Bowden allowed. "It would also make it easier to kick the slugs away from your ship if they were smaller." *And less likely to completely destroy us if the system fails or there's a glancing blow to the ship.*

"The downside to using more of the slugs," Bowden continued, "is the error ratio. Whatever the fail rate is on this, the more shots that are fired, the more likely we're going to get one off angle or out of tolerance." He shook his head. "We need something that can increase our accuracy."

"What about if we used some laser targeting for this?" Hrensku asked.

"Laser targeting?"

"Yes. We could place lasers on the ship and on Outpost, and fire them at each other. When the two beams are centered in the other's reception dishes, the system can fire the slugs. That should give the system a higher accuracy rate and reduce the chances of failure."

And take the onus of aiming off the backs of the half-witted local computers, Bowden thought. He nodded. "What do you think?" he asked, looking at Kamara.

Kamara chewed on his lower lip for a moment, then nodded slowly. "It might work."

"Good," Bowden said. "There's one more thing..."

"What?" Kamara asked. "You haven't come up with enough ways to kill us yet?"

"In order for us to be light enough for the railgun to give us enough initial velocity, we're going to have to remove a lot of the craft's cosmic ray shielding."

Hrensku nodded. "You *do* want us to die."

"No, I don't," Bowden said. "But I *do* want us to succeed. To do so, we're going to need to dump a lot of the water that provides the shielding."

"Out of the question," Kamara stated.

"It's not forever," Bowden replied. "I have a plan."

"Of course you do," Raptis said. "Can you share it with us, or are you not at liberty to tell us this, either?"

"The plan is easy. Before we launch, we use the railgun to fire several pods down our line of travel at a slower velocity than we'll be traveling. As we pass them, we scoop them up. Then, once we are safely away from Outpost, the railgun can go back to its normal operation of shooting pods, except it will be shooting pods to us that are full of the rest of the water and fuel we'll need for the mission, and we can replenish them en route. Since the pods don't have passengers, they could be launched by the railgun at extremely high gees."

"You're really serious about this," Kamara said.

"I am," Bowden replied. "It does two things for us: not only does it allow the mass of the ship to be extremely light at launch, but it doesn't increase our total signature. Each of the supply containers can be kept relatively small and made of lightweight materials that will be extremely difficult to detect."

Raptis shook her head. "There's only one problem with all that."

"What's that?"

"Who's going to go out and capture all these pods? You?"

"Don't worry about it," Bowden replied. "The cargo will handle the acquisition and retrieval of the supply pods."

"*The cargo?*" Raptis asked. "You mean there are *people* in those boxes?"

"Yes, there are, and yes, they are trained in EVA operations. They are coming to help recover the package we are going after;

they can bring the supply pods aboard and pump the additional water and fuel into the tanks. We'll need to stay in a relatively small area of the ship at the start, but as more and more of the water is brought aboard, we'll have full access to the entire ship."

Bowden looked at the faces of the crew and saw a mixture of disbelief. "Okay, I don't like it any more than you do, and I know it makes you put a lot of trust into people you don't know really well, but I am here to tell you that they can, *and they will*, get it done."

"Are you willing to bet your life on this?" Hrensku asked.

It's gotta be Tapper, and if I can't trust him, who can I trust? Bowden nodded. "I already am."

Hrensku sighed. "Then I will as well."

"I'm in, too," Fiezel said quickly.

"I'm too much of a mercenary to give up the chance to get a ship out of this," Raptis added. "I am in."

Everyone looked at Kamara. After a few seconds, he jerked his head in a single nod. "Against my better judgment, I—and my ship—are in, too."

Bowden nodded back. "Outstanding. We're pressed for time on this, so we need to get everything in place as soon as possible."

The meeting broke up immediately after, with Kamara, Raptis, and Hrensku going to see what Kamara had that could be used for the "catcher's mitt" and the laser targeting system. Fiezel stayed and pursed his lips. "Were you really going to let them leave at Outpost if they weren't onboard with the mission?" he asked in a whisper.

Bowden shook his head. "Think Murphy would have allowed that?"

"No. What were you going to do if someone had wanted to get off?"

Bowden shrugged. "Whatever it took to stop them or convince them to continue." *Including using the pistol that's in my gear if it had proven necessary.* Happily it wasn't . . . this time.

Chapter Thirty-Three

"We are ready," Kamara transmitted from the pilot's seat. He turned his helmeted head to look at Bowden in the copilot's position. "I hope this works."

Me too. "It should," Bowden said. "Attaching it directly to the rear of the fuselage and at the center of mass lets the main structural members absorb the force of the acceleration." He'd had to figure out another way to do it after looking at the nose gear of the packet again. The ship—in general—was on the spindly side, and there was no way the nose gear would have survived the railgun launch. The fuselage was marginally sturdier, assuming the mounted CONEX boxes didn't tear off.

He clicked the mic twice to let the commandos know of the impending launch, then pushed the button several times that controlled their warning light. *The railgun ride is going to provide a lot of "fun" for the commandos.* During the installation of the catcher's mitt, he'd had a wire attached to the command CONEX box that led to the bridge of the ship. Then, when he'd had a few unobserved minutes, he'd passed the word to them about the launch so that they knew to be lying down so they wouldn't get hurt. They hadn't come running out of the boxes in disapproval, so Bowden figured that their silence meant their consent.

Shitty deals for shitty SEALs.

Harry looked around and contemplated his predicament. He'd chosen the acceleration couch with the best view of the control panel. About him, five more couches, each holding a recumbent member of his assault team, were arranged in three ranks. He checked the launch warning light again. The LED sloppily epoxied onto the control panel was still green, just as it had been the last hundred times he'd looked. The abbreviated "control panel," the merest sketch of what should have been a purpose-built piece of equipment, was a joke. Comms were limited to the ship ferrying the habitat modules that housed the team. Mismatched gauges and idiot lights for the environmental control system plus a single airlock control rounded out the tools at his disposal. In fact, the construction of the entire module reeked of a "use once and recycle" philosophy that reminded Harry uncomfortably of his initial descent to R'Bak in a one-man, self-propelled tin can. They'd glued that little gem together, too.

The builder had gotten the lighting right; he'd give them that much. The feeling was akin to being in an operating room, right down to the added patient's-eye perspective, free of charge. There was the easy-to-clean blue vinyl floor, the racks of flush-mounted lockers that held their individual equipment, the abbreviated armory container fabricated from pierced steel sheeting and the small, bright red Faraday cage for the blasting caps packed in anti-shock foam. A small table-and-bench combination was permanently attached to the deck next to the ration station, which wasn't much more than a source of fresh water and a meal-warming unit. A tiny closet hid the one commode they'd be sharing.

Harry really hoped it worked as designed.

The assault force had sealed themselves into the two habitat modules hours ago, with the promise they'd launch in "thirty minutes, max!" With that guarantee, Harry had foregone the installation of the relief catheter and was now contemplating the bleak future of peeing into his Maximum Absorbency Garment, or MAG, which was a fancy name for an oversize diaper.

At last, the green launch warning light flashed three times and then dimmed before finally glowing a ruby red.

He chinned his radio switch, positioned for operation during high acceleration.

"Major, thirty-second warning," he sent over the hardwired intercom that connected him to the second hab. "Let's hope these tin cans hold together."

"I saw it, Major Tapper," Korelon replied, seemingly unconcerned. "Thank you. But there is no need for concern. And, Major?"

Harry sighed. What chestnut was Korelon going to deliver now?

"Yeah, what's up, Korelon?"

"I'm glad you are with us," Korelon said, and clicked off.

Well, what do you know about that?

"All hands stand by for acceleration," Harry announced to his own crewmates, still pleasantly puzzled over the unexpected change in the phlegmatic RockHound. "Twenty seconds. Lower your faceplates. I'd say brace yourselves, but that doesn't quite cover it."

Nonetheless, after sealing his own helmet, he pressed himself firmly into the stiff contoured padding of his couch.

"Hey, Major!" Rodriguez said on the intercom, preparing to deliver the age-old, pre-drop ritual common to those on the sharp end. "I think I changed my mind. Where do I get off?"

Nervous laughter greeted this sally.

Officially, they would experience acceleration "in excess of eight gees." Harry had asked for a more precise figure. The catapult launch control officer—whom Harry had noted with no small sense of disquiet was the same man with whom he'd exchanged words while appropriating the central hangar for his team's exclusive training use—had sidestepped the question. The acceleration figure wasn't just about the comfort of the team. The habs were temporarily affixed to the outside of an oversize mining craft while they were being ferried to the rendezvous. Harry had seen the holdfasts brazed to the hull. Eight times the mass of the hab was a lot of force to be exerted against ad hoc fasteners that connected their habs to the little ship.

It was not an inconsequential issue, but when Harry pressed a second time, the launch control officer had merely smirked and assured him the installation was quite secure, adding, "The construction is well within the limits of launch stress and design error."

Bowden expected, but still loathed, the pause as the SpinDog inside Outpost waited for the railgun to get to its optimal position, then, without another transmission, pushed the button—or however he initiated the railgun launch system—and the ship was hurled from the station. "Hurled" probably wasn't the right word, as the forces involved were more violent than an aircraft carrier catapult launch, and it certainly induced more stress than the packet was designed for.

The sounds of metal under stress filled the cockpit, and a number of caution lights flashed on the packet's dashboard, but none of the red warning lights illuminated. After a few seconds, the acceleration fell off, and Bowden began breathing again. *It worked!*

What had been called "acceleration" during all the mission preps slammed into Harry like a baseball bat to his entire body. He immediately stopped daydreaming about welds and instead imagined exploring the launch officer's guts with his Ka-Bar.

Mercifully, the launch impulse was brief, though, and Harry reflexively wiggled a bit in his bucket, checking for injury. Nothing appeared to have fallen off.

"Everybody all right?" Harry called to just the men in his hab. "Alpha, sound off."

Stunned language, colorful even by Harry's jaded standards, informed him the team was alive.

"Y'all okay over there, Korelon?" Harry commed over to the second hab. "Any exciting warning lights?"

"Situation nominal, Major," Korelon responded promptly with a familiar phrase. "As I've said, these modules are constructed well within the limits of launch stress and design error."

Huh. Must be a RockHound thing.

"All hands, that was the only big one," Harry informed the team. "We're going to stay suited for a while longer while they send a few more love taps our way. They won't be anything like the first big shove, but we stay buttoned up, just in case. Then we get to do some good training."

"The actual fuck?" seemed to be the consensus answer.

"Well, we're still alive and in one piece," Kamara said as he pushed several reset buttons. Most—but not all—of the caution lights went out. "I even think we can fix most of the failures you induced..."

"But...?" Bowden asked when Kamara left the statement dangling.

"But now we will see what happens when the gun shoots thousand-kilogram slugs at my poor ship."

While Bowden hadn't been oblivious to the dangers inherent to his plan, his scheme to catch the slugs hadn't sounded quite so dangerous until it was phrased like that. "It'll work," he said simply. *Or people will die as giant bits of metal rip through the improvised mechanism and crash through the ship.* Bowden swallowed. *Please, dear God, let this work.*

"Is the ship ready?" Kamara asked.

"As ready as it is ever going to be," Raptis said as she monitored the catching mechanism from her position in the back. "The glove is aligned."

"You may commence," Kamara reported to Outpost.

"Firing," the man replied.

A few seconds later, the craft jerked forward as the glove sequentially caught and then dumped the first six slugs the system on Outpost fired.

"It worked!" Kamara exclaimed, surprise evident in his tone, as the mitt rotated to the side to dump the slugs out of the way and realigned for the next round.

Those were the easy ones, Bowden thought. By the time Outpost rotated into position again, they would be a lot farther from the station, making the shot more difficult. A good computer system could have made the shot from the spinning platform . . . but they only had the jury-rigged laser system. "Hopefully, they can do that six more times," he said.

And hopefully, the rockets will work, too. A set of discrete solid rocket boosters had been added to the rest of the slugs. It gave the rounds a little more velocity and a limited terminal correction capability—including the ability to abort the round if there was a malfunction that would lead to an impact outside the mitt.

"The glove is aligned for the second set of shots," Raptis said, having confirmed that the mechanism was secured in its "catch" position.

"Ready," Kamara transmitted.

"Firing."

The technician at Outpost was on the money with the first several shots of the next group, but on the fourth, Bowden felt a brief moment of acceleration and then *slam!*

"What was that?" Kamara asked as a number of caution lights snapped on. This time, some of the red warning lights illuminated, too.

"The camera is out, so I can't see," Raptis said, "but from the brief glimpse I got, it looked like the fourth round tried to abort. It turned a catastrophic impact into a glancing blow, but the slug still hit the ship."

"Shit," Kamara said, pushing the button that jettisoned the device they'd been using to catch the slugs. He pointed to one of the red lights. "It looks like it must have hit the port aft thruster. I'm going to have to go out and check it."

"What do you want me to do?" Bowden asked.

"We didn't get enough velocity to get to the second planet," the RockHound said, "but we got too much to return to Outpost. I need you and Raptis to figure out where we can go from here without being seen by the Kulsians."

"Korelon, this is Tapper," Harry commed his nominal second-in-command. "Everybody can unstrap and move around."

"The acceleration maneuvers worked, I take it?" Korelon replied. "One of the last impulses was different. Is the ship damaged?"

"Not as far as I can tell," Harry said, moving toward the rack where his EVA gear was secured. "Not our problem; everything on my board that's supposed to be green *is* green. Ship repairs are strictly the province of the ship's crew.

"But don't get too comfortable; the first of the cargo pods will be heading for us pretty soon. Alpha will take the first set of them, then unsuit. Should give you time to let your guys eat comfortably before you go out to get the second. The base personnel will stagger the launches as the Outpost rotates through the best geometry for an accurate shot. Then we can alternate, watch on watch, till the loadout is complete."

"Major, I understand," the RockHound answered somewhat diffidently. "But I feel I must point out despite the improvements in Terran micro skills, we are still much more adept in freefa—"

"Negative," Harry answered, cutting off further discussion. "We've already been over this. The point is these guys need *more* time in micro, not less. Plus, we're going to spread the cumulative radiation exposure across the entire team so no one goes over the maximum amount. Let your guys get out of their gear. We're going to be in it a *lot*, and your turn is coming up."

"As you say, Major."

"The good news," Kamara said when he came back in two hours after the last, abortive pulse of acceleration, "is that I can replace the thruster. I have a spare and—with a bit of work by Hrensku and me—we can fix it and a couple of other problems the slug caused. I also just saw some of the water in the shielding being replenished, so our 'cargo' has obviously picked up the first pod on schedule, and the transfer system is working. The bad news, however, is that we're not going to be able to rendezvous with the other pods without using a good bit of thrust—so much that the signature is sure to be detected, and none of us want that to happen."

Kamara looked around the small group gathered in the galley. "The worse news, of course, is that we're headed further in-system without a way to return to Outpost without a similar thrust signature, which would be sure to bring the Kulsians to investigate. I don't see any way for us to get home or to accomplish the fool's errand we were on."

"I thought the same thing," Raptis said, "but then Bowden had an idea."

"Is this one going to be as good as your catcher's mitt idea, which worked out *so* well?" Kamara asked. "Or is it something equally dangerous and unpredictable?"

Bowden shrugged. "It's not without risks, but—like you said—we're pretty much out of options."

"And this plan is...?"

"Well, the problem, as you articulated, is that whatever we do, we have to do it without being seen."

"Correct. Leading the Kulsians to Outpost would result in the destruction of our society."

Bowden nodded. "As you also articulated, though, we're not going to make it to our rendezvous without using additional thrust. That means we need to have a burn, but we have to do it without the Kulsians seeing it."

"And the closer we get, the more likely they are to see it, so if you could just explain your plan..."

"Right. Remember when we were on the comet together?"

"Yes, but I don't see how that's going to help us."

"Bear with me. Remember how it was outgassing?"

"Yes."

"That would hide our thrust bloom if we did it on the other

side of a comet from the planet, but we'd need to be very close to the comet."

"And there is a comet we could use to hide our signature?"

"Well, yes," Bowden said. Raptis raised an eyebrow. "Okay, there's an ice-teroid headed inbound, but it isn't currently outgassing."

"An ice-teroid isn't a comet. It's just a conglomeration of rock and ice. It doesn't have the outgassing we need. How does that help us?"

"The formation of comets and such isn't uniform. Just because it isn't outgassing yet just means the star hasn't shed enough light on it to raise the temperature to the point at which the outgassing process begins. I'm suggesting we rendezvous with it and focus our thrusters on it to get an outgassing event, then we use it to conceal our thrust as we boost for the second planet."

Kamara shook his head once as he thought it through, then looked up at Raptis. "You're the expert; what do you think?"

"I think it's our only chance. Just because it's not outgassing doesn't mean it won't. I've been to dozens of comets, and a number of these have had their surface ice melted off, so it takes them a while to heat up enough for the ice inside to sublimate. Ice-teroids are similar . . . somewhat. It's possible we can do this, but we won't know until we get there and take a look."

"Where is 'there'?"

Raptis winced. "The ice-teroid is still behind us, but it's catching up quickly. We would have to start accelerating soon to match its velocity as it overtakes us."

"Won't we be seen by the Kulsians if we do that?" Fiezel asked.

"No," Raptis said. "We can use the compressed gas thrusters to speed up without tapping the main engine. I think it's possible. Once we're in the shadow of the comet, we could tap the main engine once or twice if we needed to."

"It might work," Hrensku said. "If one of the surveyor ships came over the horizon and was looking our way, they wouldn't see the thrust signature; all they'd get would be a heated particle trail. Something that would be easily passed off as comet outgassing."

"I've never thought about using one for cover that way," Kamara admitted. "It's risky, especially with Kulsians close by. Normally, we'd just snuggle up to it, go quiet, and try to hide behind it. I mean, who'd be *dumb* enough to try to get a body to outgas while you're flying in formation with it? I mean, the material spewing forth could potentially destroy the craft as easily as a Kulsian ship-to-ship missile."

"That's the greatest risk," Raptis agreed. "We're going to have to get *really* close because we're going to have to use the main engine to create the heat we need. It's going to take focusing the burn down onto the ice-teroid while using the forward thrusters at full throttle to match and counteract the main engine, maintaining our station keeping. Then, once it's going like we want, we spin the ship and use a few heavy pulses of main thrust."

"But you think it's possible?" Kamara asked.

"I never would have thought of it on my own," she said, "but I think it could work. If we can find the right area on the ice-teroid. Besides, we don't have any other choices."

"You're right." Kamara shrugged. "We can't make it back to Outpost without being seen, so I don't see how we can do anything else. A small chance of success is better than none at all."

"All right, last review of pod retrieval," Harry explained, addressing Alpha. "The name of the game is good training. I know you've been briefed, but some of you have been a little too fond of RockHound beer to reliably remember everything you've been told in the last week."

Grave de Peralto looked especially bleary. Harry caught Pham staring disapprovingly. The other members of the team had amused themselves challenging the Flea to successive drinking contests; for that matter, all hands smelled as though they'd smuggled the product of another homemade still along on the mission. Yet, the others wore the same expression of professional indifference as Harry, save Roeder, who wore his perpetual grin.

"Between the first push and the little love taps since, we're moving as fast as we can go without burning fuel. But we need to bring on board enough supplies to keep us fed and, more importantly, shielded," Harry reminded them. "We'll alternate with the RockHounds, EVAing to secure the pods, connect them to the hab's systems, and improve our overall skill moving in freefall. Just like the real thing, we're going to rely on hand signals, so the enemy isn't warned by our radio signals. Keep your tethers on and work with your battle-buddy. Any questions?"

"That launch felt like hell, actually," Grave de Peralto spoke up from where he sat on the edge of his acceleration couch. "Why does good training have to be like that, I ask you?"

"If it didn't suck, you wouldn't love it so much," Harry announced. "Besides, you get to watch me go first, Flea." He looked over his shoulder at Rodriguez. "And by me, I mean you and I, Marco. Off and on. Let's show the Hounds how we roll."

Chapter Thirty-Four

"How'd your second day of pod-herding go, boss?" Roeder asked, wrinkling his nose as he helped Harry get his helmet off.

"It's not hard in a technical sense, but it's like one long low-level workout. You never stop sweating," Harry said, vigorously scratching his chest. He felt as though he'd been marinating in a wetsuit for a week. "Ahh, damn, I've been wanting to do that for two hours. You're constantly working against the elasticity of the EVA gear and it rubs *everywhere*. All right, turn around, I'm getting this damn diaper off. The fu—the stupid catheter slid out."

He turned his back to the rest of the room and started shucking the remaining gear. In the little nook near the food warming equipment, Pham studied a magnetic chessboard, ignoring the byplay.

Grave de Peralto and McPherson were already outside, working the problem of capturing the next pair of pods fired from the distant and receding Outpost. Once the pods were safely lassoed, the EVA teams plugged the four-meter ovoids into the mass transfer system. Not much more than a hose, some valves, and a vacuum tank, the ad hoc system rapidly discharged the mass of water into the shield wall of the habs, improving the rad resistance of their temporary home. Each RockHound lived with the equivalent of an old-school dosimeter. Once they reached maximum exposure, they risked serious complications. Each pod represented a few points reduction in the radiation from the primary and increased their margin of safety. Harry, like the rest of the Lawless, also wore a dosimeter, though his lifetime total was far lower, courtesy of his planet-bound existence up to the point of the kidnapping.

"Yeah," Roeder answered, looking away. Rodriguez had also turned his back to examine his own private region. "Good training, this."

With another sigh of relief, Harry slid the swollen MAG off and dumped it into a refuse bin.

Oh, the glory and romance of space travel. Next time, stick the damn catheter in, uh, more.

"Okay, here's the deal," Roeder announced, handing little ketchup packet–sized sachets to each person. "In my capacity as acting corpsman, I strongly advise you to keep your catheter lubricated. We're only four days in, and all of you are getting considerable irritation."

"Considerable irritation, he says!" Rodriguez snarled, snatching his lube from Roeder's outstretched hand. "I'm goddamned pissed!"

"That's how you know it's really good training," Roeder quipped, trying to conceal a grin. "You need to keep the area clean and dry, except for, you know, the part where the catheter goes. Lube the hell out of that. But just the tip."

"Thanks a lot, you wanna-be chancre mechanic," Rodriguez said, studying his own equipment. "Admit it, you've been waiting to use that line all this time."

"Hey, keep it down!" McPherson called from where he sat, alone, studying the chessboard. "I've got fifty kilocredits riding on this game! I'm finally gonna take Roeder!"

"Not a chance, you Scot bastard," Roeder answered merrily. "Mate in six; nothing you can do."

"That's why we're being forced to do this now, Marco," Harry said, returning to the main topic and studying his own inflamed… parts. "We cheated too much during initial training and gave everyone pee breaks. Now we're paying for it. Should've made you wear the suits all day, then we wouldn't be suffering from, um, chaffing. Speaking of which, do you have the topical analgesic cream, Doc?"

"Here you go, sir," the big Navy chief said. "Whoops, there's the proximity alarm. Pods are early. Team One to the airlock. Time for more good training."

He ignored a baleful look from Rodriguez and extended his meaty arm again, holding a bulging plastic sack. "The bathroom is broken again. Don't forget the solid waste bag. And don't snag it on anything."

"Next pair to the airlock," Harry said after wearily undogging his faceplate. "Mind your step. Marco snagged the shitbag on the relief valve hand wheel and the freeze-dried poop is already starting to smell."

Roeder and Pham were next.

"Jesus, Rodriguez!" Roeder said, hastily locking and sealing his helmet. The external speaker came on a second later. "That reeks! What the hell are you eating?"

"Let me find it—it's the same thing I've been having for a week," Rodriguez said, exaggeratedly fishing around in the thigh-mounted cargo pocket of his EVA suit. He pulled out a closed fist and raised it toward the aggravated corpsman, lifting the middle finger at the same time. "Here it is."

"Smells like home after you Americans finished building a base," Pham said. "You could tell the foreigners had arrived from the smell of Coca-Cola, jet exhaust, gasoline, and burning shit. I almost miss it. Or is that good training?"

The room full of men chorused together, as though it had been rehearsed, "Oh, this is superior training!"

"Son of a bitch, that smarts!" Harry said, slathering a white cream on the inside of his thighs, trying to coat the raised red welts that decorated both legs. He lifted one arm to examine the matching raw areas of his underarms. "Why the hell is this happening, Doc?"

"Not enough fresh water to get the clothes or our bodies clean, sir," Roeder replied, looking at the profoundly irritated patches of skin with professional interest. "We're in and out of the suits every eight hours. I'm kinda surprised it took ten days. We're getting chafing and skin infections, and Rodriguez has a truly impressive UTI."

"Hahahaha!" Grave de Peralto laughed uproariously. "A UTI. Like a chick!"

"Fuck you, dicksmith!" The Army SF noncom was in no mood. "And Flea, if you don't shut it, I'm going to make a new lockout procedure. Step one: insert pint-sized Cubano into airlock without suit."

"Ooh, emergency egress training!" Grave de Peralto said. "The very best of all!"

Harry stood, his feet still inside the integrated EVA boots, while the rest of his gear hung down about his calves and ankles. His MAG and trishorts were likewise pulled down and he absolutely did not care who could see. He pointed at the rapidly dwindling tub of analgesic cream that was just out of reach and made "come on" gestures at Roeder.

"You need to take it easy on that stuff, sir. We have hardly any left!"

"Don't care," Harry said. "Pass it over, Doc."

"It took two weeks, but finally not having to wear that damn EVA suit every day is my kind of heaven," Rodriguez said, sniffing experimentally. "Except for the body odor, reconstituted plant-based protein pack meals, non-functioning personal waste reclamation unit, and Roeder's snoring, I'm living the dream."

"Have you recovered from your ladies' complaint, Sergeant?" Grave de Peralto inquired sweetly.

"You Navy sub guys would know about ladies' complaints, I suppose," Rodriguez replied, lying comfortably on his couch, starkers save for warm socks. "All I know is I'm finally not itching or burning, I can air everything out, and I definitely don't have to ram that catheter up my—"

A very loud, very irritating electronic warbling filled the small confines of the hab, arresting all activity.

"Shit!" Harry yelled, lurching from his seat next to the chess game. "Collision alarm!"

Wide-eyed, everyone grabbed a handhold.

"No, you morons!" Harry yelled, stuffing his first foot into his beloved EVA suit. "Suit up, strap in, and stand by. Now!"

There was a general scramble.

"I can't fucking believe it!" Rodriguez yelled, diving for his EVA gear. "Not again!"

"Hey, I think this is yours, Sergeant!" Laughing, Grave de Peralto threw a pack of catheter lube across the narrow space. "You're gonna want to get your special friend nice and slippery; Major Tapper says you need more training!"

"You're a dead man, squid!"

PART FIVE

Chapter Thirty-Five

Makarov's voice was tentative. "I have received a request for an update on mission status, sir."

Murphy tried not to sound annoyed. "Who from?"

"Primus Anseker. Private channel."

Oh, well that's *okay*. At least when Anseker read, heard, or saw something that concerned him, he also presumed that there was a good reason for it, rather than the opposite. Similarly, if there was some issue that needed resolving, it was a straightforward discussion. Not like when Murphy had to manage a passel of easily alarmed, dominion-obsessed patriarchs with egos bigger than all of space. "Tell Anseker what you told me, Pete: that Major Bowden reports the insertion is in process and on schedule. No emergency signals from the assault team, so they are presumed to be at nominal readiness."

Makarov stared quizzically at him. "Sir, that would seem to imply that you have now received Chalmers's final 'go' signal?"

"Yes, it arrived a few hours ago on Timmy's shift."

"He should have left a note." Makarov sounded more sullen than angry. "So may I tell the Primus that Chalmers's team has fashioned a plan for securing access and that you are comfortable with it?"

Murphy didn't catch his temper in time. "Pete, did you suffer an undiscovered concussion when the training exercise went south? We always knew we weren't going to have the bandwidth

293

to get a full update, and I'm not about to start lighting up comm arrays when we should be as silent as a tomb." He raised a hand to his forehead. "I'm sorry, Pete. Not your doing. Look, you remember we were never going to hear much about Chalmers's final plan, right?"

"I do, but you have obviously heard a bit more of his intents than I have."

"True, but it was so vague that if I relayed it to the Primae, they'd all lay eggs. Even Anseker."

"Because of the risk?"

"No, because there wasn't enough concrete information to even *quantify* the risk. And we're not going to tell him that because it's not a change from the operational parameters as we agreed upon them. Reassessing risk is a sleeping dog that we're going to let lie until, and if, we learn anything that changes our very wobbly best guesses."

Makarov nodded tightly. "Yes, sir. Sending reply now." After a moment, he turned back. "Sir, I understand your precaution in communicating with the Primae...but I wonder if I could ask you the same question on a personal level: given what you know of Chalmers's plan—are *you* comfortable with it?"

"I am."

"Despite Chalmers?"

"Despite Chalmers. Or maybe because of him."

"He does seem to have a gift for...for underhanded actions, sir." Makarov's tone was at once admiring and disapproving.

"Maybe," Murphy said almost defensively, "but this time, he's using that gift for the right reasons." Murphy glanced at the mission board and adjacent map. "Can't ask a man for more than that."

"Papers," the guard said.

"Right here," Chalmers said, handing the folio over. The requested paperwork was sweat-damp, but Chalmers wasn't worried—at least not about sweaty papers. That was easily explained by the absence of air-conditioning for the truck's passenger cab. The short-haul trucks were built on the cheap, and driver comfort was not a concern for the island's overlords, so the cab was still sweltering hot, even in the third hour after sunsdown, and even though the cargo container he was hauling was one of the rare refrigerated models. *Couldn't have rations bound for the survey team go bad, now could we?*

Even so, he missed his partner's reassuring presence at his side. But Jackson had other work tonight.

The guard took the papers and rifled through them in desultory fashion. The new sergeant remained in the shack beside the gate, his feet up.

Chalmers relaxed fractionally. The bribes they'd been paying were meant to ensure just this kind of laissez-faire attitude from the guards for Twin Stars trucks, but only when transporting their various cargoes to warehouses, not when moving supplies necessary for a surveyor crew.

"Supplies for flight 1517B?" the guard asked after a moment.

"So I'm told," Chalmers said. He gestured over his shoulder at the cargo container. "Where do I drop it?"

"Hangar sixteen, last but two on the left."

"Right," Chalmers said. That was good. Sixteen was the proper hangar. They hadn't been sure of that prior to launching this phase of BUCKET. So that part, at least, was according to plan.

The guard motioned at the shack. A moment later the gate dropped.

"Go ahead."

Chalmers put the truck in gear and drove slowly over the gate. He watched in his side mirrors as a hydraulic ram pushed the heavy metal plates upward from below the road surface. Once shoved almost vertical, the plates formed an inverted V that was too tall for a man to climb and tough enough to stop any truck on the island cold. Mopping his sweaty brow with the shoulder of his shirt, he picked his canteen up from the seat next to him and took a long pull. Setting the warm can of water down, he pulled his watch from his breast pocket and did the math. Five hours, fifty-five minutes to dawn. Three hours, twenty-three minutes to launch prep.

Jackson would be starting the show any minute now. Chalmers stuffed the watch back in his pocket. Wearing it was out of character. He relied on a mental countdown instead, hoping he wouldn't reach zero.

Chalmers killed the engine as he passed hangar fourteen. The truck rolled to a quiet stop a bit short of hangar 16's doors. He listened carefully before stepping down from the cab. He pulled a sap from beneath the driver's seat and slipped it into his back pocket. Bypassing the massive hangar doors, he went to the much smaller personnel door near the corner of the building and listened again. Nothing. He tried the door. It opened under his hand.

A man sat at a desk with his back to Chalmers and his feet up. He was breathing deeply, just on the edge of snoring. Chalmers recognized him and stifled a sigh of relief. Supply Officer First Class Justhines was up to his eyeballs in debt, having invested everything he had—including loans from a number of creditors—in purchasing cargo from the various brokerages.

Chalmers grinned and waited. Standing in the open doorway let him enjoy the momentary and slight artificial breeze released from the office as the cold air fled across the threshold to join the heat outside.

The dull thud of the explosion from just outside the wire made Chalmers flinch even though he'd been fully anticipating it. He heaved a relieved sigh. He'd had thirty-five left on his mental countdown.

The supply officer started awake, jumping to his feet.

"What th—"

"A fire! Over at the warehouses!" Chalmers said, standing in the doorway and pointing toward the fireball climbing into the sky.

"What?" Justhines said, face contorting as his sleepy mind tried to catch up with what was happening. The supply officer joined Chalmers at the door. His face went white with dread, but he didn't move.

Not wanting to resort to the sap if he didn't have to, Chalmers played it up. "Never thought I'd be so glad to be a simple wage slave. Those that invested too much in cargoes'll lose everything if that fire spreads much more."

That did it. Justhines rushed back into the office and grabbed his duty belt. Buckling it on, he went to the inner door, threw it open, and shouted at the men working in the hangar proper, "You men, grab firefighting gear and meet me out front!"

The pair of cargo technicians working inside leapt to do their officer's bidding.

"What should I do?" Chalmers asked.

"Wait here!"

"But the shipment…" Chalmers said, hiking a thumb over his shoulder and, in the process, positioning himself to block the door if he had to.

"Right, right." The supply officer yanked the receiver from

the cradle and put it to his ear. He started snapping orders into it a moment later.

Chalmers sweated in the doorway. He could see the fire was spreading, but he wasn't really paying attention. Instead, he strained to hear what the officer was saying.

"Looks like it started in the Fangat warehouses," he said into a lull in the phone conversation. "But now it's spreading to the others, too."

"Wha—I don't bloody care what your sergeant says!" the supply officer screamed into the phone. "We have a schedule to keep to, and I'm the duty officer. Get your men into firefighting gear and down to the warehouses—*now*!" He listened for a moment, then snapped, "I'll be there shortly, and I want everyone turned out to fight this fire." Something said to him made the officer look at Chalmers. He turned away. Despite the officer's attempt at quiet, Chalmers still heard him lower his voice and say, "Of *course* no locals. One of *them* might have started the damned fire, you idiot!"

He slammed the phone down.

Chalmers turned and raised a questioning brow. "What do I do?"

The officer looked him up and down, then came to the only decision the plan allowed for. "You'll just have to stay inside the wire for the duration of the emergency."

Chalmers frowned, said grudgingly, "Can I give you and your men a ride?"

"No, someone's coming for us. Get out of my way." He shouldered Chalmers aside and went out the door just as one of their smaller military vehicles, the Kulsian equivalent of a World War II Jeep, rolled up between the truck and the hangar. He looked over his shoulder as he jumped into the open-topped vehicle. Two men hustled out of the main hangar door, leaving it open behind them. They were moving slowly, firefighting gear weighing them down. One of the hangar doors was left ajar as they climbed in behind the driver and their officer.

"I'll bring her in, then?" Chalmers said.

The supply officer nodded. "And get that cargo aboard the lighter!"

"On my own?" Chalmers whined, hoping he wasn't laying it on too thick.

"Yes. That's why we trained you on the lift system! Oh, and get the truck out of there once you're done."

"I'll just sleep in it out here if you aren't back."

"Good. Have it done before I get back, and I'll drop you a few extra coins as well as put in the good word for your brokerage."

"Oh, thank you!" Chalmers called as the vehicle roared away. As it did, he couldn't keep a feral grin from his lips.

Not that he tried too hard.

Chapter Thirty-Six

As Chalmers hurried back to the truck, he paused to strip the tarps bearing the Twin Stars logo from its sides, revealing the Fangat logo. The paperwork inside the truck was Fangat, too. The tarps went into the back of the truck. That done, he climbed into the cab and started the engine. Leaving the truck idling to keep the refrigeration unit running, he went to open the hangar doors the rest of the way.

The lighter was inside, a vast shape that loomed almost two stories tall and stretched all the way into the far end of the hangar. The lighter's flanks were built to accommodate six of the shipping containers on each side, each bay accessible via external hatches and from a central corridor running fore and aft between them. Clamshell hatches closed over the containers in flight, protecting them from reentry stresses. All but one of them was shut tight, hiding the containers Chalmers had delivered over the last few days. The only open cargo hatch was the one just aft of the crew section. Intended to carry the crew's in-transit consumables, those containers were always loaded last.

"A lot of work for one guy," he huffed as he set his feet and started to push the first door wide.

He walked to the back of the truck and nervously tapped a specific sequence on the metal. A moment's delay, then he heard the answering sequence.

A reassured Chalmers climbed into the cab and drove the truck into the hangar.

Parking beside the massive lighter, Chalmers carefully lined up the container with the lift. Leaving the truck running, he buttoned the hangar up and hurried to the lift controls. He brought the lift bed up and under the container, raising it an inch or so off the truck bed. He took the lift system's remote and hooked it to his belt. Chalmers climbed the external ladder built into the fuselage of the lighter to enter the empty container bay of the interface craft.

Chalmers took the extendable power line from next to the central corridor hatch, returned to the ladder, and dropped the power lines down to the container. Another climb to swap the lines out, shut the truck off, and then had to spend more time he didn't feel he had making sure the load was properly balanced on the lift. He *really* didn't want to have the container slide off while he was loading it. Finalizing the check, Chalmers mopped his brow before climbing the ladder. Again.

So fucking hot, he thought.

Chalmers took a break on reaching the top, wishing he'd been smart enough to remember to clip his canteen to his belt. Parched, he pulled his watch out, put it on, and checked the time. Jackson should be here soon, assuming everything had gone according to plan on his end.

He pulled the remote from his belt and punched the "up" button. Hydraulics whined loudly as they raised the heavy load. Chalmers leaned against the hatch coaming, intending to rest a moment, but he realized he'd forgotten the hose. Which was pretty stupid, since without it, the entire mission was screwed. Cursing, he climbed down and retrieved what resembled a narrow-bore fire hose from the back of the truck cab. Looping it over his shoulder, he bent and tapped a knuckle on the passenger side fuel tank. Satisfied it was the one they'd left empty, he attached the hose.

He climbed up again, sweating bullets this time as he unwound the heavy, flattened hose a meter at a time in his wake. On reaching the open hatch, he removed the remaining loops of hose and lay there panting for a short while.

"So fucking thirsty, I forgot it again."

He was just standing up when the office door swung open to reveal Jackson.

"You made it," Chalmers called, trying to sound less relieved than he was.

Jackson smiled an immediate reply, but didn't speak. He just stood, bent over with both hands on his knees, and breathed.

Moose entered just as Jackson finally caught his breath. Both men wore dark clothing and face paint that blended easily into the night. Or rather, had worn when they began the operation. Both had sweated so profusely their paint ran from their heads in discolored rivulets.

Recovering first, Jackson closed the office door behind Moose, clapped the bigger man on the back, and crossed to the base of the ladder.

"How are my firebugs?" Chalmers asked. The lift continued to rise, cutting Jackson from view unless Chalmers wanted to poke his head out. He did not.

"We're here, ain't we?" Jackson called.

"Fair enough," Chalmers said, biting back an angry retort. What Jackson said was true. If things had gone wrong for either Moose or Jackson, the two were to make for the airport and fly out with Umaren and Vizzel.

The top of the container reached the point he could step out on it. Chalmers stopped the lift. He stood carefully at the container's edge and looked down.

Moose had crossed to join Jackson at the foot of the ladder.

"If you two are finished sucking wind down there, I could use a hand," Chalmers said.

"Right," Jackson said, beginning the climb.

Moose, wiping his brow, looked up and said, "So was this part of your plan? 'Say, let's just take the big guy out and make him run in the heat, then make him climb, then work him like a dog.' Yeah?"

"You slept since what, '69?" Chalmers asked.

"Something like that."

"I'd think you well-rested."

"Fuck you, Chalmers," Moose said, beginning the ascent.

The issue with stowing away on any spacecraft, Yukannak had told them, was that *everything* was repeatedly weighed. The need to effect a weight transfer was why he'd humped a hose up hill and over dale in thousand-degree temperatures. In theory, the weight of every container was checked and then rechecked during preflight by flight control planners and then supply officers on the ground. In practice, this procedure was not rigidly adhered to when operational demands necessitated a tight turnaround, let alone when there was some kind of emergency on the ground. The Kulsians were comfortable with this because in the extremely unlikely event of a discrepancy, both mission planners and officers knew sensors in the hold itself would detect any variance from the bill of lading to the actual weight of each cargo container and automatically abort takeoff if it was in excess of tolerances.

They'd struggled with how to get around the problem—that any stowaways would trigger those sensors—until Chalmers remembered Umaren's complaints about stripping *Loklis* of A/C parts. It was all about shedding weight in one place so you could add it to another.

Chalmers walked into the central corridor of the lighter and across to bay two, where the last container he'd brought across the wire resided. Checking the manifest to be sure it was the proper one, he smiled. He pushed a specific, palm-sized, section of the container in and to one side. A spigot not unlike a common garden hose bib was mounted within.

He turned to find Jackson stepping off the ladder.

"Hook a brother up?" Jackson said, holding the remaining loops of hose out for Chalmers to connect.

Chalmers grinned and grabbed the hose. He walked into the corridor, hooked it to the master cargo console set beside the hatch to the crew area, and then ran an integral line from the console to the concealed spigot on container two. He made sure the connections were tight and called to Jackson, "We secure down there?"

"Looks good," Jackson said.

"No kinks?"

"Only your own, brother," Moose said.

"Opening." Chalmers tapped the button on the console to begin pumping. A button next to it lit a dull amber. He pressed it home without reading the label.

Liquid gurgled, gushed, and filled the hose as a pump integral to the machinery below the console kicked on, pulling liquid from the container to the console and then on down the line and into the truck's empty passenger-side fuel tank. The empty fuel tank would hold the equivalent of seventy-five gallons.

The hose leading through the bay started smoking. Not a real smoke, more like hot Florida pavement struck with a cold rain of the Caribbean.

That's not right, Chalmers thought, sluggish and slow.

Chalmers looked from it to Jackson, who gestured at the console where the hose to the truck connected. Chalmers looked down. The fitting was rimed in smoking ice.

"Did you forget to turn on the heater?" Moose called from outside, a note of alarm in his voice. "'Cause this hose is looking mighty fat."

"Fuck," Chalmers said. He swallowed against a dry throat and stood to look down on the controls. The button that had glowed amber to warn him of the temperature difference was still lit. He slapped it, but nothing seemed to happen.

He took a second to actually read through all the markings on the console, found one below the button he'd pressed to start the water flow that was marked HEATER. He jabbed it, hard. The flow slowed as it was run through a heating coil before being pumped out, but it was already too late. The waxed-fiber hose running from the pump to the truck had been at room temperature, nearly a hundred degrees. The metal fuel tank off the truck, absorbing the heat radiated from the tarmac all day, was even hotter. The water in the cargo container was held at just above freezing. Rapid expansion of the water as it warmed made for a buildup of vapor in the line, leading to gulping backups at the truck end of the hose as the air sought a way out of the closed system. Without a release valve, pressure built. With pressure came more heat, which in turn built more air pressure in the line. The hose, made stiff and even somewhat brittle by the cold water rushing through it, was called on to expand to hold the mixture of pressurized air and water. Said pressure mounted until the local-manufactured hose split with a sound like a diarrhea-afflicted giant's extremely wet fart, if said wet fart was sufficiently powerful to tear the farter's pants apart with an accompanying ripping-fabric sound.

"Jesus!" Moose shouted from the hatch. The hangar was gray and misty beyond him as the torn hose continued to vent in great gasping burps.

Chalmers hit the emergency shut-off.

"Shut it down!" Jackson screamed.

"I did!" Chalmers yelled back.

The sound of flowing water and burping hose ends slowly diminished.

Moose, brows drawn together like a thunderhead, turned from looking below and stalked past Jackson toward Chalmers.

Chalmers thought—for just one idiotic instant—about pulling the sap from his pocket to defend himself, but the big man pushed a hand past his shoulder and turned the pump back on.

"Still gotta get all the water out of there."

"Fuck," Chalmers gulped, trembling.

"No use crying over spilt milk," Moose said, not unkindly. "Much as I want to toss you down there for a swim."

Jackson was at the cargo hatch, looking down. He turned to stare at Chalmers. His lips were a thin, bitter line. "Smooth move, ex-lax!"

Chalmers threw his hands up. "How was I supposed to know that would happen?"

"Because Yukannak told us to make sure the water was room temperature before pumping. You either didn't hear him or ignored him because you don't like him. Either way, you done fucked us all."

"Get your panties untwisted, Jackson," Moose rumbled. "That kinda shit ain't helping anyone."

"There's a freaking lake under us and you want me to calm down?!"

Moose sighed and said, "You been through a monsoon before?"

"A what?" Chalmers said at the apparent non sequitur.

"A monsoon, motherfucker," Jackson snapped. Chalmers was hard-pressed to remember when his partner had last been so angry with him.

"More accurately: when the leading edge of a monsoon hits," Moose explained. Seeing nothing but blank stares, he said, "No? Well, the air is dry enough, even on a humid coast, to dry a paved road in a very short time, even at night."

"There a lot of paved roads in Vietnam?" Jackson snarled sarcastically.

"Downtown Saigon? Yeah," Moose said. "Not to mention the airport."

Jackson calmed slightly, still muttering angrily as he climbed down the ladder to secure the tank end of the hose.

"That true?" Chalmers asked quietly.

"Fuck if I know." Moose turned on him, poking a finger into Chalmers's chest as if to emphasize his point. "I *do* know something from personal experience. Back in 'Nam, some guys got it into their heads that fragging leadership was fully justified. It isn't. At least, not during an operation. No matter how much command might deserve a Willie Pete shoved down their throat, during the mission, all is forgiven or all is lost."

Chalmers swallowed, looked away.

"Let's get the rest done, then we can start sweating Lake Chalmers." Moose was grinning as he stepped from the corridor to the container bay.

Failing to see anything funny in the big man's words, Chalmers turned and went to retrieve the necessary tools from the ship's locker.

By the time Chalmers collected the tools and returned to the hold, the mist hanging in the air outside the lighter had cleared and the container had been fully drained of water. Chalmers passed the cargo console. A different amber light glowed a steady warning above the status lights for bay two, the one they were working on. Chalmers grunted in satisfaction. Some things were going to plan. Yukannak had said the light would be red if the weight was too heavy, amber if too light as the latter was far less to worry about than the former.

Moose finished uncovering the last of the concealed bolts securing the end of container two. Chalmers knelt and set the pneumatic wrench to the first bolt. It came free after less than a minute. Nineteen more to go. The work was hot, awkward, and time-consuming, if not terribly difficult. And it was necessary, seeing as each container was inspected by the supply officer after installation and, if not intended to supply the flight crew, affixed with a chemically treated lead seal to prevent opening. Trying to reattach the seal after penetrating it was simply not something they could do on anything like the operational timeframe they'd have, so Vat had come up with this particular workaround.

"Moose, need you over here," Chalmers said, gesturing with the pneumatic wrench at the front of the container, which was now loose enough to fall forward if unsupported.

Moose dropped the coiled hose off the edge of the container and joined Chalmers.

"Make sure this shit doesn't fall on me." Chalmers blinked sweat from his eyes and blew a raspberry to clear his mouth. "So damn hot," he muttered.

"Got it," Moose said, leaning his bulk against the container front.

Chalmers resumed working. The tenth bolt came free. Eleventh. His world narrowed to the bolt, the wrench, the task. Rinse. Repeat.

"Running out of time, Chalmers," Jackson called from below. Distantly, he heard the cab door slam and the truck start.

"Got it," Chalmers said as the last bolt came free. At least he'd stopped sweating. He stood. The world swayed, steadied. He helped Moose pull the container end free and carefully wrestle the slab of composite material to the deck. The expandable bladder that had contained the frigid water was bunched up by the spigot, leaving a space approximately two meters deep and just under three meters wide on all sides.

"Get the scaffolds set up while I help Jacks?" Chalmers said. He was too tired to trust the accuracy of his work and this next phase was tricky.

Moose took the tools from him and nodded. "Good work, Chalmers."

Chalmers just nodded and staggered out of the bay onto the container top. The floor of the hangar still shone with damp, but there wasn't a lake to look at. Bone weary, Chalmers sighed and looked at his watch. The mental arithmetic was far harder now than when the night began, but he got there: one hour until flight prep. The fires would be about out by now.

They were on borrowed time.

Jackson had moved the truck outside, was struggling to push the hangar door back into place. He was too close to finishing for Chalmers to get down and be of any real help.

"Can't see the fires anymore," Jackson called. He finished closing the hangar door and jogged across the floor toward the office. He had Chalmers's canteen in his hands. He went into the office, emerged a minute later.

Chalmers did not feel at all well.

"Hey, you take your pills?" Jackson shouted. He was at the base of the ladder. How had Chalmers missed his only friend's approach?

"What?" Chalmers muttered. He staggered, almost fell forward and all the way down, leaned back in alarm, decided to take a seat and fell on his ass atop the container. He blinked, thoughts turgid and slow.

Next thing he knew, Jackson was there.

"Here, drink this." Jackson's voice was worried as he put the canteen to his partner's lips.

"I'm fine."

"No, you're not. You're burning up. Dehydrated as fuck."

Chalmers pulled at the canteen, had to admit the liquid felt phenomenal going down, but then he puked. Dry heaved, really.

"That's not right," he mumbled.

"No, it isn't. Keep drinking. Stay put."

"Mmmkay," Chalmers said. He went away for a while.

Chapter Thirty-Seven

"And . . . *now*!" Raptis exclaimed as the packet slid into the ice-teroid's shadow.

Kamara gave the ship a small boost to match the ice-teroid's velocity. A fairly large body, the object was pear shaped, nearly sixteen kilometers long and ten kilometers in diameter at its widest point. The thin end, which pointed generally away from the star as it slowly tumbled through space, was only about six kilometers.

"Okay," Kamara said when he was satisfied with the craft's positioning alongside the narrow end. His shoulders sagged as he released the breath he'd been holding. He turned to Raptis. "Your turn."

Raptis nodded and pushed off toward the airlock. "Come on, Bowden. This was your idea. You're my backup."

"We got lucky," Raptis announced once she and Bowden returned from their spacewalk two hours later. "There's a vein not too far up from this end. It's big, but the fatter end of the asteroid has blocked the seam from being heated too much prior. There is a lot of ice inside it we can use to our benefit. Because of the way the asteroid is shaped, we can burn our engine without any liminal heat being seen by the planet."

"You're sure you want to do this?" Kamara asked. "There is a possibility that this could go horribly wrong. If something

307

outgasses and hits the ship, we could find ourselves on a vector where no one will ever be able to get us."

Hrensku shrugged. "No one's going to come and rescue us in any event."

"Why's that?" Fiezel asked.

"There's no way they could get to us and get back without being seen," Hrensku said, shaking his head. "And since they can't..."

"They won't," Bowden finished. Hrensku nodded. "Therefore," Bowden continued, "it's up to us, and this is the only way we're going to get there without being seen. We have to try it. If it doesn't work or we're seen doing it, then we'll have to come up with a different plan."

"What would that be?" Kamara asked.

"I have no idea, so let's just make this work. Okay?"

Raptis chuckled. "It's our only hope, and the ice seam looked good. I say we try it."

"I agree," Hrensku said. "It really is our only chance of completing the mission...which is our only chance of getting out of this alive."

"I'm in," Fiezel said.

"As am I," Kamara said. "Anything is better than being caught by the Kulsians." He shrugged. "Even drifting off into space with no chance of rescue."

As complicated as the maneuver was going to be—to put them on a vector that would pull them into an orbit around the second planet without anything other than minor thruster corrections—Kamara booted up the computer, and they worked out the vector and thrust they'd need to intercept the planet. The results had Kamara shaking his head.

"It's going to take a big thrust pulse to get us there, which means that not only are we going to need a big outgassing screen to hide behind, we're also going to have to start our thrust for the planet much closer to the asteroid so we're not seen."

"It's what we have to do," Bowden said, "so let's do it. You take the pilot's seat, and I'll back you up as copilot."

"Very well. Everyone else is going to need to be strapped in. There is no telling what will outgas from the asteroid, nor where it will go when it does."

"Everyone's ready," Bowden said a little while later, once the packet and the people onboard were as secure as possible. Bowden had also passed the word to the commandos in the modules to secure themselves for thrust/collision; both outcomes were possible with what they were planning.

"Maneuvering," Kamara said. The ship was pointed away from the asteroid, and he walked it over sideways with the ACS thrusters, using the cameras at the back of the craft to watch his progress.

Bowden forced himself to breathe as the landscape of the asteroid passed beneath him far closer than he was comfortable with. After a few minutes, the seam appeared below them, darker in color than the rocky surface, and Kamara used the attitude control system thrusters again to stabilize their position over it.

"Here we go," Kamara said. Bowden could hear the strain in the pilot's voice as he intentionally put his ship—and everyone onboard—in danger. His fingers danced as he slowly advanced power to the engine while matching it with the ACS system to hold his position.

Nothing happened.

"We need to move closer," Kamara said.

"Give it a minute," Bowden replied. "Let it heat."

"We won't have the fuel for an extended burn if we waste it playing with this."

Bowden's eyes darted to the fuel gauge. The level was dropping—slowly, but visibly—toward the mark Kamara had drawn. When it reached the mark, they had to boost for the planetoid or they wouldn't have the fuel to reach it.

"Okay," Bowden agreed. "A little closer."

"Moving," Kamara said. He reduced thrust ever so slightly, and the ship moved toward the asteroid. Within seconds, vapor began to boil away from the ice seam.

"It's working," Bowden said.

"See, we just needed to get—" Without warning, the motor cut out completely, and the asteroid began growing quickly in the camera view. Kamara flipped the switches to restart the engine, but Bowden could see they were going to hit before the engine would be able to develop enough thrust to boost them away.

"Shit!" Bowden said, having had more than his share of bad rendezvous with asteroids. He slapped the aft ACS thrusters to full and killed the forward thrusters, which were pushing them toward the asteroid. The planetoid continued to grow in the camera view for another few seconds, then—just as it seemed Bowden could reach through the camera and touch the surface—it began to recede again. Bowden jockeyed the ACS controls to slow their velocity away from the planetoid, then stabilized the ship's position with respect to the asteroid beneath them.

"What the hell was that?" Bowden asked.

"I don't know," Kamara replied. "You saw—the engine just cut out."

"Yeah, but then you didn't do anything to stop our momentum down."

"I was trying to get the motor started."

"We were going to hit. I saved us."

"Maybe," Kamara finally allowed. "Maybe I panicked; I don't know. I thought I could get it restarted in time, but, thinking about it now, maybe not."

"Maybe we should stop and check it," Bowden said.

"No, the fuel we use isn't perfect, and the engine cuts out every once in a while. Let me run the diagnostics on the engine, and we can try again. We're already in position, and I don't want to lose any heating of the ice below that we've already done. We won't have enough fuel if we do."

Kamara restarted the engine and ran the diagnostic on it while Bowden let everyone know what was happening.

"We're ready for another try," Kamara said. "Everything is good, and I can't find anything wrong with the engine. It must have been a bit of bad fuel, as I suspected."

"Okay," Bowden replied, trying to keep his tone level. A second attempt violated most of the procedures he'd learned in the Navy.

"Here we go." Kamara moved the ship closer to the asteroid and increased power.

Bowden leaned forward and kept his hands close to the thruster panel. If it was needed again, he was going to be ready. Having done it once, Kamara moved to the position where they'd been when the motor failed and brought up the power levels again. Within seconds, the ice began to vaporize again, and the cloud of vapor grew quickly. Soon, pieces of rock and other, non-vaporized things began to spew from the crevasse, and Bowden heard a loud *bang!* as one of them hit the hull.

"Want to move a little farther from the asteroid?" Bowden

asked nervously. A rock that destroyed something in the propulsion system was just as good a mission kill as a Kulsian ship-to-ship missile.

"I've got it," Kamara said, jockeying the craft to the side slightly. The surface of the craft rang with repeated small impacts, almost as if it were raining on the hull.

Bowden glanced up, and his jaw fell. Kamara had a giant smile on his face that could be seen through his helmet as he worked the craft back and forth over the seam. When it got too hard to see the surface, he'd move slowly to the side until he could see again, slowly painting the craft's exhaust over a greater and greater swath of the ice vein.

Smash!

Something spewing forth from the vein hit the camera. There was a flash of rock, then the screen went black. Bowden's finger moved to the ACS thruster.

"No!" Kamara ordered. He looked out the ship's small canopy. "I've still got it. I can see...well enough. I think."

The qualifier didn't do Bowden's nerves any good as the rate of things hitting the hull continued to grow. Bowden would have hated to be the commandos—their boxes were probably taking a pounding and they'd have no idea what was going on. *The container walls are thick—they won't get holed...I hope.* The first yellow warning light illuminated on the control panel. A sensor on the aft portion of the ship had ceased reporting.

Bowden took a quick look out the canopy. He didn't see how Kamara was able to continue. The cloud completely enveloped them, and it continued to grow and thicken. As did the pattern of impacts with the hull.

"How much more can the ship take?" Bowden asked.

"As much as it needs," Kamara replied with a grunt as he slid it back to the right again.

Another glance to the fuel gauge; they were almost at minimum fuel for their maneuver. "The fuel..." Bowden warned.

"I know," Kamara replied.

"You're going to shave it too thin!"

"I know!" Kamara paused, nodded a couple times to himself, then stabbed the enable button on the autopilot. The ACS thrusters cut off, and the engine roared to full power. The ship accelerated a second, then spun to its intended course while the engine continued at full thrust. After about ten seconds, it cut out, and Kamara turned to look at Bowden as they started to draw ahead of the ice-teroid and angled off to the side.

"We're on our way," Kamara said. "For better or worse, we're on our way."

Chapter Thirty-Eight

On the second day outbound from the asteroid, Bowden called the team together. So far, there hadn't been a response to their maneuver from the second planet or any indication that they'd been seen. Passive sensors showed the corvette orbiting the planet as if nothing had happened. Whether that was because the corvette's crew and the planetside operators hadn't seen them, or they were just waiting for the packet to get closer, though, no one knew. Bowden, however, had more immediate concerns.

He met each of the team's eyes, but none of them had what he was looking for. Fear of being caught. A dare to be challenged. Not knowing how to proceed, he took a deep breath and just said it. "One of you is a traitor."

"What?" Kamara said. "How do you know someone is a traitor?"

"I looked at the ship's log. The engine dying while we were maneuvering near the asteroid wasn't an accident. Someone programmed it to shut down."

Bowden shook his head. "And this isn't the first time it's happened. Someone sabotaged an interface craft I was flying a few months ago." He looked at Hrensku. "It almost killed me."

"That wasn't me," Hrensku replied. "I didn't do it then, and I didn't do this, either."

"Funny that you were in close proximity to both, though, isn't it?"

"I don't find it funny at all," Kamara said. "I find it horrific. There's only one penalty for such a crime in our society."

313

"And what's that?" Bowden asked.

"We space him."

"Wait a minute," Hrensku said. "I didn't do either of those things. Why would I make a craft that I was in crash into an asteroid to highlight myself to the enemy? It makes no sense!"

"To make yourself look innocent," Kamara said. "Just like you said: Who would be dumb enough to disconnect a RATO bottle on takeoff?" He shrugged. "And, as to highlighting us, perhaps it is part of a plan for you to curry favor with the Kulsians."

Hrensku turned to Bowden. "I thought you said you believed I wasn't responsible for the crash."

"I do, actually. I believed it at the time, and I believe it now."

"Then who is responsible for this?" Raptis asked.

"I don't know," Bowden replied, "but it has to be one of you RockHounds."

"It isn't me," Raptis said. "What would I stand to gain?"

"A reward?" Hrensku asked. "Perhaps a new ship?"

"But I was promised a new ship when we returned."

Hrensku shrugged. "*If* we returned, you would get it. Maybe you weren't sure we'd make it, and you were trying to hedge your bets or get in good with the Kulsians."

Raptis turned to Bowden. "You saved my life. I *owe* you. I owe Kamara, too. Our society doesn't dismiss an honor debt so quickly."

"But—in a similar vein—Kamara owes both you and me for saving his life. If that's true, then he didn't do it, either, and we're back where we started."

"Exactly," Kamara said. "Either Hrensku did it, or one of you Terrans did."

"It wasn't me," Bowden said. "I have nothing to gain. If we get caught, I'm looking at a lot of torture, not a reward from the Kulsians. Fiezel would get the same treatment."

Kamara nodded. "Which, once again, leads us back to Hrensku."

"Who I don't think did it."

"Maybe," Raptis said. She shrugged. "And maybe not. Only one person is here voluntarily." She turned to Kamara. "You. Bowden and Fiezel were ordered here, as was Hrensku, for all intents and purposes. I lost my ship; I had nowhere else to go. But you"—she pointed—"*you* volunteered your ship and your services. Why did you do that? I've never known you to put your life at risk without a large gain."

"I saved your life, didn't I?"

"I suspect that had Bowden not been with you, you would have let me perish, then swooped in to take my ship for your own. That was probably your plan all along. You just happened to show up at the comet in time to rescue me? I'll bet you hoped to find me dead already so you could take my ship and the load it carried. Too bad I wasn't quite dead yet."

"What do you mean? That's crazy! Murphy told me to train him in the worst environments I could. That, to me, means flying near a comet."

Raptis turned to Bowden. "I never told anyone, but my ship was sabotaged. When I landed on the comet and shut down the motor, the fuel lines crimped, and I was unable to start it again. I could have avoided the outgassing—I saw it coming—but my ship wouldn't start up again. I told him"—she nodded to Kamara—"about an hour before I left that I was headed to the comet."

"An hour prior," Kamara agreed. "There wasn't time for me to do anything to your packet. And it's a good thing you told me about the comet—that's how I knew it existed. If you hadn't told me, you'd be dead now."

"Hmm..." Hrensku said. "I believe I have another perspective on this. On the day of our plane crash, I saw Kamara on the planet. I thought it strange for a RockHound to be planetside, but, in the confusion after the crash, I never got a chance to talk to him, and I never thought about it again. What were you doing there, Kamara?"

"I was down trading for needed supplies," Kamara replied. "It happens. You know RockHounds go to the planet once in a while for supplies."

"Is that true?" Bowden asked.

"Once in a *very* long while," Hrensku replied. "It isn't unheard of, but it is *very* unusual. Most can't stand the gravity."

"But not unheard of," Kamara said with a nod. "And that is what happened—I was there trading."

"You told me you were on Outpost then," Raptis said.

"I went there after my trip to the planet," Kamara said with a smile. "When I saw you, I was coming from Outpost."

"No." Raptis shook her head. "The numbers don't match. There is no way you could have gotten from the planet, to Outpost, and back in the time you had." She looked to Bowden while pointing at Kamara. "There's your traitor!"

"Wait a minute!" Kamara said. "Just because she says—"

"No," Bowden said, "she's right. You're the traitor."

"What do you mean? I never—"

"Let me ask you one question. How did you know the RATO bottle was disconnected?"

"Well, uh…" Kamara sputtered a few seconds, then said, "It was common knowledge that's what happened."

Bowden shook his head. "Fiezel was the one who saw the bottle was disconnected and—as far as I know—he never told anyone."

Fiezel shook his head. "I never mentioned it."

"Wait!" Hrensku exclaimed. "The bottle was disconnected?"

Bowden looked at Hrensku to gauge his reaction. "It was."

Hrensku launched himself at Kamara, who tried to block him and force him away. Hrensku bounced off the RockHound but got a handful of Kamara's suit and pulled himself back in. Kamara lost his handhold and the two floated free as they struggled to gain an advantage on each other.

"Stop it!" Raptis exclaimed in a voice that cut through their struggle. "Stop it *right now.*"

All four men looked to find Raptis holding a small pistol, which she pointed at Kamara. Hrensku pushed away from the RockHound, and they floated toward opposite bulkheads.

"Why did you do it, Karas'tan?" Raptis asked.

Drops of blood floated free from Kamara's nose. The larger Hrensku had obviously scored on at least one of his blows. Kamara shrugged. "To stop all of this"—he waved a hand around at the lighter—"as you *know* nothing good can come of it. You know that's true, don't you?"

Raptis shrugged. "I don't know what the plan is, but it's too late to stop it. All we can do now is try to guide it to a successful end." She stared at him a moment. "But you didn't know what we were doing before you came aboard. What is the real reason?"

"Money, of course." Kamara laughed. "People wanted Hrensku dead, and I was sent to kill him."

"Wait," Bowden said. "The RATO sabotage *was* you, wasn't it?"

"Of course. And if Hrensku had been good enough to sit in the left seat, like he was supposed to, I wouldn't be here now." He chuckled. "You Terrans, always thinking everything is about you." He stared at Bowden for a moment and then added, "It's not."

Hrensku tensed, balling his fists again.

"Stay away from him," Raptis said. "He's told us all we need to know. He's guilty of sabotage and attempted murder."

"You wouldn't," Kamara said. "After I rescued you from the comet?"

"Wouldn't what?" Bowden asked.

"Put him out the airlock," Raptis replied, never taking her eyes off Kamara. "And yes, I would. You may have saved me from the comet, but I saved you and then Bowden saved us both. And you do not gain the Death Fathers' approval for coming to the asteroid since all you *really* wanted to do was kill me and take my goods as your prize."

Kamara shrugged. "It was worth an effort."

"Move!" Raptis ordered. She motioned with the pistol. "Airlock. Now." She shepherded him to the airlock, with the rest of the team in trail. "Strip."

Kamara gave her a cruel smile. "You'd like that, wouldn't you? A chance to see me naked one more time?"

"I couldn't care less about seeing you naked; I just don't want to waste the material in your suit and clothes. They're worth more than the hundred kilos of shit stuffed inside them."

"And if I don't?"

"Then I shoot you, and we toss your bleeding body into the airlock. It'd be a waste of clothes and a pain in the ass to clean up the mess, but it'd be totally worth it. Please, *please,* give me a reason to shoot you."

Kamara slowly peeled away the suit, then floated naked in front of Raptis with his arms out to the sides. She shook her head. "Do I have to tell you to do it?"

He nodded. "Yes." He shrugged. "And you'll be sorry if you do."

"What the hell is that supposed to mean?"

"You want me alive. You need me alive."

"You're wrong." Raptis shook her head. "We need you dead. Get in the airlock."

"You'll be sorry."

"I'm already sorry. *Now get in the damned airlock!*"

Kamara opened the airlock door and moved inside, then turned and looked expectantly at her.

"If you think I'm coming any closer to you so that you can grab me, you're even dumber than I know you are." She motioned toward the door controls. "Shut it."

Kamara pushed the button and moved away from the panel. As the door closed, Raptis suddenly pushed off toward the airlock controls. Seeing her movement, Kamara tried to reverse his direction and beat her to the panel, but she was too fast. She knocked his hand back into the airlock, the door closed, and she cycled the airlock. His scream was lost as the air was ripped from his lungs, and his bowels evacuated.

Bowden looked away, having seen enough.

After a few seconds, Raptis cycled the airlock controls. "There was a point in time where he wasn't such a bad guy." She sighed. "Unfortunately, that was a long time ago."

"What do we do now?" Hrensku asked.

"Nothing's changed," Bowden replied. "We're committed and don't have a way to change our vector without being seen. We continue."

Chapter Thirty-Nine

Chalmers woke thinking a large woman was sitting on his chest to restrict his air while beating every inch of his flesh. He tried to shake her off, thrashing around, but it did no good. The large woman just clamped one of his wrists in a massive fist.

"Chalmers, cut it out!" Jackson said.

Chalmers briefly wondered why his partner was a part of this weird fetish-sex dream he was having, but then realized it was Moose who had him by the wrist and that Jackson was actually yelling at him from his other side.

"What the hell?" Chalmers croaked. He had to repeat it, louder. The roar of engines covered anything less than a shout.

"You passed out! Heat stroke!" Jackson shouted back.

Chalmers thought about things for a moment. The engine noise was a screaming rumble that made it hard to think. It dawned on him the pressure he'd felt all over and thought was someone trying to suffocate him was actually the g-forces of liftoff.

As if thoughts of the forces at play ended them, Chalmers felt the sudden removal of the weight on his chest. The subsequent full throat and swollen-head feeling of zero-gee was even less comfortable. He smiled anyway. They were on their way.

"Holy shit, we pulled it off," Chalmers said, voice reedy and thin to his own ears. His lips were parched, his throat dry where bile wasn't trying to surge up from his belly.

"No shit, Sherlock," Jackson said. His grin was violet in the dim illumination of a R'Bakuun chemlight.

"Still not done, snake," Moose said.

Chalmers nodded more soberly. "Jesus, you two had to do everything on your own?"

Jackson shrugged awkwardly against the four-point restraints rigged to the scaffolding. "Nothing new. I'm used to carrying your white ass."

Moose was more serious. "Wasn't that big a deal. I got the scaffolds built, and Jackson strapped you in."

They were side by side in the narrow space, half-seated on and half-suspended from the scaffolding that Moose had begun to rig when Chalmers walked out of the hold and passed out. The scaffold was like a seat, but relied on a suspension rig rather than cushions to prevent injury from the rattling associated with high-gee maneuvers.

"Everyone else?"

"Still good, last we checked."

"They didn't delay the launch to search for me?"

"Nope. In too much of a rush, just like Yukannak said they'd be."

"How long?"

"Were you out?"

Chalmers nodded.

Jackson checked his watch. "A bit under five hours. You were well and truly cooked, and the A/C unit took a while to chill us out."

"Speaking of which..." Moose said. He unhooked a canteen from the scaffold next to him. It had been fitted with a nipple preflight to prevent the contents from floating off in microgravity. "Drink up."

Chalmers sucked greedily. There was a weird, almost floral flavor to the water. He swallowed.

"What's in this?"

"It's laced with *hegi* petals tribal healers use to treat dehydration," Moose said.

"Where'd you pick that up?"

Moose slowly spread his hands. "Spent a lot of time around one of the SpinDog docs who trades with the healers at the poles."

"Spent time?" Chalmers said with a half-hearted leer.

"Nothing like that," Moose said flatly. "I don't like to waste time, so I try and pick up new skills as and when I can."

Chalmers wasn't sure what that meant, but the big guy clearly wasn't going to say any more on the subject, so he occupied himself with draining the rest of the canteen. He was already feeling better by the time it was done.

"Bet we smell a treat," Jackson said.

"Speak for yourself, I only smell sweeter the more I sweat," Moose said.

"Bullshit," Chalmers said.

"Just like I've only grown prettier with each passing year," Moose continued.

"And your wedding tackle's bigger?" Jackson grinned.

"Nah, can't improve on perfection," Moose said, lacing his fingers behind his head, the motion somewhat ruined when one of his elbows caught on the container wall.

The partners stifled laughter. It was unlikely they'd be heard through the container wall, the bulkhead, hatch, and several meters of corridor to the cockpit, but shit could happen and probably would, given their luck. Murphy's Law, after all.

Chalmers looked to his left and right, and decided—shit luck or no—he'd rather not have anyone else along on this particular ride with him. They just had to survive the next thirty-plus hours of claustrophobic inactivity, take over a spaceship without getting killed or breaking anything important, and then join up with a group of recently unreliable allies.

"Easy peasy," Chalmers mumbled. He waited a beat, then added, "Not that I need to, yet, but where do we piss?"

A faint vibration woke Chalmers from a half doze. It was repeated a little while later. He stretched to ease a cramp and bumped against Moose's shoulder. He checked his watch: twenty-five hours in. He looked up from it to see Jackson was watching him. His partner flicked his gaze to the container wall and pressed a finger to his lips.

"I think..." Moose's whisper was hoarse.

Chalmers looked at him, but the big veteran had his eyes closed. "What?" he said after a moment.

Moose gestured him to silence with one hand. The other was flat against the container wall in front of them.

Chalmers looked at his watch and waited a full minute without hearing anything before whispering, "What is it?"

"Shh..." Moose laid his other hand on the wall.

Chalmers did the same, just in time to feel a faint vibration through the composite. He looked over at Moose to find the other man's eyes open, and his mouth set in a thin line.

"What was that?"

Moose looked at him and whispered, "I think... a container door is open. It keeps hitting the bulkhead every ten seconds or so."

"Did one of you hear the corridor hatch open? Someone walking out there?"

"No," both men said.

"Who would leave a container doo—" Jackson started.

Chalmers popped a cold sweat. "Fucking *Yukannak.*"

"Jesus," Jackson swore.

Moose put his hands to the latch for the container doors and looked a question at Chalmers.

Chalmers hit the release on his harness. Jackson did the same beside him. They both braced themselves. Prepared to launch himself out, Chalmers nodded at Moose. He unlatched and threw open the doors, which clanged against the bulkhead and sent the torn inspection seal flying free to join the one from Yukannak and Vat's container. Jackson and Chalmers were both out and almost inside container one before the doors started to rebound.

Vat hung in his harness, unconscious or dead. Yukannak was conspicuous in his absence.

Chalmers launched himself for the cargo console and paged through some data until he found the graphic for the crew's remaining drinking water. Not quite halfway to the point they'd figured sufficient to knock them out.

"I'll take care of Vat if he's still kicking," Jackson said.

Moose bounced from the corridor wall to grab a convenient rung next to the console. He pointed with his chin at the touch panel next to the hatch.

Chalmers looked. Bypass clips were hooked into wires within the panel. The floating face of the panel still glowed a steady green, indicating the portal remained unlocked.

"Why go before they were fully dosed?" Moose asked.

Chalmers shrugged, resultant inertia nearly pulling him from the console.

Jackson didn't turn from Vat. "Because he wanted time to

talk them into backing his play, and them being a little loose
from the drugs would only make it easier . . ."

Chalmers launched himself across at the hatch leading to
the regular crew module. "And just because the *plan* called for
them to consume more, didn't mean it was strictly necessary.
We were erring on the side of caution. Wanted them good and
soused when we came out."

"Shit."

"Yeah."

"So, what do we do now?" Moose's knuckles were white where
he clutched at the rung.

Chalmers swallowed. "Go after him—them. Fast and hard."

"Right." Moose pushed off, fetched up against the hatch leading to the crew spaces.

Vat moaned. Jackson turned from him. "He's unconscious, but
he'll be fine. Looks like Yukannak slipped him the same mickey
we were giving the crew, only he got the full dose."

Relief flooded Chalmers. As much because he wanted Jacks
next to him in a fight as for the news of Vat's condition. He
pushed off for the side opposite Moose and caught himself with
a minimum of flailing. Moose already had his sap thonged to his
wrist. Chalmers pulled his out and did the same with it.

"We need to move fast once we open this," Moose said.

"Tell me again why they won't just vent the atmosphere when
we appear?" Chalmers asked.

"According to the SpinDogs, venting atmosphere is a good
way to get launched off course very rapidly, not to mention a
waste of resources," Moose said.

"But even if the Kulsis assholes think the same way guys
brought up in orbital habs do, they might try it outta spite,"
Jackson said, joining them at the hatch. "And in that case, we
should have a bunch of visible warnings as they override the
safety measures to vent atmosphere." He held up his sap. "At
which point it's crackin' crackers' faceplates till they think better of the idea."

Listening to Jackson, Chalmers felt a surge of confidence
that simply wouldn't withstand rational analysis. Deciding not
to overthink it, he rode it.

Moose looked at them both. His sweat-streaked paint job
made him look vaguely clownish—or rather, like a militaristic

version of the clown-creature in *It*. "Much as I like watching you two wind each other up, the more time we spend here, the more time Yuk has to pull shit. We need to go."

The crew module had crew cabins aft of the hatch to the cargo bays, a small mess/briefing room immediately beneath it, and the bridge—flight deck, really—forward of it. Each had its own hatch. "So," Chalmers said aloud. "Down this hatch, forward to the bridge hatch, through it, and take out whoever is at the controls. Regroup, head aft and deal with anyone behind. Jacks in the lead, me next, Moose bringin' up the rear."

"Right," Jackson and Moose chorused.

"Go."

Moose pressed the panel. The hatch irised open.

Jackson pulled himself through first, launching headfirst between the decks. Chalmers came second, turning to watch the crew cabins. The short corridor that let out on the cabins was empty and silent, their individual hatches closed.

Seeing no one, Chalmers tried to look the other way. He only succeeded in imparting a spin to his movements. "Below" him, Jackson bounced on his hands and shoved off toward the bridge. Chalmers was less graceful about it, banging his shoulder painfully as he rebounded off the deck.

Moose managed to not only grab Chalmers but hook both feet under a pair of grab bars. Grunting with effort, he hauled back and launched Chalmers toward the hatch.

Stifling the urge to puke as his ears and eyes disagreed with which way he was traveling, Chalmers prepared to stick his landing this time.

He coasted past Jackson, who was pulling himself forward hand over hand.

This hatch wasn't rigged like the one between crew module and cargo bays, leading Chalmers to wonder just where the hell Yukannak was.

Chalmers brushed a couple grip bars, slowing his rush to the hatch.

"Try it and see," Jackson said quietly.

Chalmers realized that if the hatch opened under his touch, Jacks was lined up to fly straight through without slowing. Thinking he probably looked like a shitty Superman, he reached out and punched the panel.

The hatch irised open. Jacks went through.

Neither of the crew was suited. The pilot looked over, a dopey grin on his face. That grin barely had an opportunity to congeal before Jackson was on him. Moose flew through, blocking Jackson and the pilot from view.

Chalmers pulled himself into the crowded flight deck just as Moose swung his sap at the man punching buttons at the engineering station. The engineer shoved back from his workstation. Moose missed, the momentum from his swing carrying him around in an unsteady—and uncontrolled—spin.

Chalmers launched himself at the engineer, who was struggling free of his seat webbing. He heard a meaty thump and hoped it was Jackson cracking the pilot a good one rather than Moose knocking himself out on a bulkhead. Then there was no time for thought. He grabbed the frame of the engineer's chair in his off hand, punched out with the sap in hopes of losing less body control on a miss, and clipped the engineer's shoulder instead of his chin. The man grunted, popped the rest of the way out of the restraint system, and somehow managed a strike to Chalmers's gut.

Wind whistling as it fled his lungs, Chalmers swung around the pivot-point of his death grip on the chair, wrenching his wrist with the sudden, awkward change of direction.

The engineer kicked out at Chalmers, or tried to. The odd booties Kulsis spacers wore struck a control. Something glowed an angry red in response.

Releasing the weapon to swing from his wrist, Chalmers shoved hard off the deck with his sap hand and legs. He spun back around, his pivot-wrist shrieking protest. His fist missed. The sap, on its several inches of thong, did not. Something gave way with an audible crack, but Chalmers was too busy slamming his chest against the chair to know what. Wheezing, he tried to keep station and see what was happening, what needed doing next.

The engineer was floating gently back toward the hatch, motionless.

A bloody-faced Jackson was straddling the pilot's chair while hammering his sap at the occupant. There was a lot of blood in the air around them, and the pilot didn't look like he was fighting back.

"Jackson," Moose called. "Ease up. We'll need him." The big soldier drifted slowly forward.

Jackson looked their way.

Chalmers swallowed. The hate in Jackson's eyes was limitless. His partner's face was a bleak ruin, his right eye swollen completely shut, and his jaw visibly misaligned. Bloody bubbles expanded from his nostrils with each tortured breath, expanded, grew to impossible size and popped.

"Easy, brother. Easy," Chalmers said.

Jacks mumbled something, madness fading from his eyes. He unlocked from his three-point grip on both pilot and his chair. He and the body beneath him drifted apart. If there was any question, the shit stink proved the pilot was dead.

"Hit 'm so 'rd," Jackson mumbled. "Thut I wuh dead. 'Urts."

Chalmers reached out, took Jackson gently by the arm, and eased him into the engineering seat.

An alarm klaxon sounded. Chalmers looked down. The angry red light he'd seen in the engineering console was flashing now. "What the fuck?" he said, struggling to decipher the unfamiliar data.

Moose had grabbed the engineer.

"He all right?" Chalmers asked, half-hoping the guy could be convinced to help.

"Dead," Moose said, towing the engineer toward the hatch.

"What?" Chalmers blurted.

"Temple's bashed in."

"Fuck."

"Can you shut that alarm off?" Moose asked. He opened the hatch and shoved the body out.

"I'm not even sure I know what system it is," Chalmers snapped. "Looks like a countdown of some sort."

"Countdown to what?"

"Do I look like fucking Scotty to you?"

"I'm not looking at you. I'm watching our six, like a good rear guard is supposed to. Yukannak is still outstanding. Jackson is down for the count."

Suddenly fearful, Chalmers glanced at his partner. Jackson was out cold but breathing. Even minor injuries incurred in microgravity could be a very real problem. Simple swelling could get out of control with no pull to direct the fluid in a given direction.

"Focus, Chalmers. One problem at a time," Moose said. "Get a read on what the hell is going on with engineering."

Getting a grip on his incipient panic, Chalmers started to sort through the various readouts he could access. A lot of it was locked down behind a security wall. He was sweating and his wrist throbbed, distracting him. Near as he could tell, the engineer had been busy with something to do with the power plant. He'd... Chalmers checked the readings, panic mounting.

"Fuck," Chalmers breathed. He scanned through another set of reports. The engineer had intentionally removed a section of shielding on the power plant. He tried to undo it, but ran into a request for a password or fingerprints. He ran at it another way, figured out that whatever the engineer had done, they'd also remote-locked the engineering console located in engineering.

"What?" Moose said. His usual calm voice was ground thin with impatience.

"Not sure, give me a minute," Chalmers said, checking additional radiation meters farther up the vessel. He breathed a sigh of relief. The power plant was well enough back in the ship the radiation leak wouldn't reach them with anything like a lethal dose. Not in the next few hours, anyway.

"Get me the engineer."

"I told you, he di-di-mau'd, dead as dirt."

"He's still got fucking hands, don't he?" Chalmers snapped.

Chapter Forty

The lights flickered, went out, came back on red.

"Chalmers, what the hell is going on?" Moose asked, coasting back onto the flight deck, engineer in tow.

"Automated visual warning system in case of loss of atmosphere," Chalmers read, taking the dead man by the arm.

"Warning for what?"

"Radiation levels are increasing beyond engineering..." Chalmers slapped the corpse's left hand down on the console.

Nothing happened.

"What?" Moose's voice was strained to the point of breaking. A glance showed the big guy pale beneath his paint. It figured that anyone who grew up in the late forties or early fifties could fully ignore the existential threat of nuclear radiation. Praying it would work, Chalmers grabbed the corpse's right hand and flattened it against the console.

SYSTEM UNLOCKED glowed in big red letters.

"Look man," Chalmers said, trying to play it cool as he accessed the previously secured systems beyond the print lock. "I'm no fucking engineer, but something weird was goi—" Chalmers stopped speaking when one edge of the panel started pulsing. He read it aloud. "Engineering comm."

"What?"

Chalmers ignored Moose, tapped the corner.

A speaker came to life. "Replace the shielding, and I'll surrender."

Chalmers recognized Yukannak's voice with some difficulty.

The engineering section had an ear-piercing radiation warning sounding at loud intervals.

"Wh—" Moose began. He stopped when Chalmers raised a hand.

Chalmers faked a baritone and summoned his best Kulsis accent. "Why should we not let you cook until your testicles will no longer serve to sire another generation?"

"Because I can deliver the rest of the stowaways."

Chalmers thought quickly, waved Moose out the hatch. "We have them already."

Moose looked at him for an instant, then nodded. He launched himself out the door.

"Do you have them all, though?"

Chalmers called up the hatch control graphic. "The only one outstanding is you, and I have you where I want you," Chalmers said, voice echoing as it was rebroadcast on every comm throughout the ship.

"I could do a great deal of damage here." Something in Yukannak's tone set Chalmers's teeth on edge. He watched the graphic, tracking Moose's progress through the ship.

"And die in the process?" he said, trying to visualize the position of the engine-room console in relation to the hatch. He was fairly certain the seat locked in a rear-facing position when it was unmanned, and required the occupant to unlock it when taking the position.

"I understand I wronged you by starting this the way I did," Yukannak said, even tones belying what had to be a stressful situation. "But I had limited options, and I believed you would be compromised by the drugs those who brought me aboard introduced into your supplies."

Between beats of the alarm, Chalmers remembered the dopey expression the pilot had worn on entry to the flight deck and decided he'd been only too ready with his own responses and too quick with his answers. He added a slight slur to his words. "Anger accomplishes many things."

"A wonder of evolution," Yukannak agreed.

A "lock override request" came up for the hatch leading to engineering. Chalmers's hand hovered over the accept graphic, praying Moose could get in fast and overwhelm the traitor. He paused, resolved to do what he could to distract Yukannak.

"Tell me again why you—"

"Betrayed the creatures with me?" Yukannak interrupted.

"Yes," Chalmers said.

"Once you let me out of here."

"How do I know you won't resist further?"

"Because I have lost all advantage. It would be foolish to continue. You have proven my superior."

Chalmers hesitated, thinking through the angles. "You will strap yourself into the console and remain there while we decide what to do with you."

In the relative silence between the ringing of the klaxon Chalmers half-heard a noise like an indrawn breath, but no words.

The channel went dead.

Shit. I should never have said "we." Kulsians do not reach a consensus before acting.

Another comm request light blinked, this one from the cargo bay corridor.

Making sure it was private, Chalmers tapped it open and said, "I fucked up, Moose."

"I heard. Do I go?"

"I'd join you, but there's no time delay on the door control."

"Copy. I think I can take him."

"You sure?"

"We got much choice?"

"Could just let him cook."

"And let him figure out a way to do us more harm from in there?"

"Right. Tell me when."

Chalmers swallowed. "Wait one." He muted Moose, piped the channel throughout the ship, and dialed up engineering.

A pause, then, "Chalmers?"

"Sure is," he said, dropping into his normal voice.

"I didn't kill any of you, even when I could have."

"I know." And then, because he had only one card left to play, Chalmers said, "It's the only reason you're slow roasting instead of dead already."

"How did you get control of the bridge?" Yukannak said.

"We followed the plan," Chalmers said, loading his voice with contempt. "You know, the one that would have seen us all safely in command."

"But the lockouts ... Di—"

"You can't have believed we would reveal all our capabilities to you, a traitor to your own people?"

An indrawn breath, then, "What do you want of me?"

"Surrender. Immediate and unconditional."

Chalmers heard a sound he recognized: hands slapping a console like the one in front of him. Two hands. The console was not far from the door.

"What kind o—" Yukannak started.

"That is my only, final offer!" Chalmers shouted over him, hoping the sound of his voice would cover the sound of the hatch unlocking.

"What are—?"

Chalmers heard a grunt, followed quickly by a heavy impact. A moan, then a spluttering wheeze.

"Fucker!" Moose yelled, grunting with exertion. More struggles. More gasps.

"Want me down there?" Chalmers half-shouted.

"No, he's gonna go night-night soon," Moose said, hoarse with effort.

"What?"

"Isn't that right, Yuks?" Moose hissed. "Say good night."

A gurgle. A gasp. More gurgles.

"Choked him out, Chalmers. Come get him. I ain't letting go of this asshole till you got him hog-tied."

"On my way."

"There's a big difference between swearing innocence and admitting a degree of culpability. I did attempt to take the ship alone, thinking I had a better chance of success that way. In the end, my actions assisted you in the taking of this vessel. Were it not for my actions distracting the crew, you'd not have taken them down so easily."

"Easily?" Chalmers snarled. "Look at Jackson, you smug fuck!"

Yukannak's golden gaze didn't even flick Jackson's way. He shrugged as much as his bindings would allow, which was not a great deal. He was hog-tied and suspended a good meter away from anything he could possibly reach. The muscle the Kulsian had built up while training with them was a threat they would not be underestimating again anytime soon.

"I warned you all that sons of Kulsis are not easily overcome in hand-to-hand fighting. Especially those who lay claim to a command." Yukannak cocked his head at Jackson, eyes never leaving Chalmers. "There lies proof of the truth of my words."

"Didn't stop Moose from kicking your ass, did it?" Chalmers said. Despite the brave words, he couldn't help looking at his partner's still form.

Jackson's head was a mass of bandages meant to keep his jaw in one place. They'd sedated him with some of the drugs meant for the crew, and he was breathing normally now, but none of them were real medics, let alone doctors.

"I believed your plan insufficient to the task," Yukannak said. "I told you this before we embarked on the mission. You did not listen. I only took action in order to prevent my own demise. Any miscalculation on my part worked to your benefit, landing you in command of the vessel."

Chalmers looked at the Kulsian. Yukannak didn't look that much better. His right ear was missing a big chunk where a blow from Moose's sap had torn it, his left cheek was swollen around a visible break in the underlying bone, and his lips were split in several places.

"What were you going to do if you managed to take the ship?"

"Use knowledge of your presence to assure my own survival, of course. Disrupting ongoing survey operations is an offense that carries a death sentence under normal circumstances."

"And these are anything but?"

Yukannak smiled, causing spherical beads of blood to form on his split lips. "You understand more than you let on, Chalmers."

Moose coasted into the room, sailing right past Yukannak. Chalmers took a bully's pleasure in watching the Kulsian flinch away from Moose as the big Lost Soldier hooked a bruise-mottled arm through a convenient rung to arrest his flight. He looked from Chalmers to Yukannak and said, "Vat says he's got a good read on our rendezvous."

"I hope, for all our sakes, that no emergencies arise." Yukannak's blood-dotted grin reappeared. "Emergencies such as those that require a skilled pilot at the controls of this ship."

Moose reached out and casually slapped the back of the Kulsian's head with one big mitt. "Can't exactly trust you at the controls, can we? Just like fuckin' ARVN. Never knew when they'd been bought out by the dope peddlers or the fuckin' VC."

Yukannak glared at his captors. "I only did what I knew to be the best option for my survival. My actions would have also ensured your survival as well."

"Sure, as POWs," Moose said.

"Hell, we *Untermensch* would have been accorded even less rights than any POWs the Viet Cong kept. I bet we'd have all been eager to play Russian roulette a la that scene in *The Deer Hunter* after a day or two as their prisoners."

"Chris Walken was *amazing* in that flick," Vat said, pulling himself into the galley from the flight deck.

Moose looked puzzled.

"Another great movie, brother," Chalmers explained.

"That we'll never see again," Vat added sadly.

"You are all nostalgic for so many things that mean nothing," Yukannak said, contemptuously. "And all while you should be focused on survival. It will be your undoing."

"Should have let you cook," Chalmers snapped.

Moose grinned. "I'm already nostalgic for a scene like that."

"No good if I can't watch that smug expression die," Vat opined.

Jackson mumbled something. They'd set his dislocated jaw while he was unconscious, but the hinges or whatever had swollen so big as to make him look like a chipmunk.

Chalmers drifted over toward him. "Don't speak, man. Go back to sleep."

His partner's one visible eye was open. It slowly focused on Chalmers.

"Hard to," Jackson mumbled, slowly and carefully, "with you bastards arguing."

"Hey, I seem to remember waking up all swathed in bandages—mostly *unnecessary* bandages—while you performed a little drama for my entertainment," Chalmers said, a strained feeling building in his chest. "I'm afraid arguing with the fucker who was gonna sell us out was the best I could do on short notice."

A slight stirring beneath the bandages, a sighed shadow of a chuckle that cut to a pained cough.

"Sorry, man," Chalmers whispered.

Jackson didn't reply, eye drifting closed on another wave of dope.

Chalmers felt a selfish need to keep Jackson awake: to ask him for, and receive, his approval. His absolution for everything that had gone wrong since they'd boarded the Blackhawk in Mogadishu.

Sitting on the feeling, Chalmers analyzed the need for reassurance, realized he wanted to know that he hadn't fucked everything up. That doing his best had, just this once, been *enough*.

Vat appeared at his elbow. "He's a tough bastard, Chalmers. He'll be all right."

"We're all tough bastards, ain't we?" Chalmers said. "But I'm the one who let us get blindsided."

"What?" Moose said.

Chalmers swallowed past a lump in his throat. "My decisions," he said hoarsely, "led to this. I didn't...I should have... seen that fucker coming." He fixed Yukannak with a stare. All the hate he felt—toward his situation, toward his old life, toward himself—he channeled into that withering glare.

Yukannak didn't look away, but his grin froze then broke under the stare.

Chalmers kept staring until Moose drifted between them. "I'll just move this garbage to a cabin for the time being." He untethered Yukannak from the bulkhead and towed him out of the mess.

Chalmers forced his fists to unclench as the men disappeared into the cabin. His wrist throbbed in time with his too-fast pulse.

Vat cleared his throat. "You know, I didn't think we'd pull it off."

Chalmers chuckled, said sourly, "Have we?"

"Have we what?"

"Have we pulled it off?"

"I have to believe we have," Vat said. He nodded, once and sharply, as if convincing himself. "Bowden and crew will rendezvous with us in a couple days. We get off, report, go home. Everyone is happy."

"Home?" Another, more forceful, laugh escaped Chalmers's lips. It was no less sour than the chuckle, though.

Vat shrugged. "Well, for certain values of home, anyway."

"Right. That's the thing, ain't it?"

"What?"

"We ain't ever going back. Not going home. Not in any real sense."

"You just now figuring that out?"

Chalmers looked down at his hands. "I suppose so. It's just..."
"Just what?"

"Just..." Chalmers sighed, raised his hands as he tried to explain what bothered him. "I was happy to be here at first. Had all these plans to make myself a better...person. I didn't really think that all the way through, though."

"How's that? Sounds kinda admirable to me."

Chalmers glanced at Jackson. Eyes skipping from the bandaged body back to Vat's questioning face, he shrugged. "I just realized I don't know that making me better is worth two shits if there's no one to go home to, to be better *for*, you know?"

Vat smiled crookedly. "I only know what works for me. Family—chosen or born into—is the only thing worth fighting for."

"Even when all you're fighting against is your own inclination to do wrong?"

"Especially then."

He cast another look at Jackson. "I suppose it does," Horace Earl Chalmers said with a somber nod. "I suppose it does."

Chapter Forty-One

"That's no 'package'!" Raptis exclaimed as the lighter came into view the next day. "That's a Kulsian lighter!" When Bowden raised an eyebrow at her ability to identify a ship no one had ever seen before, she glared at him. "Did you really think that we do not have microsensors of our own? That just because you 'compartmentalized' all the data from the ones left by your alien friends, that we wouldn't have our own sources?"

Bowden shrugged. What could he say? That he and Murphy had considered the possibility, realized there was no good way to ask the Primae or the Legate about it? Besides, imaging was *not* the aspect of the Dornaani data feed that restricted its distribution to those who fell under the need-to-know category.

Raptis didn't even stop to breathe, however. "Shouldn't we either be running or hiding?"

Silence.

Her head whipped from side to side as she scanned everyone's faces. "*Do you not hear me? That ship is Kulsian!*"

Bowden shook his head. "No, that ship *is* our package."

Hrensku turned away from the view screen with what appeared to be a significant effort of will. "Since Malanye seems too stunned to think, I'll ask the obvious question: What, exactly, are we doing rendezvousing with a Kulsian ship?"

Bowden smiled. "It's not a Kulsian ship. Not anymore."

"What?" Hrensku asked. "Are they traitors, too?"

"No, it was captured by a team of Lost Soldiers."

"You captured it? Are you Terrans out of your minds?"

"Murphy has a plan."

"I think it's about time you shared this plan with the rest of us," Raptis said, "because—like Hrensku—I can't see how this will lead to anything but the annihilation of our society, and I doubt *any* of us would have come on this mission if we'd known what it was really about."

Bowden shrugged. "I can't tell you about it because I don't know what it is, either. I do, however, know there *is* one, and our mission advances it." Raptis and Hrensku shook their heads, although Bowden was unable to tell whether from fear, disbelief, or some other emotion. *Or, maybe, all of them.*

"I still need the ship I was promised," Raptis said. She shook her head and sighed. "Despite the fact that I'll probably never see it, I'm still in."

"Me, too," Hrensku said with a sigh. "When the Primus asks…" He shrugged. "We also may be able to help keep things from falling totally apart. You're an okay space pilot, but I'm better. So's Raptis. Besides, I doubt you've ever flown anything that big."

"No, I haven't," Bowden said. "Have you?"

"None of us have," Raptis said. "While the SpinDogs *do* have ships as large as the lighter, those larger hulls are rare, and probably less than ten percent of their pilots have any experience with them. RockHounds have none. Still, though, we have a lot more time in space than you do and can probably understand the scope of flying it better than you."

"That's possible," Bowden allowed. He nodded to the ship on the viewer. "If we're all done discussing it, Malanye, would you do the honors and take us in?"

"Sure," she said. "One question first, though."

"Yeah?"

"What are we going to do with *this* packet? Kamara isn't going to have any use for it."

"Fiezel was supposed to fly it back, but now we don't have enough fuel to do so," Bowden said. "We could just let it go—"

"No," Raptis said. "It's a significant investment of resources, and it would be a shame to just throw it away. In fact, I know someone who could use a new ship, even one that's had a rock storm beat on its aft end."

"We can't leave it attached to the lighter," Bowden said. "It would compromise the rest of the mission."

"I think it's time you told us what you know," Hrensku said. "I know you don't know it all, but you need to tell us what you do. The traitor is gone, and we've already pledged to help you, but we can't help if we don't know what we're supposed to be trying to accomplish. What is our mission? Better yet, what's really in the modules we're carrying?"

Bowden sighed, looking at the deck, then looked up to meet Hrensku's eyes. "Commandos," he said simply. "The two modules have commandos in them."

Raptis's brows knit. "I thought you said you already controlled the lighter."

"I did, and I hope we do." He shrugged. "We'll have to confirm before we go aboard. If we don't, the commandos will get us aboard the lighter, but that wasn't their intended mission."

"Stop stalling," Hrensku said. "What *is* their intended mission?"

"We are supposed to board the lighter and get the corvette that is in orbit to come close. Then the commandos will go across and capture the corvette."

"*What?*" Hrensku and Raptis chorused. Both looked like they wanted to say something else, but neither was able to articulate their thoughts.

Fiezel chuckled. "We're not known for thinking small, I guess."

"No," Bowden agreed. "We're not." He shrugged. "That's the plan, or as much of it as I know. After we capture the corvette, we'll be given further orders, but I don't know what they'll be, and Murphy wasn't a fan of me speculating on them." He gave them a half smile. "Still with me?"

Hrensku shook his head. "If I could leave, I would, and I'd happily live in hiding from the Primus for the rest of my days. I can't, though, so I'm in."

"You could go with the packet—whatever we determine we're going to do with it."

"I could, but you're more likely to be successful if I stay. As the future of my people rests on the success of this mission, I will stay and help."

"As will I," Raptis said.

"Which leads us back to the question of, what do we do with *this* packet?"

"Is there—" Raptis started, but the engine fired, cutting her off.

Raptis, Hrensku, and Fiezel were thrown to the back of the cockpit. Bowden, seated in the pilot's chair, was barely able to keep his seat. As the gees mounted, he struggled to turn his seat to face forward, then used it to reach forward and push the Emergency Stop button. The engine immediately cut off, and Bowden hit the ACS thrusters to kill the new velocity the engine had given the craft as the lighter grew quickly in the canopy.

The reverse thrust threw the rest of the crew back into the cockpit.

After a few seconds, Bowden had the ship stabilized again with respect to the lighter, and the crew righted themselves again in the zero-gee.

"The fuck was that?" Fiezel asked.

"Apparently, our traitor wasn't done with us," Bowden said. "He must have left that command in the autopilot. That's what Kamara meant when he said we'd be sorry if we spaced him."

"Asshole," Fiezel said, rubbing an elbow. He nodded to the instrument panel. "Now I don't have enough fuel to do much of anything."

Bowden shook his head slowly as Raptis and Hrensku moved to where they could see. "No," he said, "you don't. We'll have to figure something else out."

"So, is there a moon to hide behind?" Fiezel asked. "Something like that?"

"No," Raptis said. She'd been tasked with surveying the planet and its environs to search for a good place to hide the packet as the craft approached the lighter. So far, the crew of the ship had given no indication they knew the packet was there despite their last burn. Raptis paused and swiped her tablet. "But there is...what I think is a Kulsian fuel depot in orbit."

"A what?" Fiezel asked as if he were a man in the desert, dying of thirst, who had just been handed a glass of water. "Really?"

"Really. They probably put it there so they wouldn't have to make planetfall every time." She shrugged. "It's in a medium orbit that would be easy to reach both ways."

"The packet can easily hide there after refueling," Hrensku said, warming to the subject. "That way, there's no exit signature to tip off the Kulsians since it won't leave until the rest of the operation is over. The corvette is too close to boost without being spotted."

"Also, if the mission is a success," Raptis added, "the packet won't have to boost at all. It can be hooked up to either the lighter or the corvette, and we'll be able to tow it back to R'Bak much faster." She smiled, obviously hoping it would be hers at the end of the mission.

"There's one more point to going there," Bowden said. "If we don't make it, you can hide and refuel. Then, when the corvette goes behind the planet, you can make a low power escape with a long drift back." He shrugged. "At least that way we get the word to them on what happened, and they can prepare for the arrival of the Kulsians." The thought sobered the rest of them, and Bowden hurried on. "Not that that's going to happen, of course, but just as a last resort..."

"Got it," Fiezel said.

"Good," Bowden said as he worked the packet toward the lighter. "It's agreed, then. Let's see if our people still control the lighter, or if we're going to have to call our friends upstairs."

"Do you know who they are?" Raptis asked.

"Who? The commandos or the people on the lighter?"

"Either. Both."

"Nope. I would probably know the Terrans if I saw them, but I don't, at this moment, know who they are." *Although I'd bet a lot of money that Harry Tapper is within a kilometer of me right now, one way or the other. That's where I'd want him, anyway.*

Bowden switched to the radio. "New York."

A call came back almost immediately. "Yankees."

"Seriously?" Fiezel asked. "Always hated those guys. I'm more of a Mets fan."

"I didn't pick the code words," Bowden said. "The good news is, though, that our guys are in control of the lighter."

Bowden joined with the lighter and the larger ship extended its boarding tube to them. They connected it to the packet, and Bowden led Hrensku and Raptis over to the lighter. As they reached the hatch, it opened to reveal four men, one of whom he knew.

"Hi, Max," he said to Messina. *So this is where he's been hiding.* The big sleepy-eyed bodyguard introduced his compatriots Vat, Chalmers, and Jackson. Bowden recognized them, having seen them on R'Bak a few times, but he wouldn't have expected to see them in control of a spaceship. Jackson looked a lot worse for wear; his head was a mass of bandages.

"Murphy says to tell you great job," Bowden said after he'd introduced Hrensku and Raptis, who'd then gone to check the lighter's navigation and flight station controls. Bowden nodded to the boarding tube. "I guess you'll be leaving now?"

"We talked about that," Chalmers said, "but we're going to stay. We've got too much invested in this op to turn it over completely. We're going to see it to its successful completion."

"Not done yet," Jackson said. He was hard to understand through the bandages. "Going to help out."

Bowden looked at Vat and raised an eyebrow. "I needed a break from the planet," the bunko artist and black marketeer said with a shrug. "I'm here to the end."

"Besides," Chalmers said, "we've got a wounded Kulsian I don't want to move or make someone else's responsibility. We'll just keep him here, nice and safe." He smiled. "Why don't we get your cargo loaded aboard so you can get rid of that ship before it's seen? We've got too much invested in this to blow it so close to the end."

"There he goes," Bowden said as the packet moved off to their starboard. Moving the two CONEX boxes into the lighter's hold hadn't been easy, but with the equipment they'd found on the ship—in addition to the assistance provided by Chalmers's team—they'd managed to get them strapped down in a couple of the cargo bays.

After that, they'd sealed off the hold area so the men in the boxes could get out and stretch their legs without the two groups seeing each other. Bowden thought the restriction kind of dumb at this point—if one group got captured, they were all going to get captured—but Murphy had been very clear on keeping the two groups separate. It still didn't make sense to do so, though, as it kept them from coordinating their part of the operation. *Sometimes there are operational imperatives us little guys don't need to know, I guess.*

Chalmers also kept his pet Kulsian—whose name was Yukannak—separate from Bowden's group throughout. *Maybe he thought one of the Dogs would want to kill him.* Bowden shrugged to himself. *There's no reason why—Yukannak is far more valuable alive than dead.*

"Ready?" Raptis asked a little while later once the packet was well clear of them.

"Yeah," Bowden said. "Let's get this started."

Raptis initiated the burn that would put them into orbit.

Bowden looked over his shoulder. "What's the code word for 'we're fat, dumb, and happy, and everything is fine'?"

"It's 'Riches,' believe it or not," Chalmers replied.

Bowden chuckled. "Somehow, that makes sense for them." He switched to the radio and pulled out a piece of paper on which he'd written what he wanted to say.

"Why don't I take this," Vat asked, holding out his hand. "I can speak it better than any of you."

Bowden shrugged and handed the transmitter and his script over. "Be my guest."

Vat took a minute to familiarize himself, then he keyed the mic. "Patrol Cycler PH-09, this is *Lighter 03*. Currently entering orbit. Code word: Riches."

When he didn't receive a response, he repeated the transmission.

"*Lighter 03*, Patrol Cycler PH-09. I understand code word: Riches."

"Affirmative, Patrol Cycler PH-09. We are positioned for... wait... shit! *Look out!*"

Bowden reached up, killed the drive, and gave several hard boosts with the ACS system. The ship began tumbling, and the concepts of "up" and "down" became lost as his stomach flip-flopped.

Chalmers reached forward and pulled a handle, releasing a batch of simulated accident debris to go along with the first batch he had released prior to Bowden initiating the tumble.

"Collision emergency, PH-09!" Vat continued. "The panel shows multiple hull breaches, and our attitude control is out. We're... *we're losing atmosphere. Emergency bulkheads not responding. We can't—*" He released the transmit button.

"*Lighter 03*, say again? What was the nature of the collision?" Bowden smiled.

After a few seconds, Patrol Cycler PH-09 called again. "*Lighter 03*, report your status. Respond immediately."

Bowden pantomimed dying for a few seconds, until PH-09 called. "If you can hear me, *Lighter 03*, hold on. We are on our way to you. We should be there in approximately three hours."

Bowden took the mic from Vat and attached it to the instrument panel. "Well, we've done our part. Time to wake up the folks in the hold so they can earn their pay." He pressed the button to talk to the commandos. "Bowden calling whoever's in the hold. We're being approached by the Kulsian corvette, ETA three hours. Our part of this mission is over. We got you here. Now...you're up. Go get 'em, boys!"

Chapter Forty-Two

"Korelon, stand by," Harry commed over the hardline to the second hab. "We're coming up on the precession maneuver."

Harry heard a *ka-click* on the circuit as Korelon double-keyed his comm in reply.

Obedient to Murphy's requirement, they remained strictly segregated from the packet's crew, and both teams had remained in their habs following the pod retrieval. Even during the terrifying meteor storm, or whatever the hell that had been, and throughout the heavy jostling they'd suffered during the transfer from the packet ship to the captured Kulsian lighter, the teams had accepted their lot, remaining in communications blackout. Then, almost three hours ago, they'd been rousted from the middle of the sleep period. The digital clangor of the general quarters alarm created a spasm of activity, and, while the men sorted themselves and their gear, Harry had received his first voice communication from outside the hab in nearly three weeks. He recognized Bowden, warning them of the closing distance to the target.

Despite the traditional enmity of ground pounders for the perceived cushy life of aviators and, by derivation, spaceship drivers, Harry had been surprised at the wave of emotion he rode hearing his crewmate's voice.

Damn, they didn't forget our ass.

And:

345

I'll bet that guy has been eating proper food and enjoying hot showers in a climate-controlled cockpit while we've been in here.

Now he executed the next part of Murphy's plan. The mission calculus deliberately backed the RockHounds into a corner. Harry admired the ruthlessness of it, for it could be nothing else. He knew his boss wasn't one to leave something to chance.

At Murphy's insistence, Harry had refrained from sharing the complete operational picture, instead limiting the information shared with both teams to the minimum of tactical details needed to successfully storm the corvette.

Now, per the plan, he briefed them on not only the immediate mission, but the consequences of failure. He gave them everything the RockHound Legate had been read in on. In particular, Harry laid out, in explicit terms, the significance of seizing the ship they were on right now, the enemy's lighter. There was no easy way—no way at all, really—to hide from the consequences. If it were learned that the disappearance of that ship was not some unseen accident—one that also involved the corvette—the Kulsians would know to start scouring the system for the culprits. Consequently, they had to seize the corvette so the joint piloting team could move it to the hidden manufactories where Dornaani software updates would let the SpinDogs reproduce it as fast as possible. And Bowden's team needed the freedom to ensure that the aftermath of the engagement looked consistent with some navigational or technical failure that was catastrophic for ships. If they failed, the Kulsians would learn of the existence of the space-based Families and move swiftly to destroy them. It wasn't merely a strong possibility; it was a certainty. Not only did Kulsis need to eliminate any competition, but they also had to ensure they remained in compliance with the conditions the Ktor had imposed upon their exile.

Most of the information he shared was already a matter of supposition and conjecture among the assault team. The Rock-Hounds looked especially alert. They understood the bleak outlook of failure. The Lawless were merely risking their lives; the very civilization of the Hounds was at stake. The grim silence that met Harry's info dump simmered with equal parts anger and determination.

Harry recognized the silence and understood there would be a reckoning, but that was a problem for later.

"One last thing," Harry said, holding their attention. He had to finish with something to kindle their anger, their discomfort, even their hate.

Perhaps, especially their hate. Harry would focus it like a shaped charge. *Front toward enemy.*

"Once the assault begins, we don't stop until the ship is taken and every Kulsian is neutralized. Our casualties will be treated after the fight. If you are injured, you keep fighting. Lose a hand? Doesn't matter. Lose your friend? Doesn't matter. There's only victory. Those arrogant bastards from Kulsis have no idea what's waiting for them. They've become accustomed to being the undisputed rulers of this system. For generations, they've pillaged R'Bak. They've forced the RockHounds and SpinDogs alike to hide. To conceal your very existence. They stand between us Terrans and our home.

"That's all over. We're going to tear their hearts out and take their pretty, clean ship away. They'll learn to fear leaving their own gravity well. We're going to clamp their limbs and cut them off. They'll learn respect for the Hounds. We're going to steal their air, their ship, their pride, and their very legacy. And, after today, they will fucking quail when they learn they're fighting both Terrans and Hound-Dogs *together*."

A low, aggressive growl spread through the squads, like the last sound a startled deer might hear emerging from a dense, dark thicket in the heart of wolf country.

"Rodriguez, Korelon, take your posts."

The teams emerged from the habs and took up their positions. After the training losses, Harry had reorganized the remaining men. Korelon led the Hounds of Bravo to the lighter's airlock. As its hull slowly rotated and swung the exit out of line-of-sight from the approaching ship, Bravo would exit and hide behind carefully placed debris made to look like torn hull plating and ruptured cargo containers. Harry and the other five Terrans would remain in the hangar, out of view, and wait for the Kulsians to board. As soon as the first Kulsian stepped inside, Harry would initiate.

Once the fight was joined, the assault team could resort to radio, but the chaos would be resolved by surprise and aggression. All their careful planning and detailed walk-throughs would become subordinate to whatever unexpected thing happened. Harry had been in enough fights to know nothing ever went to plan.

He wasn't disappointed.

✧   ✧   ✧

Instead of fidgeting or looking around the windowless hangar, Harry checked his commpad repeatedly. No communications were possible until the assault began, so he reined in his agitation. After a relative eon, the hangar airlock proximity alarm sounded, and Harry knew the Kulsian corvette was matching the captured lighter's slow tumble. A short time later, the airlock connection light shone green. A pressure readout began ticking up as air was pumped into the boarding umbilical.

"Initiate assault!" someone shrieked over the radio link.

Startled, Harry twitched. He realized it was the lighter pilot when the voice behind the warning continued, distorted by fear and haste, "Communication system sabotaged, we're broadcasting to the corvette. Initiate, initiate! They're being warned off!"

"Korelon, go!" Harry ordered. "Alpha, take the umbilical, now!"

Alpha, the hangar team, was already in motion, spurred by the first warning. Ahead of Harry, his five men converged on the lock. Rodriguez overrode the lighter's safety interlock, and they were tugged forward as the atmosphere in the hangar surged past them to equalize the lower pressure in the boarding tube. Rodriguez led the way, tugging the expander jack off his back. He used both feet and his remaining free hand to swarm across the connection between the ships. The entire team swung through, making the accordion-like structure sway disconcertingly. Harry watched as the veteran sergeant moved faster than thought, ramming the tool into the upper corner of the seam between the hatch and the enemy hull, immediately starting the tool.

"Another one, get it ready," Rodriguez called hoarsely, bracing himself as the door spreader bucked in his grip. "Below mine!"

Pham shouldered in, adding his entry tool to the equation. Together, the motors strained at the lock system. Designed only to contain atmosphere, it slowly began to yield.

"Enemy point defense engaging," Korelon reported coolly. "Casualties severe. Seeking shelter on the h—"

"Korelon, grab some cover!" Harry ordered unnecessarily, and immediately felt like a fool. "Give me SITREP when you can."

Harry's suit mic picked up the breaching tools automatically gearing down, the motors slowing from a fast whine to a deeper whir. He couldn't tell if the internal door mechanism was deforming, or they were overcoming the motor holding the lock shut.

An unfamiliar clanging began, and a spinning red light illuminated the narrow boarding tube.

"They're trying to undock, get the fucking door open, now!" Harry yelled. Behind him, the remaining men were stacked single file, ready to assault into the opening.

Grave de Peralto unlimbered his bulky frame charge and started forward.

With a muted *crack*, the door surged open. Opposite the door was a Kulsian in a bright red suit, hammering on the inner door with one fist. The crewman spun just in time to meet Rodriguez's charge. The furious sergeant shoved a grappler against the target's throat, and the machine snapped closed as the assault team was still swarming inside.

Without warning, the umbilical deformed and tore away. The team was buffeted by the escaping atmosphere. A moment later, there was a short surge of acceleration, and the team—as well as their first victim—were pressed unceremoniously against the aft bulkhead. Harry looked to the enemy, but a stream of white vapor from the edges of the clamp and the scrabbling hands of their victim was enough confirmation the man was out of the fight.

They untangled themselves and Harry did a quick head count.

"Where's McPherson?" he radioed.

"He was behind me," Roeder replied. "He didn't make it."

"Right," Harry answered, compartmentalizing his emotions. All that mattered was the essential understanding his team was down one. "Korelon, SITREP."

There was no reply.

"Any Bravo team member, respond."

The silent radio channel mocked him.

"Alpha, we're it," he announced. "Bravo's gone. Roeder, Flea, get the lock closed if you can. Pham, Rodriguez, check the inner lock. We need to get in right away. The enemy is warned; we need to move—*now!*"

Harry checked the slumped, still form of the Kulsian. Through the cracked faceplate, he could see the perfect features of a young, dark-haired man, mouth still yawning open in mid-scream.

"Security rounds," Harry announced, delivering a carefully aimed palm strike to the man's helmet. All he felt was a sharp crunch as the spike half-shattered the Kulsian's faceplate. A brief puff of gas emerged from the hole as liquid components of the man's blood began to boil, but then slowed to a stop.

The sounds conveyed by Harry's helmet mic also changed, taking on a tinny quality. He turned to find the outer door closed and the lock pressurizing.

"Another thirty seconds, we should be able to open the door," Pham announced calmly. "The interlocks prevent opening till pressure is equalized, or nearly so."

"We split as briefed," Harry ordered curtly. "The priority is to isolate and shut down engineering so they can't boost or sabotage the fusion chamber. Roeder, Flea, on me. Marco, Pham, go forward. Kill anyone you see and take the bridge."

"You mean, go join the Army!" Rodriguez said sardonically, checking the straps on his spike-punch.

"Travel to exotic, distant lands," Roeder continued, taking a grappler off his belt and checking the safety.

"Meet exciting new people!" Grave de Peralto added cheerfully, hands patting his holstered pistol and then dancing across his equipment belt for another check.

"And kill them," Harry finished the mordant litany. "Yeah, pretty much."

Above Pham's head, the airlock pressure indicator blinked green, and Harry stacked on the experienced NCO's side. Harry looked back at the other three men, then gave Pham a squeeze on the arm, signaling "go."

The inner door opened to a clear corridor, and Harry tried the radio again. He let Roeder lead the way toward engineering while Pham and Rodriguez headed in the opposite direction. Despite the brief surge of acceleration, they were in free fall again. Disconcertingly, the deck plates were "up," presumably to provide a walking surface if the ship was spun on its axis. He studied placards on the wall, deciphering the hybrid Ktoran script. The brushed alloy corridor was narrow, and the view forward was interrupted by airtight hatches. Employing a mixture of caution and nervous haste, Harry's trio pulled themselves past signs for medical, two small berthing compartments, and lastly environmental, although Harry made a mental note to return to the last as soon as the bridge and engineering were secure.

They reached the final airtight hatch without seeing a soul.

Like the rest, this one was closed, but the red light on the chip reader port was lit.

"Our Lady of Plastic Acceleration, don't fail me now," Harry whispered, fishing around in his suit's chest pocket. He placed the electronic lock pick against the device. In a moment, the chip reader blinked green. "And Open Sesame."

Harry gestured left and right, ordering Roeder and Grave de Peralto to either side of the door. Standing to one side, he slowly eased the hatch handle to the open position and then gave it a shove. Roeder slipped nimbly through. The short Cuban followed, bumping against both edges as he caught first one side of his suit and then the other passing the threshold. Harry followed on their heels, noting the change from deck tile to a much rougher, black nonskid surface, almost like sandpaper.

This was definitely engineering. Narrow passageways split along the bulkheads of the compartment, leaving an island of equipment and small work alcoves in the middle. Cabling and piping, archaic hand wheels sprouting from the latter, created places to snag their suits. A surprising number of analog gauges were arranged across the closed doors of cabinets, supplemented by what appeared to be red digital readouts in Ktoran script, just like Harry's digital alarm clock back in college. The space was brightly lit and a few benches were crowded against empty, shallow tables.

"Sossa?" someone queried, the sound faithfully picked up by Harry's external mic. "Sossa!"

Ahead and to the right, Grave de Peralto charged around a corner, but a frantic, high-pitched mechanical whine pierced the surprisingly quiet compartment. A powerful bound drove de Peralto forward, but as Harry watched, the muscular tension that marked his teammate's quivering readiness chopped off like a thrown light switch. Grave de Peralto drifted along his original course, passing out of sight.

Another one down.

"Doc, we got a shooter!" Harry yelled in English. "On my two, we push at the same time, got it?"

"Aye!" came the answer.

Harry drew his grappler and switched it to his left hand. Then he counted as loudly as he could.

"One! Two!"

He moved as fast as he could, knowing even speed wouldn't save him if the Kulsian was facing the wrong way. One chance for life, one chance for death. Harry planted his foot and pivoted into the alcove, catching another Kulsian facing the wrong way. This spacer had good reason, though. Roeder must have pushed up and then rebounded from the overhead, because he was descending upon his victim like the bastard love child of a rock avalanche and an angry bear, arms spread wide. The frantic whining repeated, even louder at this distance, but Roeder tackled the man, a slightly built Kulsian wearing a red coverall. By sheer mass, Roeder bore the man to the deck, falling on top of him, squeezing the Kulsian's arms to his sides. Harry took a knee. Careful not to hit Roeder with a through and through, he palm-slapped the Kulsian in the skull. The spike did its thing. The man went limp.

Harry waited for Roeder to get up, but he lay on top of the man, wheezing.

"Doc? Doc, you all right?" Harry asked, scanning the space beyond this alcove.

"He dinged me a bit," Roeder said, huffing a bit on the last syllable. With a groan, he stiff-armed himself off the corpse and twisted off to hover above the floor. Harry saw the telltale smears of blood on the fabric of Roeder's EVA suit on the lower abdomen and right leg. Harry plucked the pistol from the corpse's flaccid grip. The controls weren't suitable for EVA gauntlets. It had a very small bore, and the holes in Roeder's suit were almost needle diameter.

"Stay put, I need to check the rest," Harry said, and performed a quick search, satisfying himself that engineering was empty. He also confirmed Grave de Peralto was dead. He scavenged the man's grappler and then returned to the instrument console where they'd found the Kulsian. Nothing screamed sabotage or emergency. Aware of the time passing, Harry frantically looked for an isolation panel, recalling the plant shutdown procedures the RockHounds had diagrammed for the team. There was a series of small switches striped in the telltale yellow-and-black diagonals: the main breaker.

Harry threw the master and the lighting blinked off, instantly replaced by wall-mounted electric lanterns that cast pools of yellow light along the walkways and upon each workstation. He went along the row, flipping switches. He disabled weapons, sensors, and communications. Then, just to be certain, he moved the main engineering output control to idle and restricted the plant to local control before turning back to Roeder.

"I think I'll stay and guard engineering, boss," Roeder said, pressing a fist to his leg and wheezing heavily. "Ah shit, that smarts!"

"No problem, Doc," Harry said, patting Roeder's shoulder. "I've got this. I'll go see how many bodies Marco and Pham have got stacked, then we'll call the lighter back in to get you some first aid. Hang tough."

"Tapper to bridge team," Harry radioed, moving toward the bow of the ship, using his legs to push off helpful projections and relying on his hands to control direction. It was just a matter of retracing his route along the main corridor so far. "SITREP, over."

There was no immediate reply. He repeated the call, continuing past their original point of entry. Sweating, he licked dry lips. *Too long; this is taking too long.*

Beyond the airlock, the paired port and starboard passageways merged into what he believed must be the main, spinal corridor. To rush headlong was to invite disaster; moving too deliberately, the same.

He paused nonetheless.

Through the next hatch, drops of ruby blood floated. The walls were liberally dappled with it. One obvious source was the vacsuited Kulsian stuck to the bulkhead, both arms extended in front of the body, dangling in the odd way only found in micro. A grappling claw projected from the presumed corpse's thigh, visibly constricting the tough material to half its diameter. Harry cautiously checked the Kulsian. The back of the dead Kulsian's suit was hung up on an emergency lantern, creating an eerie glow around the body. Punch poised to strike, Harry tilted the helm to see inside. He gulped and examined the rest of the suit. Two punch holes across the chest of his—no, make that her—suit matched the spike on Harry's arm.

The trail of blood beads and smears led forward, toward the bow.

"Tapper to anyone, come back," Harry said, approaching another hatch.

He tried the radio again after opening that one and visually clearing the passage beyond. "Any station this net, respond."

"Rodriguez here," Harry heard the clear, if faint, reply. "And I'd like to officially note this op sucks, sir."

"Glad to hear your voice, Marco," Harry said, grinning in relief. "Give me a SITREP. Tell me you have the bridge."

"No such luck. Pham got one, and I winged another, but the

wounded guy made it to operations, and he's got a buddy. Pham is down. How about you, over?"

"We secured engineering," Harry answered, carefully peeking around yet another hatch. The blood trail continued. "Two enemy down and dead. Grave de Peralto's dead. Roeder's out of the fight."

"Shit, how bad?" Rodriguez asked, audibly exhaling. "Never mind. Look, they can't get out of the bridge, or whatever is behind the last damned door, and they can't lock it, either. But we're going to have a helluva time getting in."

"There isn't a door we can't blow if we have to," Harry answered, careful to sound confident.

"Maybe Bravo can help?"

"I still haven't heard from anyone from Bravo, so it's just thee and me, Marco."

There was a pause. Harry took the time to clear two more small compartments. A small refectory and a supply closet, of all things.

"About that, Harry."

Shit, not Marco.

"How bad is it?" Harry asked levelly. "Can you fight?"

"I'm holding the bridge door open," Rodriguez answered gamely. "If they try to come out, they're easy meat. But I caught a few in my leg. They got these little needle things, great penetration on anything soft, shatter on metal. I'm not losing too much blood, as far as I can tell, but it's gone numb. But since you turned off the power—wait, that was you, right?"

"Yeah, engineering is ours," Harry replied.

He must be out of it. I just told him we took engineering.

"Roeder is holding back there, so no one is turning the power back on till we say," Harry continued. "Whoever's on the bridge or operations can't call for help or move the ship."

"Good, something going as planned," Rodriguez said, sounding a bit cheerier. "My leg's pretty useless, but I can get around okay in free fall."

At that point, the ship lurched about Harry, and he grabbed a handhold, only to be pressed outward, braced against what had been the ceiling.

Ah, there it is: Murphy's Law.

The ship was under spin.

Chapter Forty-Three

Knowing the remaining Kulsians were pinned in place, Harry worked his way up the final corridor, coached by Rodriguez, forced to crawl along the notional ceiling. Ahead, he could see the bridge hatch. The coaming that surrounded the aperture was deeper, and the hatch itself partially open, so Harry could see the hatch was thicker as well. Emergency lanterns lit the surface of the door, giving it a sickly yellowish cast. He could make out the chip reader that should've locked the door. He could also see why the door remained open.

The bottom half of a Terran EVA suit projected from the opening, bent at the waist and stuck midway up the door. It was quite still. The legs dangled grotesquely toward the ceiling. A small amount of blood was dripping along the jamb.

"He dove through the door as they were closing it, boss," Rodriguez said, only the slightest catch in voice betraying any emotion. "He knew if they got it closed, we might not get it open. The guy inside sprayed him. I was on his heels and caught a few. Pham went straight away. But he's the reason the door's still open. They can't push him out without giving me—us—a shot."

Harry breathed. He packaged his emotions and evaluated the scene. Anyone trying to force the door would face at least one of those little needler things. Getting the frame charge off Grave de Peralto's body and blowing the door would startle the occupants, but it would also send high speed molten copper into a control room that Harry needed intact.

He very carefully made his way to Rodriguez's side. The sergeant had his gas gun trained on the hatch, using a man-thick bundle of cabling and pipes as cover.

"What now, boss?" he asked, the voice behind the question strained and soft.

Harry turned his helmet light onto Rodriguez's face. The man was gray and sweating. Shock.

When in doubt, talk the bastards out.

"You, in there!" Harry called as loudly as he could, relying on his suit speakers to carry his Ktoran through the partially open hatch. "Let's talk."

"Who are you?" an unseen man yelled back. "Show yourself!"

"Maybe after I know you won't shoot as soon as you see me," Harry answered, staying right where he was. He tried to spot motion in the gaps above and below Pham. *No: you have to think of it as* "the body"—*nothing more.* "You can't close the door, and I don't want to use explosives to open it. Maybe ease it open a little more so we can look at each other and talk."

There was a prolonged delay, during which Harry's speakers picked up shuffling and gasping. A man moved into view. Harry squinted. It looked more like two men, and one wore a suit of a familiar color.

Harry eeled forward, never leaving more than a bit of his body exposed in the line of fire.

"All right, I moved up," Harry announced. "My teammate has a weapon in case you do more than talk, and if we can't resolve this amicably, I've ordered him to simply blow your hatch off."

"If you attempt to force the door, he's dead!" the voice announced.

Dead? He's already dead.

The door opened to twice the previous amount, and Pham's suit, tugged by the slight centrifugal gravity, slid to the deck.

Everyone paused for a moment.

There were two figures, all right.

One was the speaker, a lean, fair-haired man of middle age, obviously Kulsian by the red coveralls and likely an officer, judging from the shoulder insignia. But Harry couldn't see much more of him, because bowed backward, helmetless, hands behind his back and an enemy's needle gun screwed into his ear, was Korelon. Dried blood crusted under his nose and across swollen lips. One leg hung at an unnatural angle, and a gash in the suit bled scarlet. "Hi, Major," Harry said after a minute. "Wondered where you got to."

"Harr—" Korelon began to reply, but was choked to silence by a thin, almost transparent filament around his neck, biting deeply into the flesh. The free end disappeared behind Korelon's back, presumably in the Kulsian's fist.

"No, you don't get to speak, dog," the Kulsian growled. The officer's accent had an odd burr, unlike the clipped speech of the SpinDogs and RockHounds. He looked keenly at Harry, then at the EVA suit holding the hatch open and back to Harry. "This is your servitor? More filth, like the rest of the garbage you brought to my ship?"

"If you choke him, the major really can't participate in our little palaver, can he?" Harry said, enunciating carefully. "Let's show a little good faith. You stop choking him, and I'll withdraw the body of my friend."

Korelon's face was purpling.

"And if I close the door and kill this one at my leisure?" the officer sneered, tugging slightly at the line, causing Korelon to bow even further backward.

"By all means, kill the only thing stopping me from blowing the hatch and everyone behind it into space." Harry replied, *not* flexing his fists. "For that matter, I also control the power plant, and I can destroy this ship at *my* leisure. Let's start small. I move the body. You stop choking him."

The man eased the line enough that Korelon inhaled, but so forcefully his breath whistled. Then the Kulsian double-checked he was covered by his hostage and cracked the hatch open further, giving Harry the most unobstructed view so far.

"Before you approach, take your helmet off!"

"Why?" Harry asked. "You have the gun."

"Because then your team cannot evacuate the air on the ship," the Kulsian pointed out angrily, his tone suggesting Harry was mentally deficient for not understanding at once. "Not without dooming you both."

Korelon shook his head microscopically.

Harry pretended not to notice. Moving slowly, he undogged his helmet and let it slowly fall to the deck.

"And your weapons, slowly."

"Sir..." From behind him, Harry heard the drawn out, cautionary syllable from Rodriguez. "This is a bad idea."

Harry kept a razor-keen focus on the Kulsian. He unclasped and lowered his equipment belt, bearing his holstered pistol and grappler to the deck, bending his knees to crouch slightly as he lowered the belt. He unbuckled the straps for his punch and let it slide downward, too, maintaining a cringing sort of posture.

"Now, I'm going to get the body of my friend," Harry said, holding his hands up, praying the Kulsian wouldn't note the small black rectangle clipped to Harry's EVA gauntlet. "All right?"

"Get that trash off my bridge, servitor!" the Kulsian said, pushing his pistol ever more firmly into Korelon's ear. "Make even a single motion I don't like, and I empty your master's skull."

Harry froze.

A familiar heat forged its way through Harry's otherwise well-controlled battle awareness, awakened by this fucker who casually dismissed Harry's dead brother as no more than trash. Incandescent anger, the deep rage that had always been there to use and be used, howled to be loosed.

And stilled, like a mirrored pool, because, as the frisson of understanding finally penetrated his thick SEAL skull, Harry understood. The man didn't merely think Korelon was his teammate. He believed Korelon was his insurance policy, that Harry wouldn't—in fact, *couldn't*—risk killing his own commanding officer.

Show no fear, show no confidence, be the fucking expressionless Sphinx. Give your opponent nothing. These are the highest possible stakes.

Harry reverted to his poker face.

Slowly, he pulled Pham's boots toward him, carefully not looking inside the helmet. He rotated the suit and gave it a little shove, sending it on a sloping trajectory behind him. As he did so, he took a step and a half closer to the door, which now opened fully to frame both his opponent and the hostage.

Immediate task complete, Harry held still, offering no threat. He kept his hands up as he regarded his opponent, taking in the arrogant expression, the haughty carriage, the golden eyes of a high-caste Ktoran exile.

He noted the tension in the man's trigger finger.

"What Family are you?" the Kulsian asked, studying Harry in return. "From where on R'Bak?"

"Not R'Bak," Harry replied evenly. "Harry Tapper, major, Consolidated Terran Republic."

"Not from R'Bak?" the man asked, confused. He gave Korelon a shake. "What is this trick?"

"This man is from beyond this system, Kulsian," Korelon slurred through battered lips. "His Republic is what the polity on Home has become. He is our legacy."

"What?" the Kulsian officer asked incredulously and then began laughing. Harry thought for a moment the man was laughing at him but realized the Kulsian was gloating for Korelon's benefit. "A rootstock aboriginal? Consigned to the Scatters? And you mean to challenge the might of Kulsis thus? You, a weakling who has devolved so far you use such detritus as servitors? Pathetic! Your blood will never prosper. You'll not take this ship, nor hold this system. Indeed, we'll scour your line, root and branch. The only pity is you won't be alive to see the true meaning of dominance."

Korelon began laughing as well, but he locked his eyes on Harry. A bit of blood floated free and began to slowly settle to the deck.

"Why do you laugh, contemptible spawn of a weakened tribe?" the Kulsian demanded, painfully shoving the pistol against his prisoner's head.

"First, because your boasting doesn't become a truly dominant man or Family," Korelon said, still trading gazes with Harry, now only two steps away. "One does not become dominant by mere assertion. Dominance is a function of knowledge and strength, leading to assured power. You have neither. Next, I mock you because you denigrate a rootstock human as somehow less than us, when they represent not only our origin, but the source of all that Ktorans may ultimately become. But mostly, I laugh at you because you've never seen a Terran move. I have. And this one is particularly quick, fool."

Harry didn't have the gas gun he'd dropped obediently to the deck, or the punch block he'd unstrapped and likewise discarded. But he did have something.

He shifted his gaze from Korelon and looked at the Kulsian. Looked deep into him.

Show no fear, show no confidence, be the fucking expressionless Sphinx. Give your opponent nothing.

But then, at last:

Fuck it. Let him see your pain. Introduce him to your rage. Show him death.

And Harry saw the sudden squint of suspicion, knew the moment his enemy saw the change in Harry's eyes.

Too late, motherfucker.

One moment, Harry was relaxed, his hands shoulder height, very slightly crouched less than a double arm span distant from his target. Cringing, cowed, unarmed.

Then Harry's hands blurred into motion, meeting in front of him, his right palm clapping to his left forearm, snatching the little holdout he'd clipped to the gauntlet cuff. His thighs bunched, straightened, launching him forward at the same time right hand flicked upward. He watched the Kulsian's shock, could see the man's trigger finger complete the first stroke, the puff-puff-puff of gas kicking from the muzzle as he tried to fan the stream of projectiles toward Harry.

The Kulsian officer's absolutely perfect golden eyes widened into absolute panic as Harry's arm reached nearly full extension, and the gravity knife took him under the point of the jaw, glittering edge and black blade burrowing deeply, severing the bundle of nerves and blood vessels before cutting into the target's fibrous windpipe. The power of the strike drove the blade into the Kulsian's spine, and all three men were launched off their feet against the backs of the piloting chairs.

Elapsed time for the Kulsian—eternity.

Chapter Forty-Four

"Permission to come up," Harry asked, drifting just outside the corvette's bridge. The ship looked about the same as Harry felt. All the blood had been cleaned up, but dimples and rough patches on the alloy hatch frame and nearby bulkheads were evidence of errant pulser needles.

Through the wide-open hatch, he saw the midnight-and-silver star field framed by the forward port. Partially obscuring his view were the gray cranials worn by Bowden and his RockHound copilot. Beyond them, several multifunction displays scrolled through screens liberally dappled with yellow alerts and at least one red caution light.

"Granted," Bowden replied, looking over his shoulder and tilting his boom mike upward. He twisted to the right as far as his straps permitted to see who it was. Grinning, he reached out a hand. "Good to see you up, Harry! How are you feeling?"

"Little sore," Harry answered, and used the hatch coaming to push off toward the flight deck. Once in range, he took Bowden's hand and used it to steady himself. The motion sent a few twinges through his left arm and shoulder, but he gripped the grab-bars on the overhead anyway. "Listen, I wanted to come sooner, but with this busted arm, I can't manage the main passageway under thrust. The skew turn is the first chance I've had to say thank you. You're most likely going to catch some shit from Murphy for delaying our return while you ran SAR, but you saved some of my guys. I owe you."

"Introductions first," the former Hornet jock replied, releasing Harry's hand and turning to the dark-haired woman in the right seat. "Meet Malanye Raptis. She's a rock miner and our Rock-Hound piloting expert. Raptis is supplying most of the know-how needed to drive this crate. Malanye, this is Harry Tapper. He's the leader of the team we carried all this way."

"Black Knife." The petite woman nodded, her eyes flicking over Harry, then over to the instrument board and back again. "It is an honor to meet you."

"Uh, thanks?" Harry asked, wondering what she was on about. "Really, I didn't do a whole lot. I passed out before you even boarded the ship, too stupid to know I'd caught some of the rounds the last Kulsian bastard sprayed at me. Frankly, I'm getting tired of waking up and seeing med-bay ceilings."

"Major Korelon hasn't stopped telling the story since we took the last survivor aboard," Raptis said, intently meeting Harry's confused gaze. "Clearing the ship single-handed. You and your hidden knife against a pulser."

"Korelon talks too much," Harry protested. "And we took—"

"Major Tapper, what the hell are you doing up here, sir?"

Harry heard the familiar bellow of his favorite Army sergeant.

"Why, Sergeant First Class Marco Rodriguez, as I live and breathe." Harry turned to see the exasperated NCO rocketing up the passageway. "Meet the pilots flying this heap."

"Sir." Rodriguez sketched a cursory salute toward Bowden as he grabbed another handhold. He turned toward Harry. "I've already met Major Bowden, Harry. While you were nobly filling up your EVA suit with blood, he helped me drag your sorry ass back to medical. Which is where Roeder says you're supposed to be, anyway."

"Black Knife, we need to start our retro-burn," Raptis said. "You should get to an acceleration couch."

"See you later, Harry." Harry saw Bowden wave as Rodriguez tugged him back to the corridor.

Harry waited until they passed the next hatch.

"What the hell is this bullshit, Marco?" Harry shook his good arm free of Rodriguez's grasp. "Are you spreading some kind of 'Black Knife' crap?"

"That's all Korelon, sir," Rodriguez answered, grinning. "You impressed the hell out of him with the itsy-bitsy holdout you tote around everywhere. I suspect he's also grateful as hell we got back half his guys, on account of you finishing the job of taking the ship. Our Dutchmen hadn't gotten too far before Bowden and his tame SpinDogs used the lighter to round up the strays."

The main passageway split, and Rodriguez led them down the starboard side.

"We didn't get them all," Harry said.

"No one ever hardly does, sir."

Ahead, Harry recognized the fully kitted figure of one of his RockHounds. The EVA suit was spotless, as was the combat gear, complete to punch spike, grappler, and gas pistol. One foot braced in a deck-mounted stirrup, the man saw the approaching pair and straightened briskly from a posture Harry recognized as "parade rest." The EVA's helmet visor was up, polished mirror bright. Drawing closer, Harry glanced over the rig, noticing an additional detail beyond the man's identity.

"Hello, Markaz," Harry said, returning the RockHound's salute. "What duty is this?"

"Major Korelon's orders, sir," Markaz replied impassively, locked into a perfect position of attention.

Harry looked at his NCO, quirking an eyebrow.

"Honor guard, Major," Rodriguez said. "We converted one of the botanical storage areas into a temporary morgue. Our guys are in there."

It hit Harry like a sucker punch.

"All of them?" He carefully kept his voice even.

"All of our boys, sir. Terrans and RockHounds. We have the Kulsians netted up outside on the hull. They'll keep."

"How long?" Harry managed. His eyes were beginning to smart.

"We're rotating through the roster, keeping watch over them," Rodriguez said solemnly. "Our honored dead are never alone, sir."

"What happens when we resume thrust?"

"No change, sir," Markaz spoke up. "The major has rigged a brace for the post, but the compartment is guarded continuously, regardless of ship operations."

Harry felt the sting of tears, but he braced against an overhead grip and assumed a modified position of attention. He carefully saluted.

"Carry on."

"Aye, aye, sir." The RockHound returned the salute, and Rodriguez led off again.

Down the corridor a bit, Harry wiped his eyes.

"Fucking allergies," he muttered. "Make a note, Rodriguez. We need to change the air filters on this scow."

Ahead, the NCO answered crisply, "Aye, aye, sir."

Harry sniffed, then repeated it even harder. Then he glanced at Rodriguez from under beetled brows.

"What's with the parade ground response business, Marco?" he asked. "Since when do you use 'aye, aye'? And what's Markaz doing with a knife clipped to his forearm? Is this some kind of joke?"

Rodriguez snagged one of the handholds lining the corridor. As he spun neatly to face Harry, the bandage on his right leg bulged against the fabric. Harry frowned, realizing he hadn't noticed it before.

"Sir, it's no joke," Rodriguez said, his face serious. "You don't get it, and that's okay since you just got up. But no one's pranking you."

Harry made "go-on" motions and grabbed himself a handhold with the other hand, halting his drift down the corridor.

"The knife, the nautical responses, it's because you're a bit of a talisman. Short version, Major, is they like you, are proud of you, and the troops want to be a bit like you."

"The ones that lived through it, you mean."

"Major," Rodriguez continued earnestly as Harry looked back over his shoulder. Markaz had returned to parade rest. "Harry, look at me."

Harry dragged his eyes off the door next to Markaz.

"Yeah?"

"Soldiers die. That's the deal. We lost a bunch, and that sucks. But every man on our team knows that such as lived, lived because of you. If you hadn't pulled a couple rabbits out of the hat, we'd all be dead or prisoners. I know it. Korelon knows it. All the lads know it. And what's more, this op you led us on has done something I haven't seen in a very long time. I'm cynical enough I still question if it's real."

"If what's real?"

"Harry, you made us into a team. The message traffic has been nonstop. The RockHounds are astounded. Volo's boss is telling everyone that will listen, 'I told you so.' Everyone on the two returning ships is strutting around with their chest out like fucking Westmoreland on a high body count day! Korelon is singing your praises, not just because you helped save his men or because you saved his ass—and by the way, I've been busting his balls about getting caught—and not just because of your nifty knife trick. He didn't wait to be told to put our dead together. He did it on his own. His idea. You welded us into a single unit, Harry. It's because you're a hell-on-wheels field commander. You lead from the front. You take your hits. And you're lucky. These guys would follow you anywhere."

Again, Harry looked over his shoulder at Markaz's post. He snorted.

"You gotta know the op was ten klicks of bad news, right?" Rodriguez explained. "If everything had gone perfectly, I figured we had no better than a break-even chance to pull it off. And surprise, surprise, it didn't go well at all. In fact, it went about as badly as possible. A spy on the lighter? Sabotage? And you still made it work. There's good leadership and there's luck. You got both. You don't believe me? Ask Pham when he wakes up, once they finish putting his shit back together again."

"Is it worth it, Marco?" Harry asked, letting go of the handhold and shoving off toward the room where he'd woken up. "Is this war worth it? Do you suppose anyone back on Earth gives a shit?"

"Well, if we can duplicate this across all of the Lawless, I figure we might pull the whole thing off, sir." Rodriguez followed Harry down the passageway. "I can't say for Earth. It *will* matter for the people on R'Bak. But that's for later. Like any self-respecting NCO, I've got my mind on the 'now.' Tell you this much, I'm not sure who's gonna catch more hell: you from Murphy for banging up his pretty new ship or me from Stella, for letting you get shot up again."

"A thousand credits on you, Marco."

"No bet, sir."

Harry nodded, but Rodriguez's reminder had spurred his thoughts elsewhere. Not toward the RockHound station that was their destination, but perhaps along a detour to the surface of R'Bak. He could see Stella's face. A detour could be just the ticket. Harry rubbed his chin.

I took control of this ship once; I could damn sure do it twice. The team would back me...

But that probably wouldn't be a good look. Be a shame to spoil the reputation the Lawless were building. He sure didn't need another ass-chewing from Murphy. And, of course, there was the annoying, if minor, impediment of hundreds of surveyors now flying, sailing, and driving all over the surface of the planet, to say nothing of enjoying a full command of its orbital space. So, on to another, even more pressing objective.

Clapping Marco on the shoulder, he led them farther down the passageway.

"First stop, coffee," Harry said. "Then we let Mama Roeder tuck us in for acceleration."

Chapter Forty-Five

Murphy stared at the three ships on the screen, two of which were decidedly worse for wear.

"It worked, sir," Makarov said. Finally.

When the corvette had been taken over a week ago, the now fully recuperated Russian had only nodded. When, along with the lighter and the RockHound packet, it reached concealment among the second planet's trailing Trojan asteroids, he announced it as if it was as a friend's wake. When the small flotilla initiated a short, hard acceleration while the body of the planet obscured their exhaust from all known surveyor ships, satellites, and drones, he drew in a great breath. When, five days later, the craft reached the spinward Trojans of the fourth planet, it was as if he was finally expelling that same breath.

Two days ago, relying upon the distant gas giant's brief cone of shadow as it interposed itself between their position and R'Bak, the tiny formation commenced a short, hard boost that set it upon the final leg of its return. Its silent coast to the cluster of asteroids in which *Spin One* was hidden had ended this morning as the ships had simultaneously initiated a final, crushing seven-gee retroboost. It generated a strong thermal signature, but so brief and so distant from any known surveyors that detection was extremely unlikely. But Makarov had simply watched the slowing blips on his tracking screen, counting down the diminishing velocity and then the shrinking distance.

The remote and manned tugs had gone out to secure them. Makarov did not react; he was too busy watching the passive scanners for any indication the three ships had been spotted during their final approach. Nothing. Even the Dornaani microsats that swept their adversaries' known locations and platforms for the trace refractions of active lascoms found no such signatures among the diffuse particles that floated in the not-quite-vacuum of open space.

But now, the Russian had spoken and, with a sigh, repeated his conclusion: "It worked, sir." And this time, he allowed hints of both disbelief and relief to creep into his voice.

"Update on the wounded?" Murphy asked.

"No change, sir. All stable."

"I want our own medical personnel on hand for assessment and treatment, even if the Primae change their minds at the last second."

"If they have reconsidered, how do you wish our personnel to proceed?"

"Straight ahead with drawn sidearms," Murphy muttered thickly. "Warnings given but safeties off. And confirm that Healer Naliryiz will be part of the receiving team. I don't trust any of the others when it comes to handling the more esoteric pharmaflora derivatives."

"Sir, I regret to point out that while Primus Anseker gave his assurances on ensuring she would be present with our own medical team, those were *personal* assurances. He made it very clear he could not speak for the other Primae, most of whom have still not responded to your request either way."

Murphy nodded sharply. "Noted. So if there is any attempt to obstruct her, the protocol is to start by appealing to reason. She's learned how to use the medicinals from the locals themselves, and is the only SpinDog who's actually used those compounds in the treatment of us Terrans."

"And if reason does not prevail?"

"Then force will. Janusz?"

"Sir!"

"You heard what I told Major Makarov?"

"Yes, sir. Every word."

"Good. Go get Captain Cutter. Relay those protocols to him. He is to arm you and two of your choice before you all report to interface bay C and link up with Healer Naliryiz of the Otlethes Family. You are her escorts and security detail. She is not to be interfered with."

"And if someone tries, sir?"

"Then you remove them."

"Do you mean with our hands, sir, or—?"

"Remove them by any means necessary. And Janusz: no comms as you head to Cutter, gather the team, or move to the bay. You are to show up unannounced and unexpected. Now, step lively, mister." Janusz frowned at the unfamiliar phrase. "Go! Now!"

He did.

"Pete, have you had a chance to look over my Homeland Manifesto?"

Makarov nodded. "I have, sir."

"Frank feedback, Mack: do you think it will fly?"

Makarov shrugged. "In a perfect world, it would, sir."

Murphy hadn't expected rave reviews on his proposal for establishing an autonomous territory—not to say, "reservation"— for the Lost Soldiers and any dependents. On the other hand, Makarov clearly had serious reservations. "Why only 'in a perfect world,' Mack?"

"I did not say *only* a perfect world, sir. I said that it surely would be accepted and succeed if this *were* a perfect world."

"Care to explain what that means in practical terms?" Murphy pointedly adopted a tone that made it clear his request was actually a cut-and-dried order.

"Yes, sir. I believe there will be no dispute over us founding a community on the second planet, sir. But in regard to a protectorate on the surface of R'Bak itself... well, I just don't know, sir."

Murphy synopsized his reasoning. "No skin off the backs of the Hounds or Dogs. They're not going to be looking to live dirtside for a long time, yet. If ever. And they need reliable interface with the surface."

"Agreed, sir. But they are always alert to agreements or conditions that could change the balance of power in any of their relationships. And while your proposal would certainly secure that necessary interface, I suspect that some Primae would be less than comfortable having us in effective control of it."

Makarov had a point—a good one—but it was one Murphy had already considered. "I suspect you're right about your suspicions," he replied with a grin. "But if they're not going to get their own hands dirty dirtside, they've got only two alternatives. One: they cut their own deal with whoever is in power at any given time and deal with the inevitable caprice and chaos of dealing with a stew of locals that distrust each other *and* them. Or, two: they strike a bargain with us and thereby secure a reliable conduit for all their needs."

Makarov smiled sourly. "And if this were a perfect world, populated by perfectly logical persons, they would obviously choose the latter. But it is not a perfect world." His frown suggested deep thought, not concern. "I would let this, uh, 'sit for a while,' Colonel. You have no need to present this to them in a rush."

Murphy laughed. "Present this to the Dogs and the Hounds? Now? Sorry for the confusion, Pete; that's not what I was thinking. Until we've tried cases with the Harvesters, this is all just a pipe dream."

Makarov's frown became one of perplexity. "Then why were you seeking my reaction to it, sir? With whom do you mean to share it?"

"Tapper. I told you about the deal I made with him."

"Yes, sir."

"Pete, I know deferential evasion when I hear it—especially from you. What gives? What's the problem sharing it with Harry?"

The Russian stiffened. "Major Tapper is a good officer, sir. But he is also quite insubordinate—"

"In our army, we called that 'proactive,'" Murphy interrupted. "Or, if you prefer, ballsy. We need that, particularly as we sketch out our collective future."

"Very well, sir, but then why, at the very outset, did you not tell him that you had already been thinking of the same issues he had?"

"You mean take him into my confidence right after he went way over the line?" Murphy shook his head. "If I had done that, he could have gotten it in his head that I was ignoring—or worse yet rewarding—his behavior. Tapper is a good guy, but he reminds me of a mastiff we had when I was a kid. Give him the least hint that he got his way in a war of wills, and he'd try to become the boss."

"That dog does not sound fully...domesticated, Colonel."

"The really useful—and loyal—dogs never are, Mack. They are excellent followers when their forever-parents—us humans—give orders and enforce discipline with determination and conviction. But if that's lacking, they reflexively take charge. Without that instinct, packs wouldn't work or be able to reorganize mere minutes after losing their leader." Seeing Makarov's alarmed look, Murphy doubled down. "Give me one mastiff over a hundred pampered lap dogs any day of the week. Or century."

Makarov shrugged. "Still, I do not understand your urgency to share your white paper with Tapper the minute he arrives. Surely it could wait a week, even a month."

Murphy shook his head. "We made a deal. He lived up to his end of the bargain at great risk, and even greater permanent pain—because he'll see the faces of the men he lost for the rest of his life. So the very least I can do is live up to my end of the bargain ASAP.

"And here's the other ASAP factor: I want him to hit the ground thinking about how to create a home in this system. The more smart people I have working on this, the better the plan we'll come up with. But Tapper's got more than a good brain; he has absolute tenacity. So, once he's determined to solve the problem, he won't stop, and he won't let go."

Makarov raised an eyebrow. "You mean like a mastiff with a bone, sir?" They exchanged a grin. "The one drawback to a tenacious breed is that it may not relent even when a better bone is waved under their nose."

"Pete, I've never met a tenacious man or dog that didn't have more than their share of stubbornness, too; that's just the flip side of the trait. So it's the price you pay for all the positives. Besides, Tapper has another crucial quality that totally offsets the costs: he doesn't simply accept conditions as he finds them."

"I have observed that also, sir, but frankly, I feel he is over-estimating the degree of unease among the others. They are unhappy, but not so deeply as he is." Makarov shrugged. "It is only natural to project one's own feelings—and the depth of them—upon others."

Yeah, Pete, and right now, maybe you are projecting your level of complacency on the rest of the Lost Soldiers. In all probability, the median of Lost Soldier morale and attitudes was somewhere between the poles defined by Tapper and Makarov. Murphy's only outward response was a shrug. "And if he is overestimating the dissatisfaction and unrest among the rest of our not-so-merry band? Well, in this case, I'm glad for it. Because even if these feelings are only stirring, failing to get out ahead of them now means risking that we won't be able to stop them later. We can't just keep kicking this can down the road."

Pistol Pete sat straighter. "With all due respect, sir, we have not exactly been lounging about, sipping Stolichnaya and picking at caviar."

Murphy leaned forward. "Yeah, we've all been busy. But firstly, some of us have been busy and *dying*. Second, busy or not, the universe doesn't hand us crises in a convenient sequence and at manageable intervals. So, if Tapper's anger is further downrange than the others, it is still a warning flag: the bow wave of dangerous seas ahead. So we start trying to solve it *now*. And the first step is the one that he put his finger on: we have to shift our focus from simply surviving to *living*."

Pyotr leaned his chin on one palm. "When did *you* start reflecting on this, sir?"

"When did I *start*? Damn; probably about thirty days after we were all awake. It was plain that we couldn't go along as we were—as we are—forever. But then, when Bo and Aliza got married—well, it pointed toward the other option open to us. The only one, really. To make this life our new life; this world, our world."

"You mean R'Bak?"

Murphy leaned back. "That's part of what we need to work out. And Tapper's definitely one of the people I want on the job." *Because he and the others will have to finish it—and a whole lot more—if this damn disease puts me dirtways before I can put a bow on it.* Which, Murphy allowed, was the universe's undisputed specialty: being maximally inconvenient. But now, even if it was, with Tapper's links to the indigs and Mara's connections to the Dogs . . .

As if she was a devil—or angel—being summoned by the mere thought of her name, Major Mara Lee tapped her knuckles against the coaming. "Permission to enter?"

Makarov was on his feet before she'd finished, hardcopy in hand. "I shall take your outline to Major Tapper personally, sir."

"I suspect he'd appreciate that. On your way. Major Lee, have a seat." Mara did, but without meeting his eyes. Not like her at all. "Major, is everything all right?"

Lee looked simultaneously nauseous and disgusted. "Damn it, I feel like I've been teleported back to fuckin' junior high."

Murphy was too perplexed to do anything other than ask, "What do you mean?"

"Well, first I had to go to Naliryiz to find out what political risks prompted her to advise against being seen with you."

"Yes...and now?"

Lee's eyes widened in a strange mix of anger, frustration, and embarrassment. "And now she sends me back to you with her answer. God damn it, Murphy! Are we passing notes in homeroom, now? What's next? You guys skip class and make out under the bleachers?"

Murphy didn't like her tone, but this was also not the time to pull rank. All things considered, it was time to shift the mood in the other direction. "Mara," he said quietly, "what the hell are you talking about?"

That seemed to calm her; anger deflated into exasperation. "Look, when you talked about going to the planet together, she told you it wouldn't be prudent, right?"

"Yes." *But you already know that...*

Mara watched his face, as if waiting to see a change there. When she waited through three full seconds of his undiminished confusion, she sighed: disappointed, but not surprised. She closed her eyes. "Naliryiz meant that you can't go together *openly*." Her eyelids parted, revealing a disbelieving squint. "Can you *really* be so blind, Murph?"

He started, not just at the realization of what Naliryiz had actually meant, but that he had completely missed it. Then annoyance rose up, and he could feel it ascending toward anger. "Well, shit: yes, I *can* be that blind. Particularly if being blind is a necessity. Chrissakes, Lee, if Naliryiz is suggesting that we—"

Mara held up her hand. "She didn't say what she has in mind...which tells me that it's none of my business. She's only pointing out that whatever you two might, er, share needs to take place on the sly."

"And that's a good idea?" Murphy paused, backing away from the abruptly spiking anger. "She's the one who pointed out what could happen if we risk that, not me. And she's right, damn it. If open, eh, fraternization is a valid concern, imagine the backlash if it was done on the sly and *then* discovered." He shook his head. "Our personal feelings don't warrant risking everyone's lives—and that's exactly what could be at stake. Hell, that was her entire point." He pushed down a surge of rage. "Except now, *I'm* the problem. Why? Because I'm sticking to the law she laid down? Because I'm willing to play the role of the dull and dutiful adult?"

Lee nodded. "I don't disagree with a thing you said. I suspect that she wouldn't, either."

Murphy heard the hanging tone. "But..."

"But sometimes maybe you're *too much* of an adult to see other possibilities, Murph." She paused, then asked in a voice that could have been his sister's, "Have you ever thought of that?"

He frowned. "No, not in those terms. But let's say I did; let's say I allowed myself to walk right up to the line Naliryiz has drawn and then decided, 'screw this straight-and-narrow shit'— and crossed over. What then?"

"Then, either way—crossing over or not—you live with that decision, Murph."

"One small problem: if I decide to cross over, then *everyone* gets to live with the consequences."

Lee shrugged and smiled. "Not being an adult every minute doesn't mean you will instantly run off and do something stupid. It might just mean daydreaming, pretending that things are different—and imagining what you might do if they were."

Murphy nodded, felt his stomach sink like a millstone the instant he allowed those hopes and dreams to tug at him. If he let himself go down that primrose path of hoping that maybe, somehow...

Before he could reconsider the action, Murphy pushed his hand up as high as he could, as if he was trying to touch the overhead. "This is what happens when I'm not concentrating on keeping it together. On what I have to do next. On staying grounded in the real world versus the one I dream about." He closed his eyes. After a dozen or so seconds, his bicep twitched: a precursor to the spasms that would follow if he kept his arm suspended motionless above him.

Keeping his eyes closed, he muttered, "That's what snaps me out of any dream I allow myself to sink into"—a small spasm ran from his shoulder to his wrist—"what happens when I leave my mind free and floating." Murphy brought his arm down before the larger spasms could start. When he was sure he was in control of himself, he opened his eyes.

And saw that Mara's were on his, liquid bright. She nodded tightly and left without a word. Not that he blamed her. Hell, what was there to say?

Besides, there was no time for reflection or feeling sorry for himself. Before he could head down to personally congratulate the teams that had saved them all, he had one more meeting. And it was anything but routine. The outcome could put a dangerous strain on the Lost Soldiers' most crucial relationship, or could mark the start of a beautiful—well, functional—friendship. But whereas most meetings led to resolutions that were someplace between those extremes, Murphy's gut told him this wasn't going to follow that comfortable paradigm.

It was going to be one extreme or the other.

Once Anseker was seated in Murphy's office, he remained silent for almost half a minute. Then, without context or preamble, he announced, "I passed an observation gallery on my way here."

Murphy just nodded.

"From its viewport, I could see all three ships." The Primus shook his head and actually chuckled. "A Kulsian corvette. Hanging in space near this habitat. A year ago, if you had asked me to speculate upon what such a sight might portend, I would have confidently predicted the certain—and imminent—death of everyone on this spinhab."

Murphy smiled, leaned back. "And now?"

"And now it signifies that your 'insanely ambitious' plans worked. Not by comfortable margins, and with no small amount of luck pushing them along, but they worked. This day is truly a turning point."

"That's more true than you know," Murphy murmured, relieved at the direction this meeting was taking. So far.

Anseker's glance was sharp, assessing. "You have more news?"

"Yes. We've been working on confirming what we've learned. And I wanted to share it with you first."

Anseker nodded slightly. "I am honored." His tone added, "as is only proper." The Primus leaned forward. "What is this news?"

By way of answer, Murphy rose and walked to the stylized wall map of 55 Tauri's stars and their respective planetary systems: a near match for what was in the larger conference room just down the corridor. "The smaller surveyor ships that have been scouring the approaches to R'Bak above and below the ecliptic apparently found nothing of interest; they've cleared the larger craft for final approach. And now that those big frames are heading farther in-system, they're dropping closer to the ecliptic. So their line-of-sight comms will soon become less reliable."

Anseker nodded. "Greater debris in the accretion plane degrades the coherence of their tight-beam transmissions. This is when surveyor flotillas typically commence a phase of final coordination with the Overlords back home."

"Yes," agreed Murphy with a slow smile, "that is exactly what they're doing. In fact, the surveyors' three highest-ranking officers are talking to the Kulsian leadership almost nonstop."

Anseker frowned, perplexed that Murphy was speaking of certainties, not conjectures. Then his eyes widened: "The Dornaani microsensors?"

Murphy nodded. "Two days ago, the big frames moved past a microsat that lies back along the course they took into this system. With a few low-power thruster puffs, we repositioned it to coordinates between them and Kulsis; it's just within the outer boundary of their comms' tight-beam diffusion cone. A lot of their messaging is simply housekeeping traffic—from which we're building a very complete roster of the surveyor flotilla. But we also discovered that the three commanders are also conferring with the Overlords regarding the composition of the *Harvester* fleet they're assembling."

"They would send such messages without encryption?" Anseker watched the smile form on Murphy's face. "Ah," he said, indulging in a smile of his own, "their encryption was no match for the repurposed Arat Kur translator, evidently."

"We cracked their codes in about twenty minutes. At the rate we're capturing their signals, we'll have a complete list of the surveyors' assets and plans within the next few days. And, by the end of the week, we should have extensive, if preliminary, intel on the elements they plan to include in the Harvester fleet."

Murphy leaned back, attempted to keep the same casual demeanor he'd maintained while making his report—because this was the inflection point of his relationship with Anseker. Either the Primus would give in to the dominion reflex in an attempt to undercut the magnitude of the Lost Soldiers' successes while reminding Murphy of their reliance upon the SpinDogs, or he'd accept them (gracefully or grudgingly; it didn't matter) as essential partners...and so, maximize the chance that they would all survive the coming of the Harvesters.